Sign up for our newsletter to hear
about new releases, read interviews with
authors, enter giveaways, and more.

www.ylva-publishing.com

OTHER BOOKS BY JAE

Under A FALLING STAR

JAE

ACKNOWLEDGMENTS

Once again, I want to thank my incredible team of beta readers—Erin, Michele, and Nicki—and my critique partners, Alison Grey and RJ Nolan. Thank you for all the time, energy, and enthusiasm you put into my manuscripts.

A big thank-you goes to Revital and Rosey for coming up with a believable scenario for one of my scenes and for completely ignoring my disclaimer to get some rest first.

Thanks to Elisa, owner of the bookstore *Another Read Through* in Portland, for selling my books and for helping me decide where Austen lives. Readers, if you live in the Portland area, pay Elisa and her bookstore a visit!

Last but not least, thanks to my editor Nikki Busch. I hope we'll work together on many more books to come!

To all my beta readers, past and present, who make the journey of writing and rewriting a book a lot easier, less solitary, and much more fun. Thank you!

CHAPTER 1

AUSTEN TUCKED THE PHONE BETWEEN her shoulder and ear and wriggled into her sheer pantyhose. "I hate first days," she said into the phone.

"Oh, come on," her best friend, Dawn, said. "What's so bad about first days? New chances, new beginnings..."

Of course, Dawn as a psychologist would see it that way. "Hey, I'm not paying you for your fabulous cognitive reframing skills, so please just let me complain."

Dawn laughed. "Go ahead."

"My first day of kindergarten, I hid in my mother's closet so I wouldn't have to go. First day of elementary school, I got sick all over the teacher."

"Ugh. Sounds like the teacher didn't have such a great first day of school that year either."

"She sure didn't. The poor woman smelled like a polecat for the rest of the day. My first days of middle and high school didn't go much better." It hadn't helped that her family had moved all over the country because her father had been in the military. She had lived in eight different towns and had gone through eight first days at new schools. Each time, the teacher would inevitably get her name wrong and call her Austin. "Then, of course, there's my first day at Kallhoff Consulting back in San Diego."

"Nothing to write home about either?" Dawn asked.

"I got into a car accident on my way to work."

Dawn sucked in an audible breath.

"No one got hurt," Austen said quickly. "Or maybe I sustained some brain damage. That would explain why I started a relationship with the woman whose rental car I hit. Needless to say, it didn't end well."

"Don't tell me...Brenda?"

"The one and only." She took up position in front of the mirror in the bathroom and gave herself a stern look, remembering her promise to move on and forget about the past. "Maybe today will be different. How bad can a company producing kids' toys be, right?"

"Right. Can't be any worse than the last company you worked for, that's for sure. So, what are you wearing?"

Austen chuckled. "Does your partner know you're having this kind of phone call with other women?"

"You wish."

They both laughed. Austen gave her reflection a once-over and grinned at herself in the mirror. In a beige pencil skirt ending just above her knees, a matching suit jacket, and a cream-colored blouse that brought out the reddish color in her hair, she was all set to make a great first impression. "None too shabby, if I may say so myself."

"Good. So go get 'em, tiger." Dawn let out a hiss and a roar.

"I'll give it my best. Thanks, Dawn."

"No problem—the bill is in the mail."

When they ended the call, Austen felt ready to face this first day. She dabbed a touch of perfume to her neck and wrists.

A quick glance at her watch showed that it was time to leave. Better to take the early train, just in case. She wanted to arrive bright and early.

On her way to the door, she blew Toby a kiss. "Wish me luck."

"Fuck you," the cockatoo warbled.

Austen groaned. "Thanks a lot for that heartfelt encouragement." She'd kill her brother the next time he visited. Apparently, he had thought it fun to teach her pet foul language. Needless to say, she didn't share his twisted sense of humor.

She snatched her purse, keys, and an umbrella from the side table and strode out the door.

When her feet hit the two concrete steps leading out to the yard, she realized that she wasn't wearing shoes. Shaking her head at herself, she unlocked the door and rushed back into the apartment.

"Loser," Toby screamed.

"I know, I know." She went on a frantic search for her camel-hued pumps and finally, after a few minutes, found them sitting on top of the closed toilet lid. "What are they doing here?" She put them on and hurried out the door a second time. She'd have to run the three blocks to the MAX station if she wanted to catch the early train.

God, she hated first days.

Even though she had hurried, she still missed the train by about thirty seconds. As she ran up to the North Killingsworth Street station, the light-rail train had just pulled away.

She slumped onto a bench and tried to slow her racing heart. No need to worry. Even though she had to transfer to another line, the next train would still get her to work on time, especially since the MAX stopped right across the street from Kudos Entertainment.

When she stepped off the train in the Lloyd District, rain began to fall. Thank God she had grabbed an umbrella on her way out; she didn't want to look like a drenched rat on her first day. As she rushed across the brick-paved plaza surrounding the high-rise building, she nearly broke a heel. She slid to a stop in front of the main entrance to close her umbrella and check her appearance in the reflective glass of the building's curving facade.

Still presentable. With a calming breath, she entered the lobby. Her heels clicked a staccato beat on the polished travertine floor but then slowed as she craned her neck and stared in open-mouthed wonder. Although she had seen the lobby when she'd been here during her job interview, it was just as impressive the second time.

Drizzle fell on the high glass roof. Despite Portland's dreary winter weather, the lobby looked as if it were bathed in sunlight. Ferns and potted plants grew in large stone troughs along two sides, and a fountain gurgled in the background. A long, crimson couch flanked one of the white marble walls.

Austen skirted the twelve-foot Christmas tree in the center of the lobby, breathing in the scent of pine. Today was the eighth of December, but for some reason, the tree was still completely bare, no ornaments hanging from its branches. *Strange. Why have a Christmas tree if you don't decorate it?* She shrugged off the distracting thought and stopped in front of the reception desk.

The receptionist looked up from her computer. Her conservative business attire contrasted starkly with a pink streak in her blonde hair.

That was encouraging. At least her new company wasn't as stuffy as the old one.

"Good morning." The receptionist smiled at her. "May I help you?" Her gaze swept across Austen, who barely restrained herself from checking if she had coffee stains on her blouse or wrinkles in her skirt.

"Good morning. I'm Austen Brooks, the new administrative assistant."

"Oh, yes. Mr. Saunders is expecting you."

Austen swallowed. She hadn't met her new boss yet, but she told herself that he couldn't be as bad as the last one.

"Take the elevator all the way up to the fifteenth floor," the receptionist said, gesturing. "It's the corner office to the left."

"Thank you." Austen walked over to the bank of elevators behind the reception desk and pressed the up button.

While she waited for the steel doors to open, steps echoed across the lobby. The reflections of the elevator's steel doors showed two people, a man and a woman, hovering behind her. Austen felt their curious gazes, but she didn't turn around.

The elevator chimed, and its gleaming doors slid open.

Austen stepped in and moved toward the back of the elevator to make room for the two other people.

"Which floor?" the man who'd entered last, dressed in jeans and a button-down, asked and gave her a questioning glance.

"Fifteenth, please."

The man and the elevator's other occupant, a woman in business attire, looked at each other before he pressed the button for the top floor.

"Did they finally hire a new admin for Ms. Saunders?" the woman asked.

Ms. Saunders? Austen had thought she would work for *Mr.* Saunders, the company's vice president of marketing and customer service. Before her job interview, she had checked out the company's website, and the organizational chart had indicated that her boss would be Timothy Saunders. Or had she misread, and had it really said Timothea? But the receptionist had said *Mr.* Saunders too, hadn't she?

"I'm an admin," Austen said, "but—"

"Well, good luck, then," the woman said. "I'm sure you'll do just fine. Don't let the rumors scare you off."

"Rumors?" That didn't sound promising. "What rumors?"

The two employees exchanged glances as the elevator propelled them upward.

"Well, they say her last admin committed suicide," the woman said in a stage whisper. "Just jumped out the window on the fifteenth floor one day."

"I thought that was her second-to-last secretary?" the man said.

The woman shrugged. "I lost track over the years. Anyway, poor Wendy. I had no idea her depression had gotten so bad."

The steel doors slid open on the third floor, and the man stepped out. "You'd be depressed too if you had to work for Ms. Saunders," he muttered just as the doors closed.

The elevator stopped once again on the seventh floor, and the woman got off, sending Austen one last encouraging glance.

Finally, Austen was alone. She stared into her own wide eyes in the mirrored wall.

Great. Apparently, her new boss was Attila the Hun.

When the elevator doors opened on the fifteenth floor, Austen stepped onto plush, gray-blue carpet. The scent of espresso wafted down the corridor. Well, at least they had good coffee. She'd need it if she really had to work for the boss from hell.

She knocked on the first door to the left but didn't hear an answer. Hesitantly, she opened the door and peeked in.

The outer office was empty and the assistant's desk unoccupied. That would probably be her new place of work. She let her gaze wander over oak-paneled walls, burgundy carpet, and a solid wood desk with a large computer screen. A smile formed on her face. The new office was a huge step-up from the tiny cubicle she'd worked in before.

As she stepped into the room, she realized that the door to the inner office was partially open. A male voice came from inside.

Was this her new boss or just someone working for the female version of Attila?

Before she could walk over to peek at the nameplate on the wall, the door opened more fully and a tall man stepped out. If this was indeed her new boss, he was not at all what she'd expected. For one thing, she had thought he would be in his fifties, but this man was only a few years older than she was, maybe in his mid-thirties. In a gray pinstripe suit that matched the color of his eyes and a dark blue tie, he looked as if he'd stepped off the cover of *GQ* magazine. He reached up to push back a strand of wavy, black hair and gave her a smile that probably made women all over the company swoon.

Austen grinned inwardly. *Good thing I'm immune to male charms.* "Good morning," she said. "I'm Austen Brooks, the new administrative assistant. I'm looking for Mr. Saunders."

His grin broadened. "You found him. Timothy Saunders. Welcome to Kudos Entertainment, Ms. Brooks."

Phew. So she wouldn't be working for Attila after all. Was the woman the employees on the elevator had talked about related to her new boss? If yes, had they just happened to get jobs at the same company, or was Kudos Entertainment a family-run business? She realized she should have studied the company's website more carefully, but there hadn't been much time to prepare before her job interview and now she didn't want to appear too nosy by asking.

They shook hands.

"Sorry for making you wait. Things are always a little crazy around here right before Christmas." He pointed toward his office, where the phone was ringing off the hook.

So that was why he seemed so happy to see her.

"Why don't we go to my office and talk for a minute?"

Austen nodded and followed him into his office.

A large, L-shaped desk faced away from a floor-to-ceiling window overlooking downtown Portland and Mt. Hood in the distance.

Wow. She couldn't help staring at the panoramic view.

He laughed. "Pretty nice, isn't it? The first week I moved in here, I didn't get any work done because I was staring out the window all the time. Take a seat, please."

Instead of sitting in the padded leather chair behind his desk, which would have given him the upper hand, he directed her to a small, round table.

Austen smiled and decided that she liked her new boss. "So what can I do to help you deal with the pre-Christmas craziness?"

"For today, probably not much. Just settle in, find out where the bathrooms are, and check out the break room. Oh, and go down to the tenth floor to fill out some employee forms before HR has my head."

"I'll do that right away."

Saunders flipped through his daily planner. "There's a staff meeting at eleven that I'd like you to attend. I'll introduce you to the rest of the marketing team."

Austen nodded.

"We also need to set up your e-mail so I can forward you a bunch of stuff that will get you up to speed on our ongoing projects. This week, I'll be busy putting together my report for the annual shareholders' meeting in January, so if anyone calls and wants to talk to me, tell them I joined the Foreign Legion."

Austen laughed. Finally, a boss with a sense of humor.

The phone in the outer office rang.

Austen jumped up, eager to prove herself. "I'll get it." She hurried over to her desk and snatched up the phone. "Kudos Entertainment, marketing department. This is Austen Brooks. How may I help you?"

"This is Danielle Saunders, COO." A contralto voice reverberated through the line. "Is my brother in?"

Austen clutched the phone more tightly. Mr. Saunders's sister was the company's chief operating officer? The one

who made administrative assistants jump to their deaths?
"Uh, I'm sorry, ma'am, he is—"

"Let me guess. He joined the Foreign Legion—again."

Austen suppressed a chuckle. At least Attila had a sense of humor too. "Yes, ma'am."

"Well, once he's back, tell him to call me." Danielle Saunders hung up before Austen could answer.

She stared at the phone. Welcome to Kudos Entertainment.

CHAPTER 2

A few minutes before eleven, Austen followed her boss to the conference room. Her first day at the new job wasn't even halfway over yet, but her head was already buzzing after sorting through mail all morning. Mr. Saunders hadn't been kidding when he'd said that they were busy right before Christmas.

About fifteen people milled around the conference room, helping themselves to coffee and chocolate cake.

Austen smiled. A team that had chocolate cake couldn't be too bad, could it?

Mr. Saunders clapped his hands to get their attention. "If I could distract you from the cake for a minute... This is Austen Brooks." He earned extra points for getting her name right on the first day. "My new secre—"

"Administrative assistant," the team shouted in unison.

"Yeah, yeah, yeah. I just wanted to see if you're paying attention."

People started shaking Austen's hand, welcoming her to the team, and introducing themselves. Someone handed her a plate with a piece of cake.

She knew she couldn't possibly remember all those names, but she was already beginning to feel like an accepted member of the team. Maybe first days weren't so bad after all.

Half an hour later, the cake was gone, and they had made it through all of the items on the agenda—expect for one.

"As you probably noticed, we're woefully behind on our Christmas decorations," Mr. Saunders said. "This year, it's our turn to decorate the company Christmas tree in the lobby. So, any takers for that assignment?"

The team members on either side of Austen stared down at the crumbs on their plates. Others busied themselves reading the papers in front of them.

Finally, the woman next to Austen looked up. "Finance did such a good job last year. That'll be hard to beat."

"Oh, please! We're marketing specialists. We can out-decorate these number crunchers with one hand tied behind our backs," Saunders said, earning enthusiastic nods around the table.

Still, no one offered to take on the project.

Saunders looked from one team member to the next. "Come on, people! I know you're all up to your necks in work, but someone has to do it. Don't make me pick a volunteer."

Paper rustled.

"How about you, Sally?"

"Me?" The brunette to Austen's right looked up from her paperwork with a horrified expression. "Oh, no, I can't."

"Why not?"

"Because…because…I'm Jewish."

The man across from her snorted. "Oh, please. You're about as Jewish as Genghis Khan. You wouldn't know a gefilte fish if it bit you in the ass."

Sally lifted her chin. "Why don't you do it, Jack?"

"You saw photos of my Christmas tree last year. Do you really want me to be the one who holds up the honor of the marketing department?"

"Come to think of it...no." Sally giggled. "That Christmas tree looked like it had dying-forest syndrome."

"That's pathetic, people," Mr. Saunders said. "We're the marketing department. Presenting things and making them look good is our job, right?"

The people around the table nodded.

"Decorating one little Christmas tree can't be that hard. Who's gonna do it?" He looked at each of his employees.

Austen hesitated. Because of Toby, she hadn't had a Christmas tree for the past five or six years. He seemed to think the tree was a giant bird toy and chewed on the ornaments, so after that first year, she had banned all Christmas decorations from her apartment. Now she was totally out of practice. Still, this was her chance to make a good impression on Mr. Saunders and her new colleagues.

Slowly, she lifted her hand. "I could do it."

All heads turned in her direction.

"Are you sure?" Mr. Saunders asked. "Wouldn't you rather ease into the new job instead of taking on a project on your first day?"

Austen squared her shoulders. "That's okay. I'd like to do it."

Mr. Saunders nodded. "All right. Thank you. How about some support for our new admin?"

"I could help her," Jack said.

Sally nodded. "Me too. We could discuss strategy over lunch."

Discuss strategy? Austen stared at her. She'd thought she would just start with the lights, add ornaments, and finally finish with tinsel. But, apparently, it didn't work that way if you were in marketing and trying to outdo the accounting team.

"All right. Please get on it right away, if possible. An empty Christmas tree is a disgrace for a company that aims to make children happy." Mr. Saunders gathered his stack of papers and got up. At the door, he stopped and looked over his shoulder at Austen. "Welcome to the team again."

This must be workplace heaven. Austen had expected a company cafeteria that served mac and cheese or lukewarm pizza, but instead she'd had her choice of four different mouthwatering dishes.

She finished her last bite of grilled chicken and got started on her cinnamon toffee muffin, which tasted just as spectacular. Clearly, Kudos Entertainment Inc. was on a mission to fatten up its employees. "Is the food always this good?"

Jack nodded while still shoveling down his second helping of curry.

"Working for Kudos is a pretty sweet deal," Sally said. "Unless you work in operations, of course." She and Jack exchanged knowing glances.

Austen swallowed a bite of muffin. "Why? What's wrong with operations?"

Sally looked left and right, then leaned across the table and whispered, "Its boss. Mr. Saunders is a sweetheart—not to mention hot—but his sister..."

"She's hot too," Jack mumbled around a mouthful of curry.

Sally rolled her eyes. "Men. She's a bitch. She fired her last assistant a few days ago, not caring that it's the holiday season. Can you believe it?"

Austen could. "My last boss was like that too."

"Yeah? What happened?" Sally's eyes gleamed. She leaned even farther across the table.

Shit. Now she'd done it. She hadn't planned to come out to her new colleagues on the first day, but maybe it was better that way. The new team seemed friendly, and she didn't want to distance herself from them by hiding in the closet, unable to join in when they talked about their private lives. She took a deep breath. "He was a homophobic chauvinist. He had it in for me ever since I brought my girlfriend to the office Christmas party the year I started working for them."

"Oh," Sally said.

Jack glanced up from his curry.

Austen clamped damp fingers around the napkin. Maybe being so open about her sexual orientation had been a bad idea.

"You should bring her to the office Christmas party the Friday after this one," Sally said.

"Who?"

"Your girlfriend."

Austen shook her head. "We're not together anymore."

Her colleagues didn't need to know the details. After breaking up with her on Christmas Day three years ago, Brenda had revealed that there was someone else. She was in a long-term partnership and had been long before they'd met. Without knowing it, Austen had been the other woman. She brushed a few muffin crumbs off her blouse, wishing she could get rid of her bitter memories as easily.

23

"Oh. Sorry." Sally reached across the table and patted her hand. "But you could still bring a date. Mr. Saunders would be fine with it. His sister is gay too."

"Attila is gay? Uh, I mean…Ms. Saunders, the COO?"

Sally chuckled. "I see you've already heard of her. Yes, she's gay. Not that anyone has ever seen her with a woman. She's married to her job."

Austen shoved back her empty plate. "So, any ideas for our Christmas tree project?"

Jack and Sally shook their heads.

"It has to be something unique," Sally said. "We can't let the guys from finance think they're more creative than us."

"Maybe we could hang little toys," Austen said. After all, that would be fitting for a games and toy company.

"That's what finance did last year," Sally said.

"Hmm." Austen searched her memory for more unusual Christmas tree decorations she'd seen in the past. "How about natural ornaments like pinecones, winterberries, and apples?"

"Already been done," Sally said.

"Gingerbread ornaments that employees baked themselves?"

Sally shook her head. "HR, four years ago."

"We could do a Christmas tree out of green beer bottles," Jack said when he finally finished the last bite of his curry.

Austen and Sally just looked at him.

"Okay, okay." He lifted his hands. "Just a suggestion."

"How did your old company decorate their tree?" Sally asked.

"We didn't have one. Instead, we donated the money to an organization that fulfills wishes of children from poor families." That had been one of the few things she liked about her old company. Austen leaned her chin on her hand and rubbed her forehead. *Wishes. Hmm, that could work.* "How about we do something less commercial?"

"What?" they asked in unison.

Austen fished for the notepad in her purse and sketched it out for them.

CHAPTER 3

AT THE KNOCK ON HER office door, Dee looked up from the reports scattered all over her desk. "Yes?" she snarled. God help whoever was interrupting her.

The door opened, and her cheerfully grinning brother appeared in the doorway. "Hey. I hear you called?"

Dee slipped out of her shoes and let them drop to the carpet. "I already took care of it."

"Took care of what?"

"Oh, nothing. Just had to go knock some heads together down in licensing. We need that licensing deal with Unicorn Pictures to go through before Christmas, or we'll lose shares in the European market. Is the marketing campaign for that ready?"

Tim nodded. "I'll send you the details before I leave for the day."

"Leave?" It was barely five.

"Yeah. Some of us have a life, you know? I don't want to end up like Dad, not getting to see my kids grow up because I'm always at work."

Part of Dee admired her brother for going against family tradition and not making work the center of his life, but she didn't have kids or anyone waiting for her at home, and she didn't see that changing anytime soon. "Are you finished with your report for the shareholders' meeting?"

"Almost. There's still plenty of time." Tim entered the office and closed the door behind him. He crossed over to her desk and set something down on a stack of spreadsheets.

Frowning, Dee studied the pile of paper snowflakes. She picked one up and looked at it. One side glimmered silver under the fluorescent lights in her office; the other side was made of white paper. "Don't tell me that's all your department came up with for the new product launch next week."

Tim chuckled. "No. It's not for the product launch. This is part of our Christmas tree decoration. We're asking our employees to write down their biggest wishes for next year on the paper side of the snowflake and then hang it on the tree. Hand them out to your team." He threw a pen at her. "And fill one out too."

Dee scrunched up her face. She didn't have time for this childish crap. Their CEO was breathing down her neck to hand in her annual report by next Tuesday at the latest. Just because he was their uncle didn't mean he'd go easy on her—quite the opposite. "Who came up with that bright idea?"

"My new administrative assistant."

"You'd better keep her on a short leash, or she'll have us knit socks for the tree next year."

Tim folded his arms across his chest. "Don't be an ass. She's an intelligent, young woman. I'm sure she'll be an asset to my team."

"If she's that good, why didn't we hire her as my new secretary?"

"It's called administrative assistant nowadays, Sis."

They grinned at each other.

"And we didn't make her your admin, because you said you didn't want one. Besides, we want to keep her around for longer than…" Tim pretended to leaf through a file, "…three weeks, six weeks, or four days."

Dee crumpled up one snowflake and threw it at him. "You make it sound like I'm impossible to work for."

He lifted an eyebrow at her. "If the shoe fits. Your track record with admins isn't the best."

"Hey, it's not my fault. The first one never got any work done. The only thing she did all day was water her plants and paint her nails. And you know what happened with the last one. She shredded my reports, and when I told her to print them out again, she somehow managed to delete my files. Which is why I have no time for this stuff." She waved at the stack of snowflakes on her desk. "I have to start over with the report."

"We've been discussing this for longer than it would have taken you to scribble down one measly wish. Come on. Get it over with."

"Jesus, you're a pain in the ass."

"Must be genetic, then, because that's what people around here say about you."

Sighing, Dee picked up a pen and thought of a wish. Only one thing came to mind. She quickly scribbled it down on the paper side of the snowflake. "There. Now get out of here and let me finish this damn report."

Tim didn't move. He narrowed his eyes at her. "You didn't wish for good fourth-quarter numbers, did you?"

She shrugged. What else was she supposed to wish for?

He picked up her snowflake.

"Hey! Isn't it supposed to be bad luck to let others read your wish?"

"That's the point of the snowflakes. We're putting them up on the tree for everyone to read." He read what she had written. "I knew it. That's pathetic. When will you finally realize that there's more to life than just work, work, work?"

"Since when?" She remembered the many nights he'd been right there with her, burning the midnight oil, both working their way up in their uncle's company.

"Since I met Janine," he said, a smile softening his expression.

Before he could go into raptures about the whirlwind romance with his wife of fifteen months, she grabbed another snowflake, wrote "world peace" on it, and shoved it at him. "There. Happy now?"

He read the two words. "No. It has to be a personal wish."

"Tim..." She rubbed her forehead and took a deep breath. It wasn't his fault that she had to write that report all over again. "Let's make a deal. I'll finish your report for the shareholders' meeting if you take care of this for me."

His eyes lit up like a Christmas tree. "Deal." He pulled a pen out of his shirt pocket, took a new snowflake from her desk, and wrote something on it. "All done. You have to hang it yourself, though."

She opened her mouth to protest.

"Just take a little detour and place it on the tree the next time you go get yourself more of that black tar you call coffee." He handed her the snowflake, turned on his heel, and strode out.

The mention of her drug of choice made Dee peek into the large mug on her desk. It was empty and probably had been for hours. She picked it up and headed for the door, leaving the snowflake behind.

A few minutes later, she returned and set the steaming mug on her desk.

The snowflake was still there.

Might as well get it over with. The coffee would still be hot once she returned. She took the snowflake and made her way down the corridor. While the elevator carried her toward the lobby, she read the two words that were written on the paper side in capital letters: NEW GIRLFRIEND.

Dee snorted. *Yeah, right.* She spent all her time at work, so how was she supposed to meet a woman? *Not gonna happen.*

The steel doors slid open, and she stepped into the lobby.

She had to admit that the Christmas tree didn't look half bad. Lights in red and blue, the company colors, had been strung around the tree, which was topped by a large, five-pointed star made of crystal. Dozens of snowflakes glimmered in the branches, and employees were swarming the tree to hang their own snowflakes and read what their colleagues had written.

Don't they have work to do? As she sent them a narrow-eyed glare, they skittered away.

Dee strode toward the tree to get it over with. When she hung her snowflake on one of the upper branches, she realized there were too many lights in this section of the tree. She moved around to get a view from different angles.

Yeah. Definitely too many lights.

That wouldn't do. Clearly, Tim's assistant had no sense of aesthetics. She jerked the first misplaced light from its branch and repositioned it.

Austen grinned when the elevator doors parted and the sparkling snowflakes on the Christmas tree greeted her as she stepped into the lobby. Her first day at the new company was over, and it hadn't been so bad after all. In fact, everything had gone great. Her new boss wasn't an asshole; the team seemed pretty nice, and she'd done a good job with her first assignment—decorating the Christmas tree. What more could you wish for?

Speaking of wishes... She still had no idea what to put on her own snowflake. Maybe a more refined vocabulary for Toby. Or she could read a few of her colleagues' wishes on her way out; that might give her an idea of what to write.

As she made her way across the lobby, another employee stepped up to the tree and hung her snowflake. Instead of then walking away, the woman began to reposition the lights on the upper branches none too gently.

What the...? The woman, clad in a pantsuit that hugged her shapely hips, definitely wasn't part of the marketing department. Austen would have remembered a colleague with such a sexy ass. *So what the hell is she doing rearranging my tree?* She rolled her eyes at herself. *My tree?* Still, she couldn't help feeling a little protective as she watched the stranger manhandle the tree.

The woman pulled another light off a branch, making the tree start to sway and dislodging a few of the snowflakes.

"Careful!" Austen shouted.

Still holding on to the tree, the woman whirled around. The top branches tilted.

Austen surged forward, but it was too late.

As if in slow motion, the star-shaped tree topper tumbled from its perch.

The woman let go of the tree and jumped back, but gravity was faster.

The heavy ornament hit her in the head and then crashed to the floor, where it exploded into fragments.

Crystal shards crunched beneath Austen's feet as she ran over. "Oh my God! Are you all right?"

"I'm fine." The woman straightened to her full height, towering over Austen, and glared at her. She ran one hand over her black hair that was pulled back into a neat chignon while clutching her forehead with the other. Blood seeped out from between her fingers. "Shit."

"You're not fine at all." Austen's mother hen instincts took over. She grabbed the woman's elbow. "Come with me."

The woman dug in her heels.

Austen tugged on her arm. "Stop being so stubborn. We need to get the bleeding stopped."

After a short tug-of-war, the woman finally followed her to the lobby bathroom, muttering curses as she went.

Ignoring the colorful language, Austen tugged her over to the sink and pressed a paper towel to the cut on her forehead. "Looks pretty bad."

"Great. What idiot puts a heavy crystal star on a tree without securing it?"

Heat rose up Austen's neck, but she forced herself not to flinch back from the woman's angry glare. "This idiot."

"What? You mean…you are Tim's new admin? The one who's responsible for decorating that damn tree?"

Austen nodded. So word about Mr. Saunders having a new assistant was all over the company already.

"Thanks a lot, then." The woman pointed at her forehead, still glowering.

"I'm sorry you got hurt, but you can't blame it on me. That star would have never crashed down if you'd just hung your snowflake, like everyone else."

"I was just rearranging the lights. A blind man could see that they were too close together."

"The lights were just fine. Everyone said so." What a control freak. She probably worked in legal or finance.

The woman blinked as if not used to people confronting her.

Blood was still dripping down, and Austen pressed a little harder to get it to stop.

"No, they weren't. I— ouch." The woman flinched back. "Careful, Nurse Ratched! There's a bleeding gash on my forehead, in case you hadn't noticed."

"I'm trying to get that bleeding stopped, in case *you* hadn't noticed." Austen shook her head. "Why is it that you tall, tough-looking types are always so squeamish?"

Smoky gray eyes blinked down at her, then narrowed. "I'm not squeamish!"

"Then hold still. We have to keep pressure on it, or it'll never stop bleeding."

Still glaring at her, the woman stopped fidgeting.

They stood like that for several minutes, with the stranger bent a little and Austen pressing the paper towel to the cut, her other hand against the back of the woman's head to keep her from moving.

The door opened, and Sally walked into the ladies' room. "Oh, hi, Austen. How was your first day at Kudos?"

When the stranger turned to face her, Sally stumbled to a stop. Her eyes widened as she took in the scene in front of the sink. "Oh." Without another word, she turned and left.

"Great," the woman mumbled. "That's how rumors are started. Now she'll tell everyone she caught me in the ladies' room in a romantic clinch with the new girl."

Austen turned her head and stared at them in the mirror above the sink. With a little imagination, their positions—with her cradling the stranger's face and the woman bending as if about to kiss her—could indeed be misconstrued as an embrace. And Sally worked in marketing, so she had imagination in spades. *Wonderful.* "So what's your name?" Austen asked.

The woman hesitated. "Why do you want to know?"

Still keeping pressure on the cut, Austen shrugged. "I'm not into anonymous encounters. I want to know who I've been caught feeling up in the ladies' room."

A hint of a smile dashed across the woman's face.

Austen couldn't help staring. With her high cheekbones and strong jaw, the woman already looked arresting, but when she smiled... *Wow.*

"Dee," the woman finally said.

Her contralto voice sounded familiar, but Austen was sure that she'd never met her before. She would remember a gorgeous woman like this. "Austen."

Dee lifted one eyebrow, nearly dislodging the paper towel from her forehead. "Like the city in Texas?"

"Like the famous author. Now hold still."

"Are you always this bossy?"

Austen laughed. "Only when I'm dealing with people who are too stubborn to know what's good for them. And why do I get the feeling that the pot is calling the kettle black?"

"Must be your vivid imagination. You're in marketing after all."

"Yes, I am. And you?"

Dee shifted her weight, earning her a warning glare from Austen when the paper towel shifted away from the cut again. After several seconds, she said, "Operations."

"Oh. My condolences. You're working for Attila, then."

"Who?"

Austen's cheeks warmed. She hadn't meant to use that nickname when talking about one of the company's executives. "I mean for Ms. Saunders."

Dee snorted. "Attila. That's a good one."

"Is she as bad as they say?"

Another wry smile crossed Dee's face. "She has her moments." She studied her forehead in the mirror. "Has it stopped bleeding? As pleasant as this has been, I need to get back to work."

Slowly, Austen lifted the paper towel, which was soaked with blood by now. *Damn.* The cut didn't look as if it would stop bleeding anytime soon. "No. Still bleeding. We should get you to the emergency room. I think that cut needs some stitches."

"I don't need stitches. It's probably not as bad as it looks. Head wounds just bleed a lot."

"I didn't know Kudos Entertainment had a physician on its payroll, Doctor."

"We don't. I'm not a doctor."

"Then you should leave the diagnosis to someone who is. Come on."

Dee didn't move an inch. "I'm fine. I just need to clean up and get back to work."

"Even Ms. Saunders can't be so horrible that she'd expect you to return to work with a bleeding head wound. Plus it's after five anyway."

Dee stared at her bloodstained forehead in the mirror for several seconds. Finally, she sighed and nodded. "All right. The emergency room it is. Just what I needed two weeks before Christmas."

CHAPTER 4

VANESSA, THE RECEPTIONIST, STARED AT them as they left the lobby bathroom.

Dee scowled at her. "Instead of standing around, staring, can you go up and get me my briefcase? My car keys and ID are in there."

"Oh. Of course." Vanessa's heels clacked over the travertine floor as she hurried to the elevator.

It took only a few minutes for her to make it back. She extended her arm as far as it would go to hand over the briefcase, either afraid to get close to Dee or to get blood on her clothes.

Dee rolled her eyes. "Thanks."

On the way to the car, Austen kept a careful arm wrapped around Dee's waist.

"You don't need to do that," Dee said. "I can walk just fine on my own." Truth be told, she didn't mind. Austen was a pain in the ass, but at least she was cute. Her auburn hair feathered around her pretty face in a sassy pixie cut, with the side fringes repeatedly falling in front of her sapphire eyes. *Down, girl.* The last thing she needed was a complaint about sexual harassment in the workplace.

Austen refused to let go. "Humor me, okay? You've got your car here, right? I'm afraid I took the MAX this morning."

"Yeah, it's over there." Dee led her across the parking lot, to the spaces reserved for senior executives. Thankfully, Austen was new to the company and had no idea about the parking arrangements.

When Dee came to a stop in front of her car, Austen's eyes widened. "You drive a BMW? Wow. I work for the wrong department, then. Maybe I should have applied for a position in operations."

"Nah," Dee said. "You wouldn't want to work for Attila, remember?"

"Right."

After getting the car key out of the briefcase, Dee pointed it at the car, pressed the unlock button, and moved to open the door on the driver's side.

Austen clutched her arm and hung on. "What do you think you're doing?"

"Uh, driving to the ER before I bleed to death?"

"You're in no condition to drive. Give me the keys." Austen held out her hand, palm up.

No one but Dee had ever driven her car, and she intended to keep it that way. She closed her hand more tightly around the key. "I'm fine. Get in." She pointed across the car to the passenger side.

Austen waved her fingers at her. "Give me the keys. I'll drive, and you can…continue bleeding. HR would have my head if I let you drive like this."

Dee had to admit that she did feel a little woozy. Blood was dripping into her eye when she forgot to apply pressure on the wound. If she wanted to get that damn cut taken care of within the next few hours, she had to give in, as uncharacteristic as that was for her. With a huff of frustration, she held out the keys.

Austen snatched them from her grasp before she could change her mind.

Grumbling, Dee walked around to the passenger side and got into the BMW. She didn't like the view from this side of the car.

Austen slid into the driver's seat and started to giggle. "Wow. How tall are you?"

Dee looked over. At the sight of Austen trying to reach the steering wheel, the brake, and the accelerator, she couldn't hold on to her annoyance and cracked a smile. "A lot taller than you, apparently."

Austen slid the seat forward and reached up to adjust the rearview mirror.

Sighing, Dee reconciled herself to the fact that she'd have to readjust everything to her liking later.

"Are you an only child?" Austen asked as she started the car and pulled out of the parking space and onto the street.

"Uh, no. Why?"

"Because it's clear as day that you don't like sharing your toys." Austen smoothed one hand over the leather of the steering wheel.

Dee didn't know what to say to that. She couldn't remember the last time someone had spoken to her so frankly.

Austen smiled. "Keep the pressure on that cut. It still hasn't stopped bleeding."

"Damn. It's a nasty one."

"Could have been worse."

What could be worse than being dragged to the ER when she should have been in her office, working on that report? "Oh, yeah?"

"Yeah." Austen's lips curled into a smile that even Dee couldn't help returning. "That star could have hit me."

Dee glared. "Shut up and drive."

"Yes, ma'am."

Austen steered the sleek BMW into a parking space as close to the emergency entrance as possible and then dashed around the car to help Dee out.

Dee waved her off. "I can walk on my own. It's not like I'm in labor or had a limb cut off or anything."

"Christ, are you always this stubborn?"

"Yeah."

Sighing, Austen stepped back and let her climb out of the car on her own. "All right, then. Let's get you sewed up."

"Gee, you make me sound like an old blanket."

Austen grinned but didn't answer, her attention already on the ER's glass doors and the bustling activity behind them. *She's not going to like this.*

When they stepped closer, the doors slid open, revealing a barely controlled chaos. The waiting room was crowded with patients. A baby cried; a man bellowed, demanding he be given the strongest pain medication they had, and the ER smelled as if at least one patient had a case of acute diarrhea.

Dee froze in the doorway. "No way am I going in there. Let me bleed to death somewhere quieter and less smelly." She whirled around and then stumbled.

With one big step, Austen was by her side and slung both arms around her, balancing her. "In you go." She directed Dee to the only free plastic chair along the wall. "Sit down before you fall down."

"I'm not gonna—" Dee paled and plopped down onto the seat, swaying a little. "Okay, okay, I'm sitting. See?"

"Good girl." Austen patted her shoulder. "Don't move an inch, okay? I'll get you the paperwork to fill out. If you're not here when I get back, I'll...I'll..."

"Yeah?" Dee drawled, smirking. "You'll do what?"

Now that she was seated and Austen was standing, Dee no longer towered over her, but she was still intimidating. No way could she physically restrain Dee or force her to stay if she didn't want to. Austen squared her shoulders. Time to pull out her ace. "I'll let Ms. Saunders know that you didn't follow company policy."

"What company policy would that be?"

"The policy to...to..."

"Well?"

That superior smirk on Dee's face made Austen want to slap her. Her thoughts raced, trying to come up with something to outwit her. "To protect valuable company assets."

"Valuable company assets?" Dee repeated slowly. "What assets would that be?"

"You, of course. The company can't afford to have one of its employees out sick with a festering head wound during the holiday season."

"Did anyone ever tell you that you're a pain in the ass?"

Austen smiled. "A time or two."

Dee threw her hands up. "Fine. Go and get me one of those clipboards."

Austen looked down at her, determined not to let Dee get away with ordering her around. "Go and get me one of those clipboards...what?"

"Huh?"

"You forgot to add the magic word."

"Abracadabra?"

Austen hid her smile. "Please."

Dee sighed. "Go and get me one of those clipboards, please. There. Magic word added. Happy now?"

Austen nodded and trotted over to the reception desk.

When Dee had filled in her information, Austen wanted to take the clipboard from her and take it back to the nurses' station, but Dee wouldn't let go. "I'm not an invalid, you know?"

"I'm only trying to help."

"I know, and I appreciate it, but it's not necessary. I'm perfectly capable of walking this over to the nurses' station all by myself."

Austen let go of the clipboard. *Wow.* She was fairly independent herself, but this was taking self-reliance to a whole new level. "Were you always this stubborn, or was it the knock on the head?"

"Why do *I* get the feeling that the pot is calling the kettle black now?" Dee asked, repeating Austen's words from earlier.

Austen tried to look innocent but knew she was failing miserably. "I have no idea."

"I'm sure you don't." Dee stood and walked over to the nurses' station, one hand still pressing a paper towel to her forehead.

Rolling her eyes, Austen watched her every step of the way. "Women."

Two hours later, even Austen was beginning to regret not turning back around.

The crowd in the ER didn't seem to thin out.

Austen leaned against the green-tiled wall, out of the way of the guy pacing back and forth next to them. His shoes squeaked across the linoleum, setting Austen's nerves on edge. To Dee's left, a drunken man wobbled in his seat. To her right, a woman whose ankle had swollen to twice its normal size was flipping through a magazine.

The guy with the squeaky shoes paused for a moment. Just when Austen wanted to breathe a sigh of relief, he started pacing again.

Dee looked up from her position, slouched in her plastic chair. Her gunmetal-gray eyes squinted at him as if she were a sharpshooter taking aim. "Jesus, stop that damn pacing." With a side-glance toward Austen, she added, "Please."

Austen chuckled.

The guy stared at her, then slunk away and resumed his pacing on the other side of the room.

Dee sank back against her chair. "Huh. What do you know? That magic word actually works."

A nurse walked toward them.

Finally. Austen watched her approach.

But at the last moment, the nurse veered a bit to the left and led the woman with the elephant-sized ankle toward one of the curtained cubicles.

Great. Austen dropped onto the now free chair next to Dee.

Dee lifted yet another blood-crusted paper towel from her forehead. "I think it stopped bleeding. That's one way to take care of patients. Just wait until they either die or heal by themselves."

"I'm pretty sure you'll survive. But keep that paper towel pressed to your forehead. We don't want it to start bleeding again." A headache was building behind Austen's eyes. She glanced toward the vending machine. "You want anything? Soda? Coffee?"

"Coffee." A beat. "Please."

Austen smiled. "Who said you can't teach an old dog new tricks?"

"Are you calling me old?"

"Me? No, never. My mother taught me not to talk about a lady's age." Austen studied the planes of Dee's face. Her age was hard to guess, but she seemed to be a few years older than Austen, maybe in her mid-to-late thirties. Crow's feet had started to form around her smoky gray eyes, but otherwise, her skin looked smooth. Austen's fingers itched to touch her and find out if that skin was as soft as it looked. *Are you crazy? She'd slap you from here to Timbuktu!*

"Your mother gave you advice on how to treat women?" Dee's eyebrow inched up her forehead, making her wince.

Had she just outed herself? Austen's cheeks warmed, and she cursed her fair complexion. "Uh, no, not really. So? Coffee?"

"Sure."

"Black?"

Dee nodded. "How did you know?"

"Call it a hunch." Austen got up and went over to the vending machine. When she returned with two plastic cups of coffee, one black, Dee had taken off her suit jacket and was now sitting there in a short-sleeved blouse. *Wow. Nice arms.* Austen forced herself to look away. She handed over one cup and sat. Her arm brushed Dee's, sending little sparks down her body. *Jesus. What's wrong with you?* Her mouth suddenly dry, she took a big sip of coffee—and promptly burned her tongue. "Ouch."

"Careful. Remember that company policy about valuable assets? We wouldn't want you to be out sick with a first-degree burn."

Not looking at her, Austen blew on her coffee.

Silence descended on them, interrupted only by the squeak of shoes across the room and the snoring of the drunken man next to them.

When the coffee was gone, Austen got up and took a magazine from the rack in the corner, but it was almost a year old already and couldn't hold her interest. Finally, she put the magazine down and turned toward Dee. "Is it true what people say about Wendy?"

"Wendy? What Wendy?" Dee's frown moved the skin on her forehead, making her wince again.

"Ms. Saunders's assistant. Did she really kill herself?"

"Oh, is that what people at the office are saying? Let me guess. Her boss drove her to jump out the window from the fifteenth floor."

Austen nodded. "Something like that, yes. So? Is it true?"

Dee jerked around and growled. "No!"

"Okay, okay, don't bite my head off." Austen lifted both hands. "I didn't know you felt so protective of your boss."

"Yeah, well..." Dee rubbed her neck. "I just don't like gossip. Don't you people in marketing have something better to do with your time? Like actually getting some work done, for example?"

Now it was Austen's turn to feel protective. "Don't make us sound like we're lazing around in the cafeteria, gossiping, for eight hours straight. From what I can tell, there are some really hardworking people in marketing."

"True. Doesn't stop them from gossiping, though."

"We have a lot of women," Austen said with a tiny grin. "They can multitask."

Dee glared at her, but after a few seconds, she couldn't hold on to her grumpy mood and returned the grin. "Apparently."

"So Wendy didn't jump?"

"No! She moved to Florida with her fiancé."

Austen couldn't help wondering. Were any of the other things that people had told her about Attila…about Ms. Saunders outright lies or exaggerations too? Well, she would find out in the near future. The woman was their COO and Mr. Saunders's sister after all, so she'd probably meet her sooner rather than later.

A woman with a severe rash on her face took a seat across from them.

Austen and Dee exchanged alarmed glances. *Uh-oh. Whatever she has, I hope it's not contagious.*

"Great," Dee mumbled. "This keeps getting better and better. And here I thought falling stars were supposed to be good luck."

Austen laughed. "Not when they hit you on the head."

Four hours. Dee fixed the clock hanging on the wall with a deathly stare. They'd been waiting for four goddamn hours now, and she was beginning to think the nurses had forgotten about her.

At least Austen was good company. The poor woman still had no idea who she was, though. In the beginning,

Dee had found it amusing, just a little game that made the time go by faster. But the longer she sat next to Austen, talking and drinking that poison the hospital called coffee, the guiltier she started to feel.

There was no easy way out, though. It was too late to come clean and tell her who she was. Truth be told, she was enjoying Austen's company, and that was rare for her. Very rare. Normally, she barely tolerated her colleagues and subordinates. Either they were busy kissing her ass, or they treated her as if she were the devil herself. Austen was different. She was friendly but didn't let her get away with anything. If she found out who Dee really was, that probably wouldn't last, and she would start watching what she said around her.

A nurse stopped in front of them and looked down at Dee's forehead. "Are you Ms. S—?"

Dee shot up. "Yes, that's me," she said before the nurse could give away her last name. She hoped the nurse had been about to say *Saunders*, not the name of some other patient who had to undergo a colonoscopy or another unpleasant procedure.

"Would you follow me, please? We'll get that cut taken care of."

As Dee was led to one of the curtained cubicles, she realized that Austen had gotten up and was following them. She tilted her head and sent her a questioning look.

"In case you need me to hold your hand," Austen said and smiled.

Dee huffed and took a seat on the exam table. "What am I? Five?"

"Oh, she's right, honey." The nurse patted her knee and gave Austen a conspiratorial smile. "It's always the big, tough ones who start whining the second they see a needle."

Dee folded her arms across her chest. "Do you hear me whining?"

Austen leaned against the exam table. "She hasn't brought in the needle yet."

Admittedly, all that talk of needles didn't sound like fun.

Dee held still as the nurse took her blood pressure, shone a pen flashlight into her eyes, and then prodded her forehead. Pain flared through her. "Ouch." She flinched back, barely resisting the urge to slap the nurse's hands away. "Careful. There's a bleeding wound up there, you know?"

The nurse and Austen exchanged glances.

"No signs of shock or trauma to her head," the nurse said, talking to Austen as if Dee weren't even there. "She'll be fine, but that cut needs stitches. The doctor will be with you in a minute."

That minute turned into half an hour. Then forty-five minutes. After an hour, there was still no sign of a doctor.

Dee was ready to just get up and walk out of the ER, but she knew Austen would drag her back.

Austen glanced at her wristwatch. "I'd better call my best friend and ask if she can come over and give Toby his dinner."

"Toby? You've got a kid?" At the thought of Austen with a child and a husband, a wave of surprise, mixed with something that felt strangely like jealousy, washed through Dee. Not that Austen had indicated that she was gay, but somehow, the subtle impression had lingered. Maybe it had been wishful thinking.

Austen laughed. "No."

"Boyfriend?"

"No, Toby is my uncouth cockatoo."

"Uncouth?" Dee found herself grinning. Somehow, Austen's smile and her good mood were contagious, even after being stuck in this hellhole of a hospital for hours.

"Yeah. When I was on a cruise last year, my brother looked after him. When I came back, he was cursing like a sailor."

"Your brother?"

"Toby. My brother taught him some new words, most of them not fit to be repeated in the company of children, priests, and old ladies." Austen held up her cell phone. "I'll be right back." She drew back the curtain and slipped out.

Dee had always thought of herself as one of the most fiercely independent women on earth. When she'd broken her leg skiing a few years ago, she'd somehow managed to get back to the lodge all alone and had driven herself to the nearest ER. But now, as she watched Austen's retreating back, she wished she'd hurry up and come back to keep her company. *Wuss.* She rolled her eyes at herself.

Within minutes, Austen returned and again took a seat on the plastic chair next to the exam table.

The waiting continued.

Finally, Dee had enough. "Can you go and remind your little friend that we're still waiting?" As an afterthought, she added, "Please."

Austen got up. "Sure."

Before she could leave, footsteps sounded and the curtain separating their cubicle from the rest of the ER was pushed aside. Austen's friend, the nurse, entered, followed by a disheveled doctor. He looked as if he was too young to even be in medical school.

Dee narrowed her eyes at him. "How old—?"

"Sssh." Austen nudged her none too gently and whispered, "If we have to wait for another doctor, we won't get out of here before midnight."

Right. Dee sank back onto the exam table.

Doctor Babyface stepped closer. "Lie down and let me take a look."

Hesitantly, Dee slid into a lying position and moved her hand with the paper towel away from her forehead.

The doctor hmm'ed—not a sound that Dee liked from a doctor. "What happened?"

"I was hit by a meteorite," Dee said.

"A meteorite?" The doctor shone a pen flashlight into both of her eyes as if suspecting severe head trauma was causing her confusion.

"Yep."

Austen rolled her eyes. "She was meddling with my Christmas tree decorations. The tree topper fell and hit her."

"Ah. Well, we're going to clean this up and then put in some stitches."

"Great. Can *we* get started, then?" Dee's patience was wearing thin. By now, it was almost ten o'clock, and she wanted to get some more work done before the day was over.

The doctor pulled a pair of latex gloves out of a dispenser and put them on. "I'm going to give you a local anesthetic."

Well, at least he had stopped talking about himself in the plural.

He gave the skin around the cut a quick swab of Betadine and then positioned the tip of the needle on Dee's forehead, where she couldn't see. She hoped Austen was keeping an eye on Doctor Babyface.

"It might sting a bit."

A burning pain flared through her forehead. She ground her teeth and glared at him. "Dammit. That's what you call a little sting?"

He ignored her. "Now we wait for the lidocaine to set in. Be right back," he said and walked out.

Great bedside manner, kid. She hoped he'd be back before the anesthetic wore off. Within minutes, she felt the upper part of her face go numb.

The doctor returned as promised and covered Dee's face with a sterile drape; it had an opening that left only the cut on her forehead free.

Not being able to see a thing made her nervous. She clutched the edges of the exam table with both hands.

"Hmmm," the doctor said from somewhere above her. "I think there's something..." Metal rattled as he took something from a nearby tray and then probed the wound.

Despite not feeling any pain, Dee winced. She wanted to pull off the drape to see what he was doing.

A small hand gently gripped her own, startling her.

"There's a sliver of glass in the wound," Austen whispered next to her. "Probably from your meteorite." Despite her teasing, her voice and the touch of her hand were warm and comforting.

Dee swallowed. Usually, people didn't treat her with such tenderness.

To her surprise, Austen didn't let go of her hand as the doctor started to stitch up the cut over her eyebrow. Dee tried not to think of the needle moving through her skin and focused on the feeling of Austen's hand in hers. She marveled at the softness of her skin and the strength she could feel in the small hand.

Finally, the doctor removed the sterile drape and taped a gauze pad over the cut. He pulled off his latex gloves with a snap and dumped them in a nearby trash bin. "All done."

Dee sat up and tried to peek at her forehead without any success. She probably looked like Frankenstein's monster now. "How many stitches?"

"Eight. You'll need to have them checked in about five days to see if they're ready to come out. You can make an appointment with your family doctor or come back here."

No, thanks. The family doc it is. She slid off the examination table and tugged on Austen's hand, which still held on to hers. "Let's get out of here."

The doctor blocked her way. "Not so fast. When did you get your last tetanus shot?"

Dee tried to remember. "I think I got one when that arrow pierced my palm."

Austen lifted Dee's hand to her eyes. "An arrow pierced your palm? How did that happen?" She ran her fingers over Dee's hand, looking for a scar.

It had been the other hand, but Dee enjoyed the gentle touch too much to point it out. "Don't ask. Let's just say the head of our safety department got fired over that debacle."

"How long ago was that?" the doctor asked.

"Hmm. Six years. Might be seven."

"If you're not sure, it's better to err on the side of caution," the doctor said. "Nurse Jones will give you a tetanus shot."

Great. Dee sat back down.

"I'll write you a prescription for some painkillers in case you need them." The doctor picked up his prescription pad and scribbled something Dee couldn't read. "Keep the area dry, and take it easy for a few days. If you start feeling dizzy or get a headache, come back to the ER immediately. Do you live with someone who can keep an eye on you tonight?"

"I don't need a babysitter."

"Ms. S—"

"Yeah, fine, okay," Dee said quickly.

He handed over the prescription, shook her hand, and was gone.

Dee watched with growing unease as Nurse Jones inserted a needle into a vile and drew a clear liquid into a syringe. She pointed the needle upward and pushed the plunger until a drop ran down.

Austen let go of Dee's hand as the nurse swiped a cotton ball over her upper arm.

Dee curled her fingers, instantly missing the soothing touch. *Oh, come on.* Since when was she the hand-holding type?

"Don't tense your arm muscles," the nurse said.

"Easy for you to say."

Nurse Jones pushed the needle into Dee's arm and then pulled it back out. "See? That didn't hurt at all."

"Yeah. Not you at least."

Smiling unrepentantly, the nurse covered the needle mark with a Band-Aid.

"Am I done?" Dee eyed her escape route with longing.

"Yes, but give me a second." The nurse stepped around the curtain and returned with a wheelchair.

"Oh, no. No way." Dee backed away. "There's nothing wrong with my legs. I walked in here without a problem, so I'll leave on my own two feet."

The nurse pushed the wheelchair closer. "It's hospital policy, ma'am."

"Then it's a stupid policy that needs to be changed."

"Dee." Austen touched her arm.

Dee pulled away. "No. I'm drawing the line here. I got a couple of stitches; that's all. It's not like they had to take a kidney."

"Can we skip the wheelchair if I promise to keep an eye on her?" Austen asked the nurse, directing her irresistible smile at her. "Please?"

The nurse sighed. "Well, if you slipped out of the cubicle while I was busy disposing of the syringe..." She turned her back and threw the needle and syringe into a hazardous-waste container.

"Come on. Let's spring you." Austen took her hand again, and they hurried out of the emergency room.

CHAPTER 5

THIS TIME, DEE DIDN'T EVEN try to get behind the wheel. She got in on the passenger side without protests or comment.

Austen glanced over at her. "Are you okay?"

"Yeah. Why wouldn't I be? It's just a few stitches, not an amputated limb."

"Well, you're letting me drive without having a half-hour discussion first. That's highly suspicious for a control freak like you."

"I'm not that bad." Dee turned her head to study Austen's expression. "Am I?"

Austen smiled a quirky little smile that could mean either yes or no.

Dee huffed. Austen had met her just a few hours ago, so how would she know?

"You'll have to give me directions," Austen said.

"Just take the same way back." Dee let her head sink against the backrest.

"Back? What do you—? Oh, no, we're not going back to the office."

"Says who?"

"Says my common sense, because you apparently don't have any. It's after ten; you've got blood all over yourself; your forehead looks like something out of a horror movie— and you want to go back to work?"

Dee had never felt guilty for her workaholic tendencies, but now she ducked her head. The way Austen had said it, her plan sounded indeed a little crazy. "Well, I have to hand in that report next Tuesday, and that doesn't give me much time to finish it."

Austen reached over and squeezed her knee. "Wow, that boss of yours must be a real tyrant if you're so worried about it. You know what? I'll help you. Together, we'll manage to hand it in on time."

Tingles shot up Dee's leg, making her shift in the passenger seat. She wanted to agree, because it meant getting to spend more time with this interesting woman. *Are you crazy? She'll find out who you are.* Of course, sooner or later, she would find out anyway. The thought made Dee's stomach clench. *God, this is so messed up.*

At a red light, Austen braked and turned her head to study Dee. "You look awful."

"Thanks."

"You know what I mean. Maybe you lost more blood than I thought. Someone really needs to keep an eye on you tonight, like the doctor said. Is anyone home? Husband, boyfriend…?"

Dee snorted. *As if.* "No, I live alone."

"Then I'll stay with you, just to make sure you're fine. So? Directions?"

"What? No, you can't stay at my house." Even though she wasn't Austen's direct supervisor, she was the company's second-in-command. Having an employee stay overnight was a big no-no. Too bad she couldn't tell her that.

The car behind them started honking when the light turned green and Austen didn't clear the intersection.

Dee gestured toward the traffic light. "I don't think it's going to get any greener."

"I'm not moving until you give me directions to your house."

"God, and you call me stubborn."

The driver behind them leaned on his horn.

Dee turned and flipped him off. "Okay, okay. Straight through. And then turn left at the next intersection."

Following Dee's directions, Austen stopped the BMW on a quiet, tree-lined side street in Irvington and sat gaping at the light sage-green Victorian across the street. Stairs with intricately carved balustrades led up to the porch, and an octagonal turret reached up into the night sky. "This is where you live?"

Dee nodded. "Something wrong with that?"

"No, it's just..." She had expected Dee to live in a sleek, modern condo, not in this lovingly restored Victorian. "I didn't take you for a closet romantic."

"I'm not." Dee looked as if she'd been insulted, making Austen laugh.

They got out of the car, and Dee led her past the green lawn and up the stairs.

Austen's heels clicked across the hardwood floor. Still a little slack-jawed, she looked around. Dee didn't offer her a tour of the house, but she got a glimpse of custom-painted cabinets in the kitchen and, when they entered the living room, a winding staircase leading upstairs. "Wow. I said it before, and I'll say it again. I clearly have the wrong job." She didn't want to even imagine what a house in this neighborhood might cost, but she knew she could never afford it. Apparently, working for Attila had its perks. "Think Ms. Saunders needs someone in operations?"

"She could use a good assistant," Dee said. "As for the house… It wasn't as expensive as you might think. I did most of the restorations myself; that saved a pretty penny."

Austen tried to imagine Dee with a sander but couldn't. She had to admit, though, that those strong hands with their long fingers certainly looked capable.

"Don't look at me like that." Dee gave her a little shove. "I really did. I had to. The living room had pink wallpaper when I moved in."

Austen looked around the living room. She liked the light cream wallpaper Dee had chosen; it made the sparingly decorated room seem cozier. Other than a couch, there wasn't much furniture, though. The walls were bare of pictures, and no personal knickknacks adorned the mantel. Half a dozen moving boxes were piled up in one corner of the living room. "Oh, you just moved here?"

Dee rubbed her neck. "Uh, kind of. I bought the house in February."

"And you still aren't unpacked? Dee, it's December!"

"What can I say? I have a more minimalistic style."

"This isn't minimalistic. This is empty."

Dee seemed unimpressed. "Well, it's not like I'm spending a lot of time here. I'm at the office almost twenty-four seven anyway."

Austen decided that she didn't want to work for Attila after all. All the money in the world wasn't worth giving up her private life.

Dee kicked off her shoes, apparently not caring where they landed, freed her long, black hair from the chignon, and shook it loose.

Instantly, the bareness of Dee's home was forgotten. Austen couldn't help staring at her. Even in her wrinkled, bloodstained pantsuit and with the row of stitches across her forehead, she was striking.

"What?" Dee asked. "Do I still have blood on my face?"

Austen wrenched her gaze away. "Uh, no."

Dee rubbed her hand over her face anyway and flinched as she touched a tender area. "Ouch. I think the lidocaine is starting to wear off." They had filled the prescription on the way to the house, and now she fumbled to get the bottle of painkillers out of her pocket.

"I don't think taking them on an empty stomach is a good idea."

"Don't worry." Dee popped the bottle open and shook out two pills. "I do that all the time."

Austen crossed the room and covered Dee's hand with hers. "Not on my watch. Why don't you go get cleaned up, and I'll see what I can scare up for a late dinner. Then you can take the pills."

Dee's brows pinched. She pointedly looked down at the hand covering hers.

Austen let go and took a step back. "Sorry. Look, I get it. I'm a total stranger, and you're obviously used to taking care of yourself. But I'm here now, so why not let me take care of dinner while you take a quick shower? Or are you worried that I'll steal your TV and the money you keep under your mattress?"

Dee snorted. "I don't have a TV, and I don't keep much cash in the house. Besides, I know where you work, so I'd have you arrested faster than you can say 'I didn't do it.'"

"Right. So?" Austen looked into Dee's eyes, fairly sure that she wouldn't be able to resist a challenge.

"I appreciate you taking me to the ER and driving me home, but you really don't have to stay. There's no reason to feel responsible for what happened with that damn star."

Austen did feel bad about Dee getting hurt, even though she knew it wasn't her fault. Dee had brought it upon herself with her ruthless repositioning of the decorations. Still, the thought of going home and leaving Dee to fend for herself didn't sit well with her. Dee didn't seem to take very good care of herself, so Austen wanted to keep an eye on her. *But that's not all, is it?* She had to admit that she also liked Dee's company. As grouchy and arrogant as she had come across at first, there was something about her that Austen couldn't help liking. "So you can log into the company server and work on that report all night?"

"Damn, you know me too well already. Am I that transparent?"

"Yes?"

Dee blinked. "Really?"

"No. I have a feeling there's more to you than meets the eye."

"Yeah, well, about that..." Dee shuffled her bare feet on the hardwood floor. "There's something I should tell you."

"Tell me over dinner," Austen said. Whatever it was, it had to wait until her stomach stopped growling and Dee had been able to take some painkillers.

Dee stared at the painkillers in her hand before sighing and putting them back in the bottle. "All right. You won't find much in my fridge, but there are some takeout menus pinned to it."

"Do they deliver this late?" By now, it was closer to eleven than to ten.

"Yes, they do," Dee said as if she knew their business hours by heart. "Just tell them you're calling on behalf of Dee. They know my address."

"Let me guess. You're keeping all of them in business." Austen imagined Dee hunched over her computer, working until late in the night and forgetting dinner until her growling stomach reminded her.

Dee shrugged. "I'm doing my best to help the economy." After glancing at Austen for a few more seconds, she moved to the winding staircase. When she reached it, she turned back around, clearly hesitant to leave a stranger downstairs while she went to take a shower.

"It's okay," Austen said with a soft smile. "Remember, you don't own a TV."

Dee gave her a look, turned, and climbed the stairs.

Austen watched her, letting her gaze trail down to Dee's firm backside. When Dee disappeared around the last curve of the winding staircase, she kicked herself into motion and walked over to the kitchen.

Dee stepped into the shower and let the hot water rain down on her back, careful to keep the stitches on her forehead dry. Her thoughts weren't on the shower, though; they still lingered on the woman in her living room.

While she had tried to send Austen away and wasn't entirely comfortable with leaving her alone downstairs, she didn't really want her to go. As much of a loner as she usually was, she found herself wanting to spend more time with her.

You've got to tell her who you are. But that was easier said than done. Austen seemed like an honest, straightforward person. Hell, Dee suspected that she was the type to feel guilty if she found she had accidentally put a Kudos Entertainment pen in her shirt pocket and had taken it home at the end of the day. She wouldn't take it well if Dee told her she'd been lying to her the whole time, even if it was a lie of omission.

Maybe it was better to tell her and have her run screaming anyway. Even making friends with an employee would not be a good idea. But as much as she told herself that, she wasn't ready to give up Austen's company.

Still struggling with her inner conflict, she shut off the water and climbed out of the shower just as a light knock came on the bathroom door.

"Dee?" Austen called through the closed door. "You didn't drown, did you?"

Apparently, she had been in the shower, trying to find a way out of her dilemma, for longer than she'd thought. "Don't worry," she called back. "I can swim."

"Good to know. I found the takeout menus. Is Chinese okay?"

"Sure."

"What do you want?" Austen called.

"Surprise me," Dee said as she reached for a button-down shirt that she didn't need to pull over her head.

"Okay." Austen's footsteps faded away.

Shirt in hand, Dee froze when she realized what she'd just said. Normally, she never, ever let anyone else order for her. That had to be the head wound and the grueling hours spent in the ER, right?

Right. She nodded to herself, got dressed, and stepped out of the bathroom.

Who would have thought that this was how she'd end the day—her first day at the new job—lugging around moving boxes in a stranger's house to build an improvised table?

Stranger, Austen repeated to herself. Realistically speaking, Dee was just that. They had met just a few hours before and barely knew a thing about each other. Still, Dee didn't feel like a stranger anymore. Maybe it was the ER experience that was binding them together.

Steps coming down the winding staircase made her look up.

Dee entered the living room, dressed in a pair of jeans and a button-down shirt. She'd looked spectacular in her pantsuit, the same gray color as her eyes, but this...

Austen touched her chin to make sure she wasn't drooling.

Then Dee stepped closer, and Austen realized that her forehead and one of her temples were still stained an orange-brown.

Smiling, Austen pointed at Dee's forehead. "You should try to wash some of that off before you go to work tomorrow. Your boss might not like the fresh-out-of-hospital look on one of her...um, what exactly is it that you do for a living?"

Dee walked around her, picked up a pair of chopsticks from the makeshift table, and twirled it through her fingers. "A little bit of this, a little bit of that. Basically, I jump in whenever it's needed."

Now that was a fuzzy job description, if she'd ever heard one. Her boss probably ran poor Dee ragged. Again, Austen thanked the patron saints of unemployed administrative assistants that she hadn't been hired by Ms. Saunders. She reached for Dee's hand. "Come on. I'll help you get the Betadine off."

With Austen leading the way, still holding on to Dee's hand, they made their way up the stairs and to the bathroom.

Dee wiped the mirror, which had fogged up during her earlier shower, and scowled at her reflection. "Great. Doogie Howser, MD, sure wasn't stingy with that stuff."

Austen chuckled at the nickname. "He wasn't that young."

Dee just arched an eyebrow and flinched when that facial expression pulled on her stitches. She took a washcloth out of the bathroom cabinet and ran water over it.

"Let me." Before she could protest, Austen stepped closer and took the washcloth from her. She put a bit of soap from the sink on one corner and slid her left hand behind Dee's head to pull her down a little so she could scrub off the stains around the stitched-up cut.

Their gazes met, and both of them froze, their bodies brushing lightly.

Austen's breath came too fast. Her body temperature, mingling with Dee's heat, shot through the roof. Tunnel vision set in until all she could see were Dee's darkening gray eyes and her full lips.

The doorbell startled them apart.

Austen pressed one hand against her rapidly beating heart. *Saved by the bell.* "Wow. That was fast." She sounded out of breath even to her own ears.

"Yeah." Dee's voice was equally rough. "They're right across the street. I'd better open the door before they turn back around with our dinner."

Dazed, Austen watched her rush out of the bathroom.

Dee suppressed a grin as she watched Austen fight with her chopsticks.

Without much success, Austen tried to pick up a piece of zucchini and some of her Gwai Wer noodles, but they kept slipping and falling back onto the plate. By the time the chopsticks reached her mouth, only bits of the Chinese barbecue sauce remained.

Admittedly, the way she licked those chopsticks was pretty sexy, so Dee said nothing and let her continue her battle. Images of pushing the Chinese takeout out of the way, pressing Austen against the improvised table, and taking her right then and there, fast and hard, flashed through her mind. Once or twice, she'd done something like that in past relationships, if you could even call them that, instantly setting the tone and letting them know that she was in control.

But with Austen, things were different. She was an employee, not some stranger she had met at a conference or on a plane. Dee had made a few mistakes in the past, having a handful of one-night stands and getting involved in relationships that were doomed from the start, because she had neither the skills nor the time to make them work. The breakups had been mostly painless, and life had gone on, with nothing to disturb her focus on work.

But she couldn't afford to make any mistakes with Austen. Giving in to the strong pull she felt could have grave consequences; she knew that. Still, watching those sensual lips slide over the chopsticks was doing things to her libido that no woman from her past had ever managed.

Austen looked up. "You're not eating. Should I have ordered something else for you?"

Dee wrenched her gaze away from her, shook off her sexual haze, and wolfed down a piece of chicken. "No," she said with her mouth full. "It's great." That was the truth. She had to admit that Austen had chosen well. "And you? Do you like what you ordered for yourself?"

"I do, but..." Austen shook her head, exasperation written all over her cute face. "It's just not logical."

"What do you mean?" Dee tilted her head. The way Austen's brain worked intrigued her.

"This." Austen lifted her chopsticks. "Of all the instruments the Chinese could have invented to eat rice, the best thing they could come up with was two thin sticks? I sure hope the inventors in our development team are more creative."

Dee laughed. She couldn't remember the last time she had laughed so much, especially not after a day like this. "Do you want a fork?"

"Yes, please. I admit defeat."

Dee put down her plate of Kung Pao chicken, got up, and went to the kitchen. She took her time, opening the fridge and getting them two more bottles of water. A moment alone, away from temptation, helped her clear her head and cool her libido.

When she returned with the water and the fork, Austen made short work of her noodles.

Finally, only the fortune cookies they had saved as a dessert were left.

"Pick your fortune," Dee said, nodding down at the two cookies.

Austen pointed back and forth between the cookies. "Eeny, meeny, miny, moe, catch a cookie by the toe. If he hollers, let him go. Eeny, meeny, miny, moe. My mother told me to pick the very best one, and that is Y-O-U." She grabbed one cookie.

Dee chuckled at her antics. "Your mother is full of wisdom, isn't she?"

"Yes," Austen said quietly. "She was."

The Kung Pao chicken sat like lead in Dee's stomach. "You mean…? She…?"

"She died fifteen years ago, when I was sixteen." Austen's eyes were dry, but full of sadness. "That's why I think you shouldn't spend all your time at the office. Life's too short."

"Work *is* my life," Dee said, still with a lump in her throat.

"It's never too late to change." Austen forced a smile. "Open your cookie. Maybe it'll have some sage advice for you." She pulled her own cookie out of its plastic wrapper and broke it in two pieces. Chewing the cookie, she opened the slip of paper—and started coughing.

"Careful." Dee handed her one of the water bottles. "Remember the valuable assets thing. HR wouldn't like it if you asphyxiated on my couch. Here, take a sip."

Cheeks flushed from her coughing spell, Austen took a sip of water.

A single drop ran down the corner of her mouth, and Dee's gaze tracked it. *Stop it, idiot!* She forced her attention back to the conversation. "So, what did you get? A tall, dark, and handsome stranger entering your life and sweeping you off your feet?"

Austen coughed again and shook her head. She curled her hand around the slip of paper. "No. Just the usual. You know. That 'you'll receive a big surprise soon' thing."

Damn. For once, the fortune cookie wisdom was accurate. Austen would receive a big surprise soon—and one she wouldn't like. *Get it over with and tell her!*

But before she could get up the courage to do just that, Austen nudged her. "And you? What great wisdom did you get?"

Dee broke her cookie, popped it into her mouth, unfolded the piece of paper, and read what was written there.

The cruelest lies are often told in silence.

She shoved that advice into the pocket of her jeans, where Austen wouldn't see it. *Wonderful.* Now she felt even guiltier for not telling Austen the truth.

"So? Wanna share with the class?"

Not particularly. She couldn't hold Austen's gaze. "Confucius says, 'That wasn't chicken. Next time, order the shrimp.'"

Austen laughed, the lingering traces of her earlier sadness disappearing. "Goof."

The return of Austen's smile felt like the sun peeking out from behind the clouds after a week of nonstop rain. The thought made her roll her eyes at herself. *Oh, come on. What's up with all this sappiness?* "Hey, I'm on medication now." She'd swallowed two painkillers after the first bites of rice. "I'm allowed to be goofy."

Austen reached out and gently touched her cheek. "I like you goofy."

Dee's breath caught. Their thighs and sides touched, even though she hadn't been aware that she'd moved closer on the couch. "I...I have to tell you something."

"Relax," Austen murmured, never looking away. "I already know."

Dee blinked. "You do?" How had Austen guessed her true identity? And why was she still so calm?

Austen nodded. "Just for the record, I'm gay too. I have fully functional gaydar, and it's been pinging like crazy since I met you. Correct me if I'm wrong, but there's a pretty strong pull between us."

Oh. That's what she means. "Yes, but that's not—"

Austen laid one finger against Dee's lips, stopping her. "Did anyone ever tell you that you talk too much?" She took her hand away.

Dee instantly missed the touch. Then all thought left her as Austen leaned forward and kissed her.

Unlike the heated battles for control Dee usually engaged in, this kiss was warm and tender and nearly made her melt into a puddle.

When Austen finally pulled back, Dee stared at her. All she could think of was the burning desire to pull her back against her body and kiss her again.

A gentle smile curled those tempting lips. "You won't blame it on the medication tomorrow, will you?"

Unable to speak, Dee shook her head.

"Good. Come on." Austen stood and pulled Dee up. "It's almost midnight. Let's clean up this mess and then go to bed."

Bed. Dee's amorous mind latched on to that one word. *Oh, yeah.*

The expression on her face must have been pretty obvious, since Austen laughed and patted her cheek. "Alone, Casanova." With all traces of humor gone, she added, "I admit that it's tempting, but I'm not the type to jump into bed with someone I just met. I want to know you in more than just the biblical sense."

Her words were like a bucket of ice-cold water being poured over Dee's head, snuffing out her overactive libido. Austen didn't even know her full name and who she really was. "Of course. You don't need to stay."

Austen wagged her finger at her. "Nice try. I'm staying. Just not in your bed. You have a head wound after all." She touched the unhurt side of Dee's forehead with one finger. "If you feel dizzy or get a headache during the night, wake me immediately, okay?"

Dee nodded. She felt plenty dizzy now, but not from the head wound. Numbly, she followed Austen to the kitchen and then led her upstairs to the guest room.

After the day she'd had, Austen had thought falling asleep wouldn't be a problem, but now she was wide awake. She lay in bed in Dee's guest room, arms folded behind her head, and stared up at the dark ceiling. Thoughts of the woman next door made her body refuse to settle down. She reached out and felt her way over to the nightstand until she found the slip of paper she'd put there earlier. In the darkness, she couldn't read what was written, but the words still rang in her head.

Normally, she was honest to a fault, but she hadn't been able to tell Dee what her fortune cookie quote really said.

The love of your life is sitting across from you. Stunned, she shook her head. *Wow.*

She wasn't in love, of course. Not yet. But there was something about Dee that just seemed to fit. Who would have thought? *Certainly not me.* She'd never been attracted to overbearing control freak types, and after Brenda, she'd become more careful about getting involved with anyone too fast.

Maybe it was a sign that she was ready to let go of the past and move on with her life.

She put the piece of paper back onto the nightstand, rolled around, and snuggled against the pillow. Was she just imagining it, or did it smell faintly of Dee's perfume? Breathing in deeply through her nose, she finally settled down. The last thing that went through her mind before she fell asleep was that she could really come to like first days.

CHAPTER 6

AUSTEN WOKE, FOR A MOMENT not sure where she was. She looked around the unfamiliar bedroom. Then the memories of yesterday rushed back. *I'm at Dee's. And we kissed.* Well, she had kissed her, but Dee had immediately returned the kiss. Maybe there'd be more kisses over breakfast.

The thought made her jump out of bed.

Dee had left a spare toothbrush and clean towels for her in the bathroom, so Austen brushed her teeth, took a quick shower, and got dressed.

The blouse was a bit wrinkled, but it couldn't be helped. Since everything Dee had in her closet would be much too big on her, making her look like a dwarf, yesterday's clothes would have to do. She just hoped that none of her colleagues would notice and comment on it.

She headed downstairs and found Dee in the kitchen, leaning against the counter in black slacks, a white blouse, and an unbuttoned vest that made Austen want to slip her hands inside and caress her curves.

"Good morning."

Dee looked up from her coffee mug. "Morning." She didn't smile and looked as if she hadn't slept a wink. Dark shadows marred the skin beneath her eyes.

Austen walked closer and peered up at her. "Are you in pain?"

"I'm fine." Dee lifted the mug to her mouth, looking more as if she was hiding behind it than drinking from it. "I already took painkillers."

"On an empty stomach?" *Christ, she really needs a girlfriend to take care of her.* Austen inwardly rolled her eyes at herself. *Yeah, and you'd gladly volunteer for the job, wouldn't you?*

Dee shrugged. "You saw my fridge. I don't have anything even remotely resembling breakfast. We can get something on the way to work. Or do you want a cup of coffee before we leave?"

"No, that's fine. I can get something to go." She had a feeling Dee couldn't wait to get to work—or maybe to get her out of the house. Her mood had changed. Gone was the playful, open woman from last night. In her place was the grouchy control freak she had first met. *Does she regret kissing me back?* Austen was afraid to ask, almost sure she knew the answer.

"All right. Then let's get going." Dee put her mug into the sink and grabbed her car keys.

Tell her. Tell her. Tell her. The words repeated themselves in Dee's mind like the refrain of a bad pop song while she guided the BMW through traffic, driving west on Northeast Broadway. The lump in her throat and the fear in her heart prevented her from speaking. What the hell was wrong with her? She usually wasn't such a coward. She'd never been afraid of telling people some hard truths. It was part of her job. Just yesterday, she had told the guys in licensing that they couldn't find their asses on a map, and now she was afraid to tell her brother's new admin who she really was. *Pathetic.*

She kept peeking over at Austen, who sat in the passenger seat, hands clutched around a paper cup and the bag holding her banana chocolate chip muffin, not saying a word. The warmth she'd exuded yesterday was gone.

Maybe it wasn't necessary to tell her anymore. From the looks of it, her interest in Dee had cooled overnight. She probably already regretted kissing her.

When she steered the BMW toward the steel-and-glass office building of Kudos Entertainment, the parking lot was still relatively empty. A quick glance at her wristwatch showed that it was too early for the nine o'clock crowd to arrive. *Whew.* If she was lucky, they'd make it into the building without anyone seeing them arrive together.

No sooner had she thought it than a red Toyota wheeled into an empty space a few rows over, and Jack Brower, one of her brother's PR guys, got out.

Great. If Jack Brower knew, Sally Phillips would find out as soon as she set foot into the building. Before lunch, the whole company would talk about how Attila the Hun had arrived at work with the new employee, who was still wearing yesterday's clothes.

Before she could stop her, Austen got out of the parked car and waved, giving Jack a friendly smile. "Good morning, Jack."

He returned her smile. "Good morning. Ready for your second day at—?" His gaze fell on Dee. "Uh, see you inside." He hurried across the parking lot toward the main entrance.

Austen watched him go. "What was that?"

"Shit," Dee muttered. "He saw us arrive in the same car."

Austen turned and studied her. "Are you worried about what he and the rest of our colleagues might think?"

Dee shrugged. "Aren't you?"

"We don't work in the same department, so this," Austen pointed back and forth between them, "shouldn't be a problem, right?"

Dee said nothing.

"Oh. I get it now. You're not out at work."

Dee snorted. "Please. Even the cleaning ladies know I'm a lesbian."

"What is it, then?"

This wasn't a conversation Dee wanted to have in the company's parking lot. She scrubbed her hands across her face. "Austen, look…"

Austen lowered her gaze. "I understand. It was just one kiss, and you were on pain medication, right? If you want us to just forget about the whole thing and not see each other again…"

Dee couldn't stand the insecure, hurt expression on Austen's face. "No!" Before she could think twice, she stepped closer and pulled Austen into her arms. "No, that's not what I want. It's just…"

Austen's arms came around her, and she leaned her head against Dee's shoulder. She exhaled as if she had waited the entire morning for a hug. "Yeah?"

The warmth of Austen's body against hers didn't exactly make thinking any easier. "It's just complicated."

Austen leaned back a little and smiled. "Aren't all good things?"

Who could resist that smile? Certainly not Dee. She smiled back. "Maybe."

"Do you want to meet after work and talk about whatever is bothering you?" She caressed Dee's back, making her tingle even through her suit jacket.

Dee squared her shoulders and nodded. Austen deserved to know the truth, no matter the consequences. She would tell her tonight. "My house, around eight? I'll even get some groceries and cook."

"Good. Want me to bring dessert?"

With any other woman, Dee would have answered with an innuendo, but they were standing in the company parking lot and she was overly aware of how inappropriate a sexual relationship between them would be. "No. You don't have to bring anything."

Just when she was about to pull back from their embrace, a silver Jaguar XJ pulled into the parking space next to the BMW and her brother got out.

Dee hastily let go of Austen and stepped back, but it was too late.

Judging by the frown on Tim's face, he'd already seen them.

"Good morning, Mr. Saunders," Austen said, smiling brightly.

Tim's gaze flicked from Dee to Austen. "Good morning." He turned his attention back to Dee, who cringed inwardly and hoped he wouldn't call her "sis" and give away her secret before she had a chance to tell Austen the truth. "Can I talk to you for a second?" he asked.

"Uh, sure," Dee said, even though it was the last thing she wanted. She knew what he would say. She was in for some brotherly ass-chewing—a well-deserved one. Shoulders slumping, she followed him to the elevator.

As soon as they reached his office, Tim took up position behind his desk and gestured at her forehead. "What happened to you?"

Dee waved him away. "Nothing."

"Okay, if you don't want to talk about it, would you mind explaining what the hell you think you're doing with my new assistant?" Tim leaned across his desk and put the two-inch height advantage he had over her to good use.

Dee glared back. "None of your business."

"None of my business? None of my business?" Tim's face took on an unhealthy color. "Oh, it damn well is my business—quite literally. This company can't afford to be slapped with a sexual harassment suit just because you couldn't keep your pants zipped. Jesus, Dee, why can't you go to a lesbian bar or a club and pick up some other hussy?"

Blood roared through Dee's ears. She slapped both palms on the desk, making it rattle, and leaned forward, right in Tim's face. "Shut up! Austen isn't a hussy!"

Tim stared at her and then dropped onto his desk chair. From there, he continued to look at her. "Okay, okay. I never said she was. But getting involved with her still isn't a bright idea. I really thought my new admin was smarter than that. To get involved with the company's COO on her very first day..."

Dee's anger deflated, and she sank onto the visitor's chair. "She doesn't know."

"Doesn't know what?"

Studying the carpet in her brother's office, Dee said, "Who I am. She thinks I'm just some grunt slaving away in operations."

Tim gave her an incredulous stare. "You slept with her without telling her who you are?"

"No."

"But you just said that she doesn't know."

Dee rocked forward onto the edge of her seat. "I didn't sleep with her." For some reason, her brother seemed to think she was a female version of Casanova, just because her relationships never lasted for very long. She didn't care what he or anyone else thought of her, but now she wanted to set the story straight because of Austen. She stood. "And you don't have to worry. Nothing else will happen between us. As soon as she finds out who I am, she won't want anything to do with me anyway."

He must have seen the regret in her eyes, because his stern expression softened. "Sorry, Sis. You really like her, don't you?"

Dee just shrugged.

"But believe me; it's better this way." He rounded his desk and slapped her shoulder in a brotherly way.

"Just promise me that you won't say anything to her. I want to tell her myself." Austen deserved that much from her.

Tim made a zipping motion across his lips. "I won't say a word. And now tell me what happened to your forehead. It looks like someone drove over you with a lawn mower."

"Thanks a lot."

"What happened?" he asked again.

"I found out that wishing on a falling star is a dangerous thing." Not just for her head, but for her heart too.

"What are you talking about?" Tim looked at her as if he was starting to doubt her sanity.

"When I went to hang up that damn snowflake, the tree topper fell and hit me. Your admin drove me to the ER and stayed the night to keep an eye on me. In the guest room."

The disapproving frown on his face faded. "Ah. So that's why you drove to work together. Sorry for jumping to conclusions."

Not all of his conclusions had been wrong, but Dee didn't want to admit that. "I'd better get to work. Talk to you later." She turned and left his office before he could ask any more questions.

CHAPTER 7

AUSTEN SAT AT HER DESK, her fingers lingering over the keyboard, but she hadn't written more than *Dear Mr. Schaefer* since booting up her computer ten minutes ago.

The shouting from behind Mr. Saunders's closed office door kept distracting her.

She had thoroughly misjudged her new boss. Yesterday, she had thought him to be fair and friendly, but clearly, he was more like his sister, Attila, than she had known.

What an asshole. Poor Dee. She tried to eavesdrop and find out why he was shouting at her, but the thick walls muffled the sounds, and she didn't dare get up to put her ear against the door.

Mr. Saunders's office door opened, and Dee slunk out. The confident stride Austen had gotten used to was gone.

"God, Dee." The letter on her screen forgotten, Austen jumped up and rushed over to her. "Are you okay?"

Not looking at her, Dee nodded.

"What did he want?" Austen marveled at how protective she already felt of Dee, even though they'd met only yesterday. She was ready to march into Mr. Saunders's office and tell him off. "You're not even working in marketing, so what gives him the right to shout at you like his maniac sister?"

Dee visibly flinched.

"Hey." Austen touched her forearm.

The door to the outer office opened, and Sally stepped in, her purse over her shoulder.

Quickly, Dee pulled back. "I need to go write that report."

Austen watched her retreating back until the door clicked shut behind her.

"Good morning," Sally said, glancing back at the door. "What did she want? Did you see those stitches on her forehead? Looks like someone tried to bash her head in. Too bad they didn't succeed."

What the...? Austen took a step toward her colleague, ready to throttle her. "That's not funny, Sally. The tree topper from our Christmas tree crashed down on her. She could have lost an eye."

Sally hooked one thumb behind the strap of her purse and gave her a disapproving look. "Jesus, don't take my head off. You're still new around here, so you don't know her as well as we do. If you did, you wouldn't defend or hang out in the ladies' room with her."

"I know her well enough to know she doesn't deserve to be hurt."

Sally shook her head at her. "Let me give you one piece of advice that'll spare you a lot of heartache. Don't get involved with her. I hear her girlfriends never last much longer than her assista—"

The door opened again, and another one of their colleagues stuck his head into the outer office. "Wow, did you see Ms. Saunders? Looks like one of the poor souls working for her finally snapped and tried to bash her head in."

It took a moment for the words to sink in. *Dee. Danielle Saunders.* That was why someone working in mid-level management could afford a BMW and a nice little Victorian in Irvington and why Dee had been able to order Vanessa to get her briefcase before heading to the ER. She wasn't just a senior manager; she was the company's COO. The blood rushed from Austen's face, and she swayed.

Sally stepped closer as if ready to catch her should she fall. "Hey! What's wrong? You look like you've seen a ghost."

No. Not a ghost. Just a pathological liar. Austen stumbled to her chair and sank onto it. Her thoughts were racing. Scenes from the hours she'd spent with Dee flashed through her mind. Had Dee secretly laughed at her when she'd talked about Mr. Saunders's sister and called her Attila? Had it all been just a game to her?

"Ms. Brooks?" Mr. Saunders called from the doorway of his office. "Can I talk to you for a minute?"

Austen looked up. *Oh, no. He's Dee's brother. He saw us arrive together, in Dee's car, with me wearing yesterday's clothes.* And now he wanted to see her in his office—probably not to have her take a letter. With a sinking feeling in her stomach, she got up and moved to his office.

He held the door open for her and ushered her inside. "Have a seat."

The soft carpet that she had admired just yesterday now felt like quicksand, pulling her into a deathly trap, as she crossed toward the visitor's chair and sank onto it. It was still warm from Dee's body heat.

Dee. She tightly closed her eyes, then opened them again as Mr. Saunders rounded his desk and sat behind it.

He regarded her across the desk. His eyes were the same color as his sister's, she realized. He really looked like a male version of Dee.

Her heart clutched as she looked at him.

After several seconds of silence, he cleared his throat.

Austen held her breath and braced herself for what he would say. Did he think she was trying to start an affair with his sister to sleep her way up the career ladder?

"Did you have a chance to get caught up on the correspondence I sent you?" he asked.

Austen slumped against the back of the seat and let the breath she'd been holding escape. He didn't know. Well, there was nothing to know. Not much, anyway. It had been just a kiss, even if it had felt like the beginning of much more. "Yes, I did."

"I need a one-page summary of every marketing campaign we've done in the last quarter. Do you think you can do that by the end of the day?"

A part of Austen's confidence returned. This was familiar territory. "Of course, Mr. Saunders. I'll get started right away." Glad to escape his office, she jumped up and rushed back to her desk. She would just focus on the job and keep up the professional facade until she could fall apart in her apartment tonight.

Dee had hidden away in her office all morning, not taking any calls. Not that it had helped with her productivity. She'd spent most of the time watching the cursor flash on her blank computer screen.

When lunchtime came, her stomach started to growl, reminding her that she'd skipped breakfast. She reached over and opened a paper bag containing a blueberry muffin. Austen had lovingly picked it out for her, insisting she have breakfast too. It smelled mouthwatering, but eating it would have felt as if she were taking advantage of a friendliness she didn't deserve. She closed the bag and leaned back.

Did Austen know who Dee was by now? Probably. Considering the look Sally had given her as Dee was leaving Austen's office, she had probably told her the instant Dee left. Had Austen become angry? Worse, had she cried?

The thought made Dee's heart hurt. She could take anger, but the thought of tears in Austen's eyes... *Oh, come on. You've barely known each other for twenty-four hours. It's not like you broke her heart.* Maybe Austen had taken it well. She seemed to be the forgiving type.

Only one way to find out—and staying in her office, hiding, wasn't it. She usually confronted whatever life threw at her head-on, so she would do the same now. If she hurried, she could still catch Austen in the cafeteria.

She took her vest from the back of her chair and put it on but left the suit jacket behind. From the way Austen's gaze had lingered on her this morning, she guessed that Austen liked how she looked in the vest.

When she reached the cafeteria, it was bustling with activity. The hum of conversation sounded like a beehive. Dee usually didn't eat there, preferring to wolf down a sandwich in her office and then to get back to work, so she had no idea who sat with whom. She stood in the aisle between tables and craned her neck, looking for the marketing team and one auburn head in particular.

Someone with a tray slammed into her back.

Growling, Dee whirled. Her sharp reprimand died on her lips, and her breath caught. *Austen.*

"Oh, I'm so sorry. I didn't pay attention to—" Austen looked up from her frantic attempts to balance the orange juice on her tray. The color drained from her face. "Dee!"

Dee smiled at her.

Austen didn't smile back. "I mean...Ms. Saunders."

So she knew. And clearly, she wasn't in the mood for forgiveness.

Before Dee could think of something to say, Austen grabbed her tray more securely and shouldered past her.

"Austen!"

Austen stopped, every part of her body stiff with tension. Slowly, she turned back around and glared at Dee. "Don't call me that." Her voice was low, but it still cut like steel.

"Aus—" Dee bit her lip. "Please. Let's talk. Give me a chance to explain."

"I'm afraid I have to get back to work, Ms. Saunders. Your brother needs a one-page summary of all marketing campaigns in the last quarter, so I have to hurry if I want to get any lunch."

Dee flinched at being called *Ms. Saunders* in such a cool, formal tone. Gone was the warmth and affection she'd seen sparkling in those gorgeous sapphire eyes yesterday. "Give me one minute. You can eat while I talk."

"You should have told me yesterday. Now there's nothing left to talk about." Austen pushed past her. Her colleagues from marketing waved at her to join them, so she walked over and sat at their table. Instead of digging into her food or engaging in conversation, she stared at her pasta without eating.

Great. Just great. Now Austen wouldn't even listen to what she had to say. Well, what was one more employee who hated her, right? She was used to uncomfortable silence and hostile glances whenever she entered a room. Somehow, though, this felt different.

Sighing, she turned and headed back to her office.

Toby's excited screams reached Austen before she even entered her one-bedroom apartment. He was hanging upside down from his cage, close to the door, waiting for her to let him out.

She dropped her wet umbrella, kicked off her shoes, and padded into the living room.

The red light on her answering machine flashed. Probably a call from her best friend, Dawn, wanting to know how her first day at the new job had gone and where she'd been last night.

Austen didn't walk over to check or call her back. She didn't know how to explain what had happened in the span of less than forty-eight hours. At least Toby didn't require any explanations. She went over to his cage and opened the door, glad to see him after the day she'd had.

Using his strong beak, he climbed out of the cage and walked up her arm toward her shoulder, where he sat and made happy grinding sounds with his beak. "Hellooo."

"Hello, you." Austen gently scratched behind his crest feathers. "How was your day?"

"Fuck," he warbled.

Austen managed a smile. "Yeah, mine was pretty fucked up too."

Toby fluffed up his feathers and started nibbling on her earring.

"Cut it out. That's not a bird toy." Austen turned her head away. With Toby still riding on her shoulder, she walked over to the kitchen to get him a few peanuts.

He squawked when he saw the treat and immediately set out to crack the first shell, dropping crumbs everywhere. Finally, when no more peanuts were forthcoming, he tugged on her earring again and imitated the ping of a microwave.

"No, thanks, Toby. I'm not hungry." She'd been looking forward to having dinner with Dee tonight, but now everything was different.

She flopped down onto the couch, making Toby flap his wings and relocate to her chest. *God, I kissed her. Kissed our COO.* She ran her fingers over her lips.

"Yummy, yummy, yummy," Toby said.

Austen scowled at him. "No, it wasn't yummy at all."

Toby let out a wolf whistle.

"Okay, maybe it was." Admittedly, the kiss hadn't been bad. Quite the opposite. But she would have never kissed her had she known who Dee was.

Dee had taken that choice from her. Worse, she couldn't shake the feeling that it had all been just a game to Dee. After three years of working hard to overcome feeling like a naive fool who fell for the smooth lines of a liar, she was right back where she had started.

"Loser," Toby warbled.

Austen squeezed her eyes shut. Yes, that was exactly how she felt.

CHAPTER 8

A FEW DAYS LATER, AUSTEN sat with Sally and Jack in the cafeteria, halfheartedly listening to their conversation without contributing to it.

"Sushi! Can you believe it?" Jack held up a piece of tuna nigiri and dipped it into wasabi.

Usually, Austen would have been as excited about sushi day at the cafeteria as her colleagues were, but she hadn't had much of an appetite all week—since finding out about Dee—so she just nibbled on her avocado maki.

At the table next to them, some employees from sales were wolfing down sushi as if there were no tomorrow. "Roy said it was one of the toy designers," one of the women said in a stage whisper loud enough to be heard in half the cafeteria. "Ms. Saunders didn't like the design for next year's Halloween costumes, so she went down to development to scream at him in person. That went on for half an hour without her running out of steam. When he couldn't take it anymore, he took one of the toy sabers and whacked her in the forehead." She made a swinging motion with her fork, demonstrating.

Austen put down the piece of sushi and shoved her tray back. She'd had to listen to stupid gossip about the cut on Dee's forehead all week. Every day, the tales about what had happened were getting more ridiculous, making her suspect that many of the rumors about Attila were outright lies or at least exaggerations. What had Dee done to earn the scorn of every single employee at Kudos Entertainment? Whatever it was, it couldn't be so bad that she deserved to be treated like that, could it?

Oh, yeah? Remember how she lied to you the entire time? So stop defending her!

"Bullshit," another guy from sales said. "That's not how it happened, Maria. I heard she tried to get fresh with a young woman during a job interview, so the lady took a letter opener from the desk and nearly stabbed one of Ms. Saunders's wandering eyes out."

Okay, now they had passed ridiculous and were quickly approaching slander. At the moment, Dee wasn't Austen's favorite person either, but she instinctively knew that Dee would never touch a woman without her consent. The urge to jump up and set the story straight swept through her, but she forced herself to stay where she was. Dee didn't deserve to be defended.

Determined to forget her, Austen popped a nigiri into her mouth and chewed vigorously. Her jaw froze mid-chew, and her eyes widened as the sting of wasabi flared along the roof of her mouth and burned her tongue. She grabbed her water and gulped it down, then snatched Jack's glass from his tray and drank his water too. "Jesus!" She fanned herself. "Who put wasabi on my plate?"

"You did," Jack said.

"No way." Austen hated wasabi. "I never eat that stuff."

Sally nodded. "You piled it on your plate like it was mashed potatoes."

Austen stared down at the heap of wasabi on her plate. *I'm really losing it.*

"What's going on with you?" Sally leaned over the table. "You seemed a little distracted all week. This spaced-out airhead routine is not how you usually are, is it?"

"No!" Austen rubbed her cheeks, which were still flushed with the aftereffects of the wasabi. God, she had to get herself together before rumors started flying about her too. "No, of course not. It's just…"

"Is it Ms. Saunders?" Sally asked, her voice low as if she were giving away state secrets. "You and she…are you… having an affair or something?"

So the rumors were already flying. As soon as she left, the guys from sales would probably start talking about how she had slept with Dee to further her career. *Great.* "No, of course not. I've never seen her in my life before I started working here, so I don't really know her." Now her cheeks flushed with more than the wasabi. She hated lying, and a lie of omission was still a lie. How was she any better than Dee?

"Better keep it that way," Sally said before swiping a salmon temaki through a puddle of soy sauce and biting down on it.

Austen nodded and got up. "Excuse me for a second. I need more water."

After five days of getting the silent treatment from Austen, Dee was admittedly getting a little desperate. They had passed each other in the hallway or had ridden up to the fifteenth floor in the same elevator a time or two. Dee had even gone to Austen's office under the pretense of having to talk to her brother. Each time, Austen had been polite and businesslike but brushed off every attempt at a more personal conversation.

Forget about her. It was only one day, one kiss, and there are other fish in the sea.

But the problem was that the other scaly creatures didn't keep her attention. Austen was gentle, friendly, and warm, but she was no pushover, and Dee secretly loved that she didn't let her get away with anything. She wanted to find out more about this fascinating woman. Plus she hated unresolved matters. She was the company's problem solver, yet she couldn't even get the newest employee to talk to her. Admittedly, it pricked her pride.

She stared at the phone on her desk. Should she try to call her? No. Austen would just hang up on her or politely direct her call to one of her colleagues.

She glanced at the clock on the wall of her office. Almost five o'clock. Time to wrap up work and head home, at least for all the other employees, who had a life beyond work and a special someone to come home to.

Austen would probably leave on time to feed Toby, her uncouth cockatoo. The memory made Dee smile. She grabbed her jacket and hurried to the elevator.

She'd try just one more time to talk to Austen. Maybe now that she'd had some time to cool down and think about it over the weekend, Austen would be more willing to listen. Christmas, the celebration of love and forgiveness, was right around the corner, after all. Or was that Easter? Dee had never been big on organized religion, so how was she supposed to know? It didn't matter anyway.

She left the building and took up position next to the main entrance.

At five o'clock on the dot, employees started to file through the doors. Most threw Dee startled glances when they found her lurking in front of the building and then hurried past her as if their shoes were on fire.

Christ. What did they think she was doing? Writing down the name of everyone who didn't work overtime to report him or her to her uncle, their CEO?

After fifteen minutes of waiting and scaring employees, Dee had enough. If she remembered correctly, Austen took the MAX to work, so she wandered over to the stop right across the street and sat on a bench to wait.

She had forgotten her overcoat in her office, and now the light drizzle soaked her suit jacket. Shivering, she crossed her arms over her chest and tried to think warm thoughts. The memory of kissing Austen did the trick.

A MAX train came and went, then another. Commuters crowded onto them, but still there was no sign of Austen. Had she not been at work today? Had something happened, or was she out sick?

The thought of Austen, all alone at home, suffering through some unknown sickness, made Dee frown. *Oh, come on. She has to be in her early thirties. So far, she made it through all the colds and stomach flus just fine without you.*

Rain dripped down her back.

Two of their toy designers walked past, doing a double take when they saw her huddling on the bench. They kept sneaking glances at her while they waited for the next train.

Dee growled. She was making a fool of herself, and she had sworn she'd never do that over a woman—yet here she was, shivering in her damp jacket, waiting for a woman who might never show up, and if she did, she might club Dee with her umbrella.

Just when Dee wanted to get up and return to work, a figure crossing the street caught her attention.

Austen! She would know that gentle sway of well-rounded hips anywhere. Slowly, she stood and waited for her to come closer. Her heart was pounding faster than it had during her very first presentation in front of the board. She knew the exact moment when Austen spotted her.

Austen paused on the edge of the sidewalk. Her hand with the umbrella dropped down, and she stood there without its protection, not caring—or not noticing—that she was getting wet.

Not sure Austen would come any closer, Dee walked over. "You're getting wet," she said softly, pointing at the umbrella that limply dangled from Austen's hand.

"You look pretty wet yourself," Austen said.

Dee shrugged and attempted a grin. "Well, what can I say? Good-looking women have that effect on me."

The moment she'd said it, she knew it was a mistake. What Austen needed—what she deserved—was a sincere apology, not a lame joke.

Austen lifted her umbrella back over her head. Now Dee couldn't see her eyes anymore.

"Sorry," Dee said. "That was inappropriate."

"Yes, it was." Austen's voice was colder than the rain dribbling down Dee's back, but Dee knew she had only herself to blame.

"Listen, can we talk? There's a coffee shop right around the corner." Dee pointed. "They even have banana chocolate chip muffins, your favorite."

Austen shook her head. "There's nothing to talk about."

"Please," Dee said.

The toy designers were looking over, observing their conversation with interest.

Dee gritted her teeth. *Oh, how the mighty have fallen. Danielle Saunders begging a woman for five minutes of her time—in front of witnesses.*

The train slid to a stop at the station, and the toy designers got on.

Austen folded her umbrella. "I have to go."

Dee stepped in front of her, between Austen and the train's still-open doors.

Another bad idea.

Austen's eyes flashed. "Let me through."

This is not the way. She couldn't boss Austen around and make her do anything she didn't want to. It had been that way from the very first moment. Dee lowered her head and stepped out of the way. She stood in the rain and watched as the train, with Austen on it, disappeared in the distance.

For the rest of the evening, Dee threw herself into work. Her job had always been her sanctuary, the one thing that really mattered in her life, but now she found thoughts of Austen intruding time and again. Everything suddenly reminded her of Austen, even the numbers on her screen.

Zero chance of Austen ever talking to her again.

One hell of a kiss they'd shared.

Two fortune cookies they'd had for dessert.

Getting just three hours of sleep the night Austen had stayed over, lying awake, trying to figure out how to tell her who she was.

Four hours of waiting in the ER until someone had finally looked at the cut on her forehead.

The five points of the star that had crashed down on her.

Six years had gone by since she'd last been so interested in someone.

It would take more than the Seven Wonders of the World for Austen to forgive her and become her friend, let alone more.

Eight stitches in her forehead that would forever make her remember their first meeting.

"Shit, shit, shit." She stabbed her fingers down onto the Ctrl+S key combo, saving the report she'd been working on, and hurled her wireless mouse across the office.

It crashed against the door and landed on the carpet.

No one came to see what had happened and whether she was all right. The outer office was empty, as it had been since she'd fired her last assistant.

She got up and walked over to pick up the mouse. "I need a goddamn admin."

What she wanted wasn't just any administrative assistant, of course. She wanted her brother's admin, to see her smiling face every time she left her office. Not that Austen would ever smile at her again.

Why the hell are you obsessing over her? She's just one woman. Was it just her pride that made her so desperate to see Austen again and set things right?

Growling at herself, she snatched up her phone and called IT.

No one answered. They had all gone home hours ago.

Dee dialed the home number of the head of the IT department. "First thing tomorrow morning, send someone up to bring me a new mouse."

A moment of silence while the head of the IT department figured out who was on the line. "Ms. Saunders? Uh, this is my home number, and it's nearly ten."

"You think I care? I need a new mouse."

"Again? Ms. Saunders, we replaced yours just last week."

"Then don't keep bringing me inferior ones that don't last long." She hung up and dropped onto her office chair. That annual report was due tomorrow, and she was supposed to work on a deal with Disney, yet she couldn't focus worth a damn. She had to set things right with Austen before she could go back to work.

But Austen refused to listen to her. Hell, she wouldn't even look at her, no matter how many times Dee lurked in the parking lot or waited for her in the cafeteria. She'd even considered calling HR and coming up with a plausible reason why she needed Austen's address and phone number. But she instinctively knew that Austen would view it as an invasion of her privacy. It would only make things worse.

Well, if the mountain won't come to Muhammad, Muhammad has to come up with another plan. First thing tomorrow morning, she would call marketing and have them send Austen over to talk to her. She was the company's COO, so Austen couldn't refuse. Not if she didn't want to get fired. A twinge of guilt shot through her, but she pushed it down. In her world, the end always justified the means.

CHAPTER 9

THE NEXT MORNING, AUSTEN WAS already at her desk, retyping the notes from their last team meeting, when the door to the outer office opened. For a second, her heartbeat sped up. She relaxed when she saw that it was only Mr. Saunders. Somehow, she kept expecting Dee to show up, wanting to talk. *You don't want to talk to her, remember?* Besides, if only half of the rumors going around were true, Dee had moved on to greener pastures by now. Apparently, no woman had ever managed to capture her attention for long.

Briefcase in hand, Mr. Saunders padded over the carpet toward her desk. "Good morning, Ms. Brooks. Any calls for me?"

"Good morning. One." She handed him a slip of paper. "Our printer is having some problems with the files for the campaign Jack came up with."

He glanced down at the piece of paper and then back up at her.

Austen was reminded of Dee and looked away from the smoky gray eyes. She had to put that lying, controlling woman out of her mind once and for all.

Instead of continuing on to his office, Mr. Saunders took another step toward her desk and picked up the paper snowflake lying there. "You still haven't hung yours?"

Austen hoped her blush wasn't visible. "I was about to, but then the accident with your sister happened, and I didn't get around to it afterward." She had stayed away from the lobby whenever possible, not wanting to run into Dee. For the last week, Dee had been stalking her all over the company and demanding to talk to her, not taking no for an answer like the control freak she was. Austen was ready to explode and shout at her to finally leave her alone—not a good move if she wanted to keep her job.

"Why don't you do it now?" Mr. Saunders asked.

"But what if someone calls while I'm downstairs?"

"I'll keep an eye—or an ear—on the phone."

"You really don't have to do that," Austen said. "I don't think I'll hang a snowflake."

Mr. Saunders arched a brow, a move that again reminded Austen of his sister. "Why not?"

"I don't know what to wish for." The only thing her life was missing was love, and her first attempt at romance after Brenda—sharing Chinese takeout and a kiss with Dee—hadn't turned out so well.

"Nonsense." Mr. Saunders handed her the paper snowflake. "Come on. It was your idea after all. We can't have you be the only one who doesn't get to make a wish."

Hesitantly, Austen took the snowflake. She cursed herself for coming up with that genius idea.

Minutes later, she stood in the center of the lobby, staring up at the tree. Someone had replaced the tree topper with a safer one, made of gold-sprayed plastic. Not that it was really necessary. No one but Dee would ever rearrange the lights just because she didn't like the way another person had done it.

She stared at the paper snowflake in her hand. What to write…? Maybe she should wish for Dee to finally leave her alone so that everything could go back to normal. But did she really want that—never seeing Dee again, except for when she absolutely had to for professional reasons?

Before she could decide, she realized she'd forgotten to bring a pen and walked over to the reception desk to get one.

The doors of one elevator opened, and Marcus, their new intern, tumbled out. When he saw her, he waved and bounded toward her. "There you are!"

She liked him. He reminded her a little of the golden retriever puppy she'd had as a child. The thought made her giggle, but it was true. He was just as eager to please as Balu had been. "Were you looking for me? I thought you were with operations today?"

He nodded. "Yeah. It's great. Ms. Saunders let me sit in on their team meeting." His eyes gleamed with hero worship—or maybe even a little crush.

Not that she could blame him. Dee was an attractive woman. *If you don't mind being lied to.*

"She sent me to get you," Marcus said. "She wants to talk to you ASAP."

Vanessa, the receptionist with the pink streak in her hair, looked up from her paperwork and gave her a worried glance. "Uh-oh. What did you do?"

Austen's hackles rose. "Nothing."

"Did she say what she wants?" Vanessa asked, looking at Marcus.

"No. Just said she wants to see Ms. Brooks in her office right away."

"Ugh. The devil's lair. That's not good. Maybe she's still mad at you for throwing that star at her." Vanessa twisted the pink strand of hair around her finger.

"I didn't throw the star at her. It fell." Dee had been right—apparently, Kudos Entertainment's employees did spend most of their time gossiping instead of working.

"Whatever it is, I really hope you didn't manage to get yourself fired after less than two weeks," Vanessa said.

Austen smoothed damp palms over her pencil skirt. "No, I'm sure it's nothing like that."

"I wouldn't be so sure about that. Once, she fired an employee after just—"

"I'd better get up there," Austen said, cutting her off. She wasn't in the mood to listen to another story about Attila the Horrible.

On her way up to the fifteenth floor, the elevator kept stopping to pick up other employees, giving Austen ample time to sweat over what was to come. Why oh why did she have to volunteer for that darn Christmas tree decoration? Her life before that had been nice and peaceful, just the way she liked it. She'd had a new job she liked and a new boss she respected, lived in a city she loved, and maybe, one day, she'd be ready to start dating again. Now nothing was the same.

The farther up the elevator traveled, the more nervous she became. Dee wouldn't fire her because she refused to talk to her, would she?

The elevator doors pinged open on the fifteenth floor.

With her heart in her throat, she stepped out and made her way over to the COO's corner office. Timidly, she knocked on the outer door.

No answer, which meant Dee still hadn't hired a new administrative assistant.

She entered, crossed the room, and knocked on Dee's office door. Her heart was beating so loudly that she was afraid Dee would hear it. *Calm down. Stay professional, whatever she wants.*

"Yes?"

Austen swallowed. Again, she smoothed her hands down her skirt to get rid of any wrinkles and realized that she was still holding the paper snowflake. Before she could turn and put it on the empty desk, the door swung open.

Dee stood in front of her, in a sapphire blouse that made her eyes look more blue than gray. "Are you going to come in, or do you want to discuss this from the doorway?" she asked, her voice soft.

Austen looked back over her shoulder. Better to get this over with once and for all. Dee had to finally get it through her thick head that she wanted to be left alone. She squeezed past Dee, careful not to let their shoulders brush, and walked toward the visitor's chair.

Instead of sitting behind the desk, Dee perched on top of it, right in front of Austen.

For several seconds, they looked at each other in silence until Austen couldn't stand it anymore. "Here I am, as ordered." She lifted her hands, indicating herself. "So?"

Dee winced at the word *ordered*. "It was the only way you'd talk to me."

"I'm not talking to you, Dee. I'm talking to our chief operating officer because she ordered me to."

Dee's shoulders lifted and dropped under a deep breath. "It wasn't the COO you kissed."

"I wouldn't have kissed you if I'd known who you are," Austen said, even when a voice in her head whispered, *Are you sure about that?* "Why didn't you tell me before I made a total fool of myself?"

Dee shuffled her feet over the carpet. "Guess it never came up. And you didn't make a fool of yourself."

"Never came up?" Austen's voice rose. "We spent the whole evening in the ER, just sitting around, waiting. I asked you about Attil—about Ms. Saunders, and yet you never thought it necessary to come clean?" She realized she was shouting at Danielle Saunders, their COO. Not a clever move if you wanted to keep your job, but at the moment, she didn't care. "Were you laughing at me the whole time?"

"What? No, please don't believe that for a second." Dee slipped from the edge of the desk and knelt next to Austen. Those irresistible gray eyes pleaded with her. "I never laughed at you."

A rapid knock came behind Austen. Before either could react, the door swung open. "Ms. Saunders? I have your new m—" The man paused in the doorway and stared at Dee, who still knelt next to Austen. "Uh, your new…um…mouse."

Dee jumped up. "Out!"

Holding up a mouse still in its package as if it were a shield, the man stuttered, "What a-about the m-mouse? Should I l-leave it or—?"

"Get out!" Dee wrenched the package from his hands and closed the door in his face. Cursing, she hurled the mouse across the office. "Great. Can you imagine what the watercooler gossip will say now?"

Austen couldn't help smiling. "Probably that you were caught proposing to your brother's assistant right here in your office."

Dee scowled at her; then her expression softened, and she smiled. She crossed the office, picked up the mouse package, and shook it.

Broken pieces rattled inside.

Sighing, Dee threw the package into the waste basket next to her desk. "That's why I didn't want to tell you." She pointed at the place where the stuttering IT guy had been standing a minute ago. "I didn't want you to look at me like that. I wanted to be Dee with you, not the company's COO."

After hearing her colleagues talk about Dee all week, Austen could understand that, but still the betrayal hurt. "How do you know I wouldn't have looked beyond your professional role and seen the woman?"

"You called me Attila, even though you'd never even met me."

Not one of her brightest moments, Austen had to admit that. "That was stupid, but don't you think I would have made up my own mind once I met you, no matter what rumors I'd heard about you?"

Dee shrugged.

"You never gave me that chance, Dee. I want complete honesty from the women I date." After Brenda, she had sworn to herself that she would never again accept anything less, so why was it that she kept attracting women who thought lying to get their way was perfectly fine? Did she have the word *sucker* tattooed all over her face?

Dee looked up, her eyes wide. "Dating? Is that where you thought this was going?"

Austen sighed. She hadn't thought at all, and that was the problem. She'd just acted on the attraction she felt, giving in to the urge to kiss Dee without allowing herself time to think and hesitate. "You didn't, apparently."

"I shouldn't have kissed you back, no matter how much I wanted to," Dee said, her voice low as if she was afraid of their conversation being overheard. "I wish it were different, but dating an employee would be a really bad idea for me."

"Yeah, I know. That's why it would have been nice if you'd told me who you are from the start." She stood and faced Dee. Maybe she was making a mountain out of a molehill. This was Dee, a stranger she still barely knew and hadn't even known existed two weeks ago, not Brenda, the woman she'd been in a relationship with for more than three years. Yes, both women had lied to her, but Dee's lie wasn't anywhere in Brenda's league. "Let's just let this go and forget about it, okay?"

"But I don't want to just forget about it." Dee looked like a petulant child who'd been told she couldn't get a sucker. "I want—"

Austen lifted her hand to stop her. Even Danielle Saunders had to get used to not always getting what she wanted. "No, Dee. Let it go."

"But can't we be friends? I rarely meet people who don't get on my nerves after two seconds, so why not be friends?"

"I don't think that's a good idea. You know I'm right." Before Dee could try to get her to change her mind, she turned and walked out. When the door closed between them, she hesitated. *Let it go,* she repeated to herself. *It was the right decision.*

Then why, she wondered, did it feel so wrong? She trudged back to her own office and knocked on Mr. Saunders's door to let him know she was back and would take over phone duties again.

"Hope you made it a good one," he said.

"Uh, excuse me?"

"Your Christmas wish," he said. "I hope you made it a good one."

The snowflake! Where was it? Austen looked down at herself. Her hands were empty, and her skirt had no pockets. She must have lost the paper snowflake somewhere in Dee's office. *How fitting.*

When Dee bent and took the package out of the waste basket to see if she could repair the mouse, her gaze fell on a silver object lying on the floor.

Austen's snowflake. She'd held it in her hand when she'd entered the office.

Dee put the mouse aside and picked up the snowflake. It was blank, with no wishes written on it. About to crumple it up and throw it away, she paused and studied it.

The pattern on this one was a little different from the one she had hung. Just like real snowflakes, each of the Christmas tree ornaments was unique. Had Austen cut out each snowflake individually?

Probably. Austen seemed like the kind of woman who'd do that.

Dee contemplated heading over to Austen's office to give back the snowflake but knew it wasn't a good idea. From now on, every contact between them had to be of a strictly professional nature. She opened a drawer, took out an envelope, and scribbled a quick message. After putting the snowflake and the message inside, she closed the envelope and threw it into her out-box. She'd take care of it later.

A knock on the door made Austen look up from the hundreds of messages in her in-box. "Come in."

Helga from HR walked in, a silver bowl in one hand and an envelope in the other. "This was taped to your door." She held out the envelope.

Austen frowned. The guy who brought their mail had already been by an hour ago, so what was this?

Only her name, Austen Brooks, was written on the envelope in bold letters, no department. She would open it later. "Thanks. What can I do for you? Mr. Saunders isn't in."

"I'm not here to see Mr. Saunders. I just realized that probably no one told you about the Christmas party the office is throwing on Friday."

"Sally mentioned it."

"Oh. Good, good. We always do a Secret Santa and swap gifts during the party. I know it's very last minute, but I was wondering if you wanted to participate in that. There's one name left." She held out the silver bowl with a folded piece of paper at the bottom.

"Sure." Why not? She liked shopping for gifts, even if it would probably go to a colleague she didn't know. She reached into the bowl, pulled out the slip of paper, and unfolded it.

The name written there made her want to throw it back and tell Helga that she'd changed her mind.

Danielle Saunders.

Luck definitely wasn't on her side. Or maybe it had nothing to do with luck. Kudos Entertainment had more than two hundred employees. What were the chances of only Dee's name remaining? Had other people drawn it and talked Helga into being allowed to put it back? Knowing Dee's lack of popularity with the people working for her, it was a distinct possibility.

She imagined Dee at the Christmas party, watching the others unwrap their gifts. She'd be the only one not receiving anything.

Austen closed her hand around the slip of paper. She couldn't do that. Not when she clearly remembered the first Christmas after her mother's death, when her father, about to be deployed to Kosovo and numb with grief, had forgotten to buy her a Christmas present.

"The spending limit is fifty dollars," Helga said, taking back the now-empty bowl. "So, you're in?"

Austen sighed. "I'm in."

When the door closed behind her colleague, she put the slip of paper into her desk drawer and opened her browser. She already knew what to get Dee. As she began her search on the Internet, she couldn't help smiling. A few minutes and a couple of clicks later, she was done. *There. Now let's see what this is.* She took the envelope from her desk and opened it.

A paper snowflake fell out, a sticky note attached to its shiny surface.

Company policy states that every employee has to make a Christmas wish. Please adhere to it.
D. Saunders

So that's how it would be from now on. All business. *That's the way you wanted it, didn't you?* Then she caught sight of the postscript.

PS: Be careful when you hang the snowflake. Beware of falling stars!

Despite everything, Austen had to laugh. She put the snowflake and the note into her desk drawer, next to the slip of paper with Dee's name, and went back to her business e-mails.

CHAPTER 10

KUDOS ENTERTAINMENT HAD GONE ALL out for the Christmas party. Austen looked around the lavishly decorated ballroom on the lower level of the Rosebud Hotel.

A band was playing, and people were mingling, chatting, or piling their plates high with food from the buffet.

Wow. What a difference to the Christmas party at her old place of work!

The only thing Austen didn't like was the alcohol flowing freely. A few of her colleagues were already sipping from their second or third Christmas cocktails. She didn't begrudge her hardworking colleagues an opportunity to let their hair down, but the alcohol was starting to loosen their tongues and they were bitching about their bosses and the company's senior executives—one in particular.

Dee. Of course. Wonder where she is? Austen craned her neck but couldn't find her anywhere. Had she stayed home? At least she didn't have to listen to all the stories being told about her. Every anecdote painted her in darker colors. Why did her subordinates and everyone else in the company hate her so much?

Austen realized that she didn't. Dee might have lied to her about who she was, but Austen still didn't believe most of what they were saying about her. To her, Dee wasn't a monster ruthlessly firing or demoting people. She was still the Dee who had made her laugh by making up fortune cookie quotes, who had let her boss her around, only grumbling a little, and who had kissed her so tenderly.

Sally stepped next to her, interrupting Austen's increasingly amorous thoughts. Her plate looked as if she'd skipped the appetizers and the main course and had started with dessert. "Hi, Austen. You clean up nicely."

Austen looked down at her black cocktail dress. She hadn't been sure what to wear since this was her first company party and had finally decided on something elegant, yet not too revealing. "Thanks. You look nice too."

And she did. Her silver sequin dress hid the extra padding on her belly and hips and made her look voluptuous instead of overweight. "Yeah, well, I've been single for ages, and I hear thirty percent of women meet their husbands at work."

Office romances. Not a good idea, Austen reminded herself.

"How about you?" Sally asked. "Are you going stag too?"

"Yeah." She'd thought about asking Dawn, her best friend, to come with her but then decided not to. Knowing her gossipy colleagues, they would have started rumors about hot kisses beneath the mistletoe if she showed up with a woman.

"Seems we're not the only ones." Sally pointed at something or someone behind Austen.

She turned.

Dee was leaning against one wall, looking over at them. When their gazes met, both looked away.

After a moment, Austen risked another peek.

So far, she had seen Dee only in her business pantsuits and in faded jeans, but now she wore an ivory dress that draped over her statuesque frame, cut high to the neck but leaving her athletic arms bare.

Her mouth suddenly dry, Austen looked around for a glass of the red Christmas cocktail.

"Come on," Sally said. "Let's get some more of those cinnamon truffles and have a seat. I think they're about to start the slideshow."

Dee leaned her head on her hand and watched as her uncle clicked through his slideshow of important or funny company events throughout the year—anniversaries, product launches, and the going-away party for Wendy, her assistant.

Yeah, people. Remember that? She didn't kill herself or end up in a sanatorium. She just moved to Florida.

Laughter echoed through the ballroom as her uncle presented the traditional company awards. People clapped as a guy from customer service stepped forward to receive the award for taking the craziest call from a customer. The woman had complained about the missing guarantee card for a toy, which, as it turned out, she had stolen.

Good thing Uncle Wade made Tim, not me, the head of customer service. Her patience for foolish customers was limited to say the least.

Of course, she also wasn't very pleased when the award for causing the most paper jams went to someone from her department. She'd have to talk to her people on Monday.

Finally, it was time for the Secret Santa gifts.

Dee sighed and glanced at her wristwatch. Would anyone notice if she snuck out?

"Don't even think about it," Tim said from across the table.

"Think about what?" Dee gave him her most innocent look, which, admittedly, wasn't very innocent.

"Leaving. You already opted out of the company picnic this summer, so you're staying for this."

Dee scowled. Their company picnic had involved a paintball battle this year. While she would have loved nothing better than to shoot a few of the idiots down in sales, she wasn't too eager to have all the employees gang up on her. They would have spattered her with paint before she could even get her finger on the trigger. *No, thanks.*

"And maybe try out a smile," Tim said. "This is the holiday season, after all, and nobody likes working for Ebenezer Scrooge."

Dee showed her teeth in an imitation of a smile. "Happy now?"

Tim sighed. "Keep working on that."

"Is this really so bad for you?" Janine, Tim's wife, asked and gestured around the ballroom. "I mean…this is nice, isn't it?"

Dee made a face. If she were Janine, she'd be happy to be here too, away from two screaming babies for the night.

"Don't bother," Tim said to his wife. "She's been like this all week, stuck in a constant grumpy mood. Not that she was Miss Sunshine to begin with, but it's been even worse lately." He tilted his head and scrutinized her closely. "What's going on, Sis?"

Unbidden, Dee's gaze darted over to another table, where Austen sat surrounded by her colleagues. She was laughing at something Jack said, throwing her head back and exposing the elegant line of her neck. Her black dress created an appealing contrast to her auburn hair.

Tim craned his head to see what she was looking at. "Don't tell me this is still about Ms. Brooks."

"Ms. Brooks?" Janine asked and leaned to the side to follow their gazes. "Who's that?"

Dee ignored the question and glared at her brother instead. She looked to her left and right to make sure no one was listening in on their conversation.

"She's my new secretary," Tim said. "I'll introduce you later."

"She's pretty," Janine said.

"Dee thinks so too."

"Would you shut up?" Her brother was totally missing the jealous undertone and the insecurity in Janine's voice. *Men. It's a wonder he's still married.* Not that she was any better at relationships. Maybe it was a genetic thing. None of her relatives seemed deliriously happy in their marriages.

"Oh." Janine took another look at Austen, then searched Dee's face. "You mean you and she...?"

"No! My mood has nothing to do with her. I just wasn't very happy to have to do my annual report all over again. She's just Tim's assistant; that's all." If she repeated it to herself often enough, she'd start to believe it.

Their uncle tapped his microphone to get everyone's attention again. "So now please all head over to the Secret Santa table and open your gift."

Chairs scraped over the floor as people jumped up.

"Come on." Tim stood. "Let's see if I got another stress ball this year."

Janine hooked her hand around his elbow and followed him.

Dee stayed where she was. No need to head over to the Secret Santa table. For some reason, no one had drawn her name since they had started the tradition a few years ago. She suspected that someone in HR was manipulating the drawing. Frankly, she didn't care. If she wanted a stress ball or some other trinket, she'd buy it herself.

When Kudos Entertainment's employees crowded around the Secret Santa table, she got up and went over to the punch bowl. She wouldn't get drunk, of course, but maybe a little alcohol would help her get through the evening.

Out of the corner of her eye, she saw someone step next to her. She didn't turn to see who had joined her, not wanting to encourage the person to start a conversation. She had no patience for small talk.

"Hi," Austen said.

The ladle fell from Dee's hand and splashed into the punch. She turned and tried to look nonchalant. "Hi."

They studied each other without saying anything else.

Up close, Austen looked even more stunning, but Dee couldn't tell her that. The COO could compliment a company employee for her touch-typing or her organizing skills but not for the way she looked in a cocktail dress.

Finally, Austen broke the silence. "You got the stitches out."

Dee resisted the urge to rub her forehead. The skin there was still tender. "Yeah, a few days ago. I had to go back and have Dr. Babyface do it because my family doctor is on vacation." This time, no one had been holding her hand when he came at her with a pair of tweezers.

"He did a good job."

Dee shrugged. "Guess he did. People finally stopped staring at me."

They looked at each other in silence, and again, it was Austen who broke it. "Aren't you going over to see what Santa brought you?"

"He didn't bring me anything." Dee smirked. "Guess I wasn't a good girl this year."

"I don't know about that, but I have it on good authority that he did bring you a little something."

Dee arched an eyebrow. "Oh, really?"

Austen nodded.

"Okay, then let's go check it out before someone steals it." She led the way over to the Secret Santa table and scanned the gifts on it. *What do you know?* Austen was right. One of the wrapped presents had a tag with her name. Like all the other gifts, this one didn't have the name of the giver on it, though.

Dee hesitated. With her luck lately, it probably was a gag gift that would embarrass her in front of everyone.

"Go on; open it," Austen said when Dee kept staring at the gift.

Bracing herself, Dee reached for the square package. She shook it and held it to her ear. No ticking. At least it wasn't a bomb.

Austen watched her, grinning.

Finally, Dee decided to get it over with. She tore off the wrapping paper, revealing a box with the logo of a technology firm. *Not a stress ball or some other cheap item.*

Her Secret Santa obviously hadn't been stingy. Beneath the transparent plastic top sat an ergonomic computer mouse. It had a nice anthracite color and looked big enough to fit her hand well. Apparently, some thought had gone into this gift.

Dee looked up, not sure what to say. "Thank you."

"Last I looked, there was no name on the present. How do you know it's from me?"

"Please. If it were from anyone else, I would have gotten an ugly reindeer sweater or something equally embarrassing." She trailed her fingertips over the box. "So, thanks."

Austen gave her a nod. "You're welcome. I know you probably replaced yours already, but you never know when having a spare one will come in handy."

"Are you saying I have a temper?"

"Are you saying you don't?"

Dee's facial muscles, tense all evening, eased into a smile. God, she really liked this woman's feistiness and her sense of humor. "I'm not admitting to anything, but I promise not to throw this one."

"Good." Austen tipped an imaginary hat and started to walk away.

Dee quickly blocked her way. She wasn't ready to give up the company of the only woman in the room who was neither a kiss ass nor someone who hated her. "Uh. How about I buy you a drink?"

"Buy me a drink?" Austen repeated. "There's an open bar, and Mr. Haggerty is footing the bill."

Did Austen know that their boss was her uncle? Dee wanted to speak on equal footing and hated saying anything that would remind Austen of their different statuses in the company. She also didn't want her to think that she had gotten her job just by being related to the boss. She'd worked hard for her position. Still, if she didn't tell her, Austen might see it as another betrayal.

"It's practically family money. You do know that he's my uncle, right?"

Austen's startled expression made it clear that she hadn't known. "Mr. Haggerty is…?"

"My mother's brother."

Austen rubbed her temples. "Any other relatives in the company that I should know of?"

"I hate to admit it, but that idiot heading the sales department is my cousin."

"Christ."

"So how about that drink? You look like you need it."

Austen nodded and followed her over to the punch bowl. "What's this?"

Dee looked at her own glass. She hadn't tried it yet. "I have no idea. It's red."

"I think I'll pass. My mother told me never to drink anything I can't identify."

Whenever she mentioned her mother, Dee didn't know what to say. Austen talked about her as if she were still an important part of her life, even though she'd died fifteen years ago, while Dee saw her own mother only a few times a year. "Smart woman." She put down her glass. "I'm not sure I want to drink it either. Let's head over to the bar and get a real drink."

Austen followed her wordlessly.

The bartender greeted them with a broad smile. "What can I get you, ladies?" He pointed to the rows of bottles behind him.

"Give me a whiskey and soda," Dee said.

"And what would you like?" The bartender slid his appreciative gaze over Austen.

Dee barely resisted the urge to tell him he should keep his eyes to himself. Austen probably wouldn't appreciate it.

Austen tapped the pineapple decoration on the bar. "How about a piña colada? Easy on the rum, please."

"Coming right up." He filled a blender with ice and added pineapple juice and cream of coconut.

Dee smirked. She would have bet good money that he'd prepare Austen's drink first.

The bartender grabbed a bottle of rum and spun it on his palm, then flipped it around his back and over his shoulder before catching it again. He grinned when Austen clapped.

Show off. "Bet you can't do it with your eyes closed." Dee knew she shouldn't, but she couldn't resist issuing the challenge. Something about the wannabe Tom Cruise irked her.

He met her challenging gaze. "Just watch me." He closed his eyes and threw the twirling bottle around his back. His hands closed a second too late, grasping only air.

The bottle crashed to the floor, splattering rum everywhere.

Dee watched without wincing. *Told you, you couldn't do it.*

"Jimmy! What are you doing?" Another bartender bustled over and pushed the red-faced Jimmy out of the way. "Why don't you take a break now?"

"It wasn't his fault." Austen nudged her with an elbow.

Dee stepped forward. "She's right. I told him to do that. Let me take over for a second."

"Uh, all right."

As Jimmy slunk away, she crossed to the other side of the bar, careful not to slip on the wet floor.

Jimmy's supervisor stepped out of the way but kept watching her.

She grabbed a new bottle of rum, flipped it over her shoulder just as Jimmy had, and caught it smoothly.

"Impressive," Austen said.

"You think that's impressive? Watch this." Dee couldn't resist showing off a little, so she repeated the maneuver with her eyes closed, catching the bottle without missing a beat. *Take that, Jimmy!*

When she opened her eyes, Austen shook her head at her instead of swooning. "Are you always this competitive?"

"Pretty much. Guess it's normal when you grow up with four brothers. We're all pretty competitive with each other."

Austen's eyes widened. "You have four brothers?"

Dee nodded. "Four brothers and," she counted quickly, "eleven cousins, all of them male. On my father's side of the family, I'm the first girl born in three generations."

"Wow. And I thought growing up with my dad and my brother was giving me testosterone overload."

After adding just a bit of rum, Dee blended the mix until it was smooth, then poured everything into a cocktail glass and garnished it with a maraschino cherry and a wedge of pineapple. "Here you go. One piña colada, easy on the rum."

Austen stared at the glass. "You've done that before."

"Yeah. More times than I can count."

"Did a lot of partying during college?" Austen wrapped her full lips around the straw and sipped from her cocktail.

Dee forced herself not to stare at her mouth. "I wish. No. I tended bar and waited tables."

"Your parents didn't pay for your college education?"

"They would have, but I wanted to pay my own way through college."

Austen gave her a respectful nod.

Dee was surprised how good that unspoken praise felt. Her family had thought it a foolish waste of time.

Austen took another sip. "This is really good."

"Glad you like it." Dee poured herself a whiskey and soda and walked back around to Austen's side of the bar. "How about you? Did you go to college?"

"I always thought I would. I had my eye on Berkeley for a bachelor of fine arts or maybe a BS in management, but then my mother died and I didn't want to leave my little brother, especially with our dad being gone so often."

Again, Dee found herself tongue-tied. She'd never been responsible for anyone's well-being but her own, and she couldn't imagine taking care of a family at the age of sixteen. "That's the brother who taught your cockatoo a bunch of four-letter words?"

"Yes. That's Brad."

"Brad?" Somehow, Dee had expected a less ordinary name from parents who had named their daughter Austen.

Austen smiled. "His full name is Bradbury William Brooks."

"Ah, finally an author I know. I could never make myself read anything by Jane Austen, but I devoured everything by Ray Bradbury I could get my hands on when I was younger."

Austen opened her mouth to answer but then closed it again. She put down her glass on the bar and looked at Dee. "You're very easy to talk to; did anyone ever tell you that?"

Dee laughed. "No. Most people aren't too fond of my style of communication."

"I can imagine. Maybe you should try not shouting at them all the time. Why don't you talk to everyone else the way you talk to me?"

"Because you're the only one who's not an idiot or a kiss ass or both. You're not constantly trying to impress me. You're just...you. I like that."

In the silence between them, the music from the band seemed overly loud.

Damn. She'd said too much. Dee took a large sip of her whiskey and soda.

"Thanks," Austen said softly. "Just for the record, I think you're a decent person too. At least away from the office."

"Thanks. I think." Dee chuckled, again appreciating Austen's honesty. So it was more than mere physical attraction. They liked each other. *One more reason to stay away from her.* Dee was good at solving any kind of problem at work, but making relationships work wasn't her specialty. Even if she, by some miracle, did manage to make it work this time, a relationship with Austen could have a serious backlash on her career—not to mention what could happen if they broke up and Austen didn't take it well.

"I think I'd better go over now and see if Santa brought me anything." Austen lifted her glass. "Thanks again for the drink."

"My pleasure." Dee leaned against the bar and watched her retreating back. Why, for Christ's sake, couldn't her brother hire an assistant who was ugly as sin and had the personality of an assembly-line robot?

CHAPTER 11

DEE PASSED HER FATHER THE mashed potatoes. "You should reinvest some of the money."

"Nah." Her father waved her away and added enough gravy to his plate to flood a small country. He looked across the table at Caleb. "What do you think, son?"

Her brother gave the same advice that Dee had. Instead of rejecting it out of hand, their father listened and hummed his agreement between bites of turkey and stuffing.

Dee pushed back her plate. She'd lost her appetite. Maybe she should have been used to it by now. God knew, this wasn't anything new.

"It's Christmas Day, for heaven's sake," her mother said after a while. "Could you stop talking about business for once?"

Silence descended over the long dining room table.

Dee chuckled inwardly. Discussions of politics or sports had already been banned years ago, when her father and Uncle Wade had gotten into a shouting match at Thanksgiving; business was the only thing left they had in common. Their family dinners looked more like meetings of Portland's most successful entrepreneurs. Without business as a topic of conversation, it would truly be a silent night.

She wondered how Austen was spending Christmas Day. No doubt she would travel to see her father and brother.

"How are the twins?" her mother asked when the silence grew awkward.

Instantly, Janine launched into a detailed explanation of colic and diaper rash.

Dee's sisters-in-law and her cousins' wives pointed out possible remedies for both.

When the discussion turned to the different types of diapers, Dee stopped listening. At least discussing tax-saving tips with her father had been familiar territory.

Finally, the last bite of pumpkin pie was eaten.

The men rose to have a glass of whiskey in the living room, recovering from doing nothing all day, while the women gathered in the kitchen to do the dishes.

Dee hated that tradition, but every time she complained and told her mother that this was the twenty-first century, her mother just smiled and said she didn't mind. *Well, that makes one of us.* She worked just as hard as her brothers, uncles, and male cousins, and she appreciated a fine glass of fifty-year-old single malt as much as they did.

"So," her mother said as she handed her a pot to dry. "When will you finally get married and give your father and me some more grandchildren?"

Several of her sisters-in-law giggled.

Dee clutched the pot and willed herself to stay calm. *Think of Austen. At least you still have your mother, even if she drives you crazy.* "I don't want children, Mom. I'm too busy with my career."

Her mother patted her arm. "That's what I said before I had you and your brothers. You'll change your mind too, just you wait and see."

Dee wanted to scream. "I don't think so. Besides, it's not like I can get pregnant by accident."

Her mother continued doing the dishes as if Dee hadn't said a word.

Even though she'd come out to her parents at sixteen—and again at twenty-one—they chose to ignore her sexual orientation and pretended she'd one day come home with a son-in-law who would go into business with Caleb Senior and his three oldest sons, helping them manage their chain of clothing retail stores.

Dee glanced at her watch and decided she'd try to make a quick escape in half an hour. Too bad she'd have to go through this again on her birthday, which, unfortunately, was in just two days.

"In case you get bored up there, you could make yourself useful, squirt," Austen said.

Her brother, now five inches taller than Austen, laughed and hopped down from the counter. "What do you want me to do?"

"Get me the milk and eggs from the fridge."

Brad opened the fridge and pulled out a carton of eggs and a gallon of milk before hopping back up onto the counter. He dangled his long legs as he watched her cook, as he'd done since he'd been a little boy.

He's not so little anymore. Sometimes, it was still hard to believe that he was all grown up now, a junior studying computer science at Cal Poly.

Austen cracked the eggs and mixed them with the flour, the milk, a bit of salt and sugar, and her secret ingredient—mashed bananas. "What did you think of Caroline?" she asked while she melted butter in a large skillet.

Brad shrugged. "She's okay, I guess."

"Yeah." She ladled a bit of pancake batter into the skillet and sprinkled chocolate chips onto it. "She seemed nice. I'm glad Dad found someone. Being alone all the time wasn't good for him."

They looked at each other, neither of them saying what Austen was sure both of them thought—how weird it was to see him with another woman. Maybe because he'd sensed the awkwardness, their father had left with his new girlfriend after dinner on Christmas Day while Brad was staying with her for a few more days.

Brad reached over and stole a handful of chocolate chips.

"Hey!" Austen smacked his hand with the spatula.

"Ouch! Don't hit me."

"Don't steal my chocolate chips."

"What about you?" Brad asked. "Do you have someone? It's been ages since what's-her-name."

"You know her name."

"Not worth remembering," Brad muttered.

Austen flipped the pancake with a bit more gusto than strictly necessary. "No arguments there from me."

"So?"

"I just started a new job. I don't have time for dating."

Brad slid closer on the counter. "I know that look on your face. That's exactly how you looked when you were fifteen and smooching Tina Baker behind the shed."

"We weren't smooching! Tina's as straight as they come." Still, Austen's face burned with heat. She'd been quite infatuated with the neighbor's daughter back then. "Besides, you were five and couldn't even tie your own shoes, so how would you know what I was doing or not doing with Tina?"

Brad just grinned. "There is someone, right?"

"No." Austen slid the pancake, cooked to a perfect golden brown, onto a plate and got started on the next one.

"What's her name?"

"I told you I'm not dating anyone."

"Did you meet her at work?"

Austen adjusted the heat and turned toward him. "Read my lips: I'm—not—dating!"

"Okay, okay." He stole more chocolate chips.

"What about you?" Austen asked when they finally sat down with a stack of banana chocolate chip pancakes. "Any hot campus romances I should know about?"

Her phone started to ring in the living room.

"Phew." Brad wiped his brow. "Saved by the bell."

Austen hurried to the living room. "Keep the pancakes warm," she called over her shoulder. "And don't eat all of them." A little breathless, she picked up the phone. "Yes?"

"Good morning, Ms. Brooks. I'm sorry for disturbing you at home on the weekend."

Austen frowned as she recognized her boss's voice. "Don't worry about it. What can I do for you?"

"I need the file on Giggles, that new electronic pet we want to launch next year."

"It's on your desk, Mr. Saunders." At least, that was where it had been when she'd left the office on Christmas Eve, three days ago.

"I know, but I'm not in the office, and I can't reach Ms. Phillips. I really need that file. Today."

Since Mr. Saunders had given all of them the rest of the week off, Sally had mentioned something about escaping for a one-week cruise in the Caribbean. "Do you want me to get the file and bring it to you?"

"That'd be great, but I'm not at home. My family and I are spending the weekend in our cabin in the foothills."

"Oh." Austen's mind churned to come up with the easiest solution. "I could fax you the documents or scan them and—"

"That won't work. I need the prototype too, and you can't fax it." Mr. Saunders paused. "I know it's a lot to ask, but do you think you could pick it up and bring it to me? The company will pay for your time and expenses, of course."

Austen sighed.

"It's less than an hour," Mr. Saunders said, "and the area is really nice. You could bring your boyfriend...uh, or girlfriend...and get away from the city for a while."

That sounded nice, actually. Maybe Brad would want to come. Even if he didn't, he was no longer the six-year-old who needed constant supervision. He could entertain himself for a few hours. "All right. I'll do it."

"Thank you. Do you have something to write with?" He gave her the address and directions to the cabin, thanked her again, and hung up.

Brad peeked into the living room. "That was her, wasn't it?"

"Who?"

"Your new girlfriend. Booty call?"

"What? No!" Austen threw her pen at him. "That was my boss, you little idiot."

"Why does he call you at home? I thought you had the rest of the week off."

"That's what I thought too, but now he wants me to drive to his family's cabin at Sandy River to drop off some stuff he needs. Want to come? I hear it's very scenic."

Brad strolled into the room and threw himself onto the couch, where he'd slept the last few nights. "No, thanks. In fact…" He peered over at her. "I didn't want to say anything after Dad took off early, but…would you mind if I take off too? Gary texted me and asked if I want to go skiing with him and the old gang."

Austen suppressed a sigh. "No, I don't mind. Have fun, but don't break anything."

He jumped up, raced around the couch, and kissed her cheek on the way out the door.

"What about the pancakes?" she called after him.

"I ate three already. The rest are all yours." Within seconds, the apartment door closed behind him.

She considered calling her friend Dawn to ask if she wanted to drive to Sandy River with her, but then she remembered that Aiden had taken a few days off, so Dawn would probably prefer spending some uninterrupted time with her partner. It seemed Giggles would have to do for some company on the way to the Saunderses' cabin.

When Mr. Saunders had said *cabin*, Austen had expected a rustic one-room log structure in the middle of the woods, but as her navigation system led her around a bend in the two-lane street, a large house with a wraparound deck and a satellite dish came into view.

Austen checked the address he had given her, just to make sure she hadn't taken a wrong turn somewhere and had landed at some luxury resort. The hastily scribbled note confirmed that this was the right place. She drove down the gravel road and parked her eight-year-old Hyundai next to a Jaguar, a Mercedes, and a Bentley.

So it wasn't just Mr. Saunders and his wife and kids at the cabin. Was Dee here too? She gave herself a mental slap as her heartbeat picked up at the thought. Still, she couldn't help looking around for the familiar BMW.

It was nowhere to be seen. Relief warred with disappointment.

"Come on, Giggles. Let's go in." She took the file and the prototype off the passenger seat and got out of the car.

The scent of firs and pines filled her nose as she slowly made her way toward the house. A river roared somewhere nearby, but she couldn't see it, because the house was blocking her view. Mountains loomed in the distance, their peaks white with snow. A light scattering dusted the steps leading up to the front porch. On the top step, Austen paused and turned to enjoy the view for a moment.

"Nice, isn't it?" came a low voice from behind her.

Austen jumped and dropped the file.

When she turned around, Dee sat on a bench, hidden in the shadows of the house.

"Jesus!" Austen clutched her chest. "You scared the hell out of me!"

"Sorry." Dee stood and crossed the porch toward her.

They bent to pick up the file at the same time, which brought them face to face, with only inches of space between them. Both froze.

After a few seconds, Dee was the first to move. She held out the file. "Here."

"What are you doing out here?" Austen asked, clutching the file and Giggles to her chest. Dee wasn't even wearing a coat, just jeans and a burgundy sweater.

Dee looked left and right before saying, "Hiding."

"From what?"

"From the testosterone brigade and their significant others."

How different they were. Austen would have loved nothing more than to spend more time with her family, whereas Dee was hiding from hers. "How bad can it be? I bet there's a nice wood-burning fireplace in there and probably the best kitchen money can buy."

"Don't forget the heated floors and the Jacuzzi on the back deck."

Was she joking? Austen studied her and took in the tense lines of her face. Probably not.

"And you? What are you doing here?" Dee asked.

"Your brother called me."

"Which one?"

"Mr. S—Timothy."

Dee cursed. "That idiot. I told him I could get the file and the prototype."

"Oh, no. If I let you take my car, you'd spend your birthday alone in the city while the whole family is here," Mr. Saunders said, stepping through the doorway.

It's her birthday, and he's calling me to bring the file so they can discuss business? Austen couldn't believe it.

He turned toward Austen. "Thanks for coming all the way out here."

Austen nodded. It wasn't as if she'd had to fight her way through the wilderness.

"Want to come in for a minute? I think you haven't met Uncle Wade, our CEO, yet."

Austen swallowed. Suddenly, hiding out here with Dee didn't sound so bad, but of course she couldn't refuse. "All right." With one last glance back at Dee, she followed him inside.

Dee hadn't been kidding about the heated floors—or about the testosterone brigade. Half a dozen men stood as Mr. Saunders led her into the formal dining room. They were all wearing business suits, only the ties were missing. Instead of a birthday cake, files, spreadsheets, and pie-chart diagrams littered the table.

Where were the women? *Do they keep them chained to the stove?*

Mr. Saunders—Timothy—introduced her to his uncle, his brothers, who all looked like male copies of Dee, and, finally, his father.

Caleb Saunders Senior shook her hand as if he expected her to kiss his ring and then went back to looking at his brother-in-law's business plans without giving her a second glance.

Gosh. Austen had been at funerals with more pleasant atmospheres. And this was supposed to be Dee's birthday party? Now she understood why Dee was hiding out on the porch. "All right. I think I'll head back now."

"Thanks again for going out of your way to do this for me." Mr. Saunders indicated Giggles and the file she'd brought. "I really appreciate it."

Before they could leave the dining room, Dee entered. "I'll drive back with her."

"What?" Austen and her boss said at the same time.

No one else reacted. Dee's father and her other brothers were still bent over a document.

"I have work waiting for me at home," Dee said. "If I don't kick some asses on Monday, we won't get that talking lizard into the stores on time."

"Oh, come on, Dee," Timothy said. "Work? On your birthday?"

Dee lifted one eyebrow and pointed at the paper-littered dining room table. "Not like we're doing anything else here."

"Yeah, but at least we get to spend some quality time together as a family."

He thinks this is quality time? Austen couldn't help staring. She wanted to grab Dee and whisk her away to the city, where she'd invite her to a real birthday dinner. But, of course, she couldn't do that.

"Call me when you get back," Dee said. "We'll have dinner or something."

Austen watched with growing disbelief as Dee shook her father's hand. *No hug?* He patted her shoulder once, then let go and went back to his discussion.

Only Timothy followed them to the door.

"I'll be right back," Dee said. "Whatever you do, don't leave without me."

Austen nodded numbly.

Dee ran upstairs, taking two steps at a time. When she returned, she carried two large bags.

"What's all that?" Austen asked as they left the house and put the bags into the trunk of her car.

"The presents I got. Can I drive?" Dee held out her hand, a hopeful expression on her face.

"No."

Still giving her the puppy dog eyes, Dee added, "Please."

Austen laughed. "The magic word doesn't help you this time. The answer is still no."

With a bit of a pout, Dee folded herself into the passenger seat.

A hawk circled overhead as Austen drove toward the highway. "Do you really have work waiting at home, or was that just an excuse?"

"I always have work waiting for me."

That didn't really answer her question, but Austen decided to let it go. "Well, at least you got nice presents. The birthday of my best friend in high school was the day after Christmas, and her family never gave her anything extra, just lumped it in with Christmas."

"No, at least my family never did that. If there's one thing they have enough of, it's money." Dee pointed over her shoulder at the trunk. "That stuff should make me a nice bundle on eBay."

Austen nearly drove the car into the ditch. "What?"

"Don't look at me like I'd said I wanted to sell my firstborn."

"But—"

"Do you want to know what I got for my birthday?"

Austen nodded.

"Well, let's see. An iPad keyboard and a wool coat from my brothers, a golf umbrella from Uncle Wade, and pearl earrings from my parents." Dee ticked it off on her fingers. "Oh, and a FDNY calendar with a bunch of half-naked firemen from my cousins. And Janine, Tim's wife, gave me a self-help book about how to heal your emotional self and lead a more balanced life."

Austen laughed. "Think she wanted to tell you something? Okay, I admit I wouldn't have liked the calendar full of naked guys either, but the rest doesn't sound so bad."

"It would be great if I had an iPad or pierced ears, played golf, and the coat wasn't two sizes too small."

Okay, that did sound bad. Didn't her family know her at all? Austen was silent for a while. "You didn't get even one thing you liked?"

"Well," Dee gave her a sidelong glance, "you showing up to spring me was pretty nice."

"That's not why I came."

"Still. I didn't like being stranded up at the cabin without a car, but Tim showed up at my house and kidnapped me this morning. He knew if I had my car, I'd try to escape early."

Austen couldn't imagine having that kind of relationship with her family. "So you're really going to sell your gifts?"

"Why not? I don't like clutter in my house."

No one could ever accuse her of having a cluttered house; that's for sure. Austen suppressed a smile as she remembered the practically bare Victorian. "Because it's rude."

"Rude?" Dee snorted. "No, rude is getting vitamins for women over childbearing age from Aunt Margaret. I'm thirty-six for crying out loud!"

Austen chuckled at Dee's outrage. "Ouch. Okay, that wasn't very nice. But why don't you at least donate whatever you don't want to Goodwill? It's not like you need the money, do you?"

"No, I don't." Dee rubbed her chin. "Okay, I'll do it—on one condition."

Austen looked away from the road for a second to eye her suspiciously. "What condition?"

"That you come with me to drop the stuff off at the nearest donation site."

Spending time with Dee outside of work wasn't a bright idea. Austen hesitated. *Oh, what the heck.* There was a donation site on Northeast Broadway, not too far from where Dee lived. It would take them only a few minutes to drop off the unwanted gifts. "Want to go see if they're open today? Or do you really have a hot date with that lizard?"

Dee chuckled. "I don't date reptiles. Although come to think of it... There was this woman a few years ago who could have been half snake. She could do some amazing things with her tongue."

Heat crept up Austen's body, and she cursed her vivid imagination. "Dee! Too much information!"

"What?" Dee gave her an innocent look. "I was talking about her ability to tie a cherry stem without using her hands."

"Yeah, right. I'm sure that's all you meant."

"Really. She could—"

"Will you shut up if I let you drive?"

Dee beamed. "Pull over."

Sighing, Austen did.

Ninety minutes later, they walked out of Goodwill, sans the two bags of gifts. "If my grandfather could see me now, practically giving family money to the unwashed masses..." Laughing, she sidestepped the slap Austen threw at her shoulder.

"Are there any non-snobs in your family?"

"Tim isn't so bad. And me, of course."

"Of course." Austen stopped in front of the driver-side door and waved. "Keys."

Reluctantly, Dee handed them over. "Anyone ever tell you that you sound like a drill sergeant?"

"My father. Good thing he's a colonel, so he still outranks me."

Dee eased into the passenger seat, careful not to hit her knees in the small car. "Your father's in the military?"

"He was. He's retired now."

Dee's admiration for Austen grew with everything she learned about her. With her father in the military and her mother dead, she must have practically raised her brother almost by herself.

A few minutes later, Austen stopped the car. "We're here."

Dee peered out through the windshield. "That's not my house." In fact, they weren't anywhere near it.

"I know," Austen said but climbed out of the car anyway.

Dee followed.

Austen crossed the street and held open the door of a café for Dee to step through first.

The tantalizing scent of coffee and chocolate wafted through the room, making Dee's mouth water. *Yum.* She sniffed like a dog.

"I know it might not be the best idea for us to spend time together outside of work, but I couldn't let you go home without cake."

Touched, Dee sat across from Austen at a small table. She couldn't remember the last time someone had done something that nice for her. "Company policy might not like it, but I do. I love cake."

Austen reached for the menu, but instead of scanning it, she just played with it.

Dee observed her. "Spit it out."

Austen made eye contact for a second before looking away. "I was just wondering. I know it's none of my business, but if you love cake, why wasn't there any at the cabin?"

Now it was Dee's turn to fiddle with her menu. "That's just not how things are done in my family. We always spend my birthday and the last few days of the year at the cabin, showing each other how well our companies did the past year."

"And how did you celebrate your birthday when you were a kid?"

"The same way." At the shocked expression on Austen's face, she added, "It wasn't so bad. Even then, I loved discussing business with my father."

The waitress came to take their orders.

Dee ordered the cream cheese pound cake while Austen, after glancing at the menu for just a few seconds, settled on the triple chocolate cake.

The waitress brought their coffee, and Austen still hadn't said anything. She stirred enough sugar into her cup to send a city full of diabetics into shock. Finally, she glanced up. "Excuse me if I'm out of line, but your father wasn't discussing anything with you. He barely looked up from his documents long enough to say good-bye to you."

"No, he—" Dee stopped herself. Why was she defending him? Austen was right. "When I was little, I spent a lot of time in my father's office. I'd just curl up on the plush carpet and listen to his pen scratch over paper. Or I'd perch on his desk, dangle my legs, and look at all the pretty, colorful diagrams."

Austen smiled. "Bet you were cute."

Dee raised one brow. "Well, everyone seemed to think so. By the time I entered school, words like *break-even point* and *degressive depreciation* were part of my everyday vocabulary. My father loved showing me off at parties he threw for his business friends."

The smile on Austen's lips faded. "With that kind of vocabulary, wasn't it difficult to talk to other kids your age?"

"I never played with kids my age. They bored the heck out of me."

The waitress brought two large pieces of cake.

Dee eyed the slice on Austen's plate, which was covered by chocolate fudge frosting and drizzled with chocolate sauce. "Think you have enough chocolate there?"

Austen licked her lips and sliced off a piece of cake with her fork. "There's no such thing as enough chocolate."

"If you say so."

After giving the chocolate cake her full attention for a minute, Austen gazed up from her plate. "So you were the apple of your father's eye. What happened to change that?"

Dee chewed a bite of cream cheese cake, enjoying the fresh lemon flavor. "Guess as I grew older, he stopped thinking it's cute for a girl to spew business terms."

"But isn't he proud as a peacock of everything you have accomplished? I mean…you're the COO of a Fortune 500 company at the tender age of thirty-six."

"Thanks for the subtle reminder about my age," Dee said. She took the sting out of her words by grinning at Austen. Taking another forkful of cake, she thought about it before she answered, "I guess in his own way, he probably is. He just has a hard time showing it."

Austen grunted, either unconvinced or because she had her mouth full of chocolate cake.

Dee didn't want to talk about her family anymore. "How about you? How did you celebrate birthdays when you were a kid?"

"Cake, clowns, candles, the whole nine yards. Mom always went crazy with decorations. She'd sneak into my room while I was asleep, and I woke up to a room full of balloons and a confetti trail for me to follow. We'd find confetti everywhere for months afterward until my dad finally convinced her to use streamers instead." Austen trailed her fork over her plate, looking as if she were a million miles away.

Dee's stomach clenched. *Stop bringing up topics that make her think of her mother, asshole!* Should she change the subject? Make a joke? Reach across the table to touch her hand?

Before she could decide, Austen looked up and smiled. "Want another piece?"

Dee glanced down and realized she'd eaten the rest of her cake without even noticing. "Bring it on."

An hour later, they tumbled out of the café, both of them clutching their bellies.

"Oh my God." Austen groaned. "I never ate so much cake in my life."

"I thought there's no such thing as too much chocolate cake?"

"I might have been wrong."

Dee stopped in the middle of the sidewalk and made a show of staring at her. "You admit to having been wrong? You?"

"I said *might*."

Dee laughed. "Right."

They climbed into the car, and Austen put the key in the ignition. For a moment, she considered asking Dee if she wanted to go get ice cream, just because she didn't want their afternoon to end. Next week, they'd be the COO and the administrative assistant again, but today, she'd had fun with Dee.

Finally, she decided that her stomach couldn't take another bite. It was a bad idea anyway.

They were both quiet on the short drive to Irvington.

When Austen stopped the car in front of the Victorian, Dee slowly unfastened the seat belt and turned to face her. "Do you want—?" She paused and shook her head. "Thanks for the cake. That was the best birthday I had in years."

If three pieces of cake were all it took to make it the best birthday in years, Austen didn't want to even imagine her other birthdays. She made a mental note to throw a big party for Dee next year, then scratched it. Assistants didn't throw birthday parties for the company's second-in-command. "My pleasure," she said with a weak smile.

Dee opened the passenger door and set one foot on the sidewalk. She shifted her weight, about to climb out of the car, but then let herself sink back and turned. "This is ridiculous."

Austen blinked. "What do you mean?"

"This." Dee waved between them. "You're the first person I've met in ages who doesn't get on my nerves, and you seem to be able to stand my company too."

Carefully, Austen nodded.

"Then why can't I invite you in for some coffee? And that, by the way, is not a euphemism for sex. I know trying for more would be a bad idea, but why can't we be friends?"

"Because even if I forgive you for lying to me, we're still on different levels of the company hierarchy."

"So what? It's not like I'm bending you over my desk and—"

"Sssh." Her cheeks burning, Austen covered Dee's mouth with her hand and then withdrew quickly when she realized how intimate that was. She reached past Dee and tried to close the passenger-side door so that no one could overhear them.

When Austen couldn't quite reach, Dee did it for her.

"You know people never care about what's actually going on," Austen said. "It's pretty much common knowledge that we're both gay, and as soon as my colleagues see us with each other, spending time together outside of the office, they'll assume that we're having a torrid affair. They'll think—"

Dee drummed her fist against the dashboard like a child throwing a temper tantrum because she didn't get what she wanted. "I don't care what those damn gossips think!"

"I know. But I do." She wanted to be recognized for her work ethic, not to be known as the secretary who'd been hired because she slept with the boss's sister.

Dee rubbed her forehead, scratching at the thin, bright red scar. "All right. I can understand that you don't want to be seen hanging out with Attila." She reached for the door.

Austen grabbed the back of her sweater. She couldn't let her leave like that. "I never thought of you that way."

Dee turned and searched her face as if looking for the truth. Finally, she nodded. "I know. That's what makes you so special."

Could it really work? Austen wasn't sure. She could think of half a dozen reasons why she shouldn't even try, but looking into those gray eyes, she couldn't walk away. Not when, by the looks of it, Dee had been deprived of friendship her whole life. "We'll have to be careful."

"I wasn't planning on introducing you as my BFF at the next board meeting. I've always kept my job and my private life separate."

"I bet that was easy to do, since you don't have much of a private life," Austen said. Every day when she left work, the lights in Dee's office were still on.

Dee grinned. "You got me there. So, friends it is?" She stuck out her hand, a hopeful expression on her face.

Austen hesitated for one more moment before sliding her hand into Dee's and shaking it. "Friends it is."

CHAPTER 12

Dee marched toward the copier, glaring at people left and right until the employees ducked back into their offices, out of her way. The new year was just three weeks old, and her cousin was already getting on her nerves. He pretended that he'd lost his copy of her report, but she had a suspicion that it was right there on his desk; he just hadn't liked her suggestions for his department.

I'll just send him another copy, and if he doesn't like my suggestions, he can shove them up his—Ouch! She slammed into someone heading the other way.

The papers she carried went flying, scattering through half of the corridor.

Cursing, she bent to pick them up.

A pair of slender hands appeared in her line of sight and helped to gather the papers. "Here."

Dee looked up, her mood instantly improving when she realized it was Austen. "Uh, hi. Thanks."

"Where are you going in such a hurry?"

"To copy some papers." Dee pointed at the copier down the hall.

Austen hooked one finger behind the strap of her purse and smiled. "You should really get an assistant, then you wouldn't have to plow down unsuspecting people on the way to the copier."

"Nah. Remember what happened to the last one? I hear she jumped out the window."

They both stood.

Dee couldn't help noticing how good Austen looked in a light blue blouse that made her eyes look even bluer. She forced her gaze away. "Heading home for the weekend?"

"Yeah. And you?"

"Not yet." Dee knew she should get back to work, but she couldn't make herself say good-bye. "Any special plans?"

"The Blazers are playing tonight. My brother gave me tickets for Christmas. Courtside seats."

Dee gave a short whistle. "Cool. Much better than a wool coat two sizes too small."

Austen chuckled. "That's for sure." She paused and looked up and down the corridor. "Do you like basketball?"

"About as much as you like chocolate."

Again the quick glance left and right. "Would you want to go with me?"

"If you're not taking anyone else."

Austen shook her head. "Most of my friends are not too crazy about basketball."

"Their loss. My gain. I'd love to go with you. When should I pick you up?"

"I already know where you live, so why don't I pick you up at six?"

Dee mock-scowled. "Does that mean you'll get to drive?"

Austen laughed. "Yes, that's what it means."

One of Tim's brand managers walked by and gave them a funny look, reminding Dee that socializing at the office was not a good idea.

"See you at six, then," she said and quickly walked away. That gave her only an hour to wrap up work, go home, and change into something more comfortable. Well, the world wouldn't end just because Danielle Saunders left work on time for once.

At least she hoped it wouldn't.

When her cell phone started to ring, Dee barely glanced up from her computer screen. She felt around for the phone with one hand while continuing to tap away on her keyboard with the other. "Yeah?"

"Where are you?"

She froze with her fingers on the keyboard. *Austen! Oh, shit.* It wasn't that late already, was it? She had barely gotten started on the paperwork she wanted to finish before leaving. Her gaze darted to the little clock on her computer. Ten minutes after six. *Double shit.* "I'm…uh… on my way."

"Don't lie to me." Austen's voice was cold. "You're still at the office, aren't you?"

"Yeah. I'm sorry. I got so involved in—"

"It's okay," Austen said, now a lot milder. "I'll just go on my own, like I'd planned."

"No!" Dee jumped up, powered down her computer, and rushed toward the elevator, not caring if she plowed into anyone else. Thankfully, Moda Center, where the Trailblazers played, was less than two miles from the office, so she would still make it in time for the game. "I'm leaving now. I'll meet you at the main entrance. Beer and hot dogs are on me."

"Oh, yes, they are," Austen said. "For the rest of the year." She didn't sound miffed anymore, though.

"You got it." The elevator doors closed behind Dee. "I'm in the elevator. See you in a minute."

"Don't speed," Austen called.

"Yeah. Yeah. I'll be careful. I'll be there long before you anyway."

No answer from Austen.

Their connection had cut out. Dee put the cell phone away and moved closer to the doors, getting ready to sprint across the parking lot as soon as they opened.

Dee was waiting in front of the main entrance when Austen arrived at the arena. Surrounded by people in jeans and sneakers, she stuck out like a sore thumb in her elegant pantsuit and expensive Italian shoes.

Austen chuckled to herself. *That's what she gets for being late.* "You're lucky we're not dating," she said instead of a greeting.

"Yeah." Dee shuffled her feet. "They tell me I'm a lousy girlfriend."

Faced with her hangdog expression, Austen couldn't be angry with her. She hooked her arm through Dee's. "Let's go in. Someone promised me hot dogs."

It was half past eight when they walked out of the arena and made their way toward their cars.

"Want to grab something to eat?" Dee asked. Her throat hurt a bit after shouting and cheering for their team.

"Oh God, no. I'm still stuffed from all the hot dogs I ate." Austen sounded equally hoarse.

Finally a woman who's not afraid to jump up and down like a maniac at a basketball game. "How many did you have? I stopped counting after the second."

Austen shrugged. "I had to make you suffer for standing me up for our first…uh, friendly outing."

"Right. Consider me duly punished." Dee slowed when they reached Austen's Hyundai. "I'm parked over there."

Austen fished her key out of her coat pocket, but instead of unlocking the car, she just played with the key and kept facing Dee. "It's still pretty early."

"Yeah." Dee took a deep breath, knowing it was on her to extend the next invitation. "Want to hang out a little longer? Maybe play some pool or—"

"Nothing that requires me and my hot dogs to move around too much," Austen said. "But I have some games at home."

"Games?" Dee eyed her, not sure what kind of games she meant.

Austen laughed. "Don't look at me like that. I'm talking about board games and card games. That kind of thing."

"Ah."

"You don't like games?"

Dee shrugged. The only time she was around games was when she had to go down to the production department to raise hell. "I don't know. I haven't tried any."

Austen's eyes widened. "You work in the game industry and you never played games? Not even as a child?"

"I played strip poker in college. Does that count?"

"No."

"Well, then I've never played any."

Austen shook her head. "That won't do. We have to remedy that. Follow me."

Who was she to argue with a pretty lady? At least not with one so stubborn. Dee walked over to her own car, waited until Austen pulled out of the parking space, and followed her.

Dee found a parking spot on the street right in front of the quiet six-unit apartment complex where Austen lived. She followed her across the lawn and up the two concrete steps to the single-story building.

An enthusiastic "hi" greeted them as soon as Austen unlocked the door to her apartment.

Dee looked around but didn't see anyone. "Uh, you do live alone, don't you?"

Austen laughed. "Yes, I do. That's just Toby. Come on. I'll introduce you."

One entire wall in the living room was taken up by a huge cage and what looked like a cockatoo play gym, complete with a ladder, climbing ropes, and a swing. The rest of the living room was equipped with Ikea furniture, some of it chewed on by a strong beak. A watercolor of a rocky beach at sunset and several drawings of a cockatoo hung on the opposite wall. The apartment looked like a comfortable, lived-in place.

Dee eyed the initials A.B. in the corner of each drawing. "Did you do these?" She gestured.

Austen followed her gaze. "All but the watercolor. That one's my mother's."

"Wow. You're good."

A faint blush covered Austen's cheeks. "It's just a hobby."

The white cockatoo portrayed in the drawings sat on the highest perch in his cage. When he saw Austen, he dropped his chew toy and extended his yellow crest feathers in her direction. "Loser," he warbled.

Dee had to laugh. "He sure knows how to talk to a lady."

"Yeah, he's a real charmer."

The cockatoo danced back and forth on his perch, bobbing up and down.

"Do you mind if I let him out for a bit?" Austen asked.

"No, go ahead."

Austen took the bird out and gave him a head scratch.

He turned his head so that she could reach every spot. For a moment, Dee thought he'd start purring, but of course, he didn't.

Austen got him a stalk of celery, and he climbed on the swing to eat it. "So let's see what games I have."

Dee followed her and peered into the hall closet Austen opened but didn't recognize any of the games. "The Quest for the Magic Carrot?" She laughed. "Sounds like the title of a really bad porn movie."

Austen slapped her on the arm.

"Hey, don't hit me, or I'll tell Uncle Wade that you have hundreds of games from the competition, but none of ours."

"Said the woman who doesn't own any games."

"Touché."

Austen pointed at one of the games. The title on the box said *Risk*. "How about this one? It's a classic."

"I think I've heard of it. Conquering the world should be right up my alley."

"That's what you think. If anyone conquers the world, it'll be me."

Challenge issued, they carried the game into the living room.

Austen leaned back against the base of the couch and took a sip of her Coke as she waited for Dee to throw the dice. *If anyone at work could see her now.*

Kudos Entertainment's second-in-command and heir apparent sat cross-legged next to her on the carpet, with the coffee table pushed out of the way to make room for the board game. She didn't seem to care that her elegant slacks were getting wrinkled. She'd taken off her suit jacket and kicked off her shoes an hour ago, and now her sleeves were rolled up above her elbows. The slender muscles and tendons in her arm bunched as she threw the three red dice. "Your turn."

Austen wrenched her gaze away and focused on throwing her own dice. Both of them showed a one. "No! Not Iceland too!"

"Oh yeah!" Chuckling evilly, Dee removed Austen's army from the board and set hers up on the little blue island. "I think I just discovered my love of games."

Five minutes later, she had captured the last of Austen's territories.

Austen slumped against the couch. "Damn, you're good at that." She had a feeling it was more than just beginner's luck. Dee seemed to put her full focus and intensity into everything she did.

"Well, I should be. I'm the leader of the Hunnic Empire after all, so conquering the world and laying waste to my enemies comes naturally."

It took Austen a moment to get the reference. "How about a rematch, Great Attila?"

"Granted, Little Napoleon."

"Hey, is that a quip about my lack of height?"

"No, it's a quip about how little land you'll own in this round. Prepare to get your ass kicked again."

"Ssssh." Austen peered over to the cage. "If Toby picks up more swearwords from you, your behind is toast."

Dee just laughed.

This is fun, Austen thought as she cleared the board for the next game. Maybe being friends with Dee hadn't been such a bad idea after all.

On Monday morning, Dee knocked and stepped into her uncle's office. "You wanted to see me?"

Uncle Wade waved her over. "Sit. I need to have a word with you."

She padded across the carpet and sat. What was this all about? Normally, he just sent her an e-mail when someone in the company had messed up and he wanted her to solve the problem.

"Someone saw you on Friday."

"Yeah? I bet a lot of someones saw me on Friday—a lot of someones who would have preferred not to." Dee chuckled. "I had to get tough with a few managers down in sales. You wouldn't believe what stuff they put on their travel expense reports."

Uncle Wade shook his head. "That's not what I meant. Someone saw you at the Blazers game. With one of our employees."

A wave of heat rushed through Dee, followed by cold dread. She forced herself to look him straight in the eyes. "So?"

"So?" His voice rumbled through the office. "Danielle, I won't have you put yourself or the company in a position—"

"We're just friends, nothing else," Dee said, trying to keep her voice down.

He scrutinized her thoroughly, as if not sure he should believe her. After fourteen years in the company, that lack of trust hurt. "You're leaving yourself wide open to a sexual harassment lawsuit. We can't have that. We're a company that produces toys for children, for Christ's sake! The competition's PR department would have a field day with our COO being dragged to court for—"

"She won't drag me to court." She pressed her lips together so tightly that she felt the blood drain from them. "I told you. We're friends, nothing more."

Finally, he shook his head. "It doesn't matter. I want you to stop seeing her."

The thought made every muscle in her body knot. "You can't tell me what I should or shouldn't do in my personal time."

Her uncle stared at her. Since the day she had started working for him fresh out of college, she had never stood up to him like this. She'd never had a reason to.

"Yes, I can," he said, his voice like steel. "You might be the COO, but you're not exempt from company rules."

"The same company rules that allow your VP of finance to play golf with his senior managers every Sunday?"

"That's different."

"Oh yeah? Because they're men?" Dee had it with the chauvinistic double standard.

He rose from behind his desk and towered over her. "No, goddammit! Because he's not a member of the family. I have to hold you to higher standards than the rest of my employees. There can't be even a suspicion of nepotism."

Slowly, Dee stood too, enjoying the two-inch height advantage she had over him. "I see. So family members are being held to higher standards."

"Yes." He held her challenging stare.

"Must be why Rick was promoted to VP of sales when he had that affair with one of his employees in customer service."

Uncle Wade's face flamed red, then went white. He dropped back into his leather chair. "You...you know about that?"

Dee sat too. "Of course I know. I know every little thing that goes on in this company. That's what happens when you spend every waking moment at work. I want to change that, Uncle Wade."

His eyes widened, though Dee wasn't sure whether it was due to her words or her using the family name at work. "You...you want to quit?"

"Jesus, no! One day, I want to sit where you're sitting now. But not at the expense of everything else. I've been working seventy-hour weeks or more—"

"No one asked you to do that."

"I know. I did it to myself. But now I'm thinking sixty hours should be enough."

He snorted. "You suddenly want to cut back your hours and expect me to believe that you and Ms. Brooks are just friends?"

"Leave her out of this." A mental image of the kiss she'd shared with Austen flashed through her mind. She could almost feel those soft lips against hers and— *Stop it!* That had been six weeks ago, long before they had decided to become friends. "Have I ever lied to you?"

He studied her through narrowed eyes. "No, but—"

"Then trust me when I say we're just friends."

"If that ever changes…"

"It won't." Dee rose and walked to the door.

Before she could make her escape, her uncle called, "Danielle?"

She turned and warily looked at him. "I prefer Dee. You know that."

He waved her away. "Yeah, yeah. Who else knows about Rick and the woman in customer service?"

"No one," Dee said.

"Let's keep it that way, okay?"

She nodded and walked out. One more reason not to start anything with Austen. She didn't want to be like her cousin who used their family's power to get away with his little escapades.

CHAPTER 13

THE LOBBY WAS EMPTY, AND Dee didn't meet anyone on her way up to the fifteenth floor. It was yet another reason why she liked coming in to work during the weekends—no employees around who watched her every move, just so they could turn around and gossip about her.

Of course, it also meant she wouldn't run into Austen on her way to the copy machine. She hadn't seen her except in passing since they had played *Risk* two weeks ago. Her grin dimmed. Growling at herself, she opened the door to her office and booted up her computer. Time to stop wondering what Austen might be doing and get some work done.

An hour later, she had outlined her PowerPoint presentation for a bid to create a line of toys for one of Disney's upcoming movies. She clicked through the slides and nodded. So far, so good. Now she only had to—

The ringing of her cell phone interrupted her mid-thought.

"Not now!" She fumbled the damn thing out of her pocket and was about to shut if off when her gaze fell on the display. Caller ID showed Austen's name. With one quick swipe of her finger, she accepted the call. "Hey there."

"Hi. How's it going?"

Dee reached out to save her presentation before turning away from the computer screen. "Good, and you? Have you recovered from losing so badly at *Risk*?"

"Oh, please. I let you win because it was your first time playing a game."

Chuckling, Dee leaned back in her desk chair. "Yeah, right. Just keep telling yourself that."

"Yep. Since it's the truth and all." A moment of silence stretched out between them, then Austen cleared her throat. "Listen, a friend of mine is coaching a basketball game, and I'm going to watch the game with another friend. I was wondering if you'd like to come with us."

Dee wasn't sure what to say. On the one hand, she would have liked to spend more time with Austen, but on the other hand, she wasn't too eager to submit herself to the scrutiny of Austen's friends. Besides, being seen out and about with Austen would be a bad idea. "I thought you said your friends weren't interested in basketball?"

"I said *most* of my friends aren't," Austen said. "So, how about it?"

"Can I have a rain check? I'm working on a presentation that I'd like to finish today."

"You're working? But it's the weekend!"

"There's no such thing as a weekend if you're the leader of the Hunnic Empire," Dee said.

"Oh, yes, there is. Or at least there should be. How can you conquer the world if you're not taking good care of yourself? We'll have to remedy that."

Normally, Dee resented anyone butting into her personal business, but Austen's concern for her felt strangely good. "Is that so?"

"Yes, it is."

"All right. But I really can't come with you today. I need to finish the bid for the Disney movie. If I manage to get this deal, my uncle will dance a jig in the lobby."

"Not sure I want to see that," Austen said. "I saw him dance at the Christmas party."

Dee laughed. "True. There's a reason my whole family is a bunch of entrepreneurs, not professional dancers. Janine, Tim's wife, very nearly didn't accept his marriage proposal just so she could avoid dancing with him at the wedding."

Austen's laughter rang through the line. "I'll have to take you dancing some time, then, just to see if you're really that bad."

The thought of dancing with Austen, holding her close while their bodies swayed together, sent shivers through Dee, and she immediately reprimanded herself. They were friends, nothing more, and that was all they were meant to be. Slow dancing was definitely out. "We'll see. Have fun at the basketball game."

"Thanks. And you don't work too long, okay?"

"I'll do my best. Bye." After hanging up, Dee stared at her cell phone for several seconds before finally turning it off. *Stop woolgathering. Back to work.* The screen sprang back to life as she reached for the mouse and started adding details to the first slide.

The high school's gym was filled to capacity. Cheering, loud music, and the squeaking of shoes on the court greeted Austen as soon as they entered. People jostled them from all sides.

"Wow, I didn't think it would get so crowded." Her friend Dawn took her arm as they squeezed through the crowd to find free seats on the bleachers.

Austen glanced at her. "You okay?"

Dawn nodded, but her full lips compressed into a tense line. "Still not too fond of crowds; that's all."

In moments like this, Austen never knew quite what to say or do. Dawn had been raped two years ago, a few months before they had met in an art class. Now her life was mostly back to normal—except for situations like this. Austen glanced around helplessly, wishing Dee had come with them. Maybe Dawn would have felt safer with a more intimidating person like Dee by her side. "Do you want us to leave?"

"No. I'm fine. Really." Dawn pressed her down onto the bleachers and sat next to her.

"You sure? Aiden will have my head if I don't take good care of you."

"Nah, she's under strict orders not to kill any of my friends. Speaking of my overprotective partner... There she is." Dawn's eyes shone as she pointed toward the court.

Aiden stood at the sideline, deeply in discussion with her assistant coach. As if feeling Dawn's gaze on her, she turned and searched the stands. It took her just a moment to zero in on them. She clapped her assistant coach on the back, sending him off, before jogging up the steps toward their seats. Her ever-present leather jacket was absent today, and the detective badge was missing from her belt. Instead, she wore khakis and a dark blue polo shirt with the school's logo. "Hey, Austen. Glad you could make it." She was speaking to Austen, but her gaze rested on Dawn. A silent conversation seemed to take place between them, with Aiden tilting her head and frowning. Finally, when Dawn gave her a smile, Aiden relented and focused on Austen. "I thought you wanted to bring a friend?"

"She had to work, so she couldn't make it." Austen tried not to let her disappointment show.

Aiden tapped her partner's nose. "And you say I'm a workaholic."

"You are." Dawn grinned up at her, her posture more relaxed now that Aiden was next to her.

Someone called Aiden's name, and she threw a glance over her shoulder. "I need to get back to my girls."

Dawn put a hand over her heart. "And here I thought I was your one and only girl."

"You are," Aiden said.

Austen watched them together, feeling like a fifth wheel. She loved seeing her friends so happy together, but at the same time, she couldn't help being just a bit envious. No one had ever looked at her the way Aiden and Dawn looked at each other. Certainly not Brenda.

Aiden bent and kissed Dawn's cheek before jogging back to gather her players around her.

The two teams took up their positions on the court, and Austen settled herself more comfortably onto the aluminum bench. "How come you've suddenly discovered your interest in basketball?" All the other times she had invited her friend to come see a game with her, Dawn had refused.

"I haven't." A smile played around Dawn's lips. "I'm just here for the hot dogs and to support Aiden's team."

"How did they get her to coach a bunch of high school kids?" Austen still vividly remembered her brother at that age. Keeping him out of trouble had been like herding cats. The thought of managing a whole team of teenagers made her shudder.

Dawn shrugged. "Her sister is the team's power forward, and they needed a new coach, so Aiden volunteered to take over for a while. 'How hard can it be?' she said."

"Famous last words."

"Exactly."

The second the game started, Aiden jumped up from the bench and paced the sideline, shouting encouragements and instructions at her players. When the game heated up, so did her shouting. She waved her clipboard at the referee. "Didn't you see that? How was that not a foul?"

Instead of watching the game, Dawn watched her partner. "Want to bet she'll get at least one technical foul before the game is over?"

"I'm not betting against that. I work too hard for my money to just give it away."

Dawn turned and studied her. "How is it going with your new job?"

"I really like it. The team is great, and my boss is letting me handle a lot of things on my own already."

"So I take it he or she isn't as much of a dimwit as your last boss?"

A mental picture of Tim Saunders rose in front of her mind's eye, only to be replaced by Dee's feminine version of his features. "Definitely not a dimwit," she murmured. Dee was intelligent and beautiful and just enough of a challenge to keep her entertained. *And she's also completely off-limits. Friends. You're just friends, remember?*

Dawn looked at her with such an intense gaze that Austen started to squirm. God, why did she have to become friends with a psychologist who seemed to be able to look right through her?

Truth be told, she was glad they had become friends, unlikely as it had seemed in the beginning. At first glance, Dawn with her degree in psychology and Austen, who had finished high school with less-than-perfect grades due to her mother's death, didn't have much in common beyond their interest in art. But on the last day of art class, they had gone out for dinner and discovered that their childhood experiences weren't all that different. Both had grown up with a brother, Dawn in a family of cops and Austen as a military brat, and both had lost one parent as teenagers.

The crowd around them burst into deafening cheers, finally making Dawn direct her gaze back to the court.

Austen blew out a breath and resolved to focus on the game for the rest of the afternoon. The last thing she wanted was to confess her stupid crush on the company's second-in-command to a psychologist, even if that psychologist was her friend. If there was a psychoanalytic complex describing her situation, she wasn't eager to find out.

CHAPTER 14

When her usually cheerful boss came back from lunch looking as if his dog had died, Austen knew something was up.

He trudged past her desk without much of a greeting.

"Mr. Saunders," she called before he could disappear into his office.

He turned, still not smiling.

"Did...? Is everything all right?"

"Yeah. Kind of. I just found out that the deal with Disney fell through. They gave the contract to our biggest rival."

Oh, shit. Austen's first thought was of Dee. She had worked like a maniac on that deal, even giving her a rain check on the basketball game two weeks ago. She hesitated. They had agreed to keep their friendship out of the workplace, but now she couldn't help herself. She glanced toward the door to the outer office, and when she found it closed, asked, "Does Dee know?"

"She's the one who told me."

"How did she take it?" Austen asked.

He grimaced. "Let's just say that it's a good thing she doesn't have an assistant, or the poor person would have fled. I sent her home before she could kill another mouse."

And Dee went without putting up a fight? That told her more than anything else that Dee wasn't in her normal frame of mind. "Um, Mr. Saunders, is it okay if I leave an hour early today?" She was itching to drive over to Dee's and make sure she was all right.

He looked at her for several moments, making her squirm. Finally, he nodded. "Why don't you take off now?"

"But I haven't gotten around to copying the agenda for Monday's meeting."

"I'll take care of it. Go."

"Thank you." At least one member of Dee's family wasn't a self-centered asshole. She powered down her computer and hurried to the elevator. Now she only had to convince Dee to open the door.

"Go away," Dee shouted.

Austen leaned her forehead against the closed door separating them. "Dee, please. I just want to make sure you're okay."

"I'm fine."

"Yeah, right." God, why did she have to befriend the most stubborn woman on the continent and possibly even on the planet? "That's why you're not opening the door."

"Nothing a little alcohol won't cure."

"Good thing I come bearing gifts, then. I've got a bottle of your favorite red wine. Come on, Dee. Open the door."

Dee didn't answer for several seconds. Finally, the sound of a deep sigh drifted through the door. "All right. Give me a minute. I have to get these damn gloves off first."

Gloves? It was February and nearly sixty degrees outside. Why did she need gloves?

The lock turned, and then the door opened.

Austen took a deep breath and entered the house.

A battered punching bag dangled by a chain from the ceiling in the living room. Dee, dressed in sweatpants and a gray tank top, gave it one last jab with her now-bare hands. Droplets of sweat ran down her sculpted arms.

Austen licked her lips and tried not to stare at the way the sweat-soaked tank top clung to Dee's chest. "Why don't you take a shower while I get us glasses?" she said, even though she felt as if she were the one needing a shower—a cold one.

When Dee trudged from the room, Austen went to the kitchen. She looked around for cheese, crackers, or anything else that might go with the wine and help soak up the alcohol, but, as usual, the fridge was empty. She carried two of the moving boxes over to the couch, again using them to build an improvised coffee table.

Once Dee returned, Austen pressed a glass of red wine into her hands. They sat at opposite sides of the couch, their feet up on the cushion between them. Dee had changed into a faded pair of jeans that emphasized her long legs, and her *COO off duty* T-shirt clung to her still-damp skin. Austen wanted to reach out and run her fingers through the wet bangs, but she forced herself to keep her hands to herself. She waited, trying to give Dee time.

When the first glass was empty, Dee just reached for the bottle and refilled her glass. She still hadn't said a word.

"Are we going to get drunk in silence?" Austen asked.

"That was the plan." Dee took a sip of her second glass of wine.

Austen swung her feet off the couch and slid closer. "Hey." She touched Dee's knee. The muscles felt like a live wire, nearly vibrating under her hand. She quickly withdrew before she could surrender to the urge to run her hand up and down Dee's leg. "It's not the end of the world."

Dee snorted into her wine. "Tell that to Uncle Wade."

"He knew there was a lot of competition for that deal. What did he expect? For you to work a miracle?"

Another big gulp of wine. "Yeah. That's what they think I am—a miracle worker."

"They?"

"My family. No matter what I'm doing, it's never enough."

Was that why Dee was such a workaholic? Was she still trying to do the impossible and earn her family's approval? "Has it always been like that?"

"Pretty much. When I graduated summa cum laude from Yale, it barely seemed to register with my father. After I got straight As all through high school, they started taking it for granted."

Austen tried to understand how something like that might have happened. "Because your brothers were straight-A students too?"

Dee snorted. "Oh, no, the boys were mostly B and C students. My father didn't push them as hard, because he knew they'd take over the family business one day, so their grades didn't matter so much."

"Wow, talk about double standard." Her parents had never treated her and her brother any differently. "I'm so sorry."

"Not your fault."

"Yeah, but I can still be sorry, can't I? If my mother's death taught me one thing, it's that you shouldn't take your family for granted."

Dee looked at her for the first time. The morose expression on her face slowly faded. "You'll make a great mother one day."

Heat shot up Austen's neck. "Thanks. What about you? Do you want kids?"

Laughing, Dee pointed at the nearly bare living room. "I can't even keep a potted plant alive." She shrugged. "But who knows…maybe with the right co-parent…"

Their gazes met.

Dee looked away and got up from the couch. "Let's order Chinese. I need some food before we empty the rest of that bottle."

Austen followed her to the kitchen to look at the takeout menu. She just hoped she'd get a different message in her fortune cookie this time.

Somewhere between a plateful of crispy seafood chow mein and her third glass of wine, Dee realized that her mood was improving. She wasn't sure whether it was the alcohol or the company. Probably both. Admittedly, she could never sulk for long whenever Austen was near.

Christ, stop waxing poetic. Maybe she should stick to water for the rest of the evening. She had to go to work tomorrow, and the alcohol was clearly messing with her head. Nursing the rest of her wine, she leaned back on the couch and put her feet up on the stack of moving boxes serving as her coffee table. "So how come you showed up at my front door before the official end of the workday? Won't my brother wonder where his admin disappeared to?"

Austen swirled the wine in her glass. "He was the one who told me to take off early."

A sip of wine lodged in Dee's throat and then shot back out. Big, red droplets ran down her chin and drenched her T-shirt as she started coughing.

Austen picked up a paper napkin and stared at Dee's chest as if debating with herself whether to mop up the mess or let Dee do it. After a moment, she wordlessly handed over the napkin.

"Thanks," Dee rasped. She dabbed at the stains and then gave up when she realized she was only making it worse. The soaked napkin landed on top of a moving box. "Let me get this straight... My brother sent you to check on me?"

"Oh, no." Austen vehemently shook her head. "But I think he suspected why I was suddenly in such a hurry to leave after finding out about the Disney deal."

"And still he let you go?"

Austen shrugged. "He's your brother. I bet he was glad to have someone check on you."

Yeah. Someone. But not you. Tim had warned her to stay away from his assistant, so why should he encourage Austen to go to her house? She gave Austen a doubtful look.

"Maybe he just thought that you could need a friend right now. Is your family really that bad that you'd doubt your brother's motives?"

"Bad?" Dee tugged on her T-shirt, pulling the wet fabric away from her breasts. It wouldn't do to have Austen think her nipples had hardened because their arms touched whenever one of them moved. "I wouldn't call it bad, but our parents raised us to take care of ourselves. We certainly weren't coddled."

Austen's eyes flashed. "Showing honest care toward each other isn't coddling."

Dee raised her hands. "I never said it was."

Both were silent for several moments.

"Can I ask you a question?" Austen finally said.

Dee tensed, unsure what was coming. Austen certainly knew how to keep her on her toes. She tilted her head in a hesitant nod. "All right. If I can ask you one too."

Austen nodded. "It's only fair, I guess. Your parents own a chain of clothing retail stores, right?"

"Right. Well, my father and my three older brothers run the company. My mother runs her kitchen."

"Why didn't you go into business with them?" Austen asked.

"That's two questions."

Austen narrowed her eyes at her.

"Okay, okay," Dee said with a laugh. "Maybe it's because I'm fashion-challenged?" She pointed at her wine-stained T-shirt.

"Bullshit," Austen said.

Christ, Austen certainly didn't let her get away with anything. Dee found that she secretly liked that. *Who would have thought?*

"You do just fine with fashion. I like the pantsuits you wear."

Do you? The compliment warmed Dee from the inside out. Or maybe it was the wine.

Austen looked away as if only now becoming aware of what she had said. Apparently, the wine was affecting her too. "So what made you join your uncle's company instead of your father's?"

For the first time in years, if ever, Dee thought about it. Joining her father's firm had never really been an option, but she had never dwelled on the reason. "When my oldest brother, Caleb Jr., finished college, my father changed the company's name to Saunders & Son. When Stuart and Matthew got their degrees, it became Saunders

& Sons. When I graduated, he bought me jewelry. Clearly, he didn't think there was a place for me in the company."

Austen touched Dee's knee. "I'm so sorry."

Overly aware of the hand on her knee, Dee tried to laugh it off. "Don't worry. I'm over it."

"Liar." Austen's answer was frank, but her tone and gaze were gentle. Her hand still rested on Dee's leg.

When the soft touch and the empathy in Austen's gaze became too much to take, Dee slipped out from under her hand and stood.

"Where are you going?"

"To get another bottle of wine." If they were continuing to talk about things like that, she would need more alcohol. She took her time rooting through the wine rack in her kitchen and finally settled on a pinot noir.

"And your uncle?" Austen's voice from the doorway nearly made her drop the bottle. "Is he less of a…um…?"

"Chauvinistic asshole?" Dee suggested and pulled out the cork with more force than necessary.

"I might have chosen another word, but…yeah."

"Uncle Wade looks at the numbers only. As long as I get him the results he wants, he doesn't care if I'm a man or a woman. Rick, his son, doesn't have the drive to lead a company of this size, so if I play my cards right, he'll suggest me as his successor once he retires."

Austen opened her mouth, probably to ask yet another question, but Dee stopped her with one raised hand. "Enough talk about my family. It's my turn to ask a question now." She led her back into the living room and poured them each a glass of pinot noir.

"Are you trying to loosen my tongue with alcohol?" Austen asked.

Dee grinned. "Is it working?"

"More than I care to admit. I'm usually not much of a drinker, so I'd better stop after this glass."

Indeed, her cheeks were a little flushed and her motions and gestures more lavish.

Cute. But cuteness or not, she wouldn't let her off the hook. She tried to think of an interesting question, but, for some reason, every question popping into her head had to do with sex. Entirely inappropriate. Finally, she settled on one that was more G-rated. "What happened at your last job?" She had heard rumors around the office, but she knew firsthand how people could come up with things that had nothing to do with what had really happened.

Austen's flush became a full-out blush, and she gulped down half of the wine in her glass.

Dee raised a brow. Maybe the rumor mill hadn't been all that far off. "Your boss really grabbed your ass?" The thought made heat crawl up her own neck, and she instantly wanted to have a little talk with that asshole.

"He tried to. He had it in for me ever since he found out I'm gay, but that didn't stop him from trying to grope me during an office party."

"What stopped him?"

"A slap to his face," Austen said, her voice rough.

"Good for you!" Dee reached over and slapped her shoulder in a buddy-like way, then gentled her touch when she realized what she was doing. God, she had passed tipsy and was heading straight for being drunk. "What happened after you slapped him?"

"I quit my job—but not before I had a serious talk with HR and threatened them with a lawsuit if they didn't do something about him. I didn't want my successor to have to go through the same thing."

Dee's admiration for Austen grew, if that was still possible. At the same time, Austen's experience at her last job made her painfully aware of how inappropriate getting involved with her would be. Sighing, she drained the rest of her glass and refilled it with none-too-steady hands. "Want to watch a movie?"

"A movie?"

"Yeah, you know, one of those things where they put together a lot of pictures to create the illusion of moving images."

Austen flicked a droplet of wine at her. "Thank you very much for that definition, wiseass. I know what a movie is."

"So do you want to watch one with me?"

"Depends."

"On?"

"What kind of movies you like."

Dee scanned her DVD shelf and realized that she had to squint to see the titles clearly. Either she was getting nearsighted or really, really drunk. Probably the latter. She dismissed the few romantic comedies she owned as well as the lesbian movies on her shelf. In her inebriated state, watching a romance with Austen was definitely not a good idea. "How about *Star Wars*?"

"Which one?"

Dee waved toward the DVD shelf. "Take your pick."

Groaning, Austen got up from the couch and made her way toward the shelf, stumbling a little to the left before correcting her course. She giggled. "Ooops. Wow. No more wine for me, please. I still need to drive home."

Images of car accidents shot through Dee's mind. She shook her head to get rid of them and clutched the couch with both hands when that caused her to become dizzy. "No," she said, a little too loudly. "You should stay over."

They stared at each other.

"On the couch," Dee added quickly.

"Why not upstairs?"

Dee's heartbeat escalated. "You want to…?"

"Sleep in your guest room."

"Oh." Dee rubbed her face with both hands. "I forgot about that."

Austen grinned. "You're drunk."

"Oh, and you aren't?"

"Maybe a tiny bit." Austen held up her thumb and index finger to indicate how drunk she was, but her movements were so uncoordinated that she held them at least three inches apart.

Dee laughed. "Yeah, right. You pick the movie, and I'll get us some water."

"Oh, God." Pain exploded in Dee's temples as soon as she tried to lift her head off the pillow. Groaning, she opened one eye. When she saw where she was, her other eye popped open as well.

She was lying on her bed, a warm body cuddled up behind her, one arm around Dee's hip, clutching her like a favorite teddy bear.

Austen! Oh, God, what did we do? Her memory got a little hazy after that first bottle of wine. Or was it the second? She remembered talking about her family and about Austen's former boss, watching one of the *Star Wars* movies, and Austen giving her a foot rub that made her tingle all over. What else had happened between them?

Carefully, she peeked over her shoulder and blew out a breath. At least Austen was still fully dressed, and so was she. Her gaze lingered on Austen's face. Sunlight danced over her cheeks, giving them a soft glow. A dusting of freckles covered her nose, and Dee found herself wanting to roll over and kiss them.

Wait a minute... Sunlight? She shot upright and then clutched her head. "Austen!" She shook her. "Wake up! We have to get to work."

Austen's lashes fluttered; then her eyes drifted open. Her gaze still hazy, she smiled at Dee.

For a moment, Dee forgot about being late. Even her headache seemed to subside.

Then Austen looked at the alarm clock that Dee had forgotten to set. Her eyes widened. "Oh, shit. We're late for work."

"Yeah. Go take a shower. I'll get us some Tylenol."

Austen stumbled to her feet. "How did we end up here?" She pointed at the bed, a hint of a blush coloring her cheeks.

"I have no idea." But, for a second, it had been a wonderful way to wake up. When Austen moved past her to the bathroom, Dee called, "Austen?"

"Yeah?"

"Thank you."

Austen's tense features eased into a smile. "For getting you drunk and making you late for work?"

"For being there for me yesterday." No one had ever done that before.

"Any time," Austen said, and Dee could tell that she meant it.

Just five more minutes. Come on. If Dawn can do it, so can you! Austen's feet pounded the belt of the treadmill beneath her. The hammering in her head echoed the loud beat, and her lungs felt as if they would spontaneously combust any second. *Oh, God, what was I thinking?* Going to the gym today had definitely not been one of her brightest ideas.

"Austen?" Dawn, who was running on the treadmill next to her, slowed her pace and looked over at her. "Are you okay? You look like you're going to puke."

She felt that way too. The five minutes weren't up yet, but she stabbed the button to slow the belt and then stop. Gripping the handles of the treadmill, she slumped over and tried to drag enough air into her burning lungs.

A warm hand touched her back through her sweat-soaked shirt.

When the pounding in her temples lessened and her head cleared, she looked up and into her friend's concerned eyes.

"Are you sick?"

Austen shook her head, straightened, and pressed both hands to the small of her back. "No. Just hungover."

"You?" A wrinkle formed on Dawn's forehead. "I've never known you to get drunk. What happened?"

"A friend of mine had a tough day at work."

"And that leads to you being hungover...how?"

"I went over to keep her company—with a bottle of wine." Now, on the day after, it didn't seem like such a brilliant idea anymore.

Dawn nodded thoughtfully. "Aha."

"What's that supposed to mean?"

"Nothing. Just 'aha.'"

"Don't aha me with that psychologist voice of yours," Austen said.

Laughing, Dawn held up both hands. "So that wine-drinking friend of yours... Is she just a friend, or does this friendship have some future romantic potential?"

"She's just someone I work with." Austen hoped that her flushed cheeks would hide her blush.

"Really?"

Dawn's knowing gaze was beginning to annoy her. "Yes, really."

"Good."

"Why is that a good thing?"

"Because if you have no interest whatsoever in this friend, you won't need to turn down the woman who's been checking you out for the last twenty minutes." Dawn nodded her head toward the row of stationary exercise bikes at the opposite wall of the gym.

When Austen looked up to see where she was pointing, a tall woman on one of the bikes grinned and waved.

Austen quickly averted her gaze. She couldn't handle this today.

Undeterred, the woman climbed off the bike and walked over. "Hi." She wiped her hand on her sweatpants and offered it to Austen. "I'm Melissa."

Austen halfheartedly shook her hand. "Austen."

"I couldn't help noticing that you seemed to be... struggling a little. Are you okay?"

How embarrassing. Even complete strangers watching her had been afraid that she'd collapse facedown onto the treadmill. "I'm fine. Just a bit out of breath."

"Can I buy you a drink?" Melissa pointed over to the juice bar.

At the word *drink*, Austen winced, even knowing that she was talking about juice. "No, thanks. Maybe another time."

"How about next weekend?"

Melissa certainly was determined, she had to give her that, and she seemed like a nice, caring human being, but Austen couldn't muster any interest in a date. "I'm sorry," she said, trying to let her down as easily as possible. "You seem nice, but I'm really busy with work right now, so…"

"All right, then. Guess I'll see you around." Melissa trotted back to her exercise bike with a slight slump to her shoulders.

From across the room, Austen could feel her gaze on her. She grabbed her water bottle and pulled Dawn toward the showers. "Let's go before this day becomes any more embarrassing."

Dawn abstained from any more comments about Austen's love life while they were showering.

Wise woman.

Finally, when they were dressed again and crossed the parking lot, walking toward their cars, Dawn put her hand on Austen's arm. "If you ever want to talk about anything…"

"Nothing to talk about," Austen mumbled. She and Dee were just friends, so what was there to talk about, right?

"If that ever changes…"

"I know." She gave Dawn a quick hug, unlocked her car, and slid behind the wheel.

When she closed the door, Dawn's penetrating gaze met her through the window. Austen waved and hurriedly drove off.

CHAPTER 15

"Why do you always get to choose what movie we're watching?" Austen asked as she slid into the seat next to Dee, carefully balancing their huge tub of popcorn with both hands.

"Always?" Dee reached over and took a handful of popcorn. "Not counting *Star Wars,* this is only the third movie we're seeing together."

"Yes, and you picked all three of them."

"That's because I have better taste in movies." Dee crunched a bit of popcorn and made a face. "And in snacks. Eating popcorn with sugar should be a crime."

Austen popped a few of the morsels into her mouth, enjoying the taste of the caramelized sugar. "Why do you eat it if you think it's gross?"

"Any popcorn is better than no popcorn," Dee said.

"True." Austen reached for another handful. "I'll let you pick our snack next time if you let me pick the movie."

"Deal."

It had been like that in each of the friendly outings they'd had in the ten weeks since they'd first watched a basketball game together. They playfully fought about who got to drive, pick the restaurant, or decide on their choice of wine for dinner.

Truth be told, Austen enjoyed not being the one who automatically made all the decisions. In past relationships, she'd often felt as if she were the adult, directing her partner to make the right choices. Thank God Dee was too headstrong for that.

Stop thinking like that. She's not your partner.

Their hands brushed as they both reached for the popcorn at the same time, sending tingles down the rest of Austen's body.

Both of them quickly withdrew their hands.

In the darkness of the movie theater, Austen curled the hand that had touched Dee's into a fist. They were friends, and that's all they'd ever be. She was entirely content with that, so why wasn't her body getting the message?

Maybe her little brother was right. It really had been too long since she'd been on a date with a woman, much less slept with one. Perhaps she shouldn't have been so quick to reject that woman at her gym when she'd asked her out a few weeks ago.

Dee nudged her. "You're not watching."

"I wasn't aware that there's a rule about having to watch the commercials," Austen said.

Dee threw a piece of popcorn at her.

Not about to be outdone, Austen grabbed a handful and threw it back.

"Hey!" Grinning like a Viking about to dive into battle, Dee reached into the paper bowl with both hands to gather ammunition.

The popcorn war quickly escalated until a woman in the row in front of them turned and shushed them.

"Sorry."

With sheepish grins, they brushed popcorn off their laps.

The woman's eyes widened, and she turned more fully in her seat. "Danielle? Is that you?"

Danielle? Austen looked back and forth between the stranger and Dee. She didn't like the familiarity in the woman's tone.

"Uh…yes, it's me. How have you been, Madeline?"

As the first trailer flickered across the movie screen, several people turned toward them. "Shhh."

"We'll talk later," Madeline said.

"Not if I can help it," Dee muttered, too low for anyone but Austen to hear.

Austen leaned over and whispered, "Who was that?"

"No one."

"An ex?"

"If you can call it that after just one night."

So Dee was into one-night stands? One more reason not to get involved with her. Austen wasn't in the market for short flings; she wanted the kind of lasting love her parents had shared.

Dee pointed at the big screen, where a trailer for a science fiction movie was playing. "That one looks good. Want to go see it with me next weekend?"

A *yes* already lingered on Austen's lips, but then she hesitated. They had seen each other every weekend, often on both days, for the last month. Maybe it was time to take a break and give her poor libido a chance to focus on someone else. Someone attainable. Clearly, Dee had redirected her attention already. Or was Madeline someone from her past, before they'd met? She mentally shook her head. It didn't matter. "I can't next weekend."

Dee turned her head and looked at her, even though the movie was now starting to play. "Oh. Hot date?" She sounded casual, but her gaze was intense.

"Kind of. A woman at the gym asked me out." The guilt Austen felt at saying it took her by surprise. It wasn't as if they were in a relationship and she was cheating on Dee.

"I see." Dee picked a piece of popcorn off her sweater and chewed it slowly before saying, "Guess we can go see the movie another time, then."

Austen tried to make out her features in the near darkness. Was she disappointed about not getting to see the movie, or—?

The man next to Dee turned. "Would you mind? Some of us are trying to watch the movie."

"Sorry."

They both fell silent, not pointing out scenes they liked or that made them laugh during the movie, as they usually did.

Austen's mind was elsewhere anyway. *Guess I'm going out on a date after all.*

Austen shot up from her seat as soon as the closing credits began to roll.

Dee raised one brow. Apparently, she wasn't the only one in a hurry to get out of here, even though she doubted that Austen was trying to avoid a former one-night stand too. As they hurried down the steps of the theater, she risked a quick glance over her shoulder.

Madeline was still in her seat. If Dee was lucky, Madeline hadn't seen her leave in the almost darkness.

Just when she congratulated herself on escaping unscathed, Austen pulled her to a stop in front of the restrooms. "Be right back. Hold this." She pressed her purse and her jacket into Dee's hands and dashed into the ladies' room.

"Uh…" Dee stared at the purse and the jacket and then back up, but before she could say anything, the door had closed behind Austen.

A line began to form, and Dee stepped out of the way to wait for Austen, keeping an eye on the door to the restroom. *Come on, Austen. Hurry up.* She craned her head and looked around, hoping Madeline wouldn't—

Before she had even finished the thought, someone tapped her on the shoulder.

Dee whirled around.

As she had feared, Madeline stood in front of her. "Hi again, stranger. Long time no see."

Dee nodded. It had been almost a year since she'd been stupid enough to sleep with Madeline. Giving in to the temptation when she knew she had no time for a relationship had been a mistake—one she hadn't repeated since then.

"You haven't made it to any of the *Women in Business* lunches since." Madeline's lipsticked lips formed a pout. "Should I take it personally?"

Dee threw a glance toward the door of the ladies' room. Why the hell did it take Austen so long to pee? "It had nothing to do with you," she said. "I was busy with work."

The truth was, she had wanted to avoid Madeline.

"Sure. Work." Madeline nodded down at the jacket and purse in Dee's arms, a knowing grin on her face. "Is that what they call it nowadays?"

"She's just a—" Dee stopped herself. She didn't owe Madeline an explanation; she didn't owe her anything. "Listen, Madeline. We had a great time together, but I'm not into relationships. You knew that."

"For someone who's not into relationships, you and your friend looked rather cozy."

Before Dee could think of a reply that would get rid of Madeline without hurting her, the door to the restroom opened and Austen stepped out. "Thanks for waiting. I shouldn't have drank so mu—" She stopped abruptly when she saw Dee with Madeline.

For a few moments, all three of them just stood there.

Finally, Austen took another step forward and reached out her hand. "Hi, I'm Austen, a friend of Dee's."

"Madeline." She eyed Austen thoroughly while she shook her hand. "Also a friend of Dee's."

Their handshake seemed to last forever.

In the past, Dee had never lost her cool around women, maybe because she never cared much what they thought about her, but now she was starting to sweat. She didn't want Austen to know about the bad choices she'd made in the past. Dee played with the strap of the purse she realized she was still holding. "Oh. Here."

Austen finally let go as she took her purse and jacket back. "Thanks."

"Well, I'd better go," Madeline said. "See you around."

Dee gave a noncommittal nod but said nothing.

When they left the building and walked toward the car, Dee felt Austen's gaze on her. She hunched her shoulders. "What?"

"Nothing."

They got into Austen's Hyundai. The silence between them continued as they drove toward Dee's house. Finally, Dee couldn't take it anymore. "I'm not proud of it, okay? Yes, I slept with her and a handful of other women, but it's not like I had one-night stands left and right. The few times I did, I always made it very clear beforehand that I don't have time for relationships and—"

Austen pulled over and shut off the engine. "You don't owe me an explanation. I'm not judging you."

She looked at Dee, her gaze open and honest, but Dee still couldn't help feeling defensive. She sensed that there was more that Austen wasn't saying. "But?"

Austen turned her head away and examined the steering wheel as if she had never seen it before. "It's just... You deserve so much more than casual flings that don't go anywhere."

"What if that's all I want?"

Austen peeked at her out of the corner of her eye. "Is it really?"

Something in her tone made Dee swallow. She had a feeling that the answer to Austen's question was *no*, but work had been her sole focus for so long that it was hard to imagine any other way of life.

"Forget I asked," Austen said before Dee could decide on an answer. "Maybe I'm more judgmental than I thought, and God knows I have no right to judge anyone when it comes to relationships."

Dee frowned at the self-loathing in Austen's tone. "Why would you say that?"

Austen sighed. "It's a long story without a happy end, and I don't want to get into it tonight. Can I have a rain check?"

Dee opened the glove compartment and pulled out the napkin they had shoved in there after eating at a food cart the previous Sunday. She took a pen, scribbled *rain check* across the napkin, and handed it over.

The sadness on Austen's face disappeared as she laughed. "Goof."

A vivid memory of the last time Austen had called her *goof* flashed through Dee's mind. Austen had kissed her then, her lips warm and soft and tender. *Stop it!* Dee slammed the bars down on the memory.

They were friends. Just friends. Next weekend, Austen would go out and possibly kiss someone else, and there was nothing she could do about it.

CHAPTER 16

At Austen's suggestion, they met in a cocktail bar—a good place for a first date. If the evening wasn't progressing so well, they could escape after one drink instead of having to suffer through a long dinner.

Her date, Melissa, was right on time. She was taller than Austen remembered, almost as tall as Dee.

While sipping their first cocktails, they talked about the usual first-date subjects: their jobs, hobbies, tastes in music, food, and movies.

Melissa didn't like basketball, board games, or chocolate cake. Austen tried not to hold it against her.

"Did you know that this used to be the most dangerous part of the city?" Melissa gestured with her straw.

Austen gazed through the glass door and down the street, filled with bars, an outdoor club, and Chinatown's gate with the two bronze lions right around the corner. "It was?"

Melissa nodded. "A hundred or so years ago, this part of town was just a bunch of saloons, brothels, gambling parlors, and opium dens."

Not much different than today, Austen thought with a glance at the party-happy crowd waiting in line in front of the club next door.

"If you weren't careful, you would wake up after a night of drinking in the hold of a ship destined for the

Orient, sold into slavery for a mere fifty bucks." Melissa took another sip of her cocktail. "I don't know if it's true, but legend has it that they were dragged to the waterfront through secret tunnels. They still exist. I took a tour through the tunnels last year."

"Sounds interesting." Maybe she and Dee could tour those tunnels one day. The second she had thought it, she mentally shook her head at herself. Why couldn't she stop thinking about Dee for even one night? She tried to focus on the here and now.

"So you didn't grow up in Portland, right?"

Austen shook her head. "No. I grew up all over."

"What do your parents do for a living?" Melissa asked.

Austen let go of her straw. She realized that she should have ordered another drink. The piña colada made her think of the one Dee had made for her at the office Christmas party. "My dad's retired now, but he used to be a marine."

Melissa smiled. "Semper fi, hmm?"

"Semper fi," Austen repeated, already dreading the question she knew was coming.

"And your mother?"

There it was. Austen swallowed. "She died fifteen years ago."

"Oh. I'm sorry."

The conversation ground to a stop. They both stirred their drinks. Finally, Austen asked about Melissa's family.

As Melissa talked about growing up in Chicago, Austen's mind started to wander, first to work, then wondering if Dee had gone to see the science fiction movie without her.

She snapped back to the here and now when Melissa paused and gave her an expectant look. "Excuse me?"

"I asked what made you change your mind."

Austen had totally dropped the ball. "Um, about what?"

"About going out with me. When I first asked you out a few weeks ago, you turned me down pretty fast. I thought you might be straight or seeing someone else already."

"No," Austen said. "I'm gay and single."

"Lucky me." Melissa smiled. "You never answered my question, though. Why did you agree to go out with me?"

The truth—*I wanted to give my libido something to play with so I can get over being attracted to a friend*—probably wouldn't go over too well, so she said, "You caught me at a bad moment, but when I had more time to think about it, I thought it would be nice to go out and meet someone new."

"To meeting someone new." Melissa clinked glasses with her.

They each ordered a second cocktail and stayed for another hour before asking for the check.

They didn't fight over who would get to pay, as she and Dee usually did. Each paid for her own drinks, and then Melissa walked her to the nearby MAX stop. The numbers on the display announced that it would be four minutes until the train arrived.

"So," Melissa said.

Austen hated that awkward moment at the end of first dates when they had to decide how to say good-bye and whether they wanted to see each other again. Melissa was nice, but Austen had no desire to kiss or date her.

Thankfully, Melissa seemed to feel the same since she just gave Austen a light hug instead of trying for a kiss. "I had a good time tonight."

"Yeah, me too."

"But," they both said at the same time and had to laugh. Austen gestured at her to go first.

"But I don't want to be your rebound girlfriend."

That was the last thing Austen had expected. "Rebound girlfriend? Why would you think that?"

"Come on, Austen! It's clear as day that you're not over her."

"You think I'm still hung up on my ex?" Had she even mentioned her tonight? "I assure you, I'm completely over her."

"Didn't sound like it. All you could talk about all evening was her. Dee mixes a better piña colada than the bartender; she—"

"What? You think Dee is my ex?" How on earth had she gotten that impression?

"She isn't?"

"No! She's just a friend."

Melissa smiled. "Sure she is."

"Really!" Austen wanted to stomp her foot in frustration but realized such a gesture wouldn't help convince her.

Melissa held up both hands. "Whatever is or isn't going on between you, it's none of my business."

Damn right, Austen nearly said but tamped down on such a childish response and instead repeated, "We're just friends."

"But you'd like to be more," Melissa said.

"No. Yes. Maybe." Austen tore at her hair with both fists. How had they gotten on this topic, in the middle of a busy MAX stop? "It's complicated."

"Of course it is. Why don't you—?"

The light-rail train slid to a stop at the station.

Saved by the train. She wasn't ready to talk about it. "I have to go. See you at the gym."

Melissa nodded and waved.

Austen got on the train, dropped onto an empty seat, and leaned her forehead against the cool glass. *Okay, maybe it's more than just attraction,* she finally had to admit to herself. She might actually be a bit infatuated with Dee. Who could blame her? Not only was Dee a good-looking woman, but she also provided just the right mix of challenging her and supporting her.

But even if Dee felt the same, one of them would have to give up her job, and it certainly wouldn't be married-to-her-job workaholic Dee. Austen had promised herself not to ever uproot her life for a woman again, and now she'd stick to her guns. Being friends with Dee would have to be enough.

When Dee put the first handful of popcorn into her mouth, she nearly spat it back out. *What the...?* It was sweet, not salty. Apparently, she had been on autopilot when she'd ordered the popcorn and requested it the way Austen preferred it. Frowning, she put the paper bucket down on the floor and focused on the big screen.

They had been showing commercials and movie previews for what seemed like an eternity. She glanced at her watch in the dim light. Seven thirty.

I wonder what Austen is doing right now. Was she having fun with that woman from the gym, or would she try to cut the evening short? What were they doing? Dinner? Drinks? Maybe a movie too? Or had they gone dancing? The thought of Austen slow dancing with some stranger made her wish the movie theater sold something stronger than the Coke in the cup holder next to her.

Would you quit thinking about her? She took a swig of her soda and tried to muster some interest in the sci-fi movie that was now starting to play.

The person next to her decided that this would be the perfect time to strike up a conversation with his seat mate.

Dee growled and sent them a deathly glare, but they just wouldn't stop discussing the movie's opening scene. Okay, admittedly, she sometimes talked to Austen during a movie too, but today her fellow moviegoers were getting on her nerves.

Or maybe it was the movie that failed to capture her interest. It was by far the worst movie she had seen in some time, and without Austen there, she couldn't even keep herself entertained by making fun of it.

Not even twenty minutes into the movie, she gave up and squeezed past the grumbling people in her row. Light drizzle greeted her as she left the movie theater and headed back to her car.

Now what? She looked around.

The office wasn't far from here. Should she drive over and get some work done? But then she remembered that, in an attempt to prove to herself that she could have a social life without Austen, she'd left the key card to get into the office at home so she wouldn't be tempted to check into work instead of seeing a movie.

What else could she do? Maybe go to a club? She rejected the thought as soon as she'd had it. She wasn't in the mood to socialize, and chatting up a stranger seemed like a waste of time and energy.

Finally, she got into the car and drove home.

She ordered Chinese and opened a bottle of red wine, but even that familiar ritual didn't help. She felt strangely unsettled tonight. *What the hell is wrong with you?* Maybe she was having an early midlife crisis.

She closed the container of only half-eaten Kung Pao chicken and got up, stumbling over the moving box serving as her coffee table.

Damn. She hopped around on one foot until the pain in her toe subsided and then glared at the moving boxes still lying around in her living room. Austen was right. She hadn't gotten much done in the year she had lived here. Well, she rarely spent any time at home and never had guests over—at least that was the way it had been before she'd met Austen. How had her life, which had consisted just of work, changed so fast and without her even noticing?

And now we're back to thinking about Austen. Great. Resolutely, she opened the first moving box and started unpacking it, just to have something to do.

CHAPTER 17

WHEN DEE REALIZED SHE HAD been staring at the same column of numbers for at least ten minutes, she shoved away the keyboard tray, making it snap back with a satisfying crash. She kicked one of the now-empty moving boxes in her home office out of the way and marched downstairs.

Coffee. More coffee. That's what she needed. *Better make it decaf,* a voice in her head said. She already felt restless enough without the caffeine overdose.

While the coffee machine ground the beans, she rifled through the fridge and the kitchen cabinets but found she wasn't hungry. With the coffee mug in hand, she wandered over to the living room.

No blinking light on the phone that lay on the couch.

Of course not. It was barely nine on a Sunday, so the rest of Portland, including Austen, was probably still asleep—and maybe not alone. *No.* Austen wasn't the kind to jump into bed with someone on the first date; she knew that. But no matter how often she told herself that, the thought of Austen with the stranger from the gym kept popping into her head.

When the phone rang, she jumped and nearly dropped her mug. Coffee spilled over, burning her fingers. "Dammit!" She wanted to ignore the ringing but then decided otherwise when she saw the name on the display. "Good morning."

"What's wrong?" Austen asked. "You sound strange."

"It's nothing. Just burned myself when I spilled my coffee."

Austen let out a dramatic sigh. "Can't leave you alone, can I?"

"It's my fourth cup, and I managed to drink the other three without any accidents, thank you very much."

"Let me guess. You've already been up for hours, getting some work done."

"Something like that," Dee said. No way she would admit that she'd mostly stared at her computer screen without really seeing it, wondering whether Austen was up yet—and whether she was sleeping alone. "And you?"

"I just got up not too long ago."

The mug in her hand forgotten, Dee settled on the couch. "Long night?" she asked, trying to sound casual, as if she weren't digging for information.

"Not really."

What did that mean? "Did you come home early because your date didn't go well?"

"No, I didn't," Austen said but didn't elaborate.

Why was it so hard to get any information about her date out of Austen? Usually, she was much more talkative.

"And what are you doing with yourself today?" Dee asked. Any plans that included a certain woman from the gym?

"I don't know yet. What about you?"

"I was thinking about doing something outdoors. I'm developing cabin fever." *Oh, is that what they're calling it now?* If she was honest with herself, she knew it wasn't Portland's spring gloom that affected her mood.

Austen laughed. "You? I thought the office was your natural habitat."

Dee didn't want her to think she was no fun at all. "I used to be the outdoorsy type."

"What happened?"

Dee shrugged, nearly spilling more of her coffee. "Life."

"Work, you mean."

"Yes."

"So how did you spend your Sundays before discovering your love of spreadsheets, contracts, and other paperwork?" Austen asked.

Dee thought back to her college days, when she'd been young and energetic enough to stay up all night, studying to keep her straight As, and then able to get up early to go hiking the next morning. "Hiking, mostly. There's nothing more relaxing than hiking through the forest, with the birds singing around you, and then settling down in some idyllic spot for a picnic." She was almost embarrassed to admit it but told herself Austen wouldn't judge her.

"Sounds great. Let's go."

"Now? It's only the end of March and—"

"Is there a law that forbids hiking in March?"

"No, of course there isn't." Dee put the mug down on the floor and jumped up. "All right. Give me half an hour to throw a few things together for a picnic, and I'll come pick you up."

"Why don't I pick you up?"

"Because I'm the hiking expert who knows where we'll be going, and that means I get to drive." Grinning at that unbeatable argument, she hurried up the winding staircase to get changed. "Oh, Austen? What are you wearing?"

Silence filtered through the line. "Uh…"

Dee laughed. "Get your mind out of the gutter, woman!"

"I'm not… I wasn't thinking…in that direction."

"Whatever you say. So, what are you wearing?"

"Jeans and one of my father's old Marine Corps sweatshirts."

A mental image of figure-hugging jeans, covered by a sweatshirt that hung down nearly to her knees, formed in Dee's mind's eye. *Too cute.* "That won't do," she said, almost regretfully.

Austen huffed. "I know. This sweatshirt isn't fit to be worn in public."

"That's not what I meant. Jeans and a sweatshirt don't make good hiking clothes. Cotton soaks up moisture and takes forever to dry."

"So what should I wear?" Austen asked.

Dee's visual imagination, already in overdrive, had a few suggestions, but she swallowed them unsaid. "Multiple layers. Synthetics, wool, fleece—whatever you have, other than cotton."

"Got it. Thanks."

"Good." One-handedly, Dee struggled out of her sweatpants. "See you in half an hour."

"Whose crazy idea was this?" Austen's voice echoed off the steep cliff wall to their left.

Dee laughed and slowed a little to allow her to catch up. "Yours."

"Going hiking with someone whose legs are twice as long as mine… What the heck was I thinking?"

"Yeah, I'm sure it's just because of my longer legs that you can't keep up. Not because of all the chocolate you eat." By now, she'd found out that Austen wasn't the vain type. She didn't seem concerned with being a pound or two over her ideal weight, so teasing her should be okay.

Austen caught up with her on the narrow path and raised her voice to be heard over the gurgling creek to their right. "Are you calling me fat?"

Dee let her gaze trail over Austen's fairly new-looking pair of hiking pants and the fleece zip top that peeked out from under her open Windbreaker. "No," she said, now completely serious. She liked her just the way she was.

"Thanks. I think."

They continued their hike in companionable silence. The trail climbed higher, leading them away from the creek and deeper into the lush forest. It wasn't raining for a change, and the late-March sun peeked through the branches of moss-covered trees.

Austen touched a dew-hung fern as they walked past. "This feels like we're a million miles away from the city. Like a scene from a fairytale."

"Yeah." Even though Dee wouldn't have chosen the same words to describe how it felt to be here, she had to agree. During the last few years, she hadn't taken any time off to go hiking and had nearly forgotten how beautiful this trail was. Coming here had definitely been a good idea. The restlessness that had plagued her all week had disappeared. She extended her hand to help Austen over a couple of slippery rocks. "Careful. There's poison oak over there."

Austen gripped her hand, the warmth of her skin mingling with Dee's. "Ugh. They don't have that in fairytales."

Dee chuckled. "Maybe they should. Would make them more interesting."

Once they were past the rocks, Austen let go.

Dee instantly missed her warmth. After they had crossed another wooden footbridge over a fast-flowing creek, she paused to take off her backpack and drink some of the water she'd brought. "So," she said when she handed Austen the second bottle, "how was your date?" She thought she did a reasonably good job at sounding interested, but not too interested. She'd waited in vain for Austen to bring up her date during the drive to Eagle Creek.

Austen took a sip of water, then another before screwing the cap back on and handing the bottle back.

Christ, she's taking forever to answer a simple question.

"It was nice," Austen finally said without looking at her.

Nice? Was that a polite way of saying it had been boring as hell? Or had it really been nice? She hadn't known this girl talk thing was so complicated, but then again, she'd never had a girl friend who was not a *girlfriend*.

Austen didn't elaborate.

Dee fidgeted with the strap of her backpack as they continued their hike. Why was Austen so tight-lipped about her date? Weren't women supposed to talk about this stuff with their friends? After a few minutes, she couldn't take it anymore. "What does she do for a living?"

"She's a project manager for a dot-com," Austen said.

Ha! COO beats project manager. Not that it was a competition, of course. "Will you see each other again?" she asked as nonchalantly as possible. This was just a friendly conversation. Friends took an interest in each other's love life, right?

"I'm not sure yet," Austen said. "I liked her, but we don't have much in common, and there wasn't any chemistry."

"No spark?"

"No spark."

Unlike between you and me. Dee banned the thought from her mind. She was Austen's friend, nothing else. Just because she'd never been friends with a woman she was attracted to didn't mean she couldn't be. Right? She was an adult and a professional, after all, not a teenager enslaved to her hormones.

"Maybe it's a good thing," Austen said as she paused to adjust her backpack.

Secretly, Dee thought so too. "Why's that?"

"By now, I probably forgot what to do with a woman." Austen lowered her voice, even though they were alone in the forest, only the birds keeping them company.

Too cute. "So it's been a while for you, huh?"

"You could say that. Three years, two months, and fourteen days. But who's counting?"

Dee stumbled over a root and grabbed hold of the cable line attached to the cliff wall to avoid tumbling down to the gorge floor.

"You okay?"

"Yeah, I'm fine. It's just…wow." There was no way no one had expressed interest in a woman like Austen for over three years. Portland's lesbians couldn't be that blind, could they? "Were you busy with your career, or…?"

"I'm a secretary—"

"Administrative assistant," Dee said.

They grinned at each other.

"Administrative assistants don't work seventeen-hour days to climb the career ladder."

"So if it wasn't the job that kept you from dating, that means your ex did a number on you."

"Guess you could say that. After Brenda, I wasn't exactly in a hurry to get involved with anyone else."

Dee bent a low-hanging branch away from the path and held it until Austen had slipped past. "Haven't you ever heard that the best way to get over someone is to get under someone?"

Austen flicked water from another branch on her. "I think that's more your style than mine."

"Yeah, you know me. I'm Attila, so making conquests is in my blood." It wasn't really. She hadn't even kissed a woman—well, other than Austen—in almost a year. *Jesus, has it really been that long?* Maybe she should put more effort into going out and meeting women, but the truth was that she enjoyed hiking with Austen much more than going to a club to pick up some stranger.

The path in front of them dropped down to an overlook. They stepped up to a cable fence. Below them, a waterfall splashed over the canyon wall and poured into a bowl-shaped basin thirty-five feet below.

"Beautiful," Austen whispered, barely audible over the roar of the waterfall.

Dee gave her a long glance, enjoying the way Austen's face lit up. *Yeah. Beautiful.*

After watching the waterfall for a while longer, they sat on moss-covered rocks and stretched out their legs. Dee opened her backpack and handed Austen all but one of the plastic boxes and bowls she'd brought.

Austen peeked into each and hummed her approval. "Wow. You came prepared."

"Of course. I learned not to go anywhere with you if there's no food within a one-mile radius."

Austen didn't even attempt to protest. "I taught you well. One day, you'll make someone a great wife."

Dee wasn't the marrying kind, but she didn't find it necessary to point that out right now. They sat in silence, watching the waterfall and sharing the food. It was strangely romantic, Dee mused as she cut an apple into slices and handed Austen her share.

They ate their sandwiches, the apples, and some cheese and grapes while the waterfall roared and birds sang above them.

"What's in there?" Austen asked after swallowing the last bite of her sandwich.

"In where?"

"In the bowl you're carefully keeping away from me."

"Oh, this?" Dee held up the bowl on her lap. "I don't think you'd be interested. It's just chocolate m—"

Austen lunged, nearly tumbling onto Dee's lap, and grabbed the bowl. She opened the lid and bounced up and down on her moss-covered rock. "Chocolate mousse!" She looked as if she was about to dive into the bowl face-first.

"Hold on." Laughing, Dee handed her a spoon.

Austen slid a spoonful of chocolate mousse into her mouth. Her eyes fluttered shut, and she moaned.

Heat rushed through Dee's body. She shifted on her rock.

"You want some?" Austen asked after the fourth spoonful.

Dee shook her head. She enjoyed watching Austen devour her favorite vice too much.

After Austen had made short work of the mousse, they put the empty boxes and bowls into the backpack and started back down the path.

"So," Dee said after a while, "your ex, Brenda... Is that the long story without a happy end that you talked about the other day?"

Austen nodded.

"How about redeeming my rain check and telling me what happened?"

Austen sighed. "Are you sure you want to hear this?"

"That bad?"

"I thought so at the time."

The pain on Austen's face made Dee want to pull her into her arms and never let go. "If you'd rather not talk about it..."

"No, it's fine. I should be over it by now." Austen hooked both thumbs under the straps of her backpack, as if needing to hold on to something. "Brenda and I met when I was still living in San Diego."

"Is that where you grew up?"

"I grew up all over...Beaufort, Washington, D.C., Quantico, Hawaii, and several cities in California, but yes, we lived in San Diego the longest. My father still lives there; that is, if he isn't spending time with his new girlfriend, who lives in Bend." Austen kicked at a pebble. It bounced along the path and then skidded down the canyon below them, quickly careening out of sight.

"So you ran into Brenda in San Diego...and then?"

Austen snorted. "Ran into is exactly right. I hit her rental car. That's how we met. Should have been a sign, right? But at first, everything was going great—at least I thought so. Three years ago, while we were opening presents on Christmas Day, she told me that she couldn't see me anymore. Totally out of the blue."

"What a bitch. How long had you been dating?"

"Nearly four years."

Dee stopped walking. "Four years? That's not dating, Austen—that's practically a marriage." None of her relationships had lasted that long. Not even close. "Were you living together?"

Austen paused in the middle of the path too and turned to face her. "Yeah. At least part-time."

"Part-time?"

"Brenda didn't live in San Diego year-round. She was a sales rep for a company that made medical equipment, so she had to travel a lot. Well, that was the reason she gave for all the canceled dinners, the phone calls, and the weekends I had to spend alone."

Oh, no. Dee could tell where this was going. "She was cheating on you?" *Gosh, what an idiot.*

Austen nodded, her lips compressed into a thin line.

Dee took a step toward her. She reached out a hand as if she could wipe away the pain so obvious on Austen's face.

Before she could touch her, Austen added, "To be more precise, she cheated on her partner with me."

"What?"

Austen nodded.

No need to ask if Austen had known. She wasn't the type of woman who'd get involved with someone who was in a relationship.

"I should have known," Austen said, staring into the canyon below. "All of the warning signs were there. My friends warned me time and again. But every time I confronted Brenda, she assured me that there was no one but me. I was stupid enough to believe her."

"It's not stupid to trust the woman you love."

"I even gave up a job I loved and moved to Portland for her, leaving all of my friends and my family behind, just because I hoped she would have more time for me if I lived in the city where her company's headquarters was. If that's not stupid, I don't know what is."

Seeing Austen beat herself up over her girlfriend's betrayal was hard to take. Now Dee understood why she had reacted so strongly to being lied to. "It's human. It could have happened to anyone."

"I bet it wouldn't have happened to you."

"No, because I never get involved with anyone."

Austen said nothing. "Let's not talk about it anymore. Come on," she called over her shoulder, already charging down the path as if trying to run from her past.

"Slow down!"

Water dripped down from the cliff wall to their right, making the path slippery.

"Austen!"

Austen slid and slipped down the trail much too fast, coming too close to the steep drop-off to their left for Dee's liking.

She lunged after Austen, managing to get one arm around her. Roughly, she pulled her back against her body, catapulting them both against the cliff wall. Her heart hammered against her ribs. "Are you crazy? You could have fallen!"

"Nonsense. Let go." Austen struggled against her embrace. Her backpack tore off a button on Dee's shirt as she turned.

Dee refused to let go.

They stood on the rocky ledge, chests heaving, their bodies pressed against each other. Austen's heat seeped through her jacket, mingling with Dee's, and a flush colored her cheeks.

Dee couldn't say who moved first or how it started. Their lips pressed against each other in a hungry kiss, fueled by fear and anger. She wound her fingers into Austen's hair and pulled her closer, feeling Austen clutch her back in return. After a moment, the kiss gentled, and their lips slid against each other like soft velvet.

Boots crunched over the path below.

They pulled away and stared at each other.

Dee had to interrupt their eye contact to flatten herself against the cliff as two other hikers squeezed past them on the narrow trail. When they were alone again, she reached for Austen, desperate to feel those warm lips on hers again.

Austen stopped her with both hands pressed against Dee's shoulders. "This is a bad idea."

It didn't feel like a bad idea at all, but maybe that was just her libido talking. Dee nodded and stepped back. "Yeah. Sorry. I don't know what—"

Austen waved her away. "Just a crazy moment, right?"

"Right."

They continued down the trail without talking or looking at each other. Two miles had never felt so long, and neither had the forty-five-minute ride back to Portland.

When Dee stopped the car in front of Austen's apartment complex, they sat in silence.

Finally, Austen said, "Listen, about next weekend…"

They had talked about driving down the coast, but now Dee wasn't so sure she could take it. After that kiss, she needed some distance and time to convince her rebellious body that friendship was all she wanted. Everything else would ruin her career—and her sanity. "Maybe we could postpone it. I need to catch up on work."

"Yeah. It'll be warmer in a month or two anyway."

A month or two. The message was clear. Better not see each other for a while. Dee nodded.

Austen nodded back as if they'd just made a silent pact. She got out of the car and closed the door between them. Their gazes met through the glass of the side window before Austen waved and walked away.

Damn, damn, damn. Dee punched the steering wheel until her fist started to hurt. After one last glance back at Austen's front door, she drove away.

CHAPTER 18

AFTER GETTING A PLATE FULL of tortellini, Austen carried her tray over to the dessert station.

Sally nudged her. "Oh, look, your favorite."

Next to cups of fruit salad, chocolate mousse waited to be devoured.

Instead of growling enthusiastically, Austen's stomach clenched. She hadn't had chocolate mousse since she'd gone hiking with Dee two months ago, and now the little bowls brought back memories she had tried to forget. Determined, she put a fruit cup on her tray.

Sally gave her a questioning look. "No chocolate mousse? Don't tell me you've gone on a diet."

"No, nothing like that."

"What is it, then?" Sally put two bowls of chocolate mousse on her tray. "You've been a little quiet lately. Everything okay?"

"Yes, of course. Everything's just fine." Austen looked away from Sally's piercing gaze—and nearly dropped her tray.

One of the two people she didn't want to see ambled through the doors of the cafeteria and took a tray from the stack.

Brenda? What the hell is she doing here?

Before she could make a quick escape, Brenda looked up and their gazes met. Brenda's empty tray clattered to the floor, making the people at the nearby tables look up.

Wonderful. Now the biggest gossips in the company were watching them. Clenching her hands around the edges of her tray, Austen decided to be an adult about it. "Can you pick a table for us?" she said to Sally. "I'll be there in a minute." Without waiting for a reply, she walked over to Brenda. "Hi."

"Uh, hi. Are you working here?"

Austen nodded.

"What a coincidence!" Brenda beamed. "Me too. Just started on Monday."

Which meant they'd keep running into each other. Austen white-knuckled the tray until she thought the plastic would crack.

Brenda looked her up and down. "You look great." She lowered her voice. "I guess you haven't heard, but Tonia and I broke up."

Austen stared at her. After what had happened between them, Brenda thought she could just compliment her and all would be well? That maybe now that she was single, they could pick up where they'd left off?

Someone cleared his throat next to them, and Austen realized that they were blocking the door.

When she stepped back, the company's vice president of sales walked past. Dee followed him.

They nodded at each other, as they always did, a simple, polite nod. Amazing how much that distanced politeness hurt. She missed her friend much more than she had thought she would.

"Want to join me?" Brenda pointed at one of the empty tables.

Austen would have rather had lunch with an alligator. "No, thanks. I'm sitting with a colleague. So if you'll excuse me, she's waiting." She walked over to Sally, who sat at a table for two, her chair positioned so she could watch them.

"Who was that?" Sally asked before Austen had even taken a seat.

She eyed the chocolate mousse on Sally's tray. "No one."

Dee put her tray down next to her cousin's and sat across from him. He prattled on about sales numbers in the Asian market while she slid her dessert to the side. *Chocolate mousse.*

She could no longer look at anything chocolate without thinking of it as an aphrodisiac—and without thinking of Austen. She craned her neck to catch a glimpse of her.

She'd seen her only in passing since their hike in March. It was better that way, she told herself. Work had begun to suffer when she'd played hooky with Austen every weekend. Sometimes, her mood had been so good on Monday mornings that her employees sent her weird looks. They were probably talking behind her back, whispering about Attila going soft. Now the old Dee who lived for her job was back. Only late at night did she allow herself to miss those weekends when she hadn't been Attila—and to miss Austen and wonder how she was doing.

Was she having lunch with that woman she'd been talking to when Dee had entered the cafeteria? She was a stunner—a clear ten on the scale Dee's cousins had used to rate women when they'd been younger. Did she and Austen know each other? The intimate way the woman had looked at Austen made her think so. Austen, however, hadn't exactly seemed happy to see her.

"That woman who was blocking the door earlier…do you know her?" Dee asked, interrupting her cousin's monologue.

"Tim's assistant?" Rick grinned around a mouthful of tortellini. "She's hot, right? Certainly fills out that blouse nicely." Waggling his eyebrows, he cupped his hands in front of his chest.

Dee gripped the edge of the table as she fought the urge to stab him with her fork. "You're an asshole, Rick."

"Jesus, calm down. Can't you take a joke?"

"No." Not when it came to Austen. "Not when it comes to one of our employees. And I meant the other woman."

"Oh, her. She's not too bad either. Brenda Van Lese, my new sales manager."

Dee nearly choked on her first bite of tortellini. A sales rep named Brenda, and Austen had stared at her as if she'd seen a ghost from her past… That couldn't be a coincidence. "She works for us?"

"Started on Monday."

Which meant that Austen would have to see her nearly every day in the cafeteria. Dee could still vividly remember the expression of self-loathing on Austen's face as she talked about Brenda's betrayal and her blind trust in her. No. She wouldn't allow the bitch to put Austen through that again. She leaned over the table. "I want you to do something for me."

Rick eyed her. "What?"

"Fire her."

"Are you crazy? I can't just—"

"Fire her, or your dad will find out about your latest affair with Vanessa, the receptionist."

Rick's Adam's apple bobbed up and down as he swallowed. "Consider her fired."

On her way out, Austen exchanged a few words with Vanessa, as she always did.

The elevator doors opened, and more colleagues leaving for the day streamed into the lobby.

Austen stiffened when she caught sight of Brenda. At least her ex didn't try to flirt with her this time. In fact, flirting seemed to be the last thing on her mind. She trudged across the lobby, looking as if she'd just had to put down her dog. Austen squinted. Were those tears gleaming in her eyes?

Brenda saw her and diverted to the reception desk. "Guess we won't see each other every day after all."

"Why? What happened?" Austen asked, trying not to do a happy dance.

"They fired me."

Austen blinked. "Just like that?"

"Yeah. Mr. Haggerty said they made a mistake when they hired me. That I wouldn't be a good fit for the company." Brenda dabbed at her eyes with a tissue.

"The big boss himself fired you?" That was unusual. Normally, he left these unpleasant tasks to Dee.

"No, his son, Richard, did."

Austen frowned. Hadn't she seen Dee talk to her cousin in the cafeteria earlier? A weird feeling prickled down her spine, and the fine hairs on the back of her neck stood on end. *Oh, no.* Even Dee wouldn't do something like that, would she?

"So I guess this is it." Brenda sniffed and looked at Austen with red-rimmed eyes. "Will you call me some time? The number is still the same."

She can't be serious! Austen dragged her through the lobby, out of earshot from the reception desk. "You broke my heart and trampled on my self-esteem. It took me three years to get my life back on track, and now you want me to pretend nothing has happened and just call you?"

"Uh…I never meant to…"

"Save it." Austen held up one hand. "I don't want to hear your excuses. The least you could do is take responsibility for your actions."

Brenda lowered her head. "Sorry, I…"

"I have to go. I forgot something upstairs." Not waiting for a reply, Austen strode back to the elevator and rode up to the fifteenth floor.

It was after five, so most offices were empty, but as she crossed the abandoned outer office of the COO, rapid typing came from the other side of the door. One hand raised to knock, Austen hesitated. Was she ready to face Dee again?

After a few seconds, she squared her shoulders. Ready or not, she couldn't let Dee get away with this. She knocked softly.

The rapid-fire typing inside continued.

Austen knocked more loudly.

"Yes? What is it?"

Dee's growl didn't exactly sound inviting, but she took a deep breath and entered.

"Better make this fast, whatever it is," Dee said without looking away from her computer screen. "I'm in the middle of—" She glanced up. Her eyes widened, and her expression softened. She stopped typing immediately. "Austen."

The way Dee said her name momentarily threw Austen off balance and threatened to make her anger drain away.

Dee took her hands off the keyboard and leaned back in her leather chair. "Come on in and take a seat."

It was tempting to do just that and allow herself to catch up on how Dee had been doing. Had she finally bought some furniture for her house? Had she taken that drive down the coast? Was she getting enough rest, or was she back to burning the midnight oil? But Austen was here for one reason only, and it wasn't to rekindle their friendship. "No, thanks," she said. "I just have a quick question."

Dee nodded. "Sure. What is it?"

How could she phrase this? She didn't want to openly accuse Dee of something she might not have done. "Brenda, my ex…"

"Don't worry. She won't bother you anymore. She's gone."

Oh God. She really did it. Austen stared at her. "You got her fired?"

Dee swished her office chair to one side and back. A shark-like grin spread over her face. "For once, having a cousin who's the VP of sales really paid off. Ding, ding, ding, the witch is dead."

Austen continued to stare. This was a side of Dee she hadn't seen before—the ruthless COO side that made employees tremble when they had to ride in the same elevator. "You can't do that."

"I just did."

"I want you to call your cousin and have him rehire Brenda."

Dee's eyebrows pinched together. "You want her to work here? But I thought it would be hell for you to see her every day. That's why I told Rick to fire her."

She did it for me. It hadn't been an impulsive thing, one of the mercurial actions Dee was famous for. She had gotten rid of Brenda to protect her, even though they weren't really friends anymore. It was touching in a way, but she still couldn't let her get away with something like that. "It would be tough, but that's no reason to fire her. Dee, you can't play with people's livelihoods like that."

"She deserves ten times worse for what she did to you!"

"That's not for you to decide."

Dee jumped up and paced through her office. "You want her back?"

"Yes. I want you to rehire her."

"No, I mean...do you want her back in your life? Don't tell me she didn't try. I saw the way she looked at you."

The tone of her voice put Austen on the defensive. "That's none of your business."

"Like hell it isn't!" Dee crossed the room in two long steps. With eyes that had gone dark, she looked down at her. "Is she the reason why you didn't call me?"

Austen folded her arms over her chest, erecting a barrier between them. "You didn't call me either."

After a few moments of silent standoff, the anger in the room deflated like a pierced balloon.

Austen sighed, suddenly feeling as if she were kicking a puppy. "I know you wanted to protect me from Brenda. Like a friend would."

"Yeah," Dee mumbled. "A friend. Right."

"But we tried to be friends. It wasn't working. It's not working now either. You can't use your family connections to get my ex fired, no matter how much she deserves it."

"But she hurt you," Dee said, sounding so childlike that Austen wanted to hug her.

"Yeah. But if I get her fired, I'm no better than she is. Do you want that?"

Dee looked away and shook her head. "I could get her rehired for one of our international offices."

"That would be great. Maybe the one in New York. Brenda always wanted to live there."

"I was thinking more along the lines of Siberia."

Austen suppressed a grin. "We don't have an office in Siberia."

"Pity."

Now Austen couldn't hold back the smile any longer. "So you'll call your cousin and have him hire Brenda back?"

Dee sighed. "If that's what you want."

"It's the right thing to do." Austen walked to the door. With every step, part of her longed to turn back around and reconnect with her friend. Should she ask whether Dee still wanted to do that drive down the coast? Or maybe invite her to get some cake on the weekend? But then what? The lure of her soft lips and her smoky gray eyes was too strong for Austen to remain just friends. Before too long, she'd do something stupid and kiss her again. She reached for the door handle.

"Austen?"

She turned, half hoping, half fearing that Dee would ask her to do something on the weekend.

They looked at each other from across the room.

"I..." Dee glanced away. "Have a nice evening."

Austen had to swallow before she could speak. "You too."

The door closing between them sounded strangely final.

CHAPTER 19

Two weeks later, Tim stuck his head into Dee's office just as she was powering down her computer. "Have you been summoned too?"

"Yeah. I was just about to go over to the conference room." She grabbed a notepad, and they headed out.

"What is he up to now?" Tim asked. "Why this last-minute super-secret meeting of department heads?"

Dee shrugged. "Hell if I know."

"You don't know? I thought he tells you everything business-related."

"That's what I thought too, but apparently, I was wrong." More and more, her uncle confided his business secrets to Rick, and she had no idea when and why things had changed. They had always talked about her one day taking over the company. Had he now decided that he wanted Rick, his son, to be his successor? Or was this her punishment for not securing the Disney deal?

Uncle Wade waited until the department heads had gathered around the big conference table before he made his grand entrance.

Rick followed him in. Judging by the expression on his face, he was just as clueless as the rest of them about what was going on.

"I'm sure you've all heard that our deal with Disney fell through back in February," Uncle Wade said.

The men around the table nodded.

Thanks for the reminder. That had been four months ago, so why did he have to keep bringing it up? Dee fought to keep her face impassive.

"So we had to look for other opportunities and potential cooperation partners. And we think we found something promising." He slid a stack of folders down the table.

Dee opened hers. "Universal Studios?"

"The theme park, not the studio itself," Uncle Wade said. "They have thirty million visitors every year, most of them willing to splurge on toys, stuffed animals, or some other memorabilia. If we could convince Universal to make us their exclusive supplier…" If he'd been a comic character, dollar signs would have popped up in his eyes.

"Don't they already have a supplier?" Tim asked.

"Yes, but the contract runs out this fall, and they haven't renewed it yet. That's our chance to convince them we're a better choice."

Dee looked at her colleagues gathered around the table. So who would the poor soul shouldering that kind of responsibility be? Maybe Alejandro, their creative director? Or would he send Rick to give him a chance to prove himself?

Uncle Wade walked down the row of leather chairs. His steps paused behind Dee's chair, and then he dropped another folder in front of her. "Here are two plane tickets and two front-of-line passes for the park. I've booked you into the Hilton for a week. I want you and your assistant to go down to LA on Monday for some research and then come up with a proposal that'll blow their socks off."

No pressure or anything. Dee gritted her teeth. "I don't have an assistant."

"You still haven't hired someone?"

"I hired three someones. None of them worked out." Truth be told, Dee would much rather work alone anyway. Sooner or later, any assistant she hired would only stab her in the back one way or another.

"I guess you can take Timothy's assistant for now. This is your chance to make up for the Disney debacle."

Dee clenched her jaw. The Disney debacle, as he called it, hadn't been her fault. It irked her that she now had to prove herself anew. After years of her bringing in one successful deal after the other, all he seemed to remember was the one deal that she hadn't been able to secure because the competition had offered better conditions.

And, to top it all off, she would travel to LA with the one woman who could manage to distract her from work. She thought about suggesting someone else to accompany her, but that would make her uncle even more suspicious, especially after she'd told him she and Austen were friends.

Was this another test to see if she could be professional and keep her hands off Austen in the more relaxed atmosphere of the theme park? Or was her uncle just sending Austen because he knew any other assistant would call in sick if he ordered him or her to go on a weeklong excursion with Dee?

She studied her uncle's face, but his expression gave nothing away.

"Any questions?" he asked.

She shook her head. The only question she had was not for him. What would Austen say when she found out?

"I have good news and bad news." Mr. Saunders perched on the edge of her desk, laying claim to her territory in the same mildly annoying way his sister did.

Austen regarded her boss carefully. "Okay. What's the good news?"

"Instead of being stuck in the office, you'll get to spend most of next week exploring an amusement park—at the company's expense."

"Really? I love amusement parks!" Wait a minute. That sounded too good to be true. And why did her boss look so worried? "Um, what's the bad news?"

He got up from her desk and stepped back as if afraid he'd get caught in the line of fire. "You'll have to work with my sister on that project."

Images of Dee and her riding a roller coaster shot through her mind, their bodies pressed together as gravity tore at them. She took a folder off her desk and fanned herself. When she realized her boss was watching her, she hurriedly set down the folder and schooled her features into impassivity. "Why me?" Had it been Dee's suggestion?

"My sister still hasn't hired a new assistant, and my uncle knows you are friends, so he probably thought chances are good that you won't quit just to avoid working with her." He searched her face. "That's what you are, right? Friends?"

Austen nodded. If she told him they were no longer friends, he'd ask why, and she didn't want to discuss it with her boss.

He studied her as if he sensed there was something she wasn't saying. "If you'd rather not go, I could tell my uncle that I need you here and he should send someone else with Dee."

The offer was tempting, but she couldn't avoid Dee forever. If she wanted to stay with the company, she had to find a way to get along with the COO—without getting along with her too well. "That's not necessary," she said. "Working with her won't be a problem at all."

She'd just have to ignore her libido and her heart for a few days, and all would be fine.

Back on the plane, Dee had been all business, discussing their schedule for the week ahead and brainstorming ideas, keeping things between them on a strictly professional level. But now, as they strolled through the theme park in more casual clothes, she stared with childlike amazement and pointed out the costumed characters roaming the park.

Austen smiled inwardly. *That's just too cute. She's like a kid in a candy store.*

"Ooh, look, Frankenstein's monster! Let's see who's got the bigger one." Dee dragged her over to a tall actor with greenish-gray makeup.

"The bigger what?"

"Scar, of course!" Dee was almost as tall as the monster, and Austen took a photo of the two of them with their foreheads side by side.

Afterward, Dee checked out the photo on the display of the digital camera. "All right, you win," she told the actor.

He nodded sagely, not breaking character by smiling.

They wandered through the park, stopping to get ice cream.

Austen licked her scoop of dark chocolate chip and hummed. "You know, we've got a tough job."

Dee nodded, the picture of the suffering businesswoman—if it weren't for the peanut butter swirl ice cream in her hand and the grin on her face. "Yeah, I know, but someone's gotta do it."

When the ice cream was gone, Dee pointed at the entrance of *Revenge of the Mummy*, a high-speed roller coaster. "Let's try that."

Austen felt herself go green around the gills at the mere thought of it. "Unless you want me to wear my ice cream on my shirt, that's not a good idea."

"I thought you loved roller coasters?"

"I did—as a child," Austen said. "But now that I'm older, they make me sick to my stomach."

Dee rolled her eyes. "Older. You sound like you're eighty."

"Let me guess. You do just fine on roller coasters."

"I have no idea. I've never been on one."

Was she kidding? "You've never been on a roller coaster?"

Dee kicked at a pebble on the path. "No. When I was a child, my parents were too busy with work to take us. And now *I'm* too busy with work."

Austen sent a quick prayer of thanks up to her mother for giving her a chance to enjoy a normal childhood. She nearly reached out and took Dee's hand but stopped herself at the last second. "We could go on one of the tamer rides. My stomach should be able to handle that."

"You sure?"

Austen nodded. What was a bit of queasiness if Dee got to experience something that she'd missed out on so far?

In front of them, a family with two kids that couldn't have been older than six or seven walked beneath a sign announcing the *Jurassic Park* water ride.

"We could do that one," Austen said. If two little kids could do it, so could she.

The company had gotten them front-of-line passes, so they didn't have to wait in line. Within two minutes, they boarded one of the yellow rafts.

The lap bar lowered over them as soon as they were sitting. *No way back now.*

The raft clattered up an incline, and Austen clutched the lap bar so she wouldn't slide back.

"Relax," Dee murmured and put one arm around her. "Remember that rule about valuable company assets? I won't let anything happen to you."

Before Austen could answer, the raft splashed down into a lagoon. A wooden gate opened in front of them, and they drifted past two long-necked dinosaurs munching on water plants.

Okay, this isn't so bad. Austen relaxed her death grip on the bar but didn't shake off Dee's supporting arm around her. It felt too good to have her near again, so she would allow herself the closeness until the ride ended.

The raft moved behind a waterfall and emerged on the other side, where a stegosaurus was looking down at them from a cliff. To their left, two smaller dinosaurs were playing tug-of-war with an empty popcorn box.

Just when Austen was beginning to think it would be a relaxing ride, they encountered another raft, empty except for the dilophosaurus munching on a yellow rain poncho. A Mickey Mouse hat drifted on the water.

Dee nudged her and grinned as she pointed at the hat. "Did you see that? I think that's a little dig at the competition."

Sparks flew as an SVU fell from the cliff overhead, nearly crushing them.

Suppressing a shriek, Austen shrunk away from it.

Dee pulled her closer against her side.

Two dilophosauruses flapped their neck frills and spit venom, one of them managing to soak Austen. She wiped water from her face and now understood why a few of the people in the row in front of them were wearing rain ponchos.

The float rumbled up a ramp into the pump building. Darkness engulfed them, interrupted only by blinking red lights overhead. The roar of an angry dinosaur echoed through the building.

Austen gripped the lap bar as her tension rose.

Warm hands covered hers in the darkness.

An alarm blared, and a voice on a loudspeaker announced that life support would fail in fifteen seconds.

A T. rex lunged down, its giant jaw open to grab them.

Austen ducked down.

At the last second, the raft escaped by plunging down eighty-four feet into a tropical lagoon.

Austen let out a startled scream. Her stomach lurched at the free fall.

Then the ride evened out and slid to a stop. The lap bar went up, and she stumbled out of the boat, with Dee gripping her elbow. After a few steps, her legs felt more steady. She tugged on her wet T-shirt and laughed. "I'm soaked."

Dee's gaze slid over her, lingering for a bit too long. "Yeah. Me too. Must be why some of the people in front of us bought a poncho."

Austen tried not to ogle Dee's now nearly see-through white T-shirt, but she was only human and caught a peek or two.

They headed into the gift shop to check out the dinosaur-themed toys, T-shirts, and memorabilia on sale.

While Dee stopped to look at some mugs, Austen continued to wander.

Photos of the water ride flashed over a row of monitors overhead. *Hey, that's us!* One of the screens showed them plunging down that steep waterslide at the end of the ride. Dee had one arm wrapped around her while clutching the lap bar with the other hand. *We look like a couple.* She sighed.

"Everything okay?" Of course, Dee chose that moment to reemerge next to her.

"Yeah, I'm fine. Just really soaked."

After a quick glance at the monitors, Dee steered her toward the exit. "Let's head back to the hotel and get into some dry clothes. We can check out everything else tomorrow."

Freshly showered and finally dry, Dee knocked on the connecting door between their rooms. "Austen?"

She heard something from inside that sounded like "come in," so she did just that.

Apparently, what Austen had actually said had been more along the lines of "give me a second." She stood next to the bed, dressed in one of the hotel's fluffy, white terry-cloth robes, toweling her hair dry.

Dee eyed the silky-looking skin peeking out from the V of the robe and instantly needed another shower—a cold one. "Uh, sorry. I'll come back." She stumbled backward and felt around for the connecting door.

"It's okay," Austen said, tugging the collar of her bathrobe closed. "You can come in if you don't mind my less-than-professional wardrobe."

Dee stopped her retreat and tried to look elsewhere. "I...uh...ordered room service. Dinner should be here in twenty minutes."

"Thanks. I feel like I could eat a dinosaur."

Dee laughed and relaxed a little. This was just Austen. She'd been around her all the time when they'd been friends. Seeing her in just a bathrobe was no big deal. She took another step into the room. "I thought maybe we could use the time to see if we can come up with some ideas for the project."

"I actually had this idea when I was in the shower. That's why I took so long. I always have my best ideas in the shower."

Dee tried not to imagine soapy water sliding down Austen's naked body, steam wafting around her, but it was like trying not to think of a pink elephant. *Work. Think of work.* She cleared her throat. "So what did you come up with?"

"Let me get dressed first; then I'll show you."

"That's okay," Dee said before she could stop herself. "We're both adults, right?" She ignored the fact that she felt more like a teenager around Austen.

Austen hesitated but then said, "Right." She tied the belt of her robe more securely. "I realize we haven't seen all of the park yet, but that water ride gave me a few ideas..."

Yeah, me too. Unfortunately, they hadn't been the professional kind. She'd spent most of the ride focused on the feel of Austen nestled against her body.

"Remember that talking lizard you were working on in December? If we modified that product line a little, it would fit nicely with the *Jurassic Park* theme."

"Damn, you're right. Of course, we'd have to add a few new products too. Something different from what they already sell."

They sat on the bed and started brainstorming.

When room service brought their dinner twenty minutes later, there were notes and sketches littering every inch of available space around them.

They sat cross-legged on the bed, Austen's bare knee lightly brushing hers, adding to the creatively charged atmosphere in the room. They ate dinner, grilled chicken and chocolate cookies for dessert, while they continued to work, sparking ideas off each other.

In the past, Dee had always preferred working alone. Most people on her team weren't able to keep up with her thought process and only slowed her down. Working with Austen was different. They effortlessly finished each other's sentences, sensing where the other wanted to go and then running with that idea and improving it.

Dee stared at the sketch of a dilophosaurus blaster, spitting water instead of venom. "Tell me again why you work as a secretary."

Austen looked up from the sketch coming alive under her skillful hands. "Uh, why wouldn't I?"

"Because your talents are totally wasted on that job. We should fire Alejandro and hire you as the head of our creative team."

Austen's gaze flickered down to the sketch, then back up. "You really think I'm that good?"

"Hell yes! You're fantastic." In more ways than she could tell her. Had no one ever told her how talented she was? Dee rose up on her knees and grabbed her shoulders to drive home her point. "Each of these ideas could be worth millions. I could kiss you!" Flushed with exuberance, she leaned forward and did just that.

The soft touch of Austen's lips against hers startled her awake as if from a dream, but before she could pull back and apologize, Austen pressed closer and returned the kiss.

Her lips were soft and parted as she moaned into Dee's mouth.

The sound made Dee's head spin. She tangled her fingers in Austen's damp hair and deepened the kiss.

Their mouths molded together, and their tongues touched.

Heat rolled through Dee. She groaned and lost herself in the taste and feel of Austen.

Austen's hands roved over her back.

Dee couldn't get enough. She pressed closer until Austen's breasts brushed the underside of hers through the thick terry cloth.

Paper crinkled as they sank onto the bed, with Dee on top. Instantly, Austen's legs parted, allowing full body contact.

Breathing heavily, they paused and stared at each other.

Austen's eyes were the most amazing shade of blue Dee had ever seen. Her cheeks were flushed and her hair messy from Dee's fingers. *Beautiful.*

"We shouldn't do this," Austen whispered, but her eyes, full of passion, said something else.

"We shouldn't." The thought of stopping, backing away from Austen and going back to her own room, hurt almost physically. "But maybe if we got it out of our system once and for all, things at work would be easier. It can be just this once if that's what you want."

"Just this once." Austen stared back at her with big, hungry eyes. "All right." Her gaze darted down to Dee's lips.

That was all it took. Groaning, Dee bent down and kissed her again. Impatient to feel Austen's skin, she slid one hand between them, loosened the sash of the robe, and pushed the garment off one shoulder. Her fingers encountered hot skin. *So soft.*

Austen gently bit down on Dee's bottom lip.

Dee grunted as the sensations, half pleasure, half pain, coursed through her body. She deepened the kiss and then broke it so she could move down and press her mouth to the shoulder she had laid bare. Goose bumps erupted under her lips, and she laved them with her tongue before raking her teeth over Austen's hammering pulse point.

Touching Austen set her blood on fire. She needed more. Much more. The need to worship every inch of Austen's body surprised her, but she didn't stop to think about it. She slipped one hand into the robe and ran it lightly up Austen's side, then back down over her waist and over the flare of her hips, studying Austen's reaction to every touch. Finally, she smoothed the pad of her thumb over the underside of one round breast before cupping it more fully.

Austen threw her head back and moaned.

The sound made Dee shiver with desire. She pushed the robe open more fully, revealing Austen's body, naked except for a pair of black panties. She bit her bottom lip as she drank her in, wanting to touch her everywhere at once.

Slow down. If this was to be a one-time thing, she wanted to make it count, but her usual suave finesse was nowhere to be found. Her hands trembled with the need to touch and bring Austen as much pleasure as she could.

Austen lay still beneath her, raw emotion in her eyes.

When Dee couldn't stand the intensity of their eye contact anymore, she stripped her T-shirt over her head and threw it on the floor. With impatient hands, she brushed the notes and sketches off the bed, not caring where they landed. "Let me take these off." She stood, gently slid the panties down Austen's legs, and used the opportunity to get rid of the rest of her own clothes too. From her position next to the bed, she gazed down at Austen, taking in the womanly flare of her hips, the auburn curls at the apex of her legs, her full breasts, and her flushed cheeks. Her skin looked like alabaster, and she longed to run her hands over every inch of it. "God, you're beautiful."

"Come here."

Dee shook off her almost poetic thoughts. *Just a one-time thing, remember?*

When she slipped back into bed, Austen immediately reached up to touch her breasts.

Oh no. If she allowed Austen to touch her now, this would be over too soon. She entwined their fingers and pressed them to the bed. With Austen immobilized beneath her, she bent and flicked her tongue over one of Austen's nipples, wanting to make her moan again.

Austen gasped.

Dee pushed her hips between her legs, earning a moan. *That's more like it.* Passion was safe, as long as she kept the rest of her feelings in check. She would allow herself one night of passionate sex with Austen, but tender lovemaking was out of the question. Despite her best intentions, she couldn't help worshipping Austen's breasts. She nibbled and sucked, enjoying the contrast of silky skin surrounding the hardened nipple. After a while, she switched to the other breast until Austen squirmed beneath her, her hips undulating. She shivered as she felt Austen's wetness against her skin.

"God, Dee." She tightened her grip on Dee's hands. "This is killing me. Just…please."

The need in her voice made Dee's breath catch. "Tell me. Tell me what you need." She let go of Austen's hands, ready to do just about anything to please her.

Instead of a verbal answer, Austen grabbed her hand and pushed it down.

They both moaned as Dee's fingertips encountered her wetness.

Dizzy with need, Dee struggled to go slow, wanting to savor every moment. She swirled her finger around Austen's clit.

Austen pressed her entire body upward, against her, opening herself to her touch. "More."

Dee kissed her once again and then dipped two of her fingers lower and into her. She slid her fingers out and watched Austen's face as she drove them back in.

Lips parted in a silent cry, Austen arched up and kissed her. As they moved against each other, she grazed her fingernails up and down Dee's back, nearly driving her crazy. Austen started panting, and her warm breath bathed Dee's ear.

Bracing herself on her left forearm, she shifted above Austen and rolled her hips in time with her hand.

Austen bucked against her, urging her on with moans and gasped encouragements. "Oh. Yes! So close."

Dee felt her own wetness grow, but she ignored it and focused solely on Austen. She curled her fingers up, searching for Austen's G-spot, intent on bringing her pleasure.

With a shout, Austen surged against her and dug her fingers into Dee's back, then collapsed back onto the bed.

Dee buried her face against her neck as Austen quivered beneath her. When Austen's breathing and her thrumming heartbeat quieted, Dee gently withdrew but kept her lips pressed to her neck, enjoying the salty taste.

Without warning, she was rolled onto her back and stared up into Austen's eyes, which had gone azure with passion.

Austen looked down at her, studying her so intently that Dee started to squirm. Then she relaxed, enjoying the intimate feeling of warm, damp skin sliding across hers.

Her fingers tangled in Dee's hair, Austen rained tender kisses over her cheeks and along her jaw and then brushed her lips over the thin scar on her forehead. Her hands followed the path of her lips, tracing Dee's features as if trying to memorize them. Finally, she lifted Dee's hand and pressed a kiss to the scar on her palm.

This wasn't how a one-night stand with one of your employees was supposed to feel. This was way too intimate, but Dee didn't have the strength to push her away. Her bones seemed to melt beneath Austen's touch, and she lay helplessly, moaning, as Austen slid lower.

Austen pressed her mouth to Dee's lower abdomen, making her feel as if her heart was about to hammer out of her chest. "Is this okay?"

Dee could only nod. She clutched the sheets beneath her as Austen teased her inner thighs with kisses before dipping between her legs. Unable to do more than hold on, Dee surrendered herself to the pleasure shooting through her body. She knew she was saying something, maybe screaming, but she had no idea what. She was close, so close already. Her nails dug into Austen's shoulders. She wanted to tell her to slow down. This was too good to be over so soon. If this was the only time, she wanted it to last. "Careful. You—oh! God, Austen!"

Shudders rippled through her as Austen sucked harder. Orgasm washed over her. She clutched Austen's head against her and held her there until she couldn't stand it any longer.

Austen crawled up the bed, and they lay in a tangle of limbs, on a nest of damp sheets, surrounded by the sheets of paper strewn around the bed.

Dee wrapped her arms around Austen and squeezed her eyes shut, trying to shut out the world for just a moment longer.

CHAPTER 20

AUSTEN WOKE AS THE FIRST rays of sunshine fell into the hotel room. She lay completely still, keeping her eyes closed. For a few moments, she allowed herself to imagine that she could just roll around, kiss Dee awake, and make love to her again.

But then reality intruded. They hadn't made love; they'd had sex. Now it was supposed to be out of their systems, so why did she want Dee more than ever? Their brilliant plan had backfired, at least for her. From what she knew about Dee's love life, she'd had casual sex before. Maybe this was no big deal for her.

Quietly, she turned around to look at her.

The bed next to her was empty. Her robe sat at the foot of the bed, neatly folded, a piece of paper on top.

Hands shaking, she reached for the note.

Gone to the gym. I'll meet you for breakfast at eight. Can you bring our notes?
Thanks,
D.

That was all. No mention of last night. *Guess I'm out of her system, and now it's back to business.* That was exactly what they had planned, so why did it hurt so much?

Dee stabbed a button, increasing the pace until she was running full out. Sweat ran down her face and dripped onto the treadmill. She tried not to think and focused just on her breathing and the pounding of her sneakers, but images of last night kept flashing through her mind.

Austen with her head thrown back in ecstasy. Austen gazing at her, her eyes darkened with passion. Austen rolling them over and kissing a trail down her belly.

Her rhythm faltered, and she nearly fell off the treadmill. She pressed another button to slow down before she broke her neck.

"Damn, damn, damn." Instead of enabling her to move on, last night had done the exact opposite. Now she wanted more. More sex? More than sex? Both? She wasn't sure. Her feelings were a big, jumbled mess.

The hotel's fitness instructor, a leggy redhead in tight spandex shorts, wandered over. "Everything okay?"

"Yeah," Dee muttered.

"Maybe you should slow down a little. You're not running for your life, are you?"

"No." Dee slowed down to a brisk walk.

"Good. Would be a pity to lose a guest this early in the day." The redhead smiled at her. The bottom of her T-shirt was tied into a knot, showing off her flat belly. She stretched her sinuous body as she leaned against the treadmill's handle next to Dee. "Are you staying here longer?"

Normally, Dee would have enjoyed the harmless flirting, but now it was just annoying her. "Just a few days."

Apparently getting the message, the redhead stepped back. "Enjoy your stay, then."

Dee didn't think she would. Now she'd have to go sit at the breakfast table with Austen and pretend that they were just two women working together.

If breakfast was as delicious as it looked, Austen couldn't tell. She pushed a piece of hash browns around on her plate, creating a mess with the sunny-side-up eggs.

Dee didn't make a dent into her Belgian waffles either. She seemed completely focused on yesterday's notes and sketches.

Looking at the crumpled paper didn't put Austen into work mode at all. All she could think of was how Dee's skin had felt against hers, how her kisses had tasted, and how Dee had touched her as they had lain surrounded by these sheets of paper.

Even though she knew she was torturing herself, she couldn't help sneaking a peek at Dee every now and then. Was Dee really focused solely on work? Could she push back thoughts of last night effortlessly?

Their gazes met, and both of them looked away.

Dee cleared her throat. "That brontosaurus umbrella will look great."

Austen bit her lip. It hurt that Dee was able to go back to work without a problem, as if last night had never happened. "Yes, it will."

They continued to eat—or pretend to eat—and to stare at the tablecloth and last night's sketches.

"I think it'll be better not to include the T. rex mug into the presentation, though," Dee said after a while.

Austen gave herself a mental kick and forced herself to be professional. "Might be better. It's not as good as the other ideas we came up with."

Dee nodded and smoothed her palms over the wrinkled paper.

Oh, God. Austen flushed at the memory of those hands running over her body.

Dee looked up and stared at her, then jerked her gaze away and continued to thumb through the notes.

Austen went back to torturing her hash browns, willing her hands not to tremble. She'd have to be strong for a little while longer. Once she'd made it through breakfast, she could lock herself in her room until they had to leave for the theme park.

Finally, Dee shoved her plate away and gathered their notes. Her expression was calm, but Austen couldn't tell whether she was really unaffected or had put on a mask of professionalism. "All right. Let's get going. We've got a theme park to explore."

The only thing Austen wanted to explore was Dee's body. She bit her lip. It was going to be a long day.

For several hours, they strolled through the park to get a better feel for Universal's style and their visitors' shopping habits. They watched a stunt demonstration, went on *The Simpsons* simulator ride, and took pictures of comic characters, but for Austen, the theme park had lost its magic.

She sat next to Dee in the tram that carted them around the studio's backlot. The subtle press of Dee's thigh against hers made it hard for her to focus on what the tour guide was saying. *Get a grip.* Dee wasn't the first woman she'd slept with, so what was going on with her? True, one-night stands were usually not her style; maybe that was why her body and her heart now expected more.

The tram rounded a corner and stopped next to a street winding through the set of an old Mexican village. Fake rain began to fall, turning the road into mud, and thunder sound effects echoed all around them.

A wall of water rushed down the hill and shot through the windows of the *mercado*, sweeping away a wooden cart next to them. People around them screamed as a wave hit the side of the tram.

Water sprayed, making Austen glad she was sitting in the middle.

Dee cursed and slid to the right to avoid getting drenched.

That move pressed their bodies together from knees to shoulders. A shudder ran through Austen as the warmth of Dee's leg permeated her jeans and Dee's arm pressed against the side of her breast.

"Sorry," Dee said. "I can't move back if I want to avoid looking like I wet my pants." She gestured to the bench to her left, which had gotten wet.

"That's okay." Did her smile look as fake as it felt? Austen hoped not. She spent the rest of the tour caught between praying that it would be over soon and hoping the ride would never end.

When the tram finally stopped and they climbed out, her legs felt a bit wobbly.

"Let's get something to eat." Dee pointed at a diner in the style of the fifties, complete with a Cadillac parked out front. "Are burgers and fries okay, or do you want something more—?"

"Whatever you want is okay," Austen said. She wasn't very hungry anyway.

"What do you want?"

As their gazes met, the question took on a deeper meaning. Was Dee asking about her food preferences, or was she ready to talk about what had happened between them?

Dee cleared her throat and looked away. "I...uh...I heard they have great milkshakes."

"Then let's go in." Austen pushed past her and stood in line with the other diners.

They waited in awkward silence until it was their turn to order and then slid into one of the red vinyl booths, still not saying a word.

Dee unpacked their notes and sketches from last night while she munched on her french fries.

Austen fiddled with her straw and wished she had never agreed to go on this business trip and, most importantly, had never agreed to have a one-night stand with Dee. *God, what was I thinking?*

Dee leafed through the notes and then pushed them away. "This isn't working."

Frowning, Austen glanced at the sketch on top, her drawing of the dilophosaurus blaster. "Why not? I think we can easily sell—"

"No. This," Dee pointed back and forth between them, "isn't working."

Dread skittered down Austen's spine. She had been afraid that this would happen. That they'd find themselves unable to work together and one of them, probably she, would have to give up her job so they wouldn't have to see each other again.

"I'm sorry," Dee said. "I know we said we'd move on after one night, but…"

"But?" Austen prompted softly. Her heartbeat hammered against her ribs, and she barely dared to breathe, afraid she'd miss the answer.

Dee gave a small smile. "After being with you, that's pretty much impossible. You're hard to forget."

Thank God. So it's not just me. Austen's muscles went limp, and she slumped against the back of the booth. "You're not quite out of my system either."

Dee's eyes smoldered.

It would have been so easy to get up, take her hand, and pull her back to their room at the nearby hotel and to bed, but Austen needed to know what it all meant first. "So you'd like to…what? Continue this when we fly back home? Meet for a quickie in the executive bathroom and sneak away to a hotel every now and then?"

She knew Dee wanted nothing to distract her from her career, so a friendship with occasional benefits might be all she wanted, but she wasn't sure she could do that.

Dee searched her face. "Is that what you want?"

Austen didn't even try to play it cool. "Christ, no. After Brenda…I don't want to be someone's dirty little secret. I want the real thing."

"The real thing," Dee repeated as if to herself. She nodded decisively. "Yeah, I want that too."

Austen felt as if she were floating. She wanted to rush around the table, crawl onto Dee's lap, and kiss her until they were both breathless, but she forced herself to stay where she was and face the hard realities. "But how is it supposed to work without one or both of us getting fired?"

"We'll have to keep it out of the office."

"That's for sure. No making out in the elevator. No quickie on your desk."

Dee stared off into space for a moment, her cheeks flushed.

Austen laughed. It was wonderful to know she was having the same effect on Dee that the other woman had on her. "You did get all the nos in that sentence, didn't you?"

Grinning, Dee rubbed her cheeks. "Yeah. Kind of." Her expression sobered. "But seriously, it won't be easy. We can't tell my family about us. We can't drive to work together. My uncle doesn't even like the thought of us being friends. If he finds out that we are…"

Yeah, what are we? Austen waited with bated breath to see how Dee would finish her sentence.

"…a couple, he won't just ignore it. If someone at work finds out, one of us will have to quit. Are you willing to risk that?"

With the word *couple* still echoing through her mind, the risk didn't seem quite so bad. "I am. I think this…we… are worth it. But what about you? You're taking the bigger risk. I know you have your eyes on the CEO position."

"Yeah. I won't lie to you…"

"Good. Even though we'll have to lie to pretty much everyone else, there can be no lies between us." Austen wanted this to be clear once and for all.

Dee nodded. "I know. That's why I'm telling you I'm not ready to give up my job. I worked toward the CEO position almost my entire life. I can't just give that up."

Austen stared at her untouched burger. "I know."

Dee reached over and covered her hand with her own. "But I don't want to give you up either. I want to at least see where this is going. Can we do that?"

It wasn't the *let's run off to Cancun and live on coconuts and sex for the rest of our lives* that a new lover wanted to hear, but it would have to do. "Yes." Austen turned her hand and entwined their fingers. "So what do we do now?"

"More research." Dee stood, pulled her up too, and led her to the diner's door, leaving behind their mostly uneaten lunch.

"Into the dinosaur project?"

"No." Dee stopped in the middle of the street and leaned over, her breath hot on Austen's ear. "Into what will make you scream my name."

Austen's knees went weak, and she slumped against Dee. "Oh, God. You can't say things like that to me in public."

Laughing, Dee pulled her toward the theme park's exit.

When they landed at PDX and got off the plane, gravity seemed to double as their lightheartedness disappeared. Austen had known that reality would set in sooner or later, but she'd chosen to ignore it during the last five days.

As if by unspoken agreement, neither had talked about what would happen when they returned to Portland. Those five days had existed as if out of time. All they had done was work on their project, make love, and feed each other morsels of the food room service brought up.

Now they sat in the backseat of the cab, cuddled together, neither of them speaking.

Austen's heart sank as the cab pulled up in front of Dee's house. After they'd spent every second of the last five days together, saying good-bye and going back to her empty apartment was nearly unbearable. *Better get used to it.* If they wanted to keep their relationship secret, they'd have to spend a lot of time apart.

With the cab's engine idling, Dee turned toward her. She trailed her hand over Austen's cheek and then kissed her, apparently not caring that the cabbie was watching them in the rearview mirror.

Austen molded herself to Dee. Her eyes fluttered shut as she deepened the kiss.

After a minute or two, the cabbie cleared his throat.

Austen jumped. She'd forgotten about him. Dee's kisses tended to make her lose track of where she was.

Dee handed him a few bills, enough to cover both of their fares. Without looking away from Austen, she fumbled for the lever, opened the door, and swung her long legs out.

God, those legs. Austen vividly remembered them wrapped around her and—

Cut it out! What are you, a sex maniac?

As the distance between them grew, she shivered, even though it was seventy-five degrees outside.

With the door still open, Dee turned back toward her. Her mouth opened as if she wanted to say something, but then she apparently thought better of it. She gave a short wave and said, "Until tomorrow, then."

"Until tomorrow." At work. Austen bit her lip. *Get yourself together. We'll have to face reality sooner or later.*

When Dee turned around, away from her, she couldn't stand it any longer. "Dee?" she called. "Can I come up?"

Dee turned back and grinned. "I thought you'd never ask."

Austen got out of the cab before one of them could change her mind. *Maybe it doesn't have to be now.* Facing reality tomorrow morning would be soon enough.

CHAPTER 21

"And, as you can see," Dee clicked through to the last slide in her presentation and pointed at the screen behind her, "the initial cost/benefit analysis I ran looks good too, since we can use some of the setup from the talking lizard toy."

A murmur ran through the vice presidents and senior managers as they studied the numbers on the screen.

Dee kept her gaze fixed on her uncle, not allowing it to wander to where Austen was sitting, taking notes for her brother.

"Thank you, Danielle," her uncle said. "I knew you could pull it off. I'll contact Universal Studios and submit our proposal."

The tension in Dee's shoulders receded. "Thanks, but it wasn't just me. Ms. Brooks contributed just as much. Most of the sketches you saw were hers."

He waved without even looking in Austen's direction. "I'll make sure she gets a nice bonus for it," he said as if she weren't in the room.

Dee clenched her teeth but said nothing. As the senior managers filed out of the conference room, she closed down her laptop and disconnected it from the projector.

"Nicely done," a low voice said next to her.

She looked up and into Austen's azure eyes. "Thanks." She rolled up the power cord and placed it in her laptop bag, trying hard not to notice how good Austen looked in her business skirt and white blouse. Part of her was tempted to compliment her, to say something to reconnect, but she knew she shouldn't. Right now, she was Danielle Saunders, COO of Kudos Entertainment, not Austen's lover.

Austen stepped closer, not inappropriately close, but close enough so Dee could feel the heat radiating from her body. "Do you think they'll go for it?"

"They'd be idiots to pass this up." She gathered the printouts of her slides, zipped the laptop bag closed, and shouldered it.

Together, they walked to the door.

"This is hard," Austen whispered right before they stepped into the hall.

So Dee wasn't the only one struggling to keep her distance at work. That made it a little easier. She nodded. "Will we see each other tonight?" They hadn't talked about how often they'd see each other or whether they would sleep over at the other's place on work nights.

Austen looked left and right before saying, "Eight o'clock, my place. And make sure you eat before you come over." She brushed past Dee and walked down the hall.

As the meaning of her words hit home, Dee's mouth went dry. She stared after her until the door to Tim's outer office closed behind her.

"Are you staying the night?" Austen called from her position nestled between the tangled sheets.

The door of the fridge banged shut, and Dee's footsteps padded through the living room. "I can't. I forgot to bring a change of clothes. Guess I was in a hurry to get here."

Austen smiled. Was it too soon to suggest that Dee might want to leave some clothes at her place, in case she wanted to stay over?

Probably. Considering they had to keep their relationship secret for now, it might not be a good idea anyway. Despite her hormones dancing a jig any time Dee was near, she told herself to take it slow. Rushing into relationships, jumping in headfirst, hadn't served her well in the past, but being with Dee made her want to forget the bad experiences.

When Dee didn't return to the bedroom, she slid out of bed, reached for one of the shirts on the floor, and put it on. The scent of Dee's perfume wafted up, and she hummed as she walked over to the living room.

She found Dee next to Toby's cage, her head bent so she could be on eye level with the cockatoo while she talked to him. She wasn't wearing a stitch of clothing, and Austen paused in the doorway to take in every inch of the body she'd worshiped just half an hour ago.

"Are you just going to stand there and ogle me?" Dee asked without turning around. Her confident posture revealed that she didn't mind, though.

Austen chuckled. "No. I wanted to see what was keeping you from coming back to bed." She walked over, pressed her body against Dee's, and wrapped her arms around her from behind, cuddling against her naked back. "What are you doing?"

"Trying to teach him some new words." Dee slid her hands along Austen's bare arms, making her shiver.

"Mmm. Which ones?"

"Sexy." Dee's fingertips trailed over the sensitive spot in the bend of her elbow. "Gorgeous." The touches wandered up her arm. "Hot. Anything more appropriate than *loser* to describe Toby's owner. Isn't that right, boy?" She reached through the bars of the cage to scratch behind Toby's crest.

"Careful! He—"

Too late. Toby sank his beak into Dee's finger.

"Ouch." Dee pulled her hand back and stared at her bleeding finger. "Dammit."

"Loser," Toby screeched.

"Oh God. I'm so sorry." Austen cradled the injured hand and tried to see how bad it was. "I should have told you how jealous he is. He doesn't like to share my attention."

"Can't say I blame him."

Austen dragged her over to the kitchen, held Dee's finger under the tap, and then dried it with a clean towel. Thankfully, it didn't seem too bad. The bleeding had almost stopped already.

"We seem to make a habit out of this—me ending up bleeding all over you."

"Yeah, but at least this time I can kiss it better." Austen pressed her lips to Dee's palm, then to the inside of her wrist. She had found out earlier how sensitive that spot was for Dee. Goose bumps formed under her lips, and she lightly traced them with her tongue.

When Austen looked up, Dee's eyes had gone dark. "My legs feel a little weak. Do you think it's the blood loss, Doctor?"

"I'd need to do a more thorough examination before I can rule out other causes."

"Maybe you should have the patient lie down for that."

"Good idea." Austen pulled her back into the bedroom, stripping off the shirt on the way.

———————— ✦

It was already close to midnight by the time Dee finally made it out of bed. Still completely naked, she stood and looked down at Austen. "I have to say, I really like your bedside manner much more than that of Dr. Babyface."

Austen laughed. "I'd certainly hope so." She marveled at how much fun it was to be with Dee. Not just the sex, but every minute spent with her. She couldn't remember ever laughing that much with a partner.

She folded her arms behind her head and watched Dee dress. *Okay, this part isn't fun at all.* She hated that Dee had to sneak back to her own bed at midnight instead of cuddling up to her all night.

Now dressed except for her missing shirt, Dee put one knee on the bed and studied her. "Are you okay?"

Austen forced a smile. "I'm fine."

Dee tapped her on the nose. "I thought you didn't want any lies between us."

Austen tugged the sheet a bit higher, feeling exposed under Dee's knowing gaze. "Yeah, I…" She peeked up at her. "I would have liked to fall asleep with you holding me."

A deep line formed between Dee's brows. "I could stay and get up an hour early tomorrow morning to—"

"No. I know you have back-to-back meetings all day tomorrow. You need your sleep."

"Yeah. I admit that being so sleep deprived has made it hard to focus at work. And some very vivid flashbacks didn't help either." Dee grinned, and then her expression went serious. "But it's worth it."

Austen pulled her down for a kiss.

It was closer to one when Dee finally made it out of the apartment, wearing only a jacket over her undershirt.

Austen stood at the window, her nose buried in the shirt she'd managed to steal from Dee, and watched the taillights of the BMW until they disappeared around the corner.

CHAPTER 22

DEE WANDERED OVER TO THE break room in search of some coffee—strong, preferably. After again spending half of the night at Austen's, she needed it. At first, they had said that they wouldn't spend time together if they had to work the next day, but that rule had been thrown overboard almost immediately.

With past girlfriends, Dee had always resented if they kept her away from work for too long, but to her surprise, she realized that she was just as eager to spend time together as Austen seemed to be.

Ergo the need for coffee.

One of the other employees apparently had the same idea. She stood with her back to Dee, refilling the coffee machine's water tank.

For a moment, Dee wanted to give up on her caffeine fix and turn back around. After just four hours of sleep and a terse conversation with her uncle, who wanted her to take over the unpleasant task of firing someone, she wasn't in the mood to exchange pleasantries with one of their employees. A closer look made her change her mind.

That sassy haircut was unmistakable. She had run her fingers through that auburn hair just a few hours ago. Softly, she cleared her throat.

Austen turned. A blazing smile transformed her features from pretty to breathtaking.

Dee wanted to return the smile but was afraid someone would see it and become suspicious. It was one thing for Austen, who was known as friendly and upbeat, to smile like that. But if she, the company's grouchy second-in-command, ran around with such a cat-that-got-the-canary grin, people would wonder what was in the coffee.

"Good morning, Ms. Brooks," she said instead. Had she ever told Austen how much she liked her unique first name? Probably not. But this definitely wasn't the time or place to make up for it.

"Good morning, Ms. Saunders."

Dee reached around Austen, their arms brushing, placed a mug under the coffee machine, and pressed a button. "So," she said while coffee splashed into the mug, "any plans for the weekend?"

To anyone passing by the break room, they sounded just like two colleagues exchanging polite chitchat.

Austen leaned against the counter and stirred what seemed like a gallon of milk and a pound of sugar into her own mug. "I'm not sure yet. A date might be nice."

"A date?" Was that supposed to be a message to her?

"Yes. You know…that activity where two people who are romantically interested in each other get dressed up, share good food and pleasant conversation, and try to get to know each other better, followed by a kiss at the front door."

They had known each other for six months and had already slept together several times, and yet Austen wanted a bona fide break-out-the-good-duds date? She picked up her mug and took a careful sip of coffee, studying Austen over the rim of the mug.

"Don't bother," Tim said as he entered the break room. "Explaining romance to my workaholic sister is like getting my uncle to give us more money for the Giggles marketing campaign—utterly useless."

Dee put down her coffee mug. "Hey, I can be very romantic."

Her brother laughed and gave her a disbelieving look. "Oh, yeah?"

"Yeah." She put her hands on her hips and tried to stare him down.

Like all of her brothers, Tim never shied away from a challenge. "So let's hear it. What's your idea of romance?"

Dee started to sweat under the curious gazes resting on her. "If I were currently seeing someone, I would...well..."

"Yes?" her brother drawled.

"I would invite her to Le Pigeon for a romantic candlelight dinner, say tonight at seven, and then take her dancing afterward. How is that?" She glanced from Tim to Austen with a challenging gaze.

"Sounds good," Austen said quietly.

"Not bad." Tim rummaged through the selection of teas and spoke over his shoulder. "But not as good as what I did on my first date with Janine."

"Whatever you say." To her own surprise, competing with one of her brothers was no longer important to Dee. So what if he thought he was more romantic or the better partner? The only opinion that mattered to her was Austen's.

"I'd better get back to work before my boss catches me lingering in the break room." With a smile at Tim, Austen carried her mug to the door. "Have a nice weekend, Ms. Saunders."

"Thanks. You too." Dee stared into the black depth of her coffee. Now how on earth was she supposed to get a table for two at Le Pigeon tonight?

Austen paraded her fifth outfit through the living room and stopped in front of the bird cage. "What do you think, Toby?" She smoothed her hands over the skirt and gave him a questioning look.

Toby stopped cleaning his tail feathers and walked closer on his perch. After eyeing her for a few seconds, he warbled, "Loser!"

"You could have said it more diplomatically, but I agree. This won't work for a date." The skirt looked too much like the ones she wore to work every day, and she wanted to wow Dee with something new for their first official date. She marched back into the bedroom, struggled out of the skirt and blouse, and threw them onto the growing pile of not-quite-good-enough clothes.

Her cell phone rang from somewhere beneath the pile.

Austen's heartbeat sped up as she searched for the phone. She hoped it wasn't Dee calling to say that something had come up at work and she had to cancel their date. Finally, her searching hand encountered the phone, and she lifted it to her ear just before the call could go to voice mail. "Hello?"

"Hi, stranger," Dawn said. "Good to see that you made it back and didn't fall off a roller coaster."

Austen flopped on top of the discarded clothes and squeezed her eyes shut. She hadn't talked to Dawn or any of her other friends since coming back from Universal two weeks ago. God, she hated people who forgot about their friends as soon as they were in a relationship, and now she was one of them. "Sorry I didn't call you. It's just... Things were pretty crazy after we came back."

"That's what I figured when you didn't show up for art class two weeks in a row. I told the others your boss is keeping you busy."

Images of the creative ways Dee had found to keep her in bed flashed through Austen's mind. "Yes," she murmured, "she's keeping me busy all right."

"She? I thought your boss is a man."

"My direct supervisor is, but the company's COO is a woman. She's the one I went to LA with."

For a few moments, only the sounds of Dawn's breathing filtered through the line.

Austen clutched the phone with one damp hand. Did her perceptive friend suspect that something was going on between her and Dee? She wasn't ready to tell anyone about her new relationship quite yet, especially since she wasn't sure what her friends would think about her starting a relationship with the company's second-in-command.

"So other than the COO keeping you chained to the desk, everything is okay?" Dawn finally asked.

Austen cleared her throat as images of Dee tying her to a desk danced through her mind. "Never been better," she said, and it wasn't a lie. The last two weeks had been amazing.

"Good," Dawn said. "Listen, I just found out that Lucille from that Chinese brush painting class we did last year managed to get some of her work included in a showing, and I thought it would be nice if we went to support her."

"Sure. When is it?"

"Tonight."

"Oh." Austen's mind raced. She hated lying to her friend, but she couldn't very well tell her that she had a date with her boss. "I'm sorry, Dawn, but I can't make it tonight. I have to... Something else came up."

Again, only silence from Dawn. Finally, when Austen couldn't stand it anymore and was just about ready to spill the beans, Dawn said, "When Aiden and I first started dating, I had a hard time getting her to open up and talk about her emotions."

It wasn't hard to imagine that. Befriending the kind, approachable Dawn had been easy, but her partner was much slower to open up. "I know, but that's not what—"

"Hush. Let me finish," Dawn said. "She would withdraw and not call me for days, just so she could avoid talking about whatever was upsetting her."

"I'm not upset. I'm just..."

"Yes?"

Austen inflated her cheeks and then blew out the breath. How could she explain without giving too much away?

"Want to hear how Aiden and I now handle situations like that?" Dawn asked.

"I'm listening."

"She tells me that something happened at work that upset her, but that she's not ready to talk about it," Dawn said. "That way, I don't feel like she's lying to me or shutting me out of her life, and she's not forced to talk about things before she's ready."

The message was clear. Austen hung her head. Initially, they had bonded over their common interest in art and the fact that they'd both lost one parent as teenagers. By now, she considered Dawn her best friend. She deserved better than this. "I'm sorry. I didn't mean to shut you out of my life."

"I know. And I didn't mean to pressure you."

Austen inhaled deeply. "I met someone. But I'm not ready to talk about it."

"Just tell me one thing. Is she good for you?"

"She's a stubborn, challenging workaholic, but she's the best thing that has happened to me since…ever," Austen answered without having to think about it.

Dawn laughed. "I know exactly what you mean. So will I see you at art class next week?"

"I'll be there." No more neglecting her friends. "Dawn?"

"Yes?"

"What did you wear on your first date with Aiden?"

A chuckle rang through the line. "A pair of ice skates."

Austen kicked a blouse off the bed. "Not helping. I don't think they'll let me into the restaurant wearing ice skates."

"Why don't you wear that emerald green dress that you bought for your cousin's wedding in November?"

Austen struggled out of the clothes pile, opened her closet, and peeked at the dress. That might work. "Thanks," she said for more than just the fashion advice.

"You're welcome."

Dee threw the folder into her out-box. Now just a quick check of her e-mails to see if Rick's salespeople had managed to keep their expenses down this month, and then she'd get out of here. That would give her just enough time to drive home, change into something less businesslike, and meet Austen for their first official date.

A last-minute reservation at Le Pigeon had nearly cost her a kidney, but if Austen wanted a date, a date was what she would get. Dee just hoped Austen had understood her secret message in the break room this morning and would meet her at the restaurant at seven.

Her fingers darted across the keyboard, entering her password.

Sixty-eight new messages since she'd last checked a few hours ago, but none of them from sales.

"What the...?" Had her cousin forgotten to CC her on the expense reports, or had he left her out of the loop on purpose? Last time she had called him onto the carpet for his team's exorbitant expenses, he hadn't been too happy about her intruding into his area. Not that Dee gave a damn about his hurt pride. She was just doing her job, and if he had been doing his too, she wouldn't have to deal with this now. Cursing, she snatched up the phone.

It took forever until someone answered, and it was neither Rick's voice nor that of his administrative assistant greeting her. "Kudos Entertainment, sales department, Brenda Van Lese speaking."

The words she had wanted to say died on Dee's lips. What was Austen's ex doing here? Hadn't they transferred her to New York or Siberia or some other, faraway place months ago? "Uh, this is Danielle Saunders."

"Oh, Ms. Saunders, what can I do for you?"

Crawl over shards of glass and apologize to Austen for what you did to her. Dee bit her tongue and said, "Is my cousin, Richard Haggerty, in?"

"He already left, and so did everyone else."

Dee frowned. "So they left you to answer the phone?"

"No. I was on my way out to catch my plane when I heard the phone ring. I was just here for our quarterly meeting."

Rick has his sales people fly in from all over the US for a meeting? Why couldn't he do it over the phone or Skype? No wonder his department's expenses were so high. And why the hell did his staff leave work so early? It wasn't even... She glanced at her wristwatch.

Oh, shit! It was much later than she'd thought. How had that happened? No time to figure it out now. She ended the call without saying good-bye and ran to the elevator, not bothering to stop to boot down her computer. As the elevator carried her down to the lobby, she bounced up and down on the balls of her feet as if that would make it move faster.

On the seventh floor, the elevator stopped.

Not now! Dee glared at the opening doors and the woman getting in before realizing who it was. *Brenda. Great. Just what I needed on top of everything else.*

"Ms. Saunders." Brenda pressed the button for the lobby. "We somehow got disconnected."

Dee waved her away. Ignoring Austen's ex, she kept her gaze on the red numbers counting down.

Finally, the number changed to zero and the doors pinged open, but Brenda still blocked the way. She turned toward Dee as if she had all the time in the world. "I hope you'll have a nice—"

"Excuse me. I'm in a hurry."

"Oh. Sure. I know how that is."

I just bet you do. Dee tried not to imagine how often Austen had sat in a restaurant, waiting for Brenda, never suspecting that she'd been held up at home, with her other partner. Nearly pushing Brenda out of the way, she sprinted across the lobby and toward her car. But no matter how fast she ran now, she'd be late. Just about now, Austen was probably arriving at the restaurant.

She'd messed up. Big time. It had happened before, more than once, actually, with past girlfriends. Her work had always come first, and she didn't care if the women in her life knew they were playing second fiddle. But with Austen, everything was different. The thought of Austen sitting alone at the table, waiting and feeling like a fool, made her cringe.

She stepped on the accelerator and took a corner a little too fast, nearly bouncing the right front wheel into the curb.

Her thoughts were racing. She had to think of something to make it up to Austen. *Flowers. Jewelry. Chocolate.* But none of that sounded right. She had a feeling that even Austen's beloved chocolate couldn't save her now. Austen deserved better than her showing up an hour late with cheap excuses and a not-so-cheap pair of earrings and a box of chocolates.

She slowed down a little, fumbled her cell phone from her pocket, and pressed number two on the speed dial. *Number two.* Work still held the number one position, on her speed dial and in her life.

"Yes?" Austen's voice interrupted her thoughts and sent her heartbeat into overdrive.

"Um, hi, it's me. Dee."

Before she could find the right words to tell her, Austen asked, "Did I misunderstand about meeting at Le Pigeon at seven? I thought that's what you were trying to tell me this morning in the break room."

Dee dug her teeth into her lower lip. "No, you didn't misunderstand. It's just…"

"How late are you running?" She sounded so calm, not angry at all, as if she had halfway expected it would happen, which made Dee feel even worse.

For once in her life, she didn't want to be an unreliable girlfriend. "I can be there in fifteen minutes if you don't mind me showing up in my work clothes."

The red and blue lights of a patrol car flashed behind her.

Dee groaned and pulled over. "Make that thirty minutes. I've just been pulled over for talking on the phone while driving."

"Dee!"

"I'm so sorry. I warned you that I make a lousy girlfriend."

Austen sighed. "Yeah, you did. You know what? Let's forget about the restaurant. Meet me at the Peninsula Park rose garden."

"Okay. Austen, I really am sorry."

A knock on the side window startled her. The police officer gestured at her to roll down her window.

"I have to go," she said into the phone. "Austen, I…"

"Go before your fine climbs even higher. And drive carefully."

"I will." Dee hung up.

Dee hurried down a few steps and then jogged along the red-paved path. The roses all around her were in full bloom, but she didn't take the time to enjoy their sweet scent or to admire the manicured hedges. Her gaze immediately zeroed in on Austen.

She was sitting on the ledge of the large fountain in the middle of the rose garden. In her emerald dress, too elegant for a visit in the park, she looked like a princess from a fairytale. She'd taken off her strappy sandals and dangled one hand into the water.

God, she's beautiful. Dee slowed and broke off one buttery yellow rose.

Austen didn't look up when she sat next to her.

Dee held out the rose, putting it into Austen's line of sight.

She took it without saying anything and fiddled with its leaves before finally turning toward Dee. "Friendship."

"Friendship?" Dee's stomach knotted. Did that mean Austen wanted to go back to being friends, now that she'd found out firsthand what a horrible girlfriend she was?

"Yeah. Yellow roses mean friendship."

Great. She couldn't even get that right. Why did relationships have to be so complicated? "Oh. I hoped it meant forgiveness."

Austen shook her head. "Only when it's fifteen of them."

Dee stole a glance at the nearby flowers. Should she…?

"Leave the poor roses alone."

Was that a hint of a smile on her face? Dee slowly reached out and put her hand on top of Austen's, hoping she wouldn't be rebuffed. "Am I forgiven anyway?"

Austen turned and entwined their fingers. "I'll let it go this time. The fine you had to pay for driving while on the phone was probably enough of a punishment."

"Ouch, yes. Five hundred dollars, can you believe it? But I don't care about the money. I only care about you." Oh, Christ. When had she started to sound like a lovesick fool? But it was the truth.

"I know you care. I also know how important your job is to you. You get wrapped up in work and forget everything around you. I knew that from the start." Austen sighed. "But sitting in the restaurant, waiting for you, and then that phone call… It was like being with Brenda all over again."

Being lumped in with Brenda, the two-timing bitch, hurt more than the five-hundred-dollar fine. "It's not the same."

"I know. I'm only telling you how it made me feel."

Dee bowed her head.

Austen squeezed her hand. "Okay, now that I made my feelings clear, let's just move on."

"I'm forgiven? Just like that?" It hadn't worked like that in any of her previous relationships. Her girlfriends would have milked it for all it was worth and laid weeklong guilt trips on her.

"On one condition. Two, actually."

Dee rubbed her thumb over the back of Austen's hand. "Anything."

"Set an alarm on your cell phone next time we have a date."

"I will. And the second condition?"

"You carry the bag over to the picnic table." She pointed at the bag at her feet.

Dee bent and peeked inside. Heavenly scents drifted out. Apparently, Austen had ordered their food to go. "Is there a chocolate dessert?"

"Is that a rhetorical question?"

Dee laughed and kissed her, not caring who was watching. "Give me a second, and we'll head over to the picnic spot. But there's something I need to do first." She pulled her cell phone from her pocket.

Austen laughed. "Are you setting the alarm already? We haven't even agreed on a time for our second date."

"No. I just have to change one of my contacts." With a few touches to the screen, she made Austen number one on her speed dial before pocketing the phone and reaching for the bag of food. "All right. Let's have a picnic."

CHAPTER 23

"DEE?" TIM'S VOICE FROM BEHIND stopped her from getting into the elevator. "Do you have a minute? I could use some feedback on the drafts for the new glow-in-the-dark animal ads."

Stopping the elevator doors from closing with her shoulder, Dee turned. "Does it have to be now?" She hadn't been late to a date with Austen since that first time nearly two months ago, and she wasn't about to change that now.

"Uh, no." Her brother studied her from head to toe. "Why? Are you heading to an out-of-the-office meeting I'm not aware of?"

"No. I...well...no. I have an appointment, but it has nothing to do with work."

Tim flashed her a smile. "I knew it. You've met someone, haven't you?"

Dee put on the poker face she had perfected in boardroom meetings, even though her stomach knotted. She hated lying to Tim, the only one of her siblings she was close to. "Why would you think that?"

"When was the last time you had an appointment that had nothing to do with work?"

"I had a dentist's appointment, a meeting with my financial adviser, and I went to the hairdresser this month." Dee ticked them off on her fingers.

"But you weren't grinning on your way to those appointments," Tim said.

Dee touched her mouth and then dropped her hand. Had she really been grinning? Probably. She'd been imagining the expression she hoped to see on Austen's face when she surprised her with the photo. "Can't I be in a good mood without it having to do with a woman?"

Tim sighed. "Okay, I'll let you keep that miracle-working woman to yourself for a bit longer. But you've got to introduce us sometime."

Dee said nothing and escaped into the elevator. *You've got to introduce us sometime,* echoed through her head all the way to the lobby. *Damn.* Now her good mood was gone.

"Keep your eyes closed," Dee whispered from behind.

As warm breath bathed her ear, goose bumps erupted all over Austen's body. She leaned back and enjoyed the safe feeling of Dee's arms wrapped around her. Without her sight, her other senses intensified, and she drank in Dee's scent and the feeling of her breasts against her back. "If you wanted to play sexy games, you didn't need to lead me out of the bedroom."

Dee chuckled. "Let's leave the sexy games for later."

"Does that mean I'm allowed to look now?"

"No. Nice try." Dee guided her through the house. Judging by their steps echoing over tiles, they had entered the kitchen now. "Okay, now you can look."

Austen opened her eyes.

A chocolate cake sat on the table, and two candles flickered on top. A gift-wrapped package lay next to it. "Um, you do know that it's not my birthday, don't you?"

"I know. And I hope you have a few more candles on your birthday cake; otherwise, I'm seriously robbing the cradle."

Austen's mouth watered as she eyed the chocolate cake. "Don't worry. Candle-wise, this is clearly not my birthday cake. What is it, then?"

Dee pulled her around to look into her eyes. "Happy two-month anniversary."

A wave of warm affection swept over Austen, and tears burned in her eyes. She threw her arms around Dee and hugged her for all she was worth.

Dee held her tightly. "I know it's a bit weird to celebrate a two-month anniversary," she said quietly, "but for me, making it to this point without messing up is kind of a big deal."

Austen rose up on her tiptoes and kissed her. "I don't think it's weird at all. It's very, very sweet." She loved knowing that their relationship was important enough to Dee to go to all this trouble.

"Don't let it get around. I have a reputation to uphold, you know?"

"Your secret is safe with me." Even if she could tell her colleagues at work, no one would believe her anyway. All they saw was Attila, not the Dee she knew.

After a few more moments, Dee let go and urged her to turn around. With both hands on Austen's shoulders, she led her over to the table. "Come on. Blow them out. And don't forget to make a wish."

Austen pulled Dee next to her. "Let's do it together. It's our anniversary after all, not just mine."

Dee wrapped one arm around her. "On the count of three. One. Two. Three."

They took deep breaths, leaned forward, and blew out the candles.

May we celebrate many more anniversaries. Austen turned and looked into Dee's eyes. Had she wished for the same?

Dee pulled out a chair and pressed Austen down onto it. "Okay, now the gift." She placed it in her lap.

Austen suppressed a grin. Dee seemed as excited as if she were the one getting the gift. "But I don't have anything for you." She had known that the two-month anniversary of their trip to LA was coming up, but after giving it some thought, she had decided that Dee might find a celebration after just two months a bit silly. *Guess not.*

"Doesn't matter," Dee said. "It's not much anyway. Now open it."

Austen slid her hands over the flat, square package. Not jewelry, that much was sure. She sniffed, shook, and tapped the package until Dee began to fidget. Finally, she slid her finger beneath the tape and removed the gift wrap.

A framed photograph was revealed. When Austen turned it around, she realized it was the picture of them on the *Jurassic Park* water ride, with her clinging to Dee. "How did you get this? I thought they erase them if no one claims them that day?"

Dee answered with a mysterious grin. "I have my ways."

"You certainly do." Austen stood to kiss her. "Thank you."

Dee linked her hands behind Austen's back and pulled her closer. "You're very welcome. Now how about some of those sexy games you mentioned?"

Austen glanced back and forth between the chocolate cake on the table and the woman holding her. Finally, she reached for Dee's hand and pulled her back to the bedroom. The chocolate cake would have to wait.

CHAPTER 24

Sally got up from the bench they had set up around the picnic tables. "I'll get myself another hot dog. Do you want something else too?"

Austen ate the last bite of her pasta salad and pushed her plate away. "No, thank you. I'm holding out for a piece of the raspberry chocolate cake later."

Laughing, Sally pulled her new boyfriend up from the table to follow her.

Austen watched them go.

Like Sally, most of her colleagues had brought their partners and even their kids to the annual company barbecue, and Austen felt a little out of place sitting alone. How ironic. She had never minded doing things with her friends and their partners, even though she'd been the only single person in her group of friends, but now that she'd finally found someone, she felt left out. She peeked over to where Dee was setting up a volleyball net with her cousin.

In a faded pair of blue jeans and a form-fitting polo shirt, Dee looked fantastic, and Austen had a hard time resisting the temptation to watch her or to walk over and join her.

"Ah, there you are." Her boss walked up to her table. He, too, was wearing jeans and a polo shirt, but he didn't look nearly as good as his sister in Austen's opinion. "I hope you're enjoying yourself."

Truth be told, Austen couldn't wait to get out of here and spend the rest of the day alone with Dee at home, where they didn't have to pretend they barely knew each other. But, of course, she smiled and said, "I'm having a great time."

"Have you ever played volleyball?"

"I played a little in high school, but I'm too short to be any good."

"Ah, come on. I'm sure you'll do just fine." Mr. Saunders waved at her to follow him. "We have to defend our honor in the annual company volleyball game, and we need a sixth player."

"Okay." At least if she played, she wouldn't have to sit around alone and stop herself from ogling her lover. She followed him over to the improvised volleyball court. "Who are we playing?"

"Us," a voice next to her said.

Austen turned.

Dee stood in front of her, one arm wrapped loosely around the volleyball. The slender muscles in her arms played beneath her smooth skin. Two of her employees lingered behind her, looking less than pleased to be on her team.

Unlike them, Austen was more than happy to drink in the way Dee looked and every little movement she made. Dee looked back with the same unblinking stare. Austen could only hope that their colleagues would think that they were sizing up the competition.

Other people from marketing and operations wandered over until both teams were complete and took their positions on the volleyball court.

After a coin toss, Dee was the first to serve. Her face was a study in concentration as she stepped back behind the inline. She threw the ball up and jumped to hit it midair.

The ball whizzed over the net at a high speed and hit the ground before anyone on Austen's team could get to it.

Austen ran after it and threw it back to Dee. "Nice serve."

"Thanks." There was something feral in Dee's grin. She hit one of her high-speed serves again, but this time, Jack managed to bump the ball at the last second.

Austen raced over and set the ball upward, and her boss sent a powerful spike across the net.

The ball headed for an empty spot on the court, but before it could hit, Dee was there again and bumped it up.

Austen nearly became dizzy as she tried to keep up with the fast back-and-forth, mainly between Dee and her brother. She seemed to be everywhere at once, making almost impossible rescues and hitting power spikes left and right while Austen watched, completely in awe.

Someone in the marketing team's back row bumped the ball into the air.

Austen wrenched her gaze away from Dee and got into position. Crouching a little, she touched the ball with her fingertips so that it just tipped over the top of the net and headed for an area of the court not covered by Dee's team.

Dee dove as if her life depended on it. A second before landing on her belly, she sent the ball back across the net. "Who had that?" she shouted before she was even back on her feet. "You have to pay attention, people!"

No one on her team answered as the game continued.

Jack blocked the ball, sending it back over the net.

"Get out of the way!" Dee rushed over. Instead of setting up for one of her teammates, she leaped high into the air and spiked the ball.

It hit the ground hard, earning another point for her team.

Austen picked up the ball, but instead of throwing it back, she carried it to the net.

When Dee approached to take it from her, Austen didn't let go. "You do know that we're playing a game and not waging World War III on each other, don't you?"

"Sure." Dee tried to take the ball, but Austen held on.

"Then maybe you should stop acting like a one-woman army and start making sure your team is having fun."

Dee's brows pinched together. "They are having fun. We're winning after all!"

"Look at them." Austen pointed at a few employees from operations, who stood with hanging arms, watching Dee warily. "Do they look like they're having fun?"

"I hate company barbecues," Dee mumbled just loudly enough for Austen to hear.

Austen gave her a look.

"Okay, okay. I'll try to behave." Dee took the ball and marched back to the inline.

The game became less aggressive after that, and Austen could go back to watching and admiring Dee in action.

A few serves later, the ball flew over the net.

One of Austen's colleagues bumped it up and another spiked it back to operations' side.

Within seconds, the ball traveled back.

Austen jumped to block it.

The ball headed straight for Dee, who moved with the intensity of a panther, wound up, and spiked the ball.

Wow. Poetry in motion, Austen thought before the ball hit her square in the face and knocked her over like a felled tree.

When she saw Austen going down, Dee forgot about the game.

The ball bounced twice before rolling off the court.

Dee dove beneath the net and ran over.

Tim and two of their teammates were kneeling next to Austen, blocking her line of sight. She shoved at his shoulder, desperate to get to Austen, who still hadn't gotten up. "Let me through, dammit!"

Finally, Tim moved a little, allowing her to drop to her knees next to Austen.

Those beautiful azure eyes were open and dazedly blinked up at her.

Oh, thank God! Dee wanted to cradle her in her arms and examine every inch of her to make sure she was unhurt, but she knew she couldn't. If she showed more concern than she would for any of her other employees, someone would start to suspect their less-than-professional relationship.

Blood trickled from Austen's nose.

Dee stared at the droplet of crimson on the alabaster skin and curled her hands to fists. Never had she felt so helpless. Finally, she jumped up and dashed over to the coolers to get some ice.

When she returned, Austen was struggling to get up.

Onlookers be damned, Dee put one arm around her and pulled her back down. "Don't move yet. Here." She handed over some tissues and the ice pack.

Austen dabbed at her bloodied nose with the tissue and tried a crooked smile. "We really have to stop meeting like this."

Dee grinned back. Her fingers itched to reach out and touch Austen, but she could feel a dozen gazes rest on her. The stabilizing arm she kept around her would be enough reason for gossip. "Yeah, we'd better not make it an annual company tradition. Are you dizzy?"

"I'm fine. Just got the wind knocked out of me."

"No headache?"

"No headache." She pulled the tissue away from her nose, showing Dee that her nosebleed had stopped too.

Her relief nearly made Dee sprawl on the ground next to Austen.

"Want me to drive you home?" Tim asked.

"No!" Dee shouted before Austen could answer. She bit her lip and lowered her voice to a more normal volume. "I mean…I can do it. It's on my way home anyway." A second later, she realized that she had just admitted to knowing where Austen lived. Thankfully, no one else seemed to have noticed.

"Way home?" Tim shook his head. "You're not going home yet. I'll follow you in Ms. Brooks's car, and then we'll drive back here together."

Dee ground her teeth until her jaw ached, but she couldn't very well tell her brother that she wanted to stay at an employee's home to make sure she was fine. "It makes no sense for both of us to go. One of us should stay and—"

"All of us are staying," Austen said, sounding much stronger than a minute before. "There's no need to drive me home. I can just sit at the table with an ice pack, and I'll be fine in a little while."

Dee opened her mouth to protest, Austen's first name already on her lips. At the last second, she held herself back. "I'm not sure that's a good idea, Ms. Brooks. Remember what I told you about valuable company assets?"

Austen got to her feet under Dee's watchful eyes. "No valuable company assets sustained any lasting damage. I promise."

Dee ran her gaze over her. The nosebleed had stopped. A few blades of grass clung to her T-shirt, and Dee's fingers itched to help brush them off. She dug her fingernails into her palms to resist temptation. "All right." Reluctantly, she stepped back and let Austen pass.

Flanked by two employees from marketing, Austen made her way toward the picnic tables.

"Want to continue playing?" Tim asked.

Dee forced herself to look away from Austen. "No, I've had enough," she said. What she wanted was to sit next to Austen, pull her against her body, and cradle her head against her shoulder while she held the ice pack to her face.

Tim narrowed his eyes. "Danielle Saunders doesn't want to savor her almost certain triumph over her brother? Did you get hit in the head too?"

A hard shove from Dee made him stumble into the net. "Just taking mercy on you. But if you insist on being embarrassed in front of your entire department... Find someone to replace Ms. Brooks, and we'll finish the game."

He patted her shoulder. "That's more like it."

When he walked away to find another player, Dee snuck a peek at Austen, who sat at the table with Sally Phillips fawning over her.

Their gazes met, and Austen lifted the ice pack away from her face to send her a quick smile.

Tim returned with the two marketing people who had walked Austen to the table and another employee whose name Dee didn't know. "Let's continue. But do me a favor and don't knock out the rest of my team, okay?"

Without answering, Dee took the ball and marched to her side of the net. She didn't care about the rest of Tim's team or even about winning the game. The only person she cared about sat at the picnic table, watching them. She threw the ball up and hit it with all her might. The sooner she ended this game, the sooner she could take Austen home.

Austen's nose was still tender, and the coldness of the ice pack against her skin was starting to become uncomfortable, but she couldn't remember ever feeling as peaceful as she did right now.

Dee lay stretched out on Austen's couch, cradling her and holding an ice pack to her face. Her warmth seeped into Austen's back, relaxing her muscles. Every once in a while, Dee lifted the ice pack away and tenderly trailed her fingertips over Austen's face.

If anyone at work could see her now... Austen marveled at the contrast between her tender lover and the competitive COO who had been so intent on winning the volleyball game as if the company's future depended on it.

They lay in companionable silence, interrupted only by the sounds coming from Toby's cage.

Dee lifted her head off the couch. "What the heck is he doing to that poor bird toy?"

Austen didn't need to answer, since Toby started throwing pieces of the bagel-shaped wooden toy out of his cage.

"Wow. You should have called him Ralph."

"Ralph?"

"Yeah, you know, after *Wreck-It Ralph* from the Disney movie."

Austen chuckled. "All cockatoos and parrots do that. It's how they entertain themselves. He can destroy most toys within seconds."

"Wow," Dee said again.

"Yes. I buy a lot of toys."

"Oh, do you?" Dee's voice rumbled through Austen's back, making her shiver.

"Bird toys, you pervert."

Dee laughed, and they lay in silence again. Every once in a while, Toby called out "loser," and Dee corrected him, trying to get him to say "sexy" instead. The cockatoo never did, but Dee was too stubborn to give up.

"Dee?" Austen finally said.

"Yes?"

Austen took the ice pack from her and threw it on the coffee table. "Would it be okay if I told my friends about us?"

Dee tensed behind her. "I guess so."

Groaning, Austen lifted herself up and rolled around, careful not to dig her hands or elbows into Dee's ribs in the process. "Really? You would be fine with that?"

"It's not like we can keep our relationship a secret forever."

Something in her tone made Austen ask, "Would you want to?"

Dee struggled to sit up, forcing Austen to move away and do the same. "No." Dee sighed. "Not really. It's just…"

Austen's stomach churned. She knew it wasn't the same; Dee wasn't Brenda, but she couldn't help being reminded of her last relationship. Brenda had been just as reluctant to be introduced to Austen's family and friends and to introduce Austen to the people in her life.

"The more people know about us, the harder it becomes to make sure no one at work finds out," Dee said.

True. What Dee said sounded perfectly reasonable, but Austen couldn't help feeling uneasy about it. "So you don't want to tell your brother?"

"Tim?"

"Yes. I thought he's the one you're closest to in your family."

"Yeah. Kind of. But he still does what my father, my uncle, and the rest of the family expect of him. He never really stood up for me and what I want."

Austen turned on the couch so that her knee was resting against Dee's thigh and took her hand. "Did you ever tell him what it is you want?"

Dee squeezed her hand, then let go and got up. She crossed the living room and stopped in front of Toby's cage to tighten a bird toy that was about to slip off the bars.

"Careful with your fingers," Austen said. "I have a vested interest in them."

Dee turned her head and grinned at her before becoming serious again. "Tim and I…we don't have the kind of relationship you and your brother do. He does want me to be happy, and he's always after me to find a nice girlfriend and settle down, but if he has to make a decision between my family's financial interests and my personal happiness, I'm not sure what he'll do. He already warned me once to stay away from you."

"But he didn't go into business with your father. He joined you at your uncle's firm. Why do you think that is?"

Dee shrugged. "Maybe he didn't want to be the fourth son in the company, the low man on the totem pole."

"But he's not exactly the top dog at Kudos Entertainment either, and he doesn't seem to mind that you outrank him. Maybe he just wanted to be closer to his big sister."

Dee walked back to the couch. "Maybe. But how about we stop talking about my brother and focus on making you feel better?"

"I already feel much better thanks to you and the ice pack."

"So this doesn't hurt?" Dee planted her hands to either side of Austen and leaned down. Her hot breath brushed over Austen's face, teasing her, before she leaned even closer and trailed kisses from her temple to the corner of her mouth.

Austen couldn't stop the moan that vibrated in her throat. "Quite the opposite."

"And this?" Dee nibbled on her lower lip.

Instead of answering, Austen pulled her down onto the couch and kissed her.

Dee's hands slipped under her T-shirt and began to wander. They were still cool from holding the ice pack, yet they instantly left trails of fire on Austen's skin.

She clutched Dee's shoulders, wanting more, wanting to—

The ringing of the doorbell startled them apart.

"Who the heck is that?" Face flushed, Dee stared toward the door. "You didn't invite your friends over, did you?"

Austen shook her head. She tried to calm her breathing and her heartbeat as she slipped out from under Dee, walked over to the window, and peeked out. A familiar silver Jaguar was parked in front of the house. *Shit, shit, shit!* She whirled around to Dee. "I think it's your brother."

"Tim? What the hell is he doing here?"

"He probably wants to check on me after you flattened me with a volleyball."

"Dammit. He's got lousy timing." Dee jumped up and straightened her clothes while Austen tucked her T-shirt back into her shorts.

The doorbell rang again. "Ms. Brooks?" Tim called through the door. "Are you okay? I was on my way home and thought I'd check on you."

If she didn't open the door, he might become worried and call an ambulance or something.

Dee's gaze darted around the room as if looking for a hiding place.

"Bathroom?" Austen whispered.

Dee took two steps in that direction and then stopped. "This is crazy. You're his assistant, not his wife, so why are we sneaking around like two cheaters?" She went into the hall, but instead of tiptoeing toward the bathroom, she opened the front door. "Hi, Tim. Come on in. She's in the living room."

"Dee? What are you doing here?"

When only silence answered, Austen took a deep breath and went out into the hall.

Dee and her brother stood facing each other across the doorway.

She cleared her throat. "Hello, Mr. Saunders. Thanks for checking on me."

He looked from Dee to her and then back. "What's going on, Sis? I thought you'd dropped her off and gone home hours ago."

"It seems your sister had the same idea you did," Austen said, praying she wasn't blushing at the bold lie. "She came back to make sure I'm all right."

"Oh. Okay. Glad she did that."

Just when the tension in the hall receded, Dee straightened her shoulders and said, "Of course I did. Any girlfriend worth her salt would do that."

Austen wasn't sure who was more surprised—she or Tim. They both stared at Dee.

"You...? She...?" He looked back and forth between them so fast that Austen was afraid he'd get whiplash.

Dee stepped back until she was next to Austen and wrapped one arm around her shoulders. "Yes." She faced at her brother with a defiant gaze. "We're together."

"Dee..." He shook his head. "Nothing personal, Ms. Brooks. You know I think very highly of you, but do you have any idea what would happen if my uncle found out?"

"He'd find a plausible-sounding reason to fire me," Austen said. Losing her job after just eight months wouldn't look good on her resume, but the more time passed and the closer she and Dee became, the less Austen cared.

Tim sighed. "Knowing my uncle, that's exactly what he'd do."

"Not if I have anything to say about it," Dee said, a threatening rumble in her tone. Her arm around Austen tensed.

"I thought you didn't like Ricky using his position in the company to protect his latest fling when Uncle Wade didn't like that pink streak in her hair, and now you're basically doing the same?"

Dee flushed and looked ready to hit him. "It's not the same thing at all!" Her mouth snapped shut. "Wait a minute... You know about Ricky's affair with Vanessa?"

"And the one with Sue from customer service before her. Just because I usually choose not to get involved in the craziness that goes on in our family doesn't mean I'm blind to it. I just thought you were different."

Dee let go of Austen and took a step toward her brother. "I am, but you are no different than the rest. Can't you just stick up for me once? You were the one who wrote *girlfriend* on my goddamn paper snowflake, and now that I have one, you—"

"I'm only looking out for you."

"Yeah, sure." Dee snorted. "You have a funny way of—"

"Stop it!" Austen shouted before she could stop herself. "Both of you."

They stopped glaring at each other and turned to look at her, identical expressions of shock and surprise on their faces.

"Neither Dee nor I were looking to get involved, least of all with each other, but now that it's happened, you as her favorite brother should be happy for her, no matter what the rest of the family is going to say."

Tim stared at her for a few seconds longer and then lowered his head. "You're right. I just can't help worrying about what will happen when Uncle Wade finds out. He hasn't been in the best mood since that Disney debacle."

Dee winced, as she always did when anyone mentioned it.

Why did they have to keep bringing it up as if Dee were to blame for that failed deal? Austen nearly told him off but then thought better of it. Shouting at her boss once was enough. "Yes," she said. "I worry too."

"So you're just going to sneak around until...what? Uncle Wade dies or chooses to retire?"

Lately, Austen had wondered the same, but she didn't want to pressure Dee into anything she wasn't ready for. Her career had been the focus of her life for too long, so she couldn't expect her to change that so quickly, if at all.

"Of course not," Dee said. "We'll tell him and the rest of the family, but now is not a good time. Not before we secure the Universal deal."

Would there ever be a good time? Or would she have to live her life stuck in the waiting loop? She tried not to let her own doubts show and stood by Dee, facing Tim.

Finally, he sighed. "Don't worry, I can keep my mouth shut. I won't breathe a word to anyone in the family until you tell me otherwise." He lightly slapped Dee's shoulder. "Keep an eye on that bump on her head." With that, he was gone. The door closed behind him.

They stood in the hall, staring at each other.

Austen wrapped her arms around Dee and kissed her cheek. "Thank you for telling him. I know you took a big risk doing that, and I'm not pressuring you to tell anyone else, okay?"

Dee nodded and then shook herself as if trying to wake from her stupor. "So, where were we?" She directed Austen back to the couch and slid on top of her. "Oh, I think I remember something like this..." She brought her lips to Austen's neck and trailed kisses and little nips down to her collarbone.

Austen's body reacted instantly, but she stopped herself from sinking into this feeling and letting Dee's touch make her forget everything else. Something about this felt off. She sensed that Dee wasn't fully present in the moment; she was probably still thinking about her brother and worrying about the future. This wasn't a time for passion. She took Dee's face in both hands, but Dee kept her head down. "Look at me."

Slowly, Dee looked up and into her eyes.

Austen smiled and trailed her fingertips down Dee's cheeks before raising herself up to kiss her tenderly.

Dee sank against her, and Austen wrapped both arms around her.

They slept that way all night, holding on to each other.

The Monday after the company barbecue, Sally popped her head into Austen's office. "Where's the raccoon look?"

Austen looked up from the letter she was typing. "Raccoon look?"

"I thought you might have two black eyes after your close encounter with the volleyball on Saturday."

"Oh, no, I'm fine. The nose wasn't broken, and I spent most of the night cooling it." Or, to be more precise, Dee had cradled her on the couch and held a cooling pack to her face, but she couldn't tell Sally that.

Sally entered more fully and perched on the edge of the desk. "Is it true that she hit you on purpose?"

Austen blinked. "Who? Oh! You mean Ms. Saunders? No, of course not! Why would you think that?"

"Catherine in finance said she probably wanted revenge for you hitting her with the tree topper."

Austen squeezed her eyes shut and groaned. When would all the ugly rumors about Dee finally stop? "For the record, I didn't hit her with the tree topper. The damned thing fell; that's all. And, of course, she didn't hit me on purpose. She'd never do something like that."

Sally tugged on her plum-colored skirt. "Hmm, yeah, she seemed a bit worried when you got hurt." She looked up from readjusting her clothing, and her gaze pierced Austen. "What's up with that? You and she... There's nothing going on, is there?"

Austen willed her fingers, still hovering over the keyboard, not to tremble. "No," she said, even though she hated lying to her colleague. "No matter what the watercooler rumors say, we're not having an affair." That much was true, at least. Dee was much more than an affair to her. "She was the one to spike the ball over the net and hit me, so why wouldn't she be worried? She's not an uncaring monster, you know?"

Time ticked by slowly as Sally continued to study her. Finally, she said, "Don't let her fool you. She's probably just worried that it could get her in trouble with HR. Take care of yourself." Before Austen could think of a reply, Sally got up, waved, and strode out the door.

CHAPTER 25

Usually, when Austen came over to pick her up, Dee was waiting by the door, ready to go. But this time when Austen rang the doorbell, no one answered.

Frowning, she tried again.

She was just about to use the key that Dee had given her to let herself in when the door finally opened.

"Come on in," Dee said, already turning and marching back upstairs. "I'm running late."

Austen followed her up the winding staircase to the bathroom. "Did you get held up at work?"

"Something like that," Dee said back over her shoulder.

Today of all days? Austen tried not to let her dismay show. She wanted Dee to make the best possible impression on her friends, and showing up late for dinner wouldn't accomplish that.

Dee took up position in front of the bathroom mirror, her back to Austen. She was wearing just a pair of black slacks and a bra.

Austen instantly forgot her annoyance as her gaze slid over Dee's firm curves and smooth skin. She stepped behind Dee and pressed a kiss to the spot above her shoulder blade while letting her fingertips trail up her bare side. "You look nice." She hummed against her skin. "And you smell nice too."

For a moment, Dee leaned back, into her, but then she shook her head and pulled away. "I'm just wearing pants so far. I couldn't decide what to wear. Or how to wear my hair." She pulled it up into a ponytail, gave Austen a questioning look in the mirror, and then let her hair drop over her bare shoulders. "Up or down?"

Was that what had made her late? Usually, Dee didn't waste any time or energy on questions like that. Austen frowned, and then a knowing grin spread over her face as she understood. "You're not by any chance nervous about meeting my friends, are you?"

Dee huffed. "Of course not. Why would I be nervous?"

Austen leaned against the sink next to her. "I don't know. You tell me."

Dee vigorously brushed her hair. "I'm not nervous."

"Is it because Aiden is a cop?" Austen asked, half teasing. "Or maybe because Dawn is a psychologist?"

"I couldn't care less about what they do for a living."

"What is it, then?" Austen gripped Dee's hips and pulled until their bodies brushed softly. "Come on, Dee. Talk to me."

Dee threw down the hair tie, apparently having decided to wear her hair down, turned, and wrapped her arms around Austen. "What if they try to talk you out of dating me because I'm your boss?"

Austen snorted. "You're constantly telling me how stubborn I am. Why do you think anyone could talk me out of dating you?"

Dee's almost desperate grip on her loosened. "Okay, they probably couldn't, but still…"

"Stop worrying and get ready." She gave Dee a playful slap on the ass. "My friends will love you, just wait and see."

The small restaurant was crowded, adding to Dee's discomfort despite its warm colors, intimate lighting, and relaxing Middle Eastern flair. She followed Austen and the hostess to the back patio, where Austen's friends were already seated. The two women rose when Dee and Austen approached.

Austen gestured to a strawberry blonde woman. "Dee, this is my best friend, Dr. Dawn Kinsley."

The blonde rolled her eyes and gave Dee a warm smile. "Dawn, please. Otherwise, I feel like I need to bill you."

Dee shook her hand and laughed. "No, please don't. I'm Dee Saunders."

Dawn directed a woman forward who had so far silently lingered next to her, observing their interaction with her sharp, amber eyes. "This is my partner, Aiden."

Aiden was as different from her partner as night and day—tall, black-haired, and a bit on the butch side. She greeted Dee with a nod and a firm handshake, eyeing her as if she were a suspect.

Dee was used to making quick judgments during business negotiations, so she knew within one minute of entering the restaurant which of the two women would be a tougher sell. She didn't worry much about the friendly Dawn; getting Aiden to accept her would be much harder.

Had Austen told them that she was her boss? Or was Aiden as a detective just naturally suspicious of people? Dee had been too nervous to ask any questions on the way to the restaurant. She never went into any meeting unprepared, and now she felt totally out of her depth. Her relationship experiences so far certainly hadn't prepared her for this evening. Since she had stuck mostly to casual dating and short flings, none of her relationships had lasted long enough for her to meet her girlfriend's friends.

They all took a seat, Austen's friends on one side of the table while Dee sat next to Austen. She busied herself with the menu, for once at a loss as to how to start a conversation. Finally, she decided on the falafel platter without the cilantro, knowing Austen, who wasn't too fond of it, would want to try her food. She grinned and mentally shook her head at herself. *Aren't we getting domestic? Who would have thought?*

The waiter came, took their orders, and left again.

Austen's hand on her leg nearly made Dee jump out of her skin. *Jesus. You've been in hostile takeover negotiations. Austen's friends shouldn't scare you.* But they did, at least a little. Maybe it was because she didn't have any friends of her own. She'd never had the time—or the interest—to pursue friendships. She put her hand on top of Austen's and squeezed.

"Did Austen tell you how she and I met?" Dawn asked.

Dee could have hugged her for breaking the awkward silence. "No, actually, she didn't." A psychologist and a secretary didn't exactly move in the same social spheres, so how had they met? She sent Dawn a questioning glance.

"Well," Dawn said, her gray-green eyes twinkling behind her glasses, "we bonded over a naked woman."

Austen, who had just taken a sip of her water, nearly spat it back out. Coughing, she pressed a napkin to her mouth and glared at Dawn. "Jesus, Dawn! You're making it sound like we went to the same swinger club."

Dee laughed and felt herself relax.

Even Dawn's more reserved partner grinned.

"What? Now you're blaming me for your dirty mind?" Dawn looked across the table at Austen, the picture of innocence.

"Me?" Austen pressed a hand to her chest. "I have a dirty mind when it was you who made that comment about—?"

"Hush." Dawn ducked her head. A hint of red dusted her cheeks.

Aiden slid forward onto the edge of her seat and leaned across the table. "Ooh, I've got to hear this. Why did no one ever tell me this story? What did she say or do?"

"Nothing," Dawn said.

"You do realize that I'll get the story out of Austen later, so you might as well tell us," Dee said.

Dawn groaned. "Fine." She peeked at her partner. "But don't say I didn't warn you. This might embarrass you."

Aiden pointed at herself with her thumb. "Me? I wasn't even there when the two of you met. So let's hear this story."

"All right." Dawn leaned forward. "Austen and I met in an art class."

Admittedly, Dee didn't know much about art, but what was so cringe-worthy about that?

"It was a figure drawing class with a nude model," Dawn said.

"And?" Dee and Aiden asked at the same time.

"The instructor told her which pose he wanted and asked her to hold it for twenty minutes. She stepped onto the platform in the middle of the room, dropped her robe to the floor, did some yoga-like twists, and then, just as I and the others had started to draw her, she asked for a break after maybe two minutes, saying her arms were cramping."

"At which point Dawn, who had the easel next to mine, put her pencil down and muttered something about her partner having much better stamina," Austen said.

"I was talking about Aiden posing for me," Dawn said, her cheeks growing red. "She can hold a pose for much longer."

Austen laughed. "Yeah, I'm sure that's all you meant."

"So," Dawn finally said after the laughter at the table had died down, "Austen told me you two met at work. Do you work in marketing too?"

Oh, shit. She had dreaded that question since Austen had told her she wanted to introduce her to her friends. "Um, no." She forced a smile. "Marketing is not my thing. I leave creative endeavors to you and Austen." Maybe that would get them back to discussing art.

The waiter chose that moment to bring their food.

Dee made a mental note to tip him well.

Thankfully, Dawn was distracted by trying the combination of Lebanese dishes on her meze platter and let the topic rest for the moment.

Aiden looked up from her chicken kebabs. "So what is it that you do for Kudos Entertainment?"

Damn. Dawn's partner hadn't swallowed the bait. "Uh, I'm..." Dee shot Austen a panicked glance. "I'm in operations."

Austen put her hand back on Dee's leg. She laid down her fork, straightened her shoulders, and said, "Actually, Dee is our COO—the chief operating officer."

The clattering of silverware on plates seemed to stop for a moment.

Dawn's ever-present smile faded. "That makes her your boss, doesn't it?"

"Technically, yes, but—"

"Will your direct supervisor also think it's just a technicality if he ever finds out?" Dawn asked. She had stopped eating and was staring at Austen with a worried frown.

So much for her quick judgment of who was going to be a tougher sell. Dee leaned forward, into Dawn's line of sight, drawing her gaze away from Austen. "Actually, he already knows. He's my brother, and he knows how to keep a secret."

Dawn's fork clattered onto her plate. "Jesus, Austen! Are you really sure it's a good idea to get involved with her?" She turned her head and looked at Dee. "No offense, you seem like a genuinely nice person, but..." She looked back at Austen. "I don't know. After everything you went through in your last relationship, is this really how you want to live? Don't you want—?"

"Honey," Aiden said and put a hand on Dawn's arm.

Here it comes. Dee gritted her teeth and braced herself for another of Austen's friends to speak out against their relationship.

"Don't you think you're jumping the gun a little?" Aiden asked, looking into her partner's eyes.

Dee stared at her, barely able to believe that Aiden was defending her.

"I'm just worried about Austen," Dawn said. "She could lose her job. Both of them could. Having to sneak around...that's no way to live."

"I know. But remember when you and I met? Getting involved with you was a big no-no for me too. I could have been fired."

Dee looked back and forth between them. Why had their relationship been a big no-no? They weren't colleagues after all, so why hadn't Aiden been allowed to get involved with Dawn? "Fired?" she repeated. "Why's that?"

Aiden glanced at her, then back at Dawn. A silent conversation seemed to take place between them. Finally, Dawn nodded.

"Dawn was a witness in one of my cases," Aiden said.

Dawn leaned against her partner's shoulder and looked Dee in the eyes. "I was a *victim* in one of her cases."

A lump formed in Dee's throat. Aiden was a detective who investigated sex crimes for a living. That meant... *Oh my God.*

Aiden wrapped one arm around Dawn's shoulders. "If the defense lawyer had gotten wind of my feelings for her, he would have told the judge and the jury that I was biased. We could have lost the case. I could have lost my badge."

"But we didn't start a relationship until long after the trial ended," Dawn said.

"Yeah, but still. Cut them some slack, okay? They can't help how they're feeling any more than we could."

Dawn's shoulders slumped, and she buried her face against her partner's neck for a moment. "You're right." She looked across the table at Austen and Dee. "I'm sorry. I know psychologists—not to mention best friends—are supposed to be understanding all the time, and here I am, acting like a horse's behind, making things even harder on you."

"It's okay," Dee said and found that she really meant it. "I appreciate you trying to watch out for Austen." She'd never had a friend who had stood up for her like that, and she was glad that Austen had one.

They nodded at each other.

Dawn reached for a piece of pita bread, and everyone at the table started to eat again.

"So you're in a big dilemma," Dawn said after a few moments of silence. "If your brother—Austen's boss—doesn't keep his mouth shut or the upper management finds out any other way..."

"Austen or I will be transferred to one of our offices on the East Coast or something," Dee said. That, of course, was the best-case scenario. With her uncle's lack of trust in her lately, who knew what would happen if he found out? He no longer seemed to think her irreplaceable.

"What are you going to do?" Dawn asked.

That was the one-million-dollar question.

"I'm going to order us a bottle of that Massaya red wine, and we'll have a relaxing evening with friends—that's what we're going to do," Austen said.

"Excuse me for sounding like a psychologist, but that's called denial." Dawn gave her a wry smile.

"I think I'm overdue for a little denial," Austen said. "After Brenda, all I did for the last three years was question myself, my judgment, my sanity. Now I just want to live my life without all the *what-ifs* and *if onlys* for a while."

Dawn seemed to consider her words for a few moments and then lifted her hand to signal their waiter. "Could we order a bottle of your Massaya, please?"

The lump in Dee's throat slowly dissolved, and she gave Dawn a grateful nod, even knowing the *what-ifs* and *if onlys* couldn't be held at bay forever.

CHAPTER 26

WHEN THE PHONE RANG, AUSTEN didn't even look at the caller ID. After three calls within half an hour, she knew who it was. She shushed Toby, who was imitating the ring tone, and picked up the phone. "Yeah, yeah, yeah. I'm all packed for tomorrow. Are you bringing the chocolate mousse again?"

Silence on the other end of the line.

"Dee?" Austen asked.

"Um, no. It's your father."

Shit. She hadn't told him about her new relationship yet and hoped he wouldn't ask any questions. "Hi, Dad. Sorry. I thought you were someone else."

"Obviously someone who knows your weakness for chocolate. Are you going somewhere?"

"I thought I'd take advantage of our nice September weather to get in a little hiking this weekend."

"Oh. Okay. Well, then…"

Austen frowned. Somehow, he sounded strange. "Is everything okay?"

"Yes. I'm in Bend right now, so I thought I'd visit you tomorrow and maybe stay until Sunday, but if you have plans, I can visit another time."

He had wanted to visit her on such short notice? That wasn't like him at all. "What's going on?"

"Nothing," he said. "I just… There's something I'd like to tell you, but it can wait."

A fist closed around Austen's throat. "I can postpone the hiking."

"No, you don't have to do that. You go hiking, and we'll see each other next weekend."

Austen knew that she'd think about the potential reasons for his visit all week. Her mind already tortured her with possible things he wanted to tell her. Was he sick? She couldn't wait a whole week to find out. "No," she said. "The hiking can wait. I want you to come tomorrow."

"Are you sure?"

"I'm sure."

"Okay. I'll try to be there around noon. See you then. I love you."

"I love you too," Austen said. "Drive safely."

As soon as they had ended the call, she dialed her brother's number. When he picked up, she said, "Dad just called me. He wants to visit me tomorrow."

"Good. It'll be great for him to get out and see you."

"Yeah, but I have a feeling there's something going on. He said there's something he has to tell me. You wouldn't, by any chance, know what it could be?"

"No idea, but he wants to visit me next weekend."

They were both silent for a few moments, pondering what that meant.

Finally, Austen cleared her throat. "Do you think he is…?"

"I'm sure he's fine," Brad said before she could say it out loud.

"Yeah." The lump in Austen's throat growing, though. She said good-bye to her brother and called Dee.

"Of course I'll bring the chocolate mousse," Dee said instead of a greeting. "I wouldn't dare leave the house without it."

"Uh…" Austen flopped down onto the couch. How could she tell Dee that she had to give her a rain check?

"What's wrong?"

Was she that obvious, or did Dee already know her so well? "How do you know there's something wrong?"

"Normally, you react with much more enthusiasm whenever I promise to bring something chocolaty."

Austen had to smile despite the tension lingering in her muscles. "Right. That's a dead giveaway."

"So what is it?"

Austen sighed. "I can't go hiking with you tomorrow. My father is coming over for a visit."

"Oh." Dee sounded a little disappointed.

"I'm so sorry. I really would have liked to go, but…"

"It's okay. We can go another time."

"Thanks for being so understanding," Austen said. "I really would have hated to postpone his visit. He said he wants to talk to me about something, and I admit it has me a little worried."

Dee was silent for a moment. "You think he has some bad news? Couldn't it be something good?"

"I suppose. Maybe it's just my old fears acting up."

"What fears?"

Austen had never confessed those fears to anyone. Her father had been too busy dealing with his own grief, and Brad was her little brother, someone to protect, not someone to burden with her own insecurities.

"If you don't want to talk about it, that's okay," Dee said when Austen remained silent.

"It's not that." Austen inhaled deeply, then blew out the breath. She knew she could trust Dee. "When my mother died, I lived in fear of something happening to my father." Just thinking about that time in her life made her shiver. "I was so afraid of losing him too. Not just for myself, but also for my brother. They wouldn't have let me keep Brad, since I was just sixteen."

"You would have found a way to be there for him," Dee said. Her voice sounded as tender as a caress. "Now you're all grown up, and so is he. Even if something were to happen to your father, the two of you would be fine. But I'm sure it'll be nothing."

"Yeah." Austen trailed her fingers over the phone as if it were Dee's hand. She would have killed to be in her arms now.

Dee was silent for a moment before asking, "Want me to come over and be there for that conversation he wants to have?"

Part of Austen longed to say yes, but she knew this wasn't the right time to introduce them. "I haven't even told him about you…about us."

"You haven't?"

"No. Does that surprise you?"

"A little," Dee said. "I just assumed that since you're so close, you'd told your dad."

"I guess I got into the habit of hiding our relationship a little too well." Admitting it dismayed her, but it was true. She had always lived her life openly and honestly. How on earth had hiding and lying become the norm?

"But you're out to your family, aren't you?"

Austen nodded before remembering that Dee couldn't see her. "Oh, yes. Have been from the beginning."

"So your mother knew too?"

"She was the first one I told." She had struggled with that decision for months, not sure if she should burden her terminally ill mother with that knowledge. When she had finally told her, her mother had thanked her. She hadn't thought about it in years, but now she remembered what else her mother had told her, and she had to smile. "She told me that she would be my guardian angel and would steer a nice, good-looking woman my way." She turned her head and looked at the framed pictures on her bookshelf. One showed her mother flanked by a much younger Brad and Austen, the other her and Dee on the water ride. *Thanks, Mom.*

"She sounds like a great person and a great mother," Dee said.

"She was. How about your parents? Do they know you're gay?" Clearly, Dee's brother knew, but she wasn't so sure about her prim and proper parents.

Dee huffed. "They know. I came out to them when I was sixteen, but they chose to believe it was just a phase, so I came out to them again at twenty-one."

"And now?" That had been over fifteen years ago, so surely they'd had enough time to get used to the thought of having a lesbian daughter.

"They still don't know what to make of my sexual orientation and choose to ignore it. My father has never even said one word to me about it."

Wow. That was hard for Austen to imagine. Her father had never just ignored her when she had told him something about herself. "So you never brought anyone home for Christmas or Thanksgiving?"

"No, never." Dee paused. "It's ironic, isn't it? You're the first person I'd like to take home with me, but I can't."

They both sighed at the same time.

"Call me if you need any support or just want to talk while your father is there, okay?" Dee finally said.

"I will," Austen said. She knew without a doubt that Dee would be there for her if anything happened with her father. "Good night. Sleep well."

"You too."

Neither of them ended the call, though.

"Austen?"

"Yes?"

"Want some chocolate mousse?"

Austen laughed, part of her tension dissipating. "You know I never say no to that."

"I'll be there in half an hour." Dee hung up.

Austen slowly lowered the phone and smiled at Dee's picture on her bookshelf. "You know what?" she said to the photo. "You're not such a lousy girlfriend after all."

Normally, her father was just as talkative as she was, and they would chat and joke over lunch, exchanging news about their lives. This time seemed different, though. They both played with their food more than eating and peeked at each other out of the corners of their eyes.

Austen studied him, trying to find evidence that he might be sick. His tan skin and his clear blue eyes looked as they always did, and as far as she could tell, he hadn't lost weight either; quite the opposite, he seemed to have gained a few pounds. It looked good on him, she decided.

But then again, their mother had looked healthy too, up until a few months before her death.

When lunch was over and they cleared the table, Austen finally couldn't take it anymore. She set the dishes in the sink with a clunk. "Would you please tell me what's going on?"

He looked at her with wide eyes, so she gentled her tone. "Please, Dad. This is driving me crazy."

He reached for her arm and led her over to the couch. Once they were seated side by side, he turned toward her and regarded her with a serious expression. "There's something I have to tell you, and I'm not sure you'll like it."

Austen's heartbeat sped up, and she wished she had taken Dee up on her offer to be there for this conversation. She longed to hold her hand. "What? What is it?"

His broad chest rose and fell beneath a deep breath. "I asked Caroline to marry me—and she said yes."

She slumped against the back of the couch as a mix of feelings washed over her—relief at finding out that he wasn't sick or even dying, surprise, disbelief, and something that felt like jealousy. Her jaw worked, but she couldn't form the words. He wanted to marry another woman—a woman who wasn't her mother. The concept was hard to grasp.

"That doesn't mean I'm trying to replace your mother," he said when she kept silent. "No one could ever replace her. But Caroline...she's a wonderful woman in her own right."

"She's all right," Austen said.

Her father gave her a look.

"Okay, she seems great."

"She is," he said. "And I'm sick of being alone. Can you understand that?"

Of course she could. She hadn't realized how sick she was of being alone until she had found Dee. She hated the nights they had to spend apart because Dee had an early meeting the next morning and couldn't stay over. After taking a deep breath, she leaned forward and hugged her father. "If she makes you happy, I'm all for it."

His knotted muscles went limp. "Thank you, honey."

After a minute or two, they let go and moved back a little.

"Do you think Brad will be okay with it too?" her father asked. Deep lines carved their way into his forehead.

"I think so. Do you want me to talk to him?"

For a moment, he looked as if he wanted to take her up on the offer, but then he shook his head. "No. You've had to be much more than a sister to him for too long already. It's not fair to you."

"It's all right. I really don't mind."

"No, it's not all right. I know that I wasn't there for you and Brad the way I should have been after your mother... after she died." His Adam's apple bobbed up and down as he swallowed. "I was so consumed with grief and barely went through the motions."

"You did what you could. Neither of us ever blamed you."

Her father looked doubtful; then he smiled wryly and ruffled her hair as he had done when she'd been a little girl. "Well, I must have done something right since you turned out so great."

"What can I say? I've got good genes."

They grinned at each other, and the tension dissipated from the room like fog in the sunshine.

"Have you set a date yet?" Austen asked.

"Caroline wants a winter wedding, so we were thinking maybe some time in January."

That was still four months away—hopefully enough time to get used to the thought of seeing her father exchange rings with another woman. She squared her shoulders. She would be supportive and smile all the way through the wedding ceremony, even if it would kill her. "I'll be there," she said.

Her father grinned. "You'll have to. Caroline wants to ask you to be her maid of honor."

Oh, wow. She and Caroline didn't know each other that well yet, but Austen vowed to be more open to getting to know her. "I'd be honored."

They hugged, and Austen let herself sink against her father's strong shoulder. When they finally let go, she wiped her eyes.

"So," her father said and then cleared his throat. "What have you been up to? Lately, you haven't told me much about your private life."

She glanced toward the framed picture on her bookshelf.

Her father followed her gaze.

Shit. She had forgotten to put away the photo before he had arrived.

"Sexy," Toby screamed at the top of his lungs. "She's sooo sexy."

Heat suffused Austen's face. Despite Dee's attempts to teach him some new words, Toby had refused to say anything but *loser* and *fuck you*. Why did he have to choose now of all times to show off his new vocabulary?

Her father raised one bushy brow. "Is there a new lady bird in his life?"

"Um, no, but there's something I have to tell you too."

He leaned forward and studied her. "What is it? You know you can tell me anything."

She squirmed under his gaze.

"Come on. Spit it out, girl." He nudged her.

"I have someone in my life too."

He pointed at the framed photo. "Her?"

Austen nodded.

"Pretty."

She nodded again, even though that word didn't do Dee justice.

"Where did the two of you meet?"

There it was: the dreaded question. "At work." She didn't want to lie to her father, but neither did she want to tell him that Dee was one of her bosses.

"And how long have you been…you know…together?" he asked, still looking at the picture.

"Fuck," Toby screamed, now back to his old vocabulary.

Exactly. Her stomach knotted. Maybe this was the question she should have dreaded. She took a deep breath and forced herself to say it. "Since June."

Her father abruptly looked away from the photo and turned his gaze on her. The hurt in his eyes made her wince. "You've been together for three months already? Why didn't you tell me before? It's not like you to suddenly start keeping secrets."

"It's…complicated."

"That's a cop-out. We never let you kids get away with it, and I don't intend to start now."

Austen sighed. "Dee is our COO."

The lines on his face deepened as he frowned. "COO?"

"Chief operating officer. Basically the company's second-in-command. And she's my boss's sister."

He winced. "That's like fraternizing with an officer."

Her shoulders slumped. "Kind of. That's why we haven't told anyone about us yet."

His blue eyes narrowed to slivers of ice. "So she's trying to keep you as her dirty little secret? Like that woman did?"

Her father always referred to Brenda that way, as if she didn't even deserve for him to remember her name.

"No," she said so fast that she almost stumbled over the word. "It's not like that at all."

His gaze didn't soften. "Then why isn't she out there, looking for another job so that you can be together without hiding? That's what your mother did when we fell in love."

"If anyone should be looking for a new job, it would be me, not Dee. She's been with the company for fourteen years, and her chances of one day taking over as the CEO are good, so my career should take a backseat to hers."

He scowled at her.

"Stop scowling. That's how Mom and you did it too."

He continued scowling. "You're not thinking about giving up your job for her, are you?"

"No," Austen said, even though it wasn't entirely true. She had wrestled with that thought for the last few weeks. Hiding their relationship introduced so much tension in their lives; some days, it just didn't seem worth it. But whenever she was ready to talk to Dee about possibly giving up her job, other thoughts intruded. Four years ago, she had given up her job for Brenda, and it had all gone downhill from there, leaving her stranded and alone in a city she barely knew and a job she didn't like.

"Call her and invite her over for dinner," her father said. "I want to meet this woman."

Austen folded her arms across her chest. "So you can get out your shotgun and force her to make an honorable woman out of me? Forget it!"

"I don't have a shotgun, but I like your idea." He finally cracked a smile. "I just want to meet her. No shotguns, I promise."

"No interrogations about her intentions toward me either," Austen said and gave him a stern look.

He held up both hands. "Okay, okay."

"All right. I'll call her." She wiped one damp palm on her pant leg and reached for the phone, hoping Dee would feel up to meeting her father.

When Dee caught a glimpse of the caller ID, she snatched up the phone, eager to hear how Austen was doing. "Hey you. How's it going with your father?"

"Uh, good, I guess. He had some big news to share. He'll get married again in January."

Austen sounded calm and supportive, but Dee knew it couldn't be that easy for her. "Oh, wow. That's big news indeed. Are you okay with that?"

"I'm happy for him."

"But?"

"It'll probably take me a while until it won't feel strange anymore. Up until two years ago, he was still wearing the ring my mother put on his finger, and now he'll replace it with another woman's."

Dee tried to imagine what it would feel like to have her father marry someone else. Her parents didn't have the happiest of marriages, but seeing them with new partners would still be strange. "I'm sure he's not replacing your mother. If she's anything like her daughter, no one could ever replace her."

"You're a sweetheart, do you know that?" Austen said.

"Me? Nah." But it was true. Austen was turning her into a person who wanted to do sweet things for her lover.

"Oh, yes, you are. I hope my father will think so too. I told him about us, and now he wants to meet you."

Dee nearly dropped the phone. She hadn't counted on that happening so fast.

"If this isn't a good time for you," Austen said, lowering her voice, "or you'd rather wait to meet my father, I'll understand."

She wasn't exactly eager to meet Austen's father. Part of her was glad that they initially hadn't shared their relationship with anyone so that it could grow without interference from their families, friends, and colleagues. But maybe that was the immature part of her, the one that wanted to keep Austen to herself and never share her with anyone. She suppressed a sigh and forced herself to be an adult and step up to the plate for Austen. "It's okay. I'd love to meet him."

Austen chuckled. "Liar. You're scared to death."

She would have growled at anyone else daring to say something like that, but with Austen, the open words just made her smile ruefully. "Yeah."

"No need to be. He promised to leave the shotgun in the car."

Dee swallowed. "Shotgun?"

"I'll explain later. So, do you want to come over for dinner?"

After taking a deep breath, Dee squared her shoulders. "Sure. What time do you want me there?"

"How about seven?"

"Sounds good. See you then." Dee wanted to send a kiss or another, more personal good-bye through the line, but Austen's father might be around, so she wasn't sure what was and what wasn't okay.

Maybe there was something to be said for a family that ignored your sexual orientation.

Austen's father, Eugene Brooks, looked nothing like his daughter. For one thing, he was much taller and could look into Dee's eyes from an equal height. His greeting wasn't quite as pleasant as Austen's either. While Austen gave her a quick peck on the lips, her father shook her hand in a forceful grip as if wanting to let her know that he could beat her up any time.

"It's a pleasure to meet you, sir," Dee said, trying to sound as if meeting her girlfriend's father was no big deal. "Austen has told me so much about you."

Eugene Brooks looked at her with his clear blue eyes, the only feature he had in common with his daughter. Dee had a suspicion that, just like Austen, he wouldn't let her get away with anything either. "I wish I could say the same, but she hasn't told me anything about you."

Ouch. Dee winced. What was she supposed to say to that?

"Stop it, Dad." Austen pulled her father away. "I already explained why I didn't tell you sooner, and you promised not to give her the third degree."

Eugene settled down on the couch but still kept an eye on Dee.

"Um, I brought dessert. Let me put it in the fridge." Dee escaped to the kitchen.

Austen followed and tried to peek around Dee's shoulder as she put the container into the fridge. "What did you bring? Does it, by any chance, have chocolate in it?"

Dee turned and nodded. "I made chocolate mousse again, hoping your father would also be amenable to chocolate."

Austen laughed. "No, sorry. I got that trait from my mother."

"Great," Dee mumbled. "Not even my famous chocolate mousse will earn me any points."

"I didn't say that." Austen lowered her voice to a seductive purr and pressed her body against Dee's. "My father might not appreciate chocolate, but it'll earn you plenty of points with his daughter, who considers chocolate an aphrodisiac."

Dee's mouth went dry, and she struggled not to lean in and capture Austen's lips with hers. "Your father is in the next room," she whispered.

"So?" Austen whispered back, an amused glint in her eyes. "He's seen me kiss my girlfriends before."

The thought of Austen's previous girlfriends made Dee scowl. She hated thinking of her with anyone else.

Austen rubbed the spot between Dee's eyebrows. "You're scowling. Are you sure you want to be here?"

It was much too late to back out now, so Dee nodded. "I'm staying. But maybe we should allow him to bring in the shotgun from the car and just get it over with."

"Oh, no. I'm not ready to give you up yet." Austen kissed her cheek and pulled Dee with her into the living room.

They settled around the coffee table and had a pleasant enough conversation about basketball and countries they had traveled to. They discovered that both Dee and Eugene had spent some time in Germany, Dee on business trips and Eugene when he'd been stationed there before Austen was born. Just when it looked as if they were starting to bond, Austen got up to check on the roast she had in the oven, leaving them alone in the living room.

Dee rubbed her hands over the outer seam of her pants and searched for another topic of conversation. Talking politics was too dangerous, since she had no idea of his party affiliation. The weather was boring, and she didn't want to talk about her work since it would only remind him of the fact that she was Austen's boss.

Before she could come up with something, Eugene spoke, "Has Austen told you about this Brenda woman and what she did to her?"

Dee held his gaze. "Yes, sir, she told me about it."

"How is what you are doing to my daughter any different?"

Dee struggled to keep her voice down. "I'm not doing anything to her. I understand that Austen is your daughter and you might feel like you need to protect her from the evils of this world, but she's an adult who can make her own decisions. We decided together that we would give a relationship between us a chance, but that we're not yet ready to announce it to the world and my family."

"Why?" He squinted over at her. "What's wrong with your family? Do they own a shotgun too?"

So he had heard what Austen had told her about the shotgun—and he had the same, slightly wicked sense of humor that his daughter had.

"No. If anyone needs killing, they'll have their people do it," Dee said. "But my uncle is the CEO of Kudos Entertainment."

The smile on Eugene's face faded. "Aren't you worried about that power imbalance in your relationship?"

"I worry that other people might think there is one, but I never perceived any power imbalance between us," Dee said. "Have you ever succeeded in making Austen do anything she didn't want to do?"

A rueful grin deepened the lines around his eyes. "You've got a point there. Did she ever tell you how she started kindergarten one week later than all the other kids?"

Dee leaned forward and propped her elbows on her thighs, finally relaxing a bit. "No, she didn't. What did she do?"

Eugene laughed. "What didn't she do? On the first day, she hid in her mother's closet until it was too late to get her to kindergarten. On the second day, she—"

"Dad!" Austen appeared in the doorway, her hands on her hips. "No embarrassing stories about me!"

"I thought the deal was no shotguns?" her father said.

"I'm extending the deal—no shotguns and no embarrassing stories." Despite her protests, she was smiling, probably just as glad as Dee was that her father was easing up a little. "Dinner is ready in five minutes. Dee, would you help me set the table?"

"Sure." Dee scrambled up from the couch and followed her into the kitchen.

"I'm sorry," Austen said as soon as they were out of earshot.

Dee stepped close and touched Austen's cheek. "No need to be sorry. I'm glad that you have someone in your life who loves you enough to protect you, even if it's not necessary." If her family ever found out, all they would worry about was their reputation and the effect their relationship might have on their businesses.

Austen put her hand over Dee's, and they stood there for a moment, the scent of roast and mashed potatoes wafting around them, until Dee's stomach started to growl. She pressed her free hand to her belly. Since Austen had called and invited her to have dinner with her father, she hadn't managed to eat a single bite.

Laughing, Austen pulled away. "Come on. We'd better feed that monster."

Her father dabbed his mouth with the napkin before putting it on the table. "Thanks for a wonderful dinner, sweetheart. The roast was every bit as good as your mother's."

Austen beamed. She wasn't a stellar cook, but after a lot of trial and error, she managed to make a handful of dishes taste just as good as her mother had.

"It was great," Dee said.

"So was the chocolate mousse." Even her father had eaten a little and declared it the best chocolate mousse he had ever had.

After they had stacked the dirty dishes and carried them to the kitchen, her father leaned against the doorjamb and watched Dee load the dishwasher.

Was he still uncomfortable with their relationship? Or just surprised that Dee was so familiar with her apartment?

"You know what?" He turned toward Austen. "I think I'll drive back to Bend tonight after all."

Austen glanced at her wristwatch. It was almost nine. "Now? But you won't make it to Caroline's until after midnight."

"I have eaten tons of food, so I won't go to sleep before midnight anyway. And that way, maybe you can go hiking tomorrow."

"You don't need to do that, Dad. We can go hiking another time."

Dee closed the dishwasher. "She's right, sir." With just a hint of hesitation, she added, "If you stay, you could even go hiking with us tomorrow."

He laughed in a way that Austen had rarely heard since her mother's death. "Oh, sure. I bet that's just what you were planning—a romantic hike to a scenic waterfall... with Austen's father tagging along."

Dee shrugged and met his gaze. "As I said, you're welcome to join us, sir."

He looked into her eyes for a while longer. "If you keep calling me *sir,* I'll start thinking I'm still in the Marine Corps. Call me Gene."

Austen wanted to hug her father, but she forced herself to stay back and watch them interact.

Only someone who knew Dee well could see the surprised expression dart across her face. "All right. Then you're welcome to join us, Gene."

"Nah. You kids will manage just fine without me." He pointed his index finger at Dee. "But I'll see you on January 10th."

"What's on January 10th?" Dee asked, her brow furrowed.

He clapped her shoulder. "My wedding day. I expect you to come."

"I'll be there, s—Gene."

When he hugged Austen, she sank into her father's arms and inhaled the scent of his cologne. "Thank you," she whispered.

"No," he said and hugged her closer, "thank you. Are you really okay with Caroline and me getting married?" He stepped back to study her face.

Austen smiled, and for the first time, she could let go of the past enough to be completely honest when she said, "I'm happy for you."

CHAPTER 27

WHEN THE LETTERS ON THE screen started to blur, Dee leaned back in her desk chair and rubbed her eyes. Several vertebrae popped when she got up and stretched. She glanced at the clock in the task bar on her screen.

Nearly seven. Everyone else, including Austen, had probably gone home long ago, but she needed to put together the new proposal for Universal before she could leave.

She reached for her cell phone and sent her a quick text message. At least she had gotten better about that and now always let Austen know when she had to work late. She also hadn't missed another date. It had been four months since they'd gone to Universal in June, so their relationship was now officially the longest Dee had ever been in. Far from feeling smothered, as she had halfway expected, she found herself wanting more. *Who knew? Maybe I'm the relationship type after all.*

Her cell phone chirped, and she grinned when she saw that it was a response from Austen.

I'm still in the office too.

Dee raised an eyebrow and typed a quick reply.

I'm not turning you into a workaholic, am I?

The answer came within seconds.

LOL. No, don't worry. Just finishing up a few things for your brother. How are things going with the Universal project?

There was no final agreement yet, so she wasn't supposed to talk about it, but she trusted Austen with every fiber of her being, so she typed a reply.

I think we've got them. They want to see a proposal for what we'd do for the new rides next year before they sign the contract. That's what I'm working on right now.

Again, the answer came within seconds.

Great. Kudos is lucky to have you. I'm about to leave. Want me to come over and bring you some coffee first?

Dee didn't have to think twice. Austen and coffee was a combination she couldn't resist.

Seconds after she had sent her reply, a knock on the door sounded.

"Wow, that was fast. Come in," Dee called.

Instead of Austen, Joseph McLendon, their CIO, entered and nearly dragged their IT systems configuration manager through the door after him.

Dee frowned. Why was everyone suddenly working late? And why did they have to do it in her office? She waved the two men into the chairs in front of her desk and sank back into her leather chair. "What's going on, Joe?"

The two men exchanged glances. The CIO crossed and uncrossed his legs.

Dee had the sinking feeling that she wouldn't like whatever he'd have to say. "Joe?"

After several more seconds, Joe cleared his throat. "We have a software license compliance issue."

If they were overdeployed by just a few licenses, Joe wouldn't have brought it to her attention. Something worse was going on. Something much worse. Dee narrowed her eyes.

"A major issue," Joe added.

No shit, Sherlock. "Do I have to drag it out of you? What happened?"

The two men looked at each other again, then the IT manager said, "My team accidentally installed a statistics software product on our standard image that got installed on all company laptops."

"The thing is, we only bought twenty licenses of that software, since it cost two thousand dollars per unit and it's really only the financial coordinators of each department that need it," Joe said.

Dee's mind spun as she did the math. If two hundred fifty computers across the company had been imaged, that could easily end up costing the company half a million, and the fines could double that.

Holy shit. She jumped up. "Accidentally?" She leaned across her desk and got into the IT manager's face. "How can you accidentally install a piece of software?"

He ducked his head. "I don't know. It just happened."

"It just happened? Do you have any idea what kind of a mess you got us into?" She whirled around and reached for the phone. "We have to get legal and PR involved right away, or this could turn into a PR nightmare."

Joe reached out a hand but stopped just short of touching her. "Calm down, Dee. I—"

"Calm down?" she shouted.

A knock on the door interrupted her, making the two men breathe a sigh of relief.

Dee threw the phone back down. "Come in!"

Austen heard the screaming halfway down the corridor. Her steps faltered. Was that Dee's voice? She slowly crept closer, crossed the outer office, and hesitated in front of Dee's closed door. The shouting from inside of the office continued.

Definitely Dee. But that wasn't the relaxed woman who had exchanged text messages with her just a few minutes ago. This was another side of Dee, one that Austen rarely saw. Not that she wanted to. She heard enough about Attila, the Ice Queen, and all the other nicknames the employees bestowed on her. Should she just walk away and come back later? But then Dee's coffee would get cold. Maybe an interruption could help defuse the situation in Dee's office.

She raised her hand and knocked timidly.

"Come in!" Dee shouted from inside.

Austen opened the door and peeked in.

Dee was towering over two men in front of her desk, scowling. When they turned to look at her, Austen recognized one as Joseph McLendon, the company's CIO.

"Uh, your coffee, Ms. Saunders."

Dee took several deep breaths, visibly gathering herself. "Thank you, Ms. Brooks. Please leave it on my desk." She turned back to the two men while Austen carried the mug across the room. "Send me everything we have on this—contracts, purchase orders, invoices, any communication with the software company."

The CIO nodded. "Do you want me to copy Mr. Haggerty, or will you let him know?"

Dee sighed. "He'll be out of the office for most of tomorrow. I'll e-mail him and explain what's going on."

Austen set the mug on the desk and looked back and forth between Dee and Mr. McLendon. Had he just foisted off an unpleasant task on Dee?

The two men were out of the door before Austen, leaving her to stare after them.

"Close the door." Dee rubbed her eyes and then added, "Please."

Austen closed the door and slowly walked closer. "What's going on? Why did you shout at them?"

"Because they deserved it."

The harsh tone made Austen flinch. She could only imagine how the two men, who had been on the receiving end of Dee's anger, had felt. "Don't you think telling them off would have worked just as well at a more moderate volume?"

Dee's head jerked up. If looks could kill, Austen would have instantly turned into a pile of ash staining the pristine carpet in the corner office. "Don't tell me how to do my job!"

They both froze and stared at each other.

"I'm sorry." Dee rubbed her face with both hands, as if that could help erase the last few seconds. "I didn't mean to shout at you." She grimaced and added, "Too."

Austen swallowed. "No, I'm the one who should be sorry. That was inappropriate. In here, you're my boss, and I shouldn't talk to you that way." She sank onto the chair the CIO had vacated. "It's just that...I don't want them to think of you as Attila. I want them to see the Dee I know."

Dee slowly shook her head. "I can't let them see that Dee. I'm the company's fixer. People come to me whenever there's a problem, because they know I'm not afraid to tell it like it is, knock some heads together, and make the hard decisions if need be."

"But doesn't it bother you? That everyone is either scared of you or hates your guts?"

Dee shrugged and reached for her mug. "It helps me do my job." She took a sip of coffee. A hesitant smile edged onto her face. "Besides, I have it on good authority that at least one employee down in marketing doesn't hate me."

"Oh, you mean your brother?"

Dee playfully glared at her until Austen relented.

"Okay, okay. I don't hate you. In fact, I'm pretty sure I love you."

Dee stopped sipping. The mug landed back on the desk with a *clonk*. "Did you just...?"

Oh, God. Austen hadn't meant for them to be in the office when she told Dee for the very first time that she loved her. "Uh. I, um... Sorry."

"Sorry?"

"Yes. This isn't the place or the time to—"

Dee rounded the desk in two long strides.

Before Austen knew what hit her, she was pulled out of the chair, pressed against the desk, and kissed senselessly. She melted against Dee and threaded her fingers through Dee's hair to feel her even closer.

Breathing heavily, Dee finally moved back a few inches. Her face was flushed, and the usually neat chignon she wore at work was coming undone. "You'd better go before the company has two crises on its hands—the licensing debacle and the COO getting caught in a compromising situation with an admin."

Austen nodded and slid out from between Dee and the desk to straighten her blouse. As the distance between them grew, her brain started to work again. "Licensing debacle? Was that why you were shouting at them?"

"Yes. They just discovered that we installed a program that we don't have the licenses for on every single company-issued laptop."

"Christ. That adds up to…"

"Half a million dollars, plus fines," Dee said, her expression grim.

Okay, maybe the shouting had been justified. "What now?"

Dee grimaced. "Lots of paperwork, negotiations, and overtime. More shouting—most of it from Uncle Wade."

And most of it at Dee. Austen hated that Dee had to be the one to shoulder the responsibility. "Let me know if there's anything I can do to help, okay? Anything at all." When Dee nodded, she walked to the door.

"Austen?"

She turned. Had Dee already thought of something she could do? "Yes?"

A gentle smile smoothed out the lines on Dee's tense face. "I love you too."

Dee reached out without looking away from her computer screen and emptied her fifth cup of coffee. Her stomach lining was starting to complain, so she rummaged through her desk drawer for some antacid. In the past, she'd always had a pack or two handy, but she hadn't needed them in some time. Not since meeting Austen. *Huh, what do you know?* Tim had been right after all. Having a life beyond work was actually good for you.

When her search didn't unearth any antacid, she gave up and threw a quick glance at her watch. It was after six already, and she was still wading through licensing contracts and reports since yesterday with no end in sight. Austen had probably long since gone home and was now snuggled up on the couch with a bowl of chocolate ice cream.

A year ago, that mental picture of domesticity would have left her cold; she would have preferred spending the evening at work to hanging out on the couch. But now thoughts of Austen made her want to get out of here at a reasonable hour.

After the software license debacle had landed in her lap, that wasn't meant to be.

She reached for her cell phone and pressed the number one on her speed dial. "Hey you," she said when Austen answered. "Just wanted to let you know that I won't be coming over today."

"Still working on that license snafu?" Austen asked.

Dee groaned and leaned back in her chair, making a couple of vertebrae pop. "Yeah. It will take me days to get through this mess."

Toby screeched in the background, and Austen shushed him. "Do you want me to bring you anything? Chinese takeout? A change of clothes?"

Dee smiled. She still thought of herself as a fairly independent person, but having someone care about her well-being felt good. *She loves me.* The thought still made her a little dizzy. "No, thanks." She wouldn't have time to eat anyway.

"You need to eat something, especially with all that coffee you're probably drinking," Austen said.

The acid burning in the pit of her stomach let Dee know that Austen was right. "Okay, I'll order something later. I'll even throw in a salad or some other healthy—"

The door to her office flew open without warning, and Uncle Wade stormed over to her desk.

"I'll call you back," Dee said into the phone and ended the call.

"Five hundred thousand?" He waved a single sheet of paper, probably the e-mail she'd sent him. "They want us to pay five hundred thousand dollars for software we're not even using?"

Dee lifted both hands. "Calm down. That's not final yet. I got legal involved, and we're still negotiating."

"Calm down?" he repeated, his face growing redder. "I'll calm down when that ridiculous demand is off the table and I have personally fired the IT manager who got us into this mess."

Dee rubbed her tired eyes. "That won't solve the problem. I told you last year that we should hire an external firm to keep track of our software license compliance. We don't have the resources to do it in-house."

Her uncle dropped into the visitor's chair. "That doesn't help us now."

"No, it doesn't." But a *you were right* or a *I should have listened to you* would have still been nice.

He stopped shouting, and his face took on a healthier color. "I expect you to take care of this."

Dee sighed. It had always been this way. Her family didn't listen to her advice and then, when the shit hit the fan, expected her to solve the problem for them. "I will."

"Good."

"What about the Universal project? We can't push that to the back burner. If we don't submit the proposal for their new rides by the end of next week, we'll lose the deal."

Her uncle rubbed his forehead as if that would help him think. "Let Rick do it."

"Rick? You can't be serious!" Her cousin had never managed an important project like this.

He glared at her. "Why not? Or do you seriously think you're the only one capable of putting together this proposal?"

A muscle in Dee's jaw jumped. She seriously doubted her cousin was the best man for the job, but she didn't have a choice. There were only so many hours in a day, and she couldn't take care of the licensing debacle and finish the proposal at the same time. "No, of course I don't think that."

"It's decided, then. E-mail Rick everything you've done so far." He crumpled up the sheet of paper and threw it in the direction of her paper basket. "There's something else that I wanted to talk to you about if you have a minute."

She hoped it wasn't another problem she was expected to take care of. "Sure. What is it?"

"The West Coast Business Symposium asked me to deliver the keynote speech at their conference next year."

"Oh, wow." Dee smiled. "That's great, Uncle Wade. What a wonderful recognition for you and the company."

He grinned, nearly bursting with pride. "I thought I'd talk about boosting productivity and sales."

Dee nodded. He had certainly managed to do that in his company over the last two decades. "Good idea."

"As the company's COO and my niece, I want you to be there. The conference is always a good opportunity to network."

"I'll be there. When is it?"

He stood and walked to the door. "January 10th."

He had already opened the door by the time Dee remembered why that date sounded so familiar. *Oh, shit. Gene's wedding.* "Uh, I'm not sure I can make it after all. I've got a previous commitment that day."

"Something more important than my keynote speech?" He turned and squinted over at her.

"Uh, well…"

"I thought so. My secretary will get you a ticket for the conference. See you tomorrow." The door closed behind him.

"Dammit!" Dee reached for the nearest object. Just when she was about to throw it against the wall, she realized that she had grabbed the mouse Austen had given her. Gently, she put it back down and threw her hole punch instead.

It crashed against the wall. The bottom fell off, and confetti rained down on her carpet.

Great. Just great. Dee crossed her arms on the desk, buried her face against them, and let out a long groan.

After crashing on the couch in her office, Dee finally made it home around eight the next evening. Instead of coming home to a quiet house smelling of stale air, she was greeted by the scent of tomato sauce, fresh basil, and Austen's perfume. Someone was singing in the kitchen, slightly off-key, but making up for that in volume and enthusiasm.

She set down her briefcase, for a moment irritated at the unexpected presence. All she wanted was a shower, a bowl of cereal or some other food that didn't take much time to prepare, and then settling down on the couch for more work. She didn't have the energy for anything else. "Austen?"

Austen's head popped out of the kitchen, her short, auburn hair disheveled. "Oh, you're home. I wasn't sure when you'd make it home, but I wanted to leave you some food in the fridge."

"You're cooking?"

"Just some spaghetti, but I didn't want you to come home to an empty fridge."

Dee's irritation melted away. She walked over and pulled Austen against her in a full-body hug.

"Are you okay?" Austen mumbled, her face buried against Dee's shoulder.

"I'm fine. It's just been a long day. A long week."

Austen reached up and massaged the knotted muscles of Dee's shoulders.

"Oh God." Dee slumped against her as she felt her muscles begin to loosen for the first time in days. "I'll tell Tim to give you a raise if you keep doing that."

"I'll do even more than that. Why don't you take a quick shower, and after I get some food in you, I'll give you a nice, long mas—"

The ringing of her cell phone from inside of the briefcase made Dee flinch. "Sorry. I have to get that. I'm waiting for a callback from Joe, our CIO."

Austen nodded and went to get the briefcase for her.

"Thanks," Dee said, not just for handing her the briefcase, but also for being so understanding about the demands of her job. That had never been a given in any of her past relationships. She lifted the cell phone to her ear before it could stop ringing. "Hello?"

"Danielle? This is your father."

Dee nearly dropped the phone. Since when did her father call her? Most of the time, her mother called and relayed any messages her father might have.

At the alarmed look on Austen's face, she mouthed, "My father," making Austen's eyes widen even more.

"Uh, hi, Dad."

"I don't want to interrupt whatever you're doing. I'm just calling to make sure you'll be at the conference."

Dee walked over to the living room and dropped down onto the couch. "What conference?"

"The West Coast Business Symposium in January," he said. "Your uncle mentioned something about you having a previous engagement. Surely that can be postponed."

Dee let her head drop onto the back of the couch. "It's a wedding, Dad. I don't think that can be postponed."

"A wedding?" her father repeated as if he had never even heard of that concept. "Who's getting married?"

"No one you know. He's…a friend." She couldn't tell him that Gene might one day be her father-in-law. *If I manage not to fuck it up for a change.*

"And he can't get married without you?"

The mild headache that had lingered all day became a throbbing pain in her temples. "He could, but that's not—"

"That's settled, then."

Dee wanted to shout at him but knew it would only make him shout back, not listen to her. She gritted her teeth. "Nothing is settled. This wedding is important to…" She looked over at Austen, who leaned in the doorway, her forehead creased as she watched Dee. "…to me."

"A stranger's wedding is more important than your family and your career?"

"It's just a keynote speech, Dad. If I'm not there to hear it, that doesn't mean I don't—"

"Just a keynote speech?" Her father's voice rose. "You don't get it, do you? But then again, you never had a head for business."

He'd said things like that before, but that didn't make it any less painful. Dee clamped her hand around the phone. She couldn't deal with this. Not after the day she'd had. For a moment, she considered just hanging up.

"This is way more than a keynote speech, girl. It's a signal," her father said, emphasizing every word. "Every member of Kudos's board will be there. If you want Wade's job one day, you'd better make sure that they see you at the conference, showing some support for him and the company."

Damn him for being right. No doubt her cousin Rick would be there, showing his pearly whites in the first row, as if he gave a shit about his father and the company. He'd make people think he was the new heir apparent of Kudos Entertainment Inc. How long before her uncle started thinking along those lines too?

She let out a long sigh. "I'll think about it, okay? But not now. We're in the middle of trying to resolve a big licensing crisis."

"I'll let you get back to work, then, and call you next week," her father said.

She knew he would continue to call until she bowed to his wishes. "Good night," she said and ended the call. Her temples were still pounding, so she pressed her hands against them and closed her eyes, shutting out the world for a few moments.

The couch dipped slightly as Austen sat down next to her. She placed one hand on Dee's leg without saying anything. Her body heat filtered through the fabric of Dee's slacks, warming her leg—and her heart.

When Dee opened her eyes, Austen slid around and took both of Dee's hands in hers. "You don't have to make any decisions today. You've got more than enough on your plate already. I just want you to know that I'd understand if you couldn't come to Dad's wedding."

Dee squeezed her hands. Her eyes burned. "I don't know what to—"

Austen gently pressed her index finger to Dee's lips. "You don't have to think about it right now." She stood and pulled Dee up with her. "Come on. Go take a shower while I rescue the spaghetti."

Not knowing what to say, Dee pulled Austen toward her by their still-joined hands and kissed her. She wasn't sure what she'd done to deserve a girlfriend like Austen, but whatever it was, she hoped she could continue doing it.

"I'm sorry about the spaghetti," Austen said as she heaped the Chinese takeout onto two plates and carried them into the living room.

"It's not your fault my father called or that I don't have enough food in my fridge to sustain a mouse."

No, it wasn't, but she still would have liked to present Dee with a homemade dinner after the stressful day she'd had. Austen had wanted to march over, take the phone from Dee, and tell Dee's father off for putting even more pressure on his daughter. What kind of father did that? Hers certainly wouldn't.

The more she found out about Dee's family, the more she understood what had made Dee the way she was. In fact, considering the way she had grown up, she was amazingly normal and had a deep capacity to love hidden beneath her I-don't-care-about-anything-but-my-job attitude.

Dee picked up a pair of chopsticks and deftly maneuvered a bit of rice and shrimp into her mouth. "Mmm, this is good," she said around a mouthful of rice. "I didn't realize how hungry I was."

Austen took her own pair of chopsticks and tried to pick up a few grains of rice but succeeded only in chasing them around her plate.

Dee laughed, and Austen was grateful to see her relax a little. She looked much better after her shower. "Come here. I'll show you."

Austen slid over on the couch, balancing her plate on her knees since Dee still didn't have a coffee table.

"You hold the first chopstick on your ring finger and tuck it into the fleshy part of your thumb. This one doesn't move." She demonstrated. "Now you place the second chopstick between your index and your middle finger. Kind of like you'd hold a pen."

Austen admired the easy way Dee's long fingers handled the chopsticks and then told herself to stop fantasizing about Dee's hands and follow her instructions instead.

Dee placed her hand over hers and gently corrected the position of her fingers. "There."

Grinning proudly, Austen moved the top chopstick up and down. "Hey, this works."

"Told you. Now try some rice."

At first, all went well. Austen managed to pick up a small clump of rice, but then her chopsticks crossed at the tips. Soy-sauce-covered rice spattered all over her lap. "Ugh. You need a coffee table."

"Then maybe we should buy one," Dee said.

The *we* made Austen smile. "How about next weekend?"

Dee sighed. "Better make it the weekend after that. I'll have to work through this weekend."

She looked so tired, and her shoulders slumped as if she had the weight of the entire company resting on them. Austen wanted to protest and tell her not to work so hard, but she knew Dee needed her support, so she nodded.

Once Austen had finally managed to empty her plate, they ate the fortune cookies that had come with the takeout.

Austen nearly choked on her cookie when she read what was written on the slip of paper. "You'll receive a big surprise soon."

"They should really put in some new quotes. That's the exact same saying that you got when we ordered Chinese the day we met, isn't it?"

Austen swallowed the cookie through a suddenly dry throat. "Um, no, it isn't."

"But I remember—"

"I lied," Austen said and bit her lip until it hurt. "I know that makes me a hypocrite, and I'm sorry I did it, but I wasn't ready to tell you what was really in my fortune cookie. I mean, we'd only just met that day and—"

Smiling, Dee leaned over and covered Austen's mouth with her hand for a moment. "You're rambling. So, are you ready to tell me now?"

Austen nodded and took a deep breath. Her voice was a bit husky when she said, "The love of your life is sitting across from you. That's what it said."

"Oh, wow. No wonder you didn't want to read that to me. I probably would have laughed it off." Dee brushed a handful of cookie crumbs off her slacks and then peeked over at Austen, no longer looking like the confident COO but more like a shy teenager. "Am I? The love of your life, I mean."

After Brenda, Austen hadn't thought that she would ever fall in love again and give someone so much power over her, but now she found herself nodding.

Dee took her hand and pressed a soft kiss to her knuckles. "Just for the record, I think you're mine too."

"You think?" With any other woman, Austen might have been hurt by the careful, hesitant phrasing, but she knew Dee had never really learned to express her feelings.

"I'm fairly sure."

Austen smiled. "That's good enough for me."

"Is it?" Dee searched her face.

"Yes." Now Austen was the one to place a kiss on Dee's knuckles. "Come on. Let's clear the nonexistent table so you can get some sleep."

"I'm not going to bed yet. I've got more work to do."

"Dee, you look like you're about to fall over. Why don't you at least take a short nap?"

Dee reached for her briefcase and unzipped it. "Later."

Suppressing a sigh, Austen got up, carried the dishes into the kitchen, and put them into the dishwasher. The pots with the overcooked spaghetti and the burned tomato sauce still sat on the stove, but she'd clean up that mess later, once she'd gotten Dee to take a nap.

When she returned to the living room, she found Dee staring at the screen of her laptop with red-rimmed eyes.

"Will you stay a little longer and keep me company while I work?" Dee asked.

"I'll stay. I promised you a massage, remember?"

"I need to check my e-mails first and see if—"

"Massage first, e-mails later." Austen reached over and closed the lid of the laptop.

Dee didn't stop her. She let herself be pulled off the couch and up the stairs. "Just a quick massage, then I need to get back to work."

"Just a quick massage. Five minutes, tops."

Five minutes later, Austen tiptoed back downstairs to clean the kitchen, leaving Dee behind in the bedroom, sound asleep. She would wake her in an hour or two, but for now, Dee needed some sleep much more urgently than she needed to check her e-mails.

CHAPTER 28

By the time they left the second furniture store, Dee was ready to commit hari-kari. After working nonstop for the last ten days, her patience for furniture shopping was limited, to say the least. "We could have just ordered everything online, you know?" she said when they got back into the car.

Austen fastened her seat belt and looked up as if Dee had said something blasphemous. "You can't buy a recliner or a desk chair online. You have to sit in them to see if they are comfortable."

"But none of them were comfortable."

"That's why we have to continue searching."

Dee groaned. She hated shopping for anything but computers, laptops, and other gadgets. "Can we stop to have lunch first?"

Austen reached over and patted her knee. "Sure. I'm even letting you drive today."

"You're *letting* me drive?" Dee repeated and raised one eyebrow.

Austen nodded and smiled.

"That's very generous of you, Your Majesty." Dee reached over and pinched Austen's hip, then gentled her touch and rubbed the spot she'd just pinched.

Austen gave a queenly wave, making Dee laugh.

Intent on enjoying the reprieve from shopping, Dee drove toward Twelfth Avenue, where her favorite seafood restaurant was. She could almost taste the stuffed salmon and the clam chowder. When traffic slowed at an intersection, she remembered that the menu was on the pricey side. She didn't care and would have happily paid for both of them, but Austen was a proud woman. She seemed fine with being invited to dinner at a nice restaurant every now and then, but probably wouldn't be happy with such an expensive lunch when all she wanted was a quick bite between furniture stores.

She sighed inwardly. *Oh, the sacrifices we make for love...* She changed direction, and instead of frowning, she smiled to herself. *Love.* There had been something special about Austen from the very first moment they met, and after so many failed relationships, it felt good to finally admit that she was in love with her.

They found a parking space only one block away from a more affordable restaurant and walked in holding hands.

While the hostess greeted them, Dee looked around. The restaurant was as small and cozy as she remembered from a previous visit. At this time of the day, it wasn't very busy. Only three couples sat at the tables, enjoying their lunches.

One of the couples looked awfully familiar. Dee narrowed her eyes. There probably weren't many blondes with pink streaks in their hair having lunch with a burly man in a suit, were there?

"Austen," she whispered and tugged on her sleeve. "I think we should go somewhere else."

But before she could drag Austen out of there, the burly man looked up.

Shit. Just my luck. It was indeed her cousin Rick.

His eyes widened when he saw her, and he choked on a bite of food. His face turned the color of a tomato as he coughed and gasped for breath.

The blonde hurried around the table and patted his back.

His gaze still on Dee, he tried to fend her off. Finally, he stopped coughing, managed to free himself of the blonde's hands, and pointed over to them.

The blonde turned and immediately snatched her hands away from him. It was indeed Vanessa, Kudos Entertainment's receptionist.

He doesn't learn, does he? She had thought he had ended the affair months ago, but apparently, he was still seeing Vanessa behind his wife's back.

Rick came over and shuffled his feet. "Hi, Dee. I didn't know you frequent this restaurant."

Yeah, obviously you didn't, or you wouldn't have taken your mistress here. He had probably thought taking her to this restaurant was safe, because the rest of the family preferred more upscale dining.

The hostess looked back and forth between them. "Will you be having lunch together?"

"No," Dee said more sharply than intended. "Could you give us a moment, please?"

"Of course."

When she walked away, Rick peeked up. His gaze fell on Austen. His posture, meek and submissive before, immediately straightened. "I can't believe it! You're busting my ass about Vanessa, and here you are, showing up at a romantic little restaurant with Tim's assistant!"

Blood roared through Dee's ears. "That's not the same. Unlike you, I'm not married and cheating on my wife, you asshole! Austen is just helping me shop for furniture." Okay, now that she had said it out loud, it sounded a bit too domestic.

Her cousin snorted. "Yeah, sure. I bet Dad would love to hear all about your furniture shopping."

Dee gritted her teeth until her jaw began to hurt. "Are you blackmailing me, Ricky? Because if you are, let me tell you that it's a very dangerous pastime."

He showed his teeth in a shark-like grin. "Oh, blackmailing is such an ugly word. I'd rather call it a mutual agreement. You forget that you've ever seen me with Vanessa, and I won't mention that you're doing the horizontal mambo with Tim's secretary."

Dee wanted to spit, preferably in his face. She peeked at Austen out of the corner of her eye.

She stood frozen, her cheeks flaming red and her gaze lowered to the floor.

It hurt to see Austen so embarrassed about herself and their relationship.

God, this is such a mess. I can't believe I'm related to this slimy asshole.

"So?" Rick said. "Do we have a deal?"

Dee had made a few deals in her life that weren't exactly kosher, but she knew this one would keep her up at night. She didn't have a choice, though. No doubt her cousin would run straight to his father if she didn't agree to the terms of his deal. She glared at him. "All right."

Beaming, he reached out to shake her hand.

Dee ignored it. She took Austen's arm and marched out of the restaurant as fast as she could. Outside, she stopped and kicked the nearest street lamp. Pain shot through her toes, only adding to her anger. "Damn, damn, damn! I'm so, so sorry, Austen."

"It's not your fault." Unlike her, Austen looked completely calm. Too calm. "I can't believe your cousin would blackmail you. Would he really go to his father?"

"Oh, yeah, he would do that in a heartbeat. My family is not the warm and fuzzy type. Blackmailing each other to gain the upper hand is a family tradition, and Ricky has been waiting for years to get one over on me. He hates that his father wants me to be his successor instead of him."

Austen hugged her, ignoring the people who had to veer around them on the sidewalk.

The anger drained from Dee's body as they rested against each other.

"I'm sorry," Austen whispered. "You deserve better than that."

Dee had never thought about it before seeing Austen with her father. She had never had that kind of loving relationship with her own father or anyone else in the family. "It's okay. I have you." But for how much longer? A woman like Austen didn't deserve to be treated like one of Rick's mistresses. Something had to change—and soon, but Dee wasn't sure she was ready for it.

"Come on." Austen ended the embrace and reached for her hand. "Let's go have lunch somewhere else."

After having lunch at a sushi restaurant, they continued on to the third furniture store. Austen hoped it would be the last one because Dee looked as if her patience was waning. Maybe it had been a stupid idea to go furniture shopping. After working like a maniac all week, Dee needed rest more than she needed furniture. Austen vowed that they'd go home after this store, no matter what.

A salesman greeted them as soon as they entered. "Hi. My name is Josh. What can I do for you?"

Dee just returned the greeting with a pained smile, so Austen took over the conversation. "We need some furniture for her house—a desk, a desk chair, a coffee table, and a recliner for starters."

"I'm sure we have just what you need." He glanced at Dee. "So what style is the furniture in your house? I want to make sure whatever you choose is a good fit."

Austen laughed. "We don't have to worry about it. We're pretty much starting with a blank slate."

"I understand. If you'd follow me…" He led them through the store, showing them coffee tables first.

Austen ran her hand over a polished oak table and then inspected one made of birch.

Dee trailed behind them.

After looking at a few coffee tables, Austen turned toward her and asked, "What do you think about this one?" She pointed at a table that seemed like the perfect height for Dee's couch. She liked the warm, honey-colored oak, but maybe Dee would prefer a darker color.

"Looks good to me. That's decided, then." Dee wandered over to the recliners.

Austen joined her and lightly bumped her with one hip. "You are not just saying that to get out of here quickly, are you?"

"No. You probably have better taste when it comes to stuff like this anyway." She flopped down into a recliner and reached for its remote control. The recliner started to vibrate. Her eyes lit up, and she appeared interested for the first time. "Oooh, it gives massages. We're definitely getting this."

Austen looked at the price tag and the brownish olive-green color and cringed. Not only was the recliner ugly, but it was also horribly overpriced. They could get three much nicer ones for that price. She shook herself like a dog with fleas. "Over my dead body."

For a few moments, everything was silent in the store, just the recliner continued humming.

From her reclining position, Dee stared up at her with a wrinkle on her forehead. "Um…"

"Sorry, that was out of line. It's your house and your recliner, so you get to choose whatever you want." Austen ducked her head and quickly walked away. She couldn't believe she'd said that.

The massage function of the recliner was shut off, and footsteps hurried after her. "Austen, wait!"

Austen turned back around, ready to face the music.

"I don't like to be told what I can or cannot do," Dee said, her expression stern.

Austen swallowed. "I know. And that wasn't my intention."

Dee lifted up one hand to stop her. "But I do value your opinion, even if it differs from mine."

"I know. But that doesn't give me the right to act like I can veto your decisions. We don't live together, so you should be the one to pick the furniture."

Dee searched her face for so long that Austen started to fidget. "Would you want to?"

"Pick your furniture?"

"Live together."

Austen sighed. Truth be told, she would have liked nothing better than to go to sleep cuddled up to Dee every night and to wake up next to her every morning. But that was just wishful thinking. "It's a moot point. Even if we were both ready for such a big step in our relationship, we can't. If I let HR know that my address has changed and I now live in the same house you do, it would raise a big, red flag at work."

Dee slumped into the nearest armchair, put her elbows on her thighs, and massaged her neck with both hands. "Yeah, you're right, of course."

Had she wanted them to move in together? Austen walked over and knelt in front of the armchair. She slung one arm around Dee's leg and pressed their foreheads together. Before she could gather the courage to ask if Dee wanted them to live together, Dee stood and pulled Austen up with her.

"Let's look for another recliner with a massage function and then…" She pulled Austen against her side and whispered into her ear, "…we'll go home and break in the furniture."

The tone of her voice made Austen tingle all over. For a moment, she thought about telling Dee that they weren't buying a bed and even if they were, the new furniture wouldn't be delivered until next week, but then she just followed her. When Dee looked at her like that, protesting was the last thing on her mind.

Austen was unusually quiet on the ride home. She kept her hand on Dee's thigh but stared out the window.

Dee kept sneaking peeks at her and finally took one hand off the steering wheel to rub Austen's fingers. "You okay?"

Austen nodded.

At the next red light, Dee turned her head to study her.

Austen met her gaze and smiled, but she still appeared to be deep in thought.

A heavy weight settled on Dee's shoulders. She couldn't do this to Austen for much longer. Austen was honest to a fault; keeping their relationship secret was taking its toll on her. Especially after living through canceled dinners, nights alone, and solo vacations when she'd been with Brenda, Austen wanted to live her relationship out in the open—and Dee wanted the same thing.

In the past, the thought of moving in with someone would have made her feel as if she were stuck in a straitjacket, unable to move, to breathe, to achieve any of her goals. Now, though, the thought of sharing her house and her life with Austen didn't make her panic at all. It felt right. Like something that would help her achieve her goals and happiness instead of holding her back.

But, unfortunately, there was just one way to secure their future together. Well, two ways. One of them had to give up her job.

CHAPTER 29

Dawn peeked over at Austen's easel and started to laugh. "You are such a lesbian! The instructor hires a male nude model for us to sketch—and you're painting a forest!"

Frowning, Austen eyed the canvas in front of her. "It's not a forest. It's his chest hair."

Dawn giggled. "Whatever you say."

The instructor sent them a glance, making them duck behind their easels like schoolgirls who had been caught talking in class.

"Are you okay?" Dawn whispered once the instructor had redirected her attention somewhere else. "You don't seem really into art today."

Austen sighed and lowered her brush. Dawn was right. "Tomorrow is the eighth of December."

"And that's significant…why?"

"It's the day Dee and I met last year."

"One year. Wow. Time sure flies, doesn't it?"

Austen nodded and dipped her brush into more of the black paint.

"So why do you look like just thinking about your anniversary is giving you constipation?" Dawn reached over and touched Austen's forearm. "Things not going too well between the two of you?"

"That's just it," Austen said, keeping her voice low so the other people in their art class couldn't overhear.

"Things are wonderful whenever we're together—which is almost never right now. Except for a few hours of furniture shopping, I've barely seen her since that licensing snafu started, and that was six weeks ago. We can't even share a few moments together at work, because no one can know about us."

"I see." Dawn rubbed her chin, leaving a pink paint spot behind. "It's the same with Aiden whenever she gets obsessed with a case."

"How do you make it work?" Austen asked. Her friends seemed so happy together that she'd never considered that they might have some of the same problems she and Dee had.

"I try to be supportive and mostly just let her do whatever she needs to do, but if it gets to be too much, I kidnap her for a weekend in some remote location, away from case files and crime-scene photos."

Getting away for a weekend, to a location where they could be themselves and didn't need to hide their relationship...that sounded like heaven. "I'm not sure Dee could get away right now. She—"

The instructor took up position between their easels. "How is it going, ladies?"

"Um, good," they said in unison.

Their instructor craned her neck around one easel to glance at Austen's painting.

"It's his chest hair," Austen said.

"Oh, I love it. What a fresh outlook!" She patted Austen's arm. "Please continue."

When she walked away, Austen stuck her tongue out at Dawn. "See? She loves my fresh outlook." Maybe that was really all she needed—a fresh outlook. A weekend away would provide that. She would ask Dee as soon as they had a moment alone.

Dee watched her uncle pace back and forth in his office. "We got them to drop the noncompliance fines because we were able to show that we didn't overdeploy on purpose."

That stopped his pacing. "Oh, good." He turned toward her, accidentally swiping a framed picture off his desk.

Dee leaned forward, out of her chair, and caught it before it could crash to the floor. She held it in her hands for a moment. It was the photo she had taken of her aunt and uncle at their cabin on Sandy River two years ago. "How is Aunt Margo?"

"She's fine. Busy with her book club." He took the photo from her and placed it back on his desk.

At least he could have a picture of his significant other in his office, displayed for all to see. Dee couldn't. Not that a picture could replace the real thing. She had practically worked nonstop for the last six weeks, so she and Austen hadn't gotten to spend much time with each other. She had worked late every evening, sometimes even sleeping on the couch in her office. Austen hadn't made her feel guilty about it, but Dee found that she missed it. Missed her. They hadn't even gotten to spend any time together on the one-year anniversary of meeting each other.

"What about the rest of the costs?" her uncle asked, interrupting her thoughts. "Could we negotiate a discounted price, or are they still planning to charge us the full price for the licenses?"

"We're still negotiating. We might be able to prove that we didn't use most of the installations, since the software creates a log file when it's used. Hopefully, most of our laptops don't have the log file. We can use that for negotiation leverage. I think we can at least get them to agree on last year's list price, not the higher one from this year."

Her uncle sighed and dropped onto his office chair. "What a mess."

Tell me about it. She'd been the one who had to deal with lawyers for weeks, and she was heartily sick of it.

"All right," he finally said. "Keep me posted."

Dee nodded and stood. Back to work. At the door, a spontaneous thought made her turn back around. "Uncle Wade?"

He looked up from some paperwork on his desk. "Yes?"

"Are you using the cabin this weekend?"

"No. Why?"

Dee resisted the impulse to shuffle her feet. "Well, I was thinking that if no one else is using it, I'd like to get away for a day or two."

He shrugged. "Why not? It's not like these lawyers will make a decision anytime soon." He went back to his paperwork, dismissing her.

Austen wasn't sure how to broach the subject. Would Dee just blow off her suggestion to go away for the weekend? Maybe even tell her she didn't understand the demands of her job? *Well, you'll never find out if you don't ask.*

She took a deep breath and dialed Dee's cell phone number.

Dee picked up almost immediately. "Hi there."

Her voice still caused butterflies to take flight in Austen's stomach, even after half a year together. "Hi. Are you still at work?"

"Yes. Same old, same old."

"Want me to call back later?" Austen asked.

"No. I was just about to call you anyway."

Dee sounded more cheerful than she had in weeks. Maybe this was indeed a good time to talk to her about going away for the weekend.

"Listen, I was thinking..." they both said at the same time.

Austen laughed. "Go ahead." Her suggestion could wait.

"I was thinking that we both could use some time away from work and everything else," Dee said. "I asked my uncle, and he said we could use the cabin this weekend. I mean, of course he said I could use it, since he doesn't know about us. We could drive up tomorrow after work and stay until Sunday. So? What do you think?"

Austen sat on her couch with the phone in her hand, mouth agape.

"You don't like that idea, do you?" Dee asked when Austen remained silent.

"Oh, no. No, I love it. I'd love to go to the cabin with you."

"Really?"

"Really." Austen stretched out on the couch and smiled. "In fact, I was just about to ask you if you'd like to get away with me for the weekend."

"It seems great minds think alike," Dee said, the grin obvious in her voice.

Austen hummed her agreement. "Do I need to pack anything special?"

"No." She lowered her voice to an intimate whisper. "There's a Jacuzzi on the back deck, but don't you dare pack a bathing suit."

Austen's skin started to tingle at the thought of being in the Jacuzzi with Dee, warm water swirling around their naked bodies. "I won't," she said, her voice husky.

Both were silent for a few moments.

"Dee? I'm looking forward to tomorrow. We really need this."

"I know," Dee said, all playfulness gone from her tone. "I'm sorry if I neglected—"

"No. Don't apologize. Your job is important to you; I knew that from the start."

"Yeah, but so are you."

Austen hadn't realized how much she needed to hear that until Dee said it. She exhaled slowly. "I'll see you tomorrow after work, then."

"I'll pick you up at six. I love you."

Hearing it from Dee still made her breath catch. "I love you too."

They hung up, and Austen lay on the couch, staring at the ceiling, for a few moments more. Then she jumped up and went to the bedroom to pack, doing a little happy dance on the way.

Darkness had fallen by the time they made it out of the office and to the cabin. Gravel crunched under Austen's feet and the roaring of the river behind the cabin greeted her as she got out of the car. She breathed in the scent of fir and pine. A few light snowflakes fell, adding to the enchanted feeling.

Dee led her up the few steps to the porch, unlocked the front door, and held it open for her.

With just her and Dee there, the cabin felt much more welcoming than the last time Austen had entered it. She set her small bag down in the hall and twirled playfully. "I can't believe it. Almost two whole days. No work. No hiding our relationship."

Dee watched her with a grin. "No laptop," she added.

Austen stopped twirling and stared at her. "You left your laptop at home?"

"Yes. I also turned off my cell phone before we left. I want this weekend to be just for us."

They came together in the middle of the hall for a deep kiss. When they finally separated, Dee took her hand and pulled her down the hall. "Come on. You can unpack later."

Someone had lit a fire in the wood-burning fireplace, but Dee didn't give her a chance to stop and admire it or ask who had lit it. She pulled her through the living room and slid open the glass door leading to the back deck that ran the entire length of the house.

Dee let go of Austen's hand, crossed the deck, and removed the cover of the Jacuzzi.

Steam rose into the cool night air. Candles flickered in a large circle around the tub, and a bottle of wine and a bowl of chocolate-covered strawberries were chilling within easy reach.

Austen stared at the candles and the strawberries, and it took a few moments before she could speak. "Wow. Are you trying to seduce me?"

"Is it working?"

"Oh, yes, it is. How did you manage to do this?" She gestured at the Jacuzzi, the candles, and the food.

Dee grinned. "I have my ways." She dipped a foot into the water to test it. "Perfect."

Yes. Everything was indeed perfect. Who knew her girlfriend was such a romantic?

Dee stripped off her slacks and her blouse without an ounce of self-consciousness. Not that she had any reason to feel self-conscious. For someone who sat behind a desk all day, she had a fantastic body.

Austen watched transfixed as Dee unhooked her bra and slid her panties down her long legs. Her skin gleamed in the candlelight, making Austen want to run her hands over every inch of it.

Naked, Dee stepped closer until Austen could feel her body heat. "Now you." She hooked two fingers under the bottom of Austen's sweatshirt and pulled upward.

Austen raised her arms, allowing her to slip the garment off. Her bra followed with an expert flick of Dee's fingers. The cool air formed goose bumps on Austen's skin and made her nipples harden—or maybe it was the way Dee looked at her. The muscles of her lower abdomen tightened as Dee unbuttoned her pants and slowly slid the zipper down.

Dee knelt and pushed the pants down Austen's legs, taking the panties with her as she went. From her kneeling position, she looked up at Austen, who now stood completely naked. Her breath fanned over Austen's belly.

Slowly, she leaned forward and pressed a kiss to the spot right below Austen's navel before standing and holding out one hand. "Come on," she said, her voice husky. "Let's get in."

The water frothed invitingly.

Holding on to Dee's hand, Austen made her way down the two steps that were nearly invisible beneath the bubbling water. With a hum of appreciation, she lowered herself onto the tiled bench.

Dee sank into the churning water next to her until it engulfed her up to her chest, interrupting Austen's admiration of her body.

Their sides pressed together as they lounged in the Jacuzzi, letting the pulsing jet streams massage their backs. Tendrils of steam rose off their shoulders like a curtain separating them from the rest of the world.

"Here." Dee handed her a glass of wine and took one for herself. "To an uninterrupted weekend, just for the two of us."

"To our weekend."

They clinked glasses and sipped wine while the warm water swirled around them.

A droplet of water splashed onto Austen's face.

Dee reached out and tenderly wiped it away. She bent her head, keeping her eyes open until their lips connected.

Austen moaned into the kiss. Dee tasted of wine and passion. Not interrupting their kiss, she slid around until she straddled Dee on the bench.

Their bodies pressed together, the warm water making each touch feel like silk sliding over silk.

Dee kissed a hot trail down Austen's neck, chasing drops of water with her lips while her hands slid down her back until she clasped her ass.

Austen gasped and threw her head back.

Dee used the opportunity to nibble on the exposed line of her throat.

Finally, Austen couldn't take the sweet torture anymore. "Let's go inside."

Dee nodded, her cheeks flushed from more than the heat of the water surrounding them.

Before Austen could step out of the Jacuzzi, the sound of the glass door sliding back made her pause.

"Danielle? Where are you?" Wade Haggerty, Dee's uncle and their boss, stepped onto the back deck. "We've got a situation with Universal. You didn't answer the urgent e-mail I sent, and my calls went straight to voice mail, so I—" He stumbled to a stop. "What the hell?"

Oh no! No, no, no. Austen sank even lower in the water and pulled up her arms, covering as much of herself as she could.

Dee stepped in front of her, blocking Wade's line of sight with her own body. "Could you give us a moment, please?" she asked, her voice shaking.

"I…yeah. I'll wait inside." He took two steps toward the sliding doors but then said over his shoulder, "You know what? This can wait. I've got more important things to deal with. Come and see me first thing Monday morning. And check your damn e-mail, Danielle."

He was already through the glass door when Dee shouted after him, "I don't have my laptop."

"Then forget about it. Rick and I will deal with it." The door clicked shut behind him. Barely a minute later, an engine howled on the other side of the house and tires crunched over gravel as Wade sped away.

"Dammit!" Dee sank back into the Jacuzzi and hit the surface of the water, accidentally splashing Austen.

Austen swallowed a mouthful of water and had to cough.

"Sorry."

"It's okay." She moved closer and wrapped her arms around Dee, relieved when she wasn't rebuffed. "It'll all be okay."

"Yeah," Dee mumbled but didn't sound as if she believed it.

They clung to each other in the tub until their toes and fingers started to prune. Austen felt a bit woozy as she climbed out of the Jacuzzi, but she wasn't sure if it was from being in the hot water for too long or from having her world tilt on its axis.

Their fingers brushed as Dee wordlessly handed her a bathrobe.

Austen grabbed Dee's hand before it could retreat. "Dee? If you need us to go home and deal with this, that would be okay."

Dee shook her head, her lips forming a grim line. "No. You heard Uncle Wade. He wants to talk to me on Monday. For now, let's just enjoy the weekend."

Austen nodded, but they both knew neither of them would be able to relax. She vowed to make the best of it and distract Dee as much as she could. Not letting go of Dee's hand, she bent and picked up the bowl of fruit. "Come on. I hear some chocolate-covered strawberries calling our names."

CHAPTER 30

AFTER AGONIZING OVER HER DECISION the entire weekend, Austen knew what she had to do when she entered the lobby on Monday morning. She waved at Vanessa behind the reception desk but didn't hang around to chat. She headed straight for the elevator that brought her to the fifteenth floor.

The scent of espresso wafted down the corridor, as it had the first day she had started working at Kudos Entertainment. For a moment, she was tempted to veer off to the break room and delay the inevitable, but then she shook her head and continued to the corner office on the left.

Mr. Saunders was already at his desk with the door open when she entered the outer office. He looked up and smiled. "Good morning, Ms. Brooks. Did you have a nice weekend?"

It had been nice—up until the moment Dee's uncle had stepped onto the back deck. Instead of answering, she walked over and hesitated in the doorway. Was this really what she wanted to do? She had promised herself to never uproot her life for a woman again.

Mr. Saunders frowned. "Is everything okay?"

Austen hesitated for a few moments longer before deciding that things were different with Dee, so she could no longer stick to the promises she had made herself in the past. Her future with Dee was more important than clinging to the past, and if she had to decide between her job and her relationship, her decision was clear. The lump in her throat prevented her from speaking, so she just handed him the letter she had typed up when they had returned from the cabin.

He took it and held it in his hand without opening it. "What's this?"

Austen took a deep breath and said, "My resignation letter."

The word hung between them for a few moments.

He tried to hand the letter back, but Austen shook her head and refused to take it. "No," she said. "I mean it. It's not a decision I made lightly, but there's no other way. I quit."

"But why? Am I handing you too much work, or—?"

"No. I love my job, but..." She shrugged and smiled. "I love your sister more. I should have done this months ago."

He set the resignation letter on his desk and looked at it for a few more seconds before rising slowly. He stood before her, and for the first time since she'd met him a year ago, the suave businessman looked as if he didn't know what to say. Finally, a small smile crept onto his face. "I understand. I hate to lose you as an admin, but who knows, maybe I'll have you as a sister-in-law one day."

Austen grinned. "Who knows." If Dee ever asked her, she certainly wouldn't say no.

They shook hands, and Austen said, "I know my contract says I have to give two weeks' notice, but I would appreciate it if I didn't have to finish my two weeks. That could be awkward for Dee now that your uncle knows."

"Shit. Uncle Wade knows about the two of you?"

Austen nodded and pressed her lips together. "Yes. He's probably reading her the riot act right now."

"Shit," he said again.

"Yeah."

"Don't worry about the two weeks. Head home and start looking for a new job. And if you need any references, come straight to me. I will highly recommend you to any future employer."

"Thanks, Mr. Saunders."

"Tim."

She shook his hand again and repeated, "Thanks, Tim." She headed for the door but turned as she reached it. "Do you think you could go over and make sure your uncle doesn't rip her head off?"

He rubbed his chin. "Do you really think that's a good idea? Uncle Wade would only get angrier, and Dee never wanted me to get involved in her business."

By now, Austen knew Dee well enough to realize that wasn't entirely true. Dee had gotten used to fighting her battles alone; that was all.

"You really have no idea how lonely Dee feels in this company." She paused, surprised about the sharpness of her tone, but Tim was no longer her boss, so she could afford to be completely honest. "Everyone seems to hate her, just because your uncle keeps giving her all the dirty jobs. Her position in her family isn't any better. No one asks her how she's doing; they just expect her to function. She's been fighting all the battles alone for fourteen years, and she never gets any appreciation. For once, having a little support from someone in the family would mean the world to Dee."

Tim stared at her and straightened the collar of his shirt as if it had gotten a little too tight. "I hate to admit it, but you're right."

"Yeah." Austen rubbed her neck. "Sorry for coming off to you like this. I didn't mean to speak so candidly."

"No problem. I think I needed it." He crossed the room, rotating his shoulders like a boxer preparing for a fight. "All right. Let me go and rescue our damsel in distress. Want to come?"

Austen nodded. "But I'd better wait in front of his office, or the dragon will slay us all."

Dee hesitated in front of her uncle's office and slid her hands over her vest to make sure it was properly buttoned.

Two of the company's admins walked past, eyeing her and whispering to each other.

Great. Dee gritted her teeth. She could only imagine what kind of gossip would circulate among the employees by lunchtime. She took a deep breath and knocked.

Uncle Wade waved her in but didn't offer her a seat, so she stood in front of his desk like a naughty child who'd been called into the principal's office.

He leaned back in his two-thousand-dollar executive chair and regarded her for a while without saying a word, letting her sweat.

Dee didn't give him the satisfaction of fidgeting. She stood with her head held up high. Yes, she was in deep shit, but she wasn't ashamed of her relationship with Austen.

Finally, Uncle Wade sighed. "I'm very disappointed in you, Danielle."

That pierced Dee's emotional armor. She winced. If there was one thing she had always strived for, it was a little recognition from her family. She wanted to say something, but he cut her off with one impatient movement of his hand.

"I warned you to stay away from her, didn't I?"

"Yes, and I tried, but—"

"But, of course, you didn't listen. You went ahead and created another problem for the company. Like we don't already have enough on our plate with Universal and that licensing mess. I really expected better of you."

Dee pressed her lips together, not happy with him equaling her relationship with the projects that had given her headaches for weeks.

After a few more minutes, he ran out of steam, slumped against his high-backed leather chair, and waved her into the visitor's chair. "You know I can't ignore this affair. I wish I could, especially since you are my niece, but I have to do what's best for the company."

"Relationship," Dee said quietly.

He frowned. "What?"

"It's not an affair, Uncle Wade. We're in a relationship."

"Whatever it is, we only have two options here." Leather creaked as he leaned forward. "Either you break up with her, or we have to fire her."

It shouldn't have been a surprise, but the open words were still like a slap to the face. Her hands went cold, and heat shot into her cheeks. "No! I'm not breaking up with her."

"All right." Her uncle nodded. "That leaves the second option. Do you want to let HR know, or should I—?"

Dee jumped up. "I don't want her to get fired either. She's the best admin in this whole damn company. She doesn't deserve—"

"Careful," her uncle said, a warning snarl in his voice. "She brought this upon herself. I mean, what do you expect me to do?"

She dropped back into her chair. "Nothing," she said. "I don't expect you to do anything."

"You want me to just put my head into the sand and ignore the whole thing?" His brows climbed up his forehead. "You know I can't do that."

You manage just fine with Rick's flings. She bit her lip and held herself back from saying it. "No, that's not what I meant. You don't need to do anything about the situation, because," she took a deep breath and looked him in the eyes, "because I quit."

The words seemed to echo through the room.

They stared at each other.

Dee blinked. Had she really said that? Had she really just quit her job and given up the position she had worked for all her life?

Judging by the expression on Uncle Wade's face, she had. He looked as if someone had thrown a bucket of toads into his face.

Oh, shit. Was it too late to take it back?

But after her initial shock waned, she realized she didn't want to. This felt amazingly right.

His face as red as a fire truck, her uncle finally managed to say, "But...but what about the Universal project?"

She had worked her ass off for this company for fourteen years, and that was all he had to say? "You wanted to give it to Rick anyway."

"But he can't do it on his own. He—"

"That's no longer my problem." How freeing it felt to say that. Only now did she realize how much the constant power games, company politics, and family entanglements had gotten on her nerves. She stood and walked to the door.

"You are out of your mind," her uncle shouted after her.

Dee turned back around and shrugged. "Maybe I am, but I don't think so."

"You could have been my successor one day. No woman is worth giving that up for."

"That's where you are wrong." With a feeling as if she were sleepwalking, she left his office. One foot went in front of the other, but it felt as if she wasn't in full control of what she was doing. It was like watching a movie with herself as the main character. She couldn't stop it. Nor did she want to. The sound of the office door closing behind her for the last time echoed through her ears all the way down the hall.

Austen slowed her hurried jog down the hall and gripped Tim's arm. "We're too late."

Dee walked toward them without seeing them. Her stride, normally long and confident, was now unsteady and searching, as if she wasn't sure how firm the ground in front of her was.

Austen's heart clenched. She wanted to rush over and embrace her, but this wasn't the place. "Dee! Um, Ms. Saunders." She bit her lip and looked left and right to make sure they were alone in the hall. "How did it go?"

Dee looked up and blinked. It took a few seconds for her gaze to focus on Austen. Slowly, her face creased into a smile. "You don't have to worry about what you call me anymore. I just quit."

Austen pulled at her earlobe, sure she couldn't have heard correctly. "Did you just say...?"

"I quit."

Austen reached out for the wall to steady herself. "But...but this job meant everything to you. It was the focus of your life."

"Not anymore. I was too busy working my ass off to realize it, but my job hasn't been really fulfilling for quite some time. The resentment from the employees, having to prove myself to Uncle Wade like some greenhorn fresh out of college, that constant feeling that he might pull the rug out from under me anytime and make Rick his successor instead of me..." Dee shrugged. "I didn't want to admit it, but it got to me."

Tim started to laugh and slapped his thighs. "You two are quite the pair."

Dee narrowed her eyes at him. "You really think me quitting my job is funny?"

"No, but she," he pointed at Austen, "did the same."

"You did...what?"

"I quit my job," Austen said quietly.

Dee stared at her and then shook her head with a wry smile. "Tim is right. We really are a pair." She pulled Austen into her arms in the middle of the hall.

Sally squeezed past them, watching them with wide eyes, but Austen no longer cared. She pressed her face to Dee's shoulder and held her more tightly. She had been fine with giving up her job to save Dee's. It had been the logical thing to do, since Dee was a COO and she just a lowly admin. But logical or not, she now realized how good it felt to know she wasn't the only one willing to make sacrifices for their relationship.

Finally, they let go and looked at each other.

"What now?" Austen asked.

"I have no idea." For the first time in her life, Dee didn't seem to have a plan.

"Well," Tim said, "now that Dee is no longer our COO, I could just tear up your letter of resignation and you could keep working as my admin."

Austen had enjoyed working for him, and that way, at least one of them would have a steady paycheck, but going back to her job while Dee gave up hers didn't feel right. She'd have to talk to Dee before she made a final decision. "Why don't I finish out my two weeks? That would give us time to think about it and you a chance to find a replacement."

Tim nodded. "All right. Then we'd better get back to work. We can't all be people of leisure." He winked at his sister.

Dee slapped his shoulder and kissed Austen's cheek. "See you later." She walked toward her office.

"Hey, where are you going, Sis?" Tim called. "The elevator is over there."

Dee turned. "There's something I need to grab from my office before I go."

She had already disappeared around the corner when Austen realized what it was—the mouse she had given Dee at the Christmas party.

This year, there would be no Secret Santa and no office Christmas party for them, but Austen knew she wouldn't miss either as long as she had Dee.

CHAPTER 31

AUSTEN THREW A GLANCE UP the curving facade of Kudos Entertainment's headquarters as she stopped in front of the entrance to close her umbrella.

It would feel strange not to come here nearly every day anymore, and she could only imagine how Dee must feel. Not that either of them regretted their decisions or had the time to miss their old places of work.

Her heels clicked over the polished travertine floor as she entered the lobby and walked past the potted ferns and the crimson couch.

The Christmas tree in the center of the lobby was even larger than last year's. The sales department had decorated it with little red plastic apples and candy canes that were just as fake.

She went up to the fifteenth floor, said good-bye to Sally and Jack and the rest of her colleagues, and then went to clean out her desk.

Most of the office supplies belonged to the company, and she'd never been able to put a framed picture of Dee on her desk, so there wasn't much to pack. She placed her dictionary, her squishy stress ball, and the stapler that belonged to her into the box she'd brought and then went through the desk drawers to make sure she hadn't forgotten anything.

All but one drawer were empty already, but when she peeked into the last one, something white and silver caught her attention.

The paper snowflake! She'd put it in there last December and had then completely forgotten about it. She took it out and smoothed her fingers over the blank paper.

Beneath the snowflake lay two pieces of paper. One was the slip of paper with Dee's name on it that she had drawn for Secret Santa. The other was the sticky note Dee had written when she had given back the snowflake. Smiling, Austen read it.

Company policy states that every employee has to make a Christmas wish. Please adhere to it.
D. Saunders

Oops. She had never followed that order. Her paper snowflake was still as blank as freshly fallen snow. She laughed as she read the postscript Dee had scribbled beneath the message.

PS: Be careful when you hang the snowflake. Beware of falling stars!

That falling star had certainly led to a turbulent year, but Austen didn't regret any of it. She put the snowflake and the two pieces of paper into the box and turned to say good-bye to Tim.

His door was closed, so he was probably on the phone or in a meeting.

No big deal. She would see him later this week for Christmas dinner anyway. After Dee had quit her job, her father had announced that he didn't want to see her or talk to her until she came to her senses, so instead of going over to spend Christmas with Dee's family, they would have dinner with Austen's family. Tim and his wife would join them.

With the box in her arms, she took the elevator back down to the lobby.

On the twelfth floor, the elevator stopped and two employees from sales got on. They leaned against the mirrored wall, staying away from Austen's side of the elevator, but eyed her the whole twelve floors down.

When the doors pinged open and Austen stepped out into the lobby, one of them whispered to the other, "Did you hear what happened?"

"No. What?"

"That bitch, Ms. Saunders, fired her on her very last day."

Austen whirled around. She couldn't take all the rumors people spread about Dee anymore. "No, that's not what happened. I quit because I couldn't take the stupid gossip around here anymore!"

One woman took a step back until she crashed into her colleague. "I-I didn't think..."

"That's right. You didn't think. You just repeated a rumor you heard, without bothering to check if it's true first. How would you feel if people did that to you for fourteen years?"

The woman just stared at her.

Austen took a deep breath and tried to rein in her thudding pulse. She forced a smile, said, "Merry Christmas," and walked away.

Vanessa waved at her from behind the reception desk. "Hey, Austen. Last day?"

Austen nodded, even though it felt more like the first day of her new life.

"So you and Ms. Saunders…?"

Austen just smiled, not wanting to contribute to the rumors going around.

"I gave my notice this morning too," Vanessa said, her voice lowered to a whisper.

"You did?"

"Yes. It just…it wasn't working out, and I deserve better than waiting around for…" Vanessa bit her lip.

Austen let go of the box with one hand and patted her arm. "You do. Take good care of yourself and merry Christmas."

"You too."

The box in her arms, Austen circled the Christmas tree and headed for the glass doors. At the last moment, she turned back and stopped in front of the tree. She took the slip of paper with Dee's name out of the box, pinned it to the snowflake with the stapler, and hung both on the tree.

There. She had finally made a wish. Having Dee in her life was really the only thing she wanted—needed—for this Christmas and all future Christmases.

After one glance back at the silver snowflake gleaming against the background of red plastic apples, she stepped through the glass doors and stopped to suck in a lungful of the fresh winter air.

"Austen!" someone called from the visitors' parking spots.

Austen turned.

Dee leaned against her BMW and waved.

Their gazes met across the parking lot.

Austen dropped the box and sprinted over, right into Dee's arms.

Dee held her tightly and then kissed her.

"Hi," Austen mumbled against her lips when the kiss ended. "This is a nice surprise. Your appointment with your banker didn't take long."

"No, it didn't."

"How did it go?"

"Great." Dee smiled broadly. "I'll tell you everything on the way home. Let's get your box and go."

When Dee wanted to walk over to the box, Austen held on to her. "You know what? I think I don't need it anymore. This is the first day of my new job, and I'm sure my new boss will buy me a new stapler."

"How come you're in such a good mood? I thought you hated first days?"

Austen grinned. "Not anymore. The curse is broken."

"All right. But you don't have a new boss. We're partners, Austen—in life and in business."

That would take some getting used to. Austen still tended to think she didn't have much to contribute to their newly founded company, but Dee obviously thought otherwise. "Okay, partner. Then let's go home." She walked over to the box and took out the note Dee had written her last year before returning to Dee's side and reaching for the car key in her hand. "Can I drive?"

Dee snatched the key out of her reach. "No."

"But if you are not my boss anymore, you don't have the authority to tell me I can't drive."

"It's my car."

Grinning, Austen shook her head. "It's the new company car, so it's ours."

Dee rolled her eyes and looked up at the gray sky. "Why oh why did I have to fall in love with the only woman on earth who's more stubborn than me?"

"Because your brother wished for it upon a star."

Dee seemed to consider it for a moment and then nodded slowly. "I knew he was my favorite for a reason. But you still don't get to drive."

Laughing, Austen walked around the car and got in on the passenger side.

EPILOGUE

D EE STOOD WITH EVERYONE ELSE as the organist started playing the wedding march.

The doors at the back of the chapel opened, and Austen's father and his bride walked down the aisle arm in arm. Dee chuckled as she remembered Caroline's energetic response at being asked who would walk her down the aisle. "I'm not some maiden to be given away for three goats and a gaggle of geese," she had said. "We're in this together, so we'll walk in together."

Dee liked that sentiment, and she also liked Gene's spunky bride.

Austen and her brother—maid of honor and best man—had already taken their places at the altar.

The ceremony was short and a bit of a blur to Dee because she couldn't look away from Austen, who stood holding the bouquet of white roses for Caroline. In her turquoise dress that made her eyes appear even bluer and revealed glimpses of her shapely legs, she outshone the bride—at least in Dee's opinion.

As the couple exchanged rings, a ray of sunlight streamed through the stained-glass windows, making a rainbow of color flicker across Austen's face.

Beautiful.

Over the head of her father, who was now kissing his new wife, Austen smiled at her.

At this very moment, Dee's parents, her brothers, and her eleven cousins were all at the West Coast Business Symposium, listening to Uncle Wade's keynote speech, but Dee knew that there was no place else she would rather be than here—with Austen.

Carrying two empty plates, Austen stood in the line that had formed in front of the chocolate wedding cake. She glanced over at their table while she waited.

Her father stood next to the table, talking to Dee. He looked just as good in his classic black tuxedo as Dee did in her cream-colored pantsuit.

Wonder what they're talking about?

He laughed about something Dee had said and then bent to kiss her cheek before walking away.

Oh, wow. What a relief to see them get on so well!

Someone cleared his throat behind her, and Austen realized it was her turn to get cake.

Carrying two pieces of the delicious-looking dessert, she made her way back to their table. She stopped to talk to one of her father's friends, back from his days in the Marine Corps. "I hear you're a grandfather now."

A pleased smile spread over his bearded face. "Yeah. Thank God she doesn't look anything like her grandfather."

Austen laughed. "Congratulations." As she hugged him, she gazed over his shoulder—and then quickly pulled back. "Excuse me for a moment. I'd better go rescue my partner."

"Oh, sure, go."

Austen hurried toward the table, where Grandaunt Elisa had her arm looped through Dee's and was chatting her ear off. She slid one of the plates in front of Dee and took a seat next to her. "Hi, Auntie."

Her grandaunt lifted her glasses, which dangled on a golden chain around her neck, to her eyes. "Oh, Austen, it's you. I was just telling your friend about the day I married my Paul, God rest his soul."

Had anyone told Auntie Elisa that Dee was more than just a friend? Austen wasn't even sure her grandaunt knew she was gay. She hesitated for a few moments but then decided that she was through hiding their relationship. "Dee is more than just my friend, Auntie."

Her grandaunt patted Dee's arm and smiled. "Oh, yes, she just told me."

"She did?" Austen looked back and forth between her grandaunt and Dee.

Grandaunt Elisa nodded. "She's your partner, right?"

Wow, for a ninety-year-old woman, she was really matter-of-fact about lesbian relationships. *Who knew?* Austen beamed. "Yes, she is."

"That's wonderful, honey. I always told your father he should have sent you to college, no matter what. You never could fulfill your potential as a secretary."

Uh…what? What did college have to do with her relationship? She sent Dee a helpless gaze.

"Your grandaunt thinks it's great that we partnered up to open our own company."

"Yes!" Auntie Elisa clapped her hands. "A company producing toys for pets is such a wonderful idea. I'll be your first customer. My Coco will love it."

"Oh." Austen slid her chair a little closer to the table. "Um, but, Auntie, Dee isn't just my partner in business."

A frown deepened the lines on her grandaunt's face. She let go of Dee's arm so she could point from her to

Austen and back. "You mean... You...? She...? The two of you are...?"

Sitting up as straight as she could, Austen nodded. "We are a couple and just as much in love as Uncle Paul and you were."

Grandaunt Elisa looked thoughtful. "That's a lot of love."

"Yes," Austen said and glanced at Dee. "It is."

Her grandaunt shook her head as if she still couldn't quite process it but then shrugged and reached for Dee's arm again. "So tell me, dear. How did you meet my grandniece?"

Austen blew out a breath. That hadn't gone too badly.

Dee looked over at her, and they smiled at each other. "Well," Dee said and wrapped her free arm around Austen, "we met under a falling star, and the rest, as they say, is history."

If you liked reading about these characters, you might want to check out the novel *Conflict of Interest*, which tells the story of Austen's best friend, Dawn, and her partner, Aiden.

ABOUT JAE

Jae grew up amidst the vineyards of southern Germany. She spent her childhood with her nose buried in a book, earning her the nickname *professor*. The writing bug bit her at the age of eleven. For the last eight years, she has been writing mostly in English.

She used to work as a psychologist but gave up her day job in December 2013 to become a full-time writer and a part-time editor. As far as she's concerned, it's the best job in the world.

When she's not writing, she likes to spend her time reading, indulging her ice cream and office supply addictions, and watching way too many crime shows.

Connect with Jae online

Jae loves hearing from readers!
E-mail her at: jae@jae-fiction.com
Visit her website: jae-fiction.com
Visit her blog: jae-fiction.com/blog
Like her on Facebook: facebook.com/JaeAuthor
Follow her on Twitter: @jaefiction

EXCERPT FROM

CONFLICT OF INTEREST

BY JAE

"I'm going to throw up," Dawn Kinsley said, rubbing her nervous stomach.

"No, you won't." Her friend and colleague Ally just grinned. "Come on, you're a therapist. You're used to talking to people."

"Not to one hundred cops who would rather be elsewhere and who won't give me the time of day." Dawn knew what the police officers sitting on the other side of the curtain were thinking. Most of them would view her lecture as a waste of time.

Ally rolled her eyes. "A psychologist with glossophobia. I wonder what the APA would say about that."

"I'm sure the American Psychological Association would be much more concerned about a psychologist with your lack of compassion," Dawn answered, now with a grin of her own. Usually, she didn't have a problem with public speaking. She had held her own in front of gum-chewing high school kids, earnest college students, and renowned psychologists twice her age, but cops were a special audience for her. It was almost as if she was expecting to see her father sitting in one of the rows and was trying to impress him. *Oh, come on. This is not the time to start analyzing yourself.*

"Touché," Ally said.

Both of them had to chuckle, and Dawn felt herself relax.

"There are a few techniques that can help in these situations, you know," Ally said.

"Let me guess—picturing everyone in the audience naked?" Dawn grinned at her friend. "And how would that help with my nervousness?"

Ally shrugged. "Well, maybe it won't." She peeked out from behind the curtain, letting her appreciative gaze wander over the men in the first few rows. "But it might be nice nonetheless."

"Maybe for you, but how would it be nice for me to picture a room full of naked men? Hello?" Dawn gave a little wave. "Did you miss the office memo informing everyone about my sexual orientation?"

"Office memo? Is that what they call it nowadays when spotted kissing your girlfriend in the office parking lot?"

"What?" Dawn sputtered. "I never did that!"

Ally rubbed her forehead and pretended to think about it. "No? Must have been Charlie, then." She pushed the curtain aside to glance at the audience again. "There are also a few female officers down there. You could look at them."

"All two of them?" Dawn joked but stepped closer to follow Ally's gaze. There were more than two female cops in the audience—but not that many more.

"Pick one," Ally said.

Dawn nudged her with an elbow. "I'm here to give a lecture, not to pick up women, Ally."

Ally ignored her protests. "Pick one and concentrate on her during your lecture. Ignore the rest of the crowd. It'll help with the nervousness. So?" She pointed to the seated police officers.

Well, it can't hurt. Dawn craned her neck and peeked past the taller Ally. Her gaze wandered from woman to woman, never stopping for long until... "Her!" she said, pointing decisively.

In the very last row, between a tall African American man in his forties and a younger man whose posture screamed "rookie," a female plainclothes detective was just taking her seat. She had short, jet-black hair, and a leather jacket covered what Dawn could see of her tall, athletic frame.

"Ooh!" Ally whistled quietly. "Nice choice! Didn't know you liked them a little on the butch side, though. Maggie isn't nearly—"

"Compared to Maggie, even you look butch," Dawn said.

"Dr. Kinsley?"

Dawn looked away from the detective and turned around. "Yes?"

One of the seminar organizers stepped up to them. "Here are your handouts." He handed her a stack of paper. "Are you ready to begin?"

Dawn clutched the handouts and swallowed. "Yes."

"Good luck," Ally said. Behind the seminar organizer's back, she mouthed, "Remember to picture her naked."

How's that supposed to calm my racing heart? Dawn stepped out from behind the curtain and made her way over to the microphone with a confidence she didn't really feel.

⸻ ✦

Aiden slumped into a seat between her partner and Ruben Cartwright. The chair next to Ruben was suspiciously empty. "Where's your partner? Terminal back pain again?" If she had to be at this stupid seminar, so did everyone else, even hypochondriacs like Jeff Okada.

Ruben looked up from the paper airplane that had once been his seminar brochure. He shoved a strand of brown hair out of his boyishly handsome face and glanced from Aiden to her partner. "Uh, what?"

Ray leaned over to him with a grin. "There's one thing you have to know about your new partner, rookie. His back acts up every time a seminar comes along."

"It acts up whenever I have to sit in one of these seats designed for first graders," Jeff Okada said as he walked up to them. Gingerly, he eased himself down next to his rookie partner.

Aiden sighed and glanced at her watch. She had a stack of unfinished reports on her desk, and their thirty open cases didn't get any closer to being solved while she sat here. The seminar also stopped her from spending her lunch hour in the courtroom's gallery, watching her favorite deputy district attorney at work. Maybe she would have even worked up the courage to ask Kade to lunch today.

Sighing again, she wrestled herself into a standing position and pointed to the back of the conference room. "I'm going for coffee."

"If you want to live long enough to enjoy your hard-earned pension, I'd advise against that, my friend." Okada raised his index finger in warning. "In more than twenty-five years on the job, I've never been to a law enforcement seminar with even halfway decent coffee."

Ray smirked. "In twenty-five years on the job, you've never been to a law enforcement seminar, period."

Over the top of his sunglasses, Okada directed a withering glance at Ray before he turned back to Aiden. "The lack of drinkable coffee is obviously a nationwide conspiracy from law enforcement brass to make sure nothing distracts their officers from the lectures. For the same reason, you'll never encounter donuts or attractive female lecturers at a law enforcement seminar."

"Or comfortable chairs," Ray said.

Okada threw up his hands. "Now you're starting to get it."

Aiden sank back into her chair. Giving up on her caffeine fix, she pulled the now crushed seminar program out from under her. The wrinkled paper announced the title of the first lecture: Special Needs and Issues of Male and GLBT Survivors of Rape and Sexual Abuse. The speaker was some PhD named D. Kinsley.

"Great," Aiden murmured. They hadn't even hired a cop or someone who knew the reality of handling sex crimes to give the lecture. Instead, some antiquated Freudian in a stiff suit would bore them to tears with his academic theories.

A young woman carrying a stack of handouts stepped out from behind a curtain and crossed the podium— probably the Freudian's assistant or the poor soul who had the questionable honor of introducing the speaker. The woman tapped the microphone to test its volume and nodded. "Good morning, ladies and gentlemen. I'm Dawn Kinsley, your lecturer for the first part of the seminar."

Aiden's head jerked up. That was D. Kinsley?

Nothing reminded Aiden of the academic Freudian she had imagined except the glasses on the freckled nose. Instead of a suit and tie, slacks and a tight, sleeveless blouse covered a body that was petite, yet not frail. The strawberry blonde hair wasn't pulled back into an old-fashioned bun, but cascaded in curls halfway down to softly curved hips.

Seems she's the PhD, not the assistant. That's what I get for stereotyping. Of course, looking at her instead of an old man is not exactly a punishment. However boring the lecture might be, at least she would have something captivating to look at.

The lecture began, and to her surprise, Aiden found herself looking away from the pretty speaker to jot down interesting details about dealing with male rape victims. The lecture turned out to be informative, practice-oriented, and witty. She even caught Okada bending his aching back to take notes. The psychologist spoke with passion and sensitivity, never even glancing down at her notes.

Instead, Aiden felt as if the psychologist was looking right at her, focusing on her as if there were no one else in the room. *Oh, come on. Stop dreaming. There are a few other people in the room, you know?* Aiden listened with rapt attention to the rest of the lecture.

Forty-five minutes passed almost too soon.

"I knew I should have tried the coffee," Ruben mumbled when they began to file out of the room with the last of the seminar participants. "If there's an attractive female lecturer, there's a chance the rest of your seminar conspiracy theory is bull too."

Okada stretched and shook his head. "I wouldn't bet your meager paycheck on it, partner. Some government employee obviously failed to check the lecturer's picture, but there's no way they would overlook a bill for Blue Hawaiian beans at forty dollars per pound."

Someone chuckled behind them.

Aiden turned and looked into the twinkling gray-green eyes of Dawn Kinsley, their lecturer. The faint laugh lines at their corners indicated that the psychologist was closer to thirty than to twenty as Aiden had first assumed.

"Sorry," Aiden said, pointing at Okada and Ruben. "They're not used to being out and about. We normally keep them chained to their desks."

Dawn didn't seem offended. Her full lips curved into an easy smile that dimpled her cheeks and crinkled the skin at the bridge of her slightly upturned nose, which made the freckles dusting the fair skin seem to dance. "Don't worry, Detective, I've been called worse things than attractive."

Aiden tilted her head. "How do you know I'm a detective?"

"Oh, I don't know, could it be the fact that we're at a law enforcement conference?" Okada said.

Dawn smiled at him, but she spoke to Aiden. "The way you stand, walk, and talk pretty much screams 'cop' in capital letters. And the way you dress suggests you're a detective. Sex crimes unit?"

Aiden nodded. "Aiden Carlisle." She extended her hand.

"Dawn Kinsley, but I guess you already knew that." The psychologist nodded down at her name tag. Her handshake was as genuine and warm as her smile.

"Hey, Aiden." Ray, already halfway out the door, waved her over. "We're gonna make a run for the nearest coffee shop before the next lecture starts. You up for it?"

Forty-five minutes ago, Aiden would have jumped at the chance to leave the seminar room, but now she found herself hesitating. "Um, sure." She glanced at Dawn. "Would you like to come with us?"

"I don't drink coffee." The psychologist laughed at the look on Aiden's face. "Don't look so shocked, Detective. I'm a tea drinker, and I'd love to accompany four of Portland's finest, but regrettably, I've got an appointment."

"Maybe next time, then," Aiden said, knowing they would likely never see each other again. Not as eager to get a caffeine fix as before, she said good-bye and followed her colleagues out of the conference room.

Conflict of Interest is available as a paperback and in various e-book formats at many online bookstores.

OTHER BOOKS FROM
YLVA PUBLISHING

www.ylva-publishing.com

SOMETHING IN THE WINE

JAE

ISBN: 978-3-95533-005-7
Length: 393 pages

All her life, Annie Prideaux has suffered through her brother's constant practical jokes only he thinks are funny. But Jake's last joke is one too many, she decides when he sets her up on a blind date with his friend Drew Corbin—neglecting to tell his straight sister one tiny detail: her date is not a man, but a lesbian.

Annie and Drew decide it's time to turn the tables on Jake by pretending to fall in love with each other.

At first glance, they have nothing in common. Disillusioned with love, Annie focuses on books, her cat, and her work as an accountant while Drew, more confident and outgoing, owns a dog and spends most of her time working in her beloved vineyard.

Only their common goal to take revenge on Jake unites them. But what starts as a table-turning game soon turns Annie's and Drew's lives upside down as the lines between pretending and reality begin to blur.

Something in the Wine is a story about love, friendship, and coming to terms with what it means to be yourself.

CONFLICT OF INTEREST

(revised edition)

JAE

ISBN: 978-3-95533-109-2
Length: 467 pages

Workaholic Detective Aiden Carlisle isn't looking for love—and certainly not at the law enforcement seminar she reluctantly agreed to attend. But the first lecturer is not at all what she expected.

Psychologist Dawn Kinsley has just found her place in life. After a failed relationship with a police officer, she has sworn never to get involved with another cop again, but she feels a connection to Aiden from the very first moment.

Can Aiden keep from crossing the line when a brutal crime threatens to keep them apart before they've even gotten together?

DEPARTURE FROM THE SCRIPT

JAE

ISBN: 978-3-95533-195-5
Length: 240 pages

Aspiring actress Amanda Clark and photographer Michelle Osinski are two women burned by love and not looking to test the fire again. And even if they were, it certainly wouldn't be with each other.

Amanda has never been attracted to a butch woman before, and Michelle personifies the term butch. Having just landed a role on a hot new TV show, she's determined to focus on her career and doesn't need any complications in her life.

After a turbulent breakup with her starlet ex, Michelle swore she would never get involved with an actress again. Another high-maintenance woman is the last thing she wants, and her first encounter with Amanda certainly makes her appear the type.

But after a date that is not a date and some meddling from Amanda's grandmother, they both begin to wonder if it's not time for a departure from their usual dating scripts.

HEART'S SURRENDER

EMMA WEIMANN

ISBN: 978-3-95533-184-9
Length: 305 pages

Neither Samantha Freedman nor Gillian Jennings are looking for a relationship when they begin a no-strings-attached affair. But soon simple attraction turns into something more.

What happens when the worlds of a handywoman and a pampered housewife collide? Can nights of hot, erotic fun lead to love, or will these two very different women go their separate ways?

BITTER FRUIT

LOIS CLOAREC HART

ISBN: 978-3-95533-213-6
Length: 270 pages

Fuelled by booze and boredom, Jac Lanier accepts an unusual wager from her best friend. Victoria, for reasons of her own, impulsively challenges Jac to seduce Lauren, her co-worker and a young woman Jac's never met. Under the terms of their bet, Jac has exactly one month to get Lauren into bed or she has to pay up. Though Lauren is straight and engaged, Jac begins her campaign confident that she'll win the bet. But Jac's forgotten that if you sow an onion seed, you won't harvest a peach. When her plan goes awry, will she reap the bitter fruit of her deception? Or will Lauren turn the tables on the thoughtless gamblers?

BARRING COMPLICATIONS

BLYTHE RIPPON

ISBN: 978-3-95533-192-4
Length: 374 pages

It's an open secret that the newest justice on the Supreme Court is a lesbian. So when the Court decides to hear a case about gay marriage, Justice Victoria Willoughby must navigate the press, sway at least one of her conservative colleagues, and confront her own fraught feelings about coming out.

Just when she decides she's up to the challenge,—she learns that the very brilliant, very out Genevieve Fornier will be lead counsel on the case.

Genevieve isn't sure which is causing her more sleepless nights: the prospect of losing the case, or the thought of who will be sitting on the bench when she argues it.

COMING FROM YLVA PUBLISHING IN WINTER 2014/2015

www.ylva-publishing.com

GOOD ENOUGH TO EAT

JAE & ALISON GREY

Robin's New Year's resolution to change her eating habits is as unusual as she is. Unlike millions of other women, she isn't tempted by chocolate or junk food. She's a vampire, determined to fight her craving for a pint of O negative.

When she goes to an AA meeting, hoping for advice on fighting her addiction, she meets Alana, a woman who battles her own demons.

Despite their determination not to get involved, the attraction is undeniable.

Is it just bloodlust that makes Robin think Alana looks good enough to eat, or is it something more? Will it even matter once Alana finds out who Robin really is?

THE CAPHENON

FLETCHER DELANCEY

On a summer night like any other, an emergency call sounds in the quarters of Andira Tal, Lancer of Alsea. The news is shocking: not only is there other intelligent life in the universe, but it's landing on the planet right now.

Tal leads the first responding team and ends up rescuing aliens who have a frightening story to tell. They protected Alsea from a terrible fate—but the reprieve is only temporary.

Captain Ekayta Serrano of the Fleet ship Caphenon serves the Protectorate, a confederation of worlds with a common political philosophy. She has just sacrificed her ship to save Alsea, yet political maneuvering may mean she did it all for nothing.

Alsea is now a prize to be bought and sold by galactic forces far more powerful than a tiny backwater planet. But Lancer Tal is not one to accept a fate imposed by aliens, and she'll do whatever it takes save her world.

Under a Falling Star © by Jae

ISBN: 978-3-95533-238-9

Also available as e-book.

Published by Ylva Publishing, legal entity of Ylva Verlag, e.Kfr.

Ylva Verlag, e.Kfr.
Owner: Astrid Ohletz
Am Kirschgarten 2
65830 Kriftel
Germany

http://www.ylva-publishing.com

First edition: October 2014

Credits
Edited by Nikki Busch
Proofread by Akilesh Sridharan
Cover Design by Streetlight Graphics

Lightning Source UK Ltd.
Milton Keynes UK
UKOW02f1114290115

245342UK00001B/52/P